RAVES FOR ROBERT DALEY'S
A FAINT COLD FEAR

"Fine, engrossing."
—*Los Angeles Times Book Review*

"This is a book that can be read for entertainment: It's well plotted and written with clarity and power. Or it can be read for insight: It offers an accurate depiction of the drug industry at ground zero."
—*New York Newsday*

"Daley know whereof he writes. His experiences, plus widely recognized talent for spinning thrillers are put to good use in this, his twentieth book."
—*Pittsburgh Press*

"Never less than informative and fascinating, often exciting and always ringing true . . . Daley grabs our attention and doesn't let go until the last line."
—*Publishers Weekly*

"Another fine piece of work from the author of *Prince of the City* and *Hands of a Stranger*. Highly recommended."
—*Library Journal*

"Robert Daley draws masterfully on his experience in this insistently absorbing adventure story."
—*Raleigh News and Observer*

"Daley's strongest police thriller since *Year of the Dragon* . . . a sober, steadily gripping narrative whose finely observed love story infuses the intense cops-vs.-dealers action with a resounding humanity."
—*Kirkus Reviews*

"May well be the best effort of Robert Daley since *Prince of the City*."
—*Worcester Telegram and Gazette*

P9-BIY-665

BOOKS BY ROBERT DALEY

NOVELS
The Whole Truth
Only a Game
A Priest and a Girl
Strong Wine Red as Blood
To Kill a Cop
The Fast One
Year of the Dragon
The Dangerous Edge
Hands of a Stranger
Man with a Gun
A Faint Cold Fear

NONFICTION
The World Beneath the City
Cars at Speed
A Star in the Family
Target Blue
Treasure
Prince of the City
An American Saga

TEXT AND PHOTOS
The Bizarre World of European Sport
The Cruel Sport
The Swords of Spain

ATTENTION: SCHOOLS AND CORPORATIONS

WARNER books are available at quantity discounts with bulk purchase for educational, business, or sales promotional use. For information, please write to: SPECIAL SALES DEPARTMENT, WARNER BOOKS, 666 FIFTH AVENUE, NEW YORK, N.Y. 10103.

ARE THERE WARNER BOOKS
YOU WANT BUT CANNOT FIND IN YOUR LOCAL STORES?

You can get any WARNER BOOKS title in print. Simply send title and retail price, plus 50¢ per order and 50¢ per copy to cover mailing and handling costs for each book desired. New York State and California residents add applicable sales tax. Enclose check or money order only, no cash please, to: WARNER BOOKS, P.O. BOX 690, NEW YORK, N.Y. 10019.

ROBERT DALEY

A FAINT COLD FEAR

WARNER BOOKS

A Time Warner Company

The characters and events in this book are fictitious.
Any similarity to real persons, living or dead,
is coincidental and not intended by the Author.

If you purchase this book without a cover you should be aware that this book may have been stolen property and reported as "unsold and destroyed" to the publisher. In such case neither the author nor the publisher has received any payment for this "stripped book."

WARNER BOOKS EDITION

Copyright © 1990 by Riviera Productions Ltd.
All rights reserved.

Excerpt from "The Waste Land" in *Collected Poems 1909–1962*, copyright 1936 by Harcourt Brace Jovanovich, Inc. and copyright © 1963, 1964 by T. S. Eliot, reprinted by permission of the publisher.

This Warner Books Edition is published by arrangement with Little, Brown & Company, 34 Beacon Street, Boston, MA 02108.

Cover illustration by Marvin Mattelson
Hand lettering by Carl Dellacroce
Cover design by Jackie Merri Meyer

Warner Books, Inc.
666 Fifth Avenue
New York, N.Y. 10103

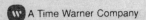 A Time Warner Company

Printed in the United States of America

First Warner Books Printing: January, 1992

10 9 8 7 6 5 4 3 2 1

And I will show you something different from either
Your shadow at morning striding behind you,
Or your shadow at evening rising to meet you
I will show you fear in a handful of dust

T. S. Eliot,
"The Waste Land"

BOOK I

BOOK 1

1

IT WAS A LOW apartment house at the end of a short, tree-lined, dead-end street in a residential neighborhood in Forest Hills, supposedly the richest section of Queens. Behind it ran a chain link fence and below the fence ran the Grand Central Parkway. There was no way to watch the building from the parkway side. Since the street dead-ended at the fence, the front side was not much better. You could approach from one direction only and not at all without being noticed. Across the street was a row of one-family brick houses with slate roofs. The houses were rammed in side by side. They had driveways and garage doors in front and tiny front lawns, with maybe an alley between each pair of them. They were occupied by families with children—no chance of setting up anything in those houses. Some of them had a few bushes out front that maybe you could hide in at night, if you scrunched up real small. Since there was so little traffic, a stakeout in parked cars was not possible. To work a surveillance truck into such a street without attracting attention was not possible. There were no overhead wires to service. You could repair the pavement or work the manholes but only for a few days at a time. You could send in "delivery" men, but not too often. You could put a man on the roof, but you couldn't protect him there. You could send a dog walker down the street twice a day every day, provided it was the same guy and the same dog; but how long could they linger?

In short, a difficult building to watch, and chosen no doubt for that reason. A problem. A series of problems that Ray Douglas had come upon during a period of immense unhappiness in his life, and had attacked with increasing intensity.

In the end he had used all of the above techniques and some others, switching back and forth, doubling back on himself, and the surveillance had not been burned, as far as he could tell, though it had lasted now four months. He had lost himself in this case. After four months it would end within the hour.

Douglas was forty-four years old, a tall man with black hair and nearly black eyes. He had been a cop from the age of twenty-two. From college, needing a job because he wanted to get married, he had gone simultaneously into the Police Academy and into the N.Y.U. graduate school of business administration. His ambition in life had nothing to do with being a cop. It was to become a businessman like his father. The department for him was in no sense a calling, though it became one soon enough. The young husband, the earnest student, was a patrolman on patrol and as such no different from the others. He spent his days and sometimes nights arresting villains, coping with trauma and tragedy, helping where he could help. He found he loved the helping. But he loved the violence too. He loved the camaraderie of the station houses.

He loved everything about being a cop.

A daughter was born. There was no longer enough money for graduate school. Rather than ask his father for help he had dropped out and taken a second job painting houses. He never went back. Within four years he was a sergeant, moving up fast within the department.

By now his rank was deputy chief. He commanded the narcotics division, a thousand men. He had an office in headquarters and was supposed to be in it, his eye on his entire division. Like everyone else in headquarters, he was supposed to be protecting his career and his back, and politicking in the halls. But he did not care about any of that anymore. He was not supposed to be concentrating on any particular investigation but he had organized this one personally and then, to the astonishment of his detectives, had joined them. He had ridden with his men in tail cars, had sat with them on wiretaps, had sometimes brought them coffee in the night.

And he was with them now, lying under a bush across the street from the apartment building. The case had become more real to him than his life. Panel trucks had been driving up all day. Boxes had been going inside. Douglas supposed he knew what was in them, and on this supposition had based his decision. The case ended tonight.

The lobby had glass doors. It was empty and he watched it. The people they were watching, as he had told his men, were disciplined, organized, and as heavily armed and dangerous as any of the world's terrorist gangs. They were richer than the government of the country they came from, which his detectives thought beside the point. Douglas did not. Rich meant they could buy gear his side was not permitted or could not afford. They had recoilless submachine guns that made no noise, and perhaps hand grenades. They had night-vision goggles, and electronic detection devices that perhaps picked up police transmissions. They might have night scopes too. The crosshairs could be fixed on his forehead at this moment. Most felons were afraid to fire at cops. Not these people, who had orders from base to shoot it out. Usually they obeyed, why not? If arrested they faced astronomical bail, meaning no bail, and after that astronomical sentences. They were all illegal aliens anyway. To them a shoot-out made sense. They either died or, if they escaped, went home and were safe forever.

Douglas's career was as much at risk as his life. Perhaps more so.

If tonight's results did not measure up to the prodigious number of police man-hours he had expended and the hopes he had raised; if too few arrests were made or if they did not stand up in court; if the evidence to be seized was less than he had imagined; worse, if a cop or cops got killed—then most likely he would lose his command, and his career would be over. In the New York Police Department his personal involvement would be taken certainly as incompetence and probably as stupidity—not because he had mangled the case, but because he had risked his personal prestige on it—in the world of police commanders, proof of the worst sort of bad judgment.

It was August, and the night was hot. Douglas wore jeans and a polo shirt, and lay with stones pressing into him, beside a detective named Sullivan. The young man seemed dumbstruck by such intimate proximity to rank; in any case, he had been silent for an hour. The police radio was in Douglas's hand, and his briefcase, which contained the warrants, leaned against his leg. He was waiting for five men to come out. He could not go up and get them; the apartments in that building had steel fire doors. In the case of the suspects' apartment, this made it a fortress. Assault the fortress and cops would get killed. The five might come out together. He hoped they would come out separately. He did not want a pitched battle in the street either.

There were two detectives parked down on the verge of the highway below the fence, watching the back of the building, an unlikely escape route; they would be useless in any shoot-out up here. Others were crouched between the houses—once darkness had fallen it had become possible to move them up that close but no closer. The rest were out on the avenue, waiting.

Five perpetrators. Although an educated man, Douglas thought in police jargon, same as street cops. Perpetrators.

Suddenly the first of them appeared. The elevator doors opened and there he was, crossing the lobby. He was alone, and this was what Douglas had hoped for, and he slapped the radio to his mouth and whispered: "Salvador's coming out."

It was two o'clock in the morning. He had felt Detective

Sullivan stiffen beside him. He could almost hear the department cars start up out on the avenue.

Salvador in the doorway eyeballed the street and sidewalk. Nothing alarmed him. He came out, climbed up into his double-parked van, and started it up. As it moved away, Douglas again whispered into the radio: "Don't anyone follow him."

Salvador had a wife and children, just like other people. His address was known, his habits. You never arrested everyone in a conspiracy like this. You left a loose end to lead to a new case. You stayed away for two weeks, then put the tail back on and watched where the loose end took you. At the end of two weeks of looking over his shoulder, Salvador would imagine the heat was off, he had been overlooked. He would make contact with someone, or someone would make contact with him, and the case would resume. Of course, sometimes this tactic got the loose end killed. He was assumed by his colleagues to have been overlooked because he was an informant, and he got hit. If this should happen to Salvador, it would cause Douglas's detectives, though not Douglas, to laugh. "Couldn't have happened to a nicer guy," they would joke. But it would end the case.

With Salvador gone, Douglas ordered more men up close, but left several detectives at the head of the street to stop any residents who might be coming home late. He was trying to think of everything—and to protect his career as much as he could under the circumstances. If there was to be a shootout, he could not afford to get some bystander caught in the crossfire.

Presently he had a van double-parked in front of the door with detectives inside it. Douglas was standing now. A three-quarter moon hung low over the trees, and he could feel a faint cool breeze against his face. He was like an orchestra leader about to make music. It could not be long now. A crescendo was about to be heard. He was the man who controlled what was to happen next, and he felt the power of it—power such as few men ever feel. He was about to change people's lives.

For fifteen minutes, perhaps more, he watched the open elevator doors. When finally they slid shut, he ran across into the lobby and watched the floor numbers light up.

The elevator had stopped on the third floor. "They're coming," he breathed into his radio, and he ran back out and hid behind the van, radio in one hand, gun in the other.

What was now supposed to occur he had written down on paper, diagrammed, explained, but the behavior of criminals, like the behavior of bullets, could not be predicted, and Douglas knew this, and had so warned his men who knew it also but sometimes forgot. Since the remaining perpetrators had arrived in two cars, then logically they should split up at the sidewalk, for the cars were parked at either end of the street. Douglas had assigned separate teams to rush them. The idea was to take them simultaneously with overwhelming force.

This was the way the book said to do it, and he believed in the book as far as it went. The New York Police Department made a hundred thousand felony arrests a year, a few of them as dangerous as these, and when the book was followed there was almost never any shooting. Particularly there was almost never any shot or dead cop. Almost never.

Peering over the hood of the van, Douglas watched the elevator doors open.

Only three suspects stepped forth. Where was the last of them? Was he asleep up there? Was he watching from the roof? Would he erupt shooting from the stairwell as soon as the arrests were in progress?

The three were each carrying attaché cases. They were relaxed and jabbering to each other in their own language, for he could hear them.

Out on the sidewalk they shook hands all around the way foreigners did, then separated. Two went one way, one the other. And one still upstairs.

What to do?

When they were about twenty paces apart, Douglas shouted "Now!" into his radio, and tossed it in the window of the van. As he rushed forward he was aware that in a moment he might be dead, an exhilaration he had experienced before and that was like no other. Jamming his gun into someone's belly he shouted: "Police, freeze."

He wasn't dead and the danger was almost past.

"Move, motherfucker, and you're gone," said Sullivan, who was beside him.

Douglas's heartbeat began to slow.

Their astonishment was pleasant to see, though it was followed almost instantly by something colder, more calculating. But as detectives from the van, from the alleys, from the bushes kept pouring forward, the three sets of hands rose into the air.

Douglas ordered them stripped of their attaché cases, pushed up against the van, patted down, handcuffed. While this was done he watched the lobby, the open elevator doors.

He was nervous again. "Hurry up," he urged his men.

One of the prisoners squealed. "Too tight, man."

Another said: "*Abogado.*"

"Fucker wants his lawyer," Sullivan said.

"Shove them into the van," ordered Douglas.

The elevator doors were still open, the lobby still empty. One was still upstairs. Douglas tried to decide what to do next.

The apartment's steel door was as much a fortress with one man behind it as with five. Kick it down and there would be widows to notify. To wait or not to wait? The perpetrator might come out five minutes from now, or not at all. He might be waiting for them to hit the door. He might be in bed asleep, and in the morning come down surrounded by people on their way to work.

The prisoners' pockets had been emptied out, and their belongings spread out on the hood of the van. Douglas stirred through coins, wallets, cigarette lighters, keys. He studied the keys and thought: We won't have to kick the door down at all.

He took the keys and started toward the lobby.

A crowd of detectives tried to enter the building with him. Kicking doors down was the most dangerous work cops did, but there was never any shortage of volunteers. They all wanted to do it. But four men was enough for a thing like this. You didn't want your men lined up in a narrow hallway. He kept three detectives, and sent the others back.

Having tiptoed along the third-floor hallway, Douglas put his ear to the apartment door. But he could hear nothing. His heart was beating very fast again. Danger had the effect of stopping time in its tracks. This moment he was alive. The next moment he might not be. The dichotomy was absolute. Once through that door he could not go back. Risk was intellectual and physical both. To Douglas this was police work at its best, he loved it, could never give it up. He glanced behind him at the other three men who shared this risk, this moment with him, and they gave each other nervous grins, and he loved them too.

There were two locks. One was a Lori, the other a Blocker. Lori was a fairly uncommon lock, and Blocker was rare. They could both have been Yales. He went searching through the three rings of keys. Luckier still: there was only one key of each make. Having detached them, he slid them as silently as possible into the two locks.

He nodded at the detectives he had with him, got three nods back, turned both keys at once, and burst into the room.

He was in a short hallway furnished only by a cardboard box. On the box lay a gun, and it was cocked. Beyond the box was the bathroom door, open, steam coming out. A man stood stark naked at the sink, half-turned from the mirror, staring toward them, lather on half his face. He held an old-fashioned razor in the air and stared as if stupefied.

Two of the detectives rushed forward and wrestled him naked into handcuffs, while Douglas reached for the gun and uncocked it. He found he was panting, though he had not exerted himself at all. As he tried to catch his breath, he glanced around, and as he did so a new exhilaration came on.

It was a one-room apartment and it was crammed nearly to the ceiling, nearly wall to wall, with cartons. It was unbelievable! There was a kitchen table and some chairs and no room for any other furniture at all. The cartons where he stood were stacked chest-high and he ripped one open, and lifted out and hefted two plastic packages. They weighed about a kilo each, and he dropped them back into that box and ripped open another, and then another. He glanced all around him. Not an apartment, a drug locker.

His detectives were ripping open cartons too. When the ripping stopped, they gaped at the cartons. They gaped at each other. Their awe was almost religious. They had seen cartons going in today but had not been able to get close enough to count them. Douglas had expected to find a good many, everybody had, but nothing of this magnitude.

A detective came out of the bathroom with a small suitcase. "It was behind the john," he said.

An expensive attaché case, rather large. Glove-soft leather. Hand-stitched. Brass hinges and clasps. Locked. Heavy.

Douglas knew what was in it without being told. "What's the combination?" he asked the naked man.

"*Abogado,*" the man said.

A detective handed Douglas a clasp knife.

"It's a nice case," Douglas said to the prisoner, "don't make me do this."

The naked man stared at him with black eyes.

He worked the blade under the heavy brass clasps. His own attaché case back in the van was scuffed from years of carrying around the tools of his trade on jobs like this one. Tonight, in addition to the warrants, it contained two boxes of bullets, an extra set of handcuffs, a flashlight, a sap, a hunting knife in a leather sheath, a second gun, and a cheese sandwich in a plastic bag.

He forced the blade in deeper, ripping the leather, prying the clasps loose. He lifted the lid.

Inside was money. Stacks of bills of all denominations. It was crammed with them.

He picked up a radio and spoke to his men outside. "We've got one additional prisoner plus a roomful of stuff, plus an attaché case full of cash." He paused to let this news sink in, then said: "Congratulations to you all."

He wanted the prisoners brought up, and when this was

done he ordered them manacled, along with the nude, to the kitchen chairs, knees under the table to save space. The outer door was closed and the apartment was now filled almost to bursting with boxes and people.

"Now comes the hard part," Douglas told his detectives. Each package in each carton had to be counted, and initialed. The money had to be counted bill by bill, and there were tens of thousands of them. "The sooner it's done," Douglas said, "the sooner we can leave."

The brilliant work was over and the slave work began. The detectives counted and the prisoners watched them: twelve men on a hot night in August in a room whose air space was occupied mostly by cartons. The only window was a sliding glass door that seemed to have been bolted shut. They could not get it open. The outer door had to be kept not only shut but locked. The temperature went up and up. The apartment came to seem hermetically sealed. There were scores of cartons, and they were heavy, and Douglas, the deputy chief, moved as many as anyone, helping count over two thousand packages, taking his turn counting bills as well. The detectives begged for the outer door to be propped open, but Douglas would not permit it, for the money count was too high, the package count as well, and slinging the packages around made noise. He did not want some freelance stickup man peering in. He did not want the neighbors peering in or, worse, calling the police. He imagined trying to fend off a few carloads of blue uniforms. Or suppose while the door was open one of the prisoners' cohorts turned up to see what was keeping them?

He was trying to control this case to the smallest detail to the very end.

When he knew approximately what the totals would be he went out to the call box on the avenue to report to headquarters. The police commissioner had been informed in advance, as had other high-ranking commanders. Any of them might have called in to ask about results. He supposed they all had.

He got the PC's duty sergeant on the line. Douglas knew

him. The only occupant of the police commissioner's office each night. An older man, officious. At night he considered himself to outrank everyone.

"The PC cannot be disturbed," he said stiffly.

A sergeant was no fit recipient for Douglas's news, particularly this sergeant, but his ebullience was so great he could not help himself. "It's the biggest seizure in the history of the city," he blurted out, "two tons."

It changed the sergeant's tune, for he had once been a street cop himself. "Jesus," he breathed.

"Yeah."

"Used to be, if you took five kilos it was enormous."

"Yeah," said Douglas.

"And it had to be heroin. If it was only cocaine you apologized as you turned it in."

"And over two million bucks in cash as well. Did anybody call?"

No one had. The sergeant was effusive with his praise, though. "Should I wake everybody up?"

"Let 'em sleep," Douglas said, and hung up. For no reason he began to laugh. He laughed most of the way back to the apartment. Once he stopped to peer up at the stars. He breathed in the hot night air. The streets were empty, the city as quiet as he had ever heard it. This was what any man became a cop for, he thought. This was a night such as cops dreamed about their whole careers, and most never got it, and he was the luckiest man alive.

The apartment, when he stepped back in, seemed hotter than ever. Guns lay atop cartons. Bulletproof vests lay in a pile. The men worked stripped to the waist, dripping, and he joined them. A round of jokes began. Can you top this? Some were old and stale. The men brought them forth one after another. All sounded uproarious now. They laughed until they could hardly stand.

The prisoners glowered and said nothing.

The pace of the counting, of the heaving around of cartons, had slowed. Their exhaustion approached hysteria, and even the blandest jokes made them reel and heave with laughter.

"Here's one you haven't heard," said Sullivan. "Why did the chicken eat the cocaine?"

"I don't know."

"I don't know either," said Sullivan, and he broke into gales of laughter. As did everybody. They staggered around, they socked each other in the arms.

Through the still-sealed glass slider Douglas watched the sky lighten. His cheeks ached from laughing. The sun came in on the cartons and painted them red.

He called in the police trucks by radio. Uniformed men lined the street with shotguns while he and his detectives heaved cartons up onto the tailgates. A small group of neighbors, some in bathrobes, had come out of the houses to watch. The perfect case perfectly controlled from beginning to end.

Later he sat between Sullivan and another detective at the counter in a Forest Hills coffee shop. He drank coffee and ate a piece of yesterday's danish, for the place had just opened for the day. As the air conditioning came up, the sweat dried on his body and his clothes dried and he was cool finally. There were detectives at two of the tables, and he kept half turning on his stool, glancing around at them fondly. He wanted the night never to end.

2

THE SLEEPING BEAUTY was awakened not by a kiss but by the window shade, which sprang open to the top, and then slapped round and round itself. Her eyes blinked open with it, and then, in time with the slapping, continued blinking.

Prince Charming, namely her husband in his pajamas, was standing over the bed with a cup of coffee for her and she glared at him and he glanced from her to the window shade and back again.

He laughed. "I didn't do it on purpose."

The sunlight washing into the room made her blink several times more but she sat up and took the saucer in both hands. He had a second cup for himself and he perched on the edge of the bed as always.

After a moment she said: "Did the paper come?"

Carrying his coffee he went out of the room and down the corridor. Her name was Jane Hoyt Fox, and she waited. She heard the apartment door open, then close.

George Fox came back into the room, his coffee in one hand, the paper in the other, and stood above her scanning the front page. "Dress lightly," he said cheerfully. "Paper says we're in for another scorcher."

The paper came in four sections. Today as always he took the financial section, the only one that interested him, apparently. As she reached for the other three, Jane said: "I was having a nightmare. Something had me by the throat."

His smile got broader. "That was life had you by the throat, imagine."

Not a new thought, but it sobered her.

Fox took the financial section with him into the bathroom. Also as he did every morning.

Turning to Metro news first, she scanned the headlines and bylines, all the while sipping her coffee, then read enough of each story to know what it was about and how well it was done.

Presently, shaved and reeking of after-shave lotion, Fox came out, and she put the paper down and went into the bathroom in her turn.

Later, both dressed, husband and wife sat at the dining room table. Jane was working her way through the national and international sections of the paper and sipping more coffee.

"What do you have on today?" Fox asked.

He was a tall, well-built man with a ruddy complexion and

hair that was beginning to thin out, and she looked at him. "You can read it in the paper tomorrow."

"The piece about the working mothers," he said. "Do you think they'll run it?"

"They'll run it, but I'll have to ruin it first." She had lain awake last night plotting her strategy. Perhaps that was where the nightmare had come from. How much of the piece could she preserve?

Fox rose to leave. "Ask me what I have on today?"

"I know what you have on," she said. "How's it going?"

A corporate lawyer, he was writing a contract whereby one of the divisions of Texaco acquired one of the divisions of Mobil. "It's nearly finished," he told her.

The last time he had spoken of it, the contract had reached 360 pages in length. Three younger lawyers were helping him write it. "Two or three more weeks," he said.

No one who signed such contracts ever read them. The principal lawyers on each side read them and told the signers where to sign. The two chairmen would sign at a ceremony. Then the contract would go into a vault never to be read again. Her husband was writing a book for an audience of two or three people, whereas her stories appeared in the paper the next day, or within a week anyway, and were read by hundreds of thousands. She felt a bit sorry for him.

"What do the stockholders get out of this?" she asked him.

"I don't know."

"On which side do they get screwed?"

He laughed. "I don't know."

"Why don't you?"

He smirked at her. "You're a good reporter. You ask indiscreet questions."

He went back into the bedroom, then came forth carrying his briefcase. "We need milk, sugar, and paper towels," he said, standing over the table with his hand on her shoulder. "And can you please drop off my two suits to be cleaned."

Normally Jane went to work an hour later than he did. Therefore this job kept falling to her. "I can't today."

"Come on, Jane."

"I have to get to the office right away and the cleaners won't be open this early."

"What am I supposed to do?"

His needs, she felt, did not always take precedence over hers, but she forbore telling him so. Still, she was so worried about the working mothers piece, and about what today would bring, that she snapped at him. "If it's that important to you, put them in a bag and hang them on the cleaner's doorknob."

"In this city? Those suits cost almost a thousand dollars each."

"You could always wear the suit you have on two days in a row." But it made Jane defensive. "I'll take them for you tomorrow."

He moved toward the door. Jane said hurriedly: "Can I share your taxi?"

"It'll take me ten minutes out of my way."

She got up from the table.

"Oh, all right," said Fox.

"Never mind, I'll take the subway."

The city was Jane's beat and therefore, she sometimes felt, she should live in it twenty-four hours a day, and she tried to. The subway was where she felt she belonged.

She carried the cups into the kitchen. They rode the elevator down in silence, wished the doorman good morning, and went out onto the sidewalk under the awning where Jane kissed Fox on the cheek and strode off toward the entrance on the corner. She could feel the sun already hot on her bare arms. The subway this morning was going to be unbearable.

"I wish you'd let me give you a lift," Fox called after her. She gave him a wave without turning around and kept going. She could easily have got her own taxi, but was not going to. Let him feel like a shit.

After a moment Fox stepped between parked cars and a taxi stopped and he got into it.

The subway station was jammed and smelly and hot and there were homeless people down there on the platform— two men in ragged clothes still asleep on benches, their ragged bundles serving as pillows; and then a bit farther on a woman clutching a similar bundle who reclined against the wall snoring. Most of the homeless were harmless enough; they just weren't very pleasant to look at. Not many years before such people would have been referred to as derelicts or bums. There were too many to call them that now. They could not be dismissed so easily. They were a municipal failure, or perhaps a national failure. They were people with no place else to go.

Most of the other waiting passengers simply pretended they were not there. For Jane this was impossible. Having been assigned to do a piece about the problem, she had interviewed more than thirty of them in all parts of the city, and then had written not a single piece but a three-part series about the proliferation of the homeless in the richest city in the richest country in the world. When published, the series had caused some consternation at City Hall. The mayor had promised to do something, and maybe he would. Jane was not a cynical person but she knew better than to trust the public utterances of politicians under pressure from newspapers.

Jane was thirty-six. In college she had majored in English literature, had written poems and mooned over various young men, all of whom had tried to get her into bed, and a number of whom had succeeded. This had begun the process of hardening her for life. She had acted in college plays, and had found it enthralling. After graduation she had tried to become an actress. She had had photos made up, and had begun the round of auditions. She had thick, dark brown hair, blue eyes, and a fair complexion—whenever she got angry or blushed it showed. Otherwise there was a softness to her face. She had auditioned for producers, agents, casting directors. She had tried to attract anyone who might help her. She had attracted them, and then had had to fight them off.

For three years she had auditioned, waitressing on the side, taking money from her father. She had got only a few small parts. Sometimes she was one of two hundred girls, many of them truly beautiful, auditioning for the same part. She could be rejected one day, cry herself to sleep that night, and go

back into a theater the next day and try again. She was
determined to succeed. People were always surprised to find
she was a competitor, for she looked so vulnerable. But at
last she turned away from the stage.

She decided to become a newspaper reporter. This goal
seemed to her almost equally romantic, and it proved to be
almost equally elusive.

She got a job on the paper as a copygirl running errands;
her father still had to send her money to live. After a year
she had been promoted to clerk, and she had begun writing
articles on her own time for certain of the paper's Sunday
sections. Journalism, she now saw, was unromantic in the
extreme. Which is not to say it did not excite her. It excited
her more every day. If she could not become a great actress,
then she would become a great reporter and do good with
her life. Change the world, or at least small corners of the
world. She dreamed of investigating scoundrels, of exposing
something really disgusting and stopping it. About this time
she also met Fox, who had been full of energy and enthusiasm
then, and who dreamed, so he said, of becoming a famous
trial lawyer. The two dreamers moved in together and, soon
after, married. All her friends were married. It seemed to her
the right time. She was not exactly head over heels in love,
but blamed this on too much previous experience.

Jane did get promoted to reporter, but Fox never became
a trial lawyer. He took no steps in that direction. He became
instead a specialist in corporate mergers. Corporate mergers
was the way America was going, he told her. The legal
technicalities that he seemed to find so fascinating, the
hundreds of pages of small print, did not fascinate her, though
she tried to show interest. He was her husband and marriage
had to be worked at, she realized. But before long she realized
also that this particular husband was not the man she thought
she had married. Fox's mergers absorbed him totally. He
brought work home, was preoccupied, was rarely funny anymore, and he did not seem very interested in her.

By now Jane had been on the paper twelve years, had been
a reporter for nine. She had driven one scoundrel from office,

the chairman of the Landmarks Preservation Commission. The man had accepted money so that a midtown theater could be condemned. The thrill of nailing someone who was betraying the public was as terrific as she had imagined. She was the one who had broken the story, and during the first few days, before the other papers got up the nerve to help, she was the only one writing it. She wrote it nervously each day: Who am I to be attacking this man, am I so sure I'm right? She was filled with fear and at night did not sleep. But she was right, and the chairman went to jail for six months.

She had grown into a tough and determined person. She would fight other reporters for stories, she would fight men for stories, she would come back with details others did not get.

She was five feet seven and weighed 125 pounds, meaning she could wear clothes well. She liked clothes and spent a lot of her money on them. She had a firm chin and nice eyes and fleshy lips that made her look, to many men, sexy. She certainly did not look like an aggressive reporter. She had never had any trouble attracting boys and then men which, once she was married, was a nuisance. Especially in her professional life it was a nuisance. Most men thought every woman available, and when she was working she sometimes did not have the leisure to say no nicely. But she had no intention of catting around. To Jane, marriage was marriage, and perhaps they were all like hers, rather tame once the initial gloss had worn off. Sometimes she considered divorce, but the very idea frightened her. If she divorced Fox, what did she do next? Perhaps there was nothing better out there, and besides, Fox had done nothing to deserve such a step. He did not cheat on her that she knew of, was often thoughtless but never deliberately cruel, did not harass her, was scrupulously fair about money, and he certainly never hit her. It was just that he did not seem to need her for anything. They rarely had fun together. He seemed to think that what she did for a living was sordid. He never praised her and perhaps did not read her stories at all. In any case he never talked about them.

As a reporter Jane was more or less satisfied with what she had accomplished. As a woman she was less so. She accused herself of indecisiveness, lack of direction. She felt unfulfilled, and was not entirely sure why. She wished in a vague way that she might fall in love again.

She waited on the subway platform.

When the train came she wedged her way inside into the crush and rode that way for seventeen minutes, not very long compared to the rides some people endured every day. But by the time she had come up the stairs into the sunlight again her armpits were moist, and sweat had run down her backbone, and she was extremely annoyed at Fox.

She rode the elevator up to the newsroom on the seventh floor. She was alone in the elevator car, and alone in the newsroom too when she came into it, except for two janitors who moved along the rows of desks emptying wastebaskets. An hour from now the editors and reporters would come in. The energy level would go up and up, something she still found exciting, people moving, talking, joking, telephones ringing, the floor—the whole building—humming with computers. But at this hour the newsroom was another thing: a vast, windowless space, low-ceilinged, empty, almost oppressive, row after row of unoccupied desks stretching from one wall to the other, the distance of a full city block.

She moved to her own desk, which was almost in the exact center of the floor, put her handbag down and switched on her terminal almost with the same motion. When the screen lit up, she leaned over the keyboard and tapped out the commands that called up her story on the working mothers. When it appeared, tears of frustration popped into her eyes, and she pulled her chair out and sat down. Last night after she had gone home her story had again been tampered with—for the second night in a row—and by the same editor, judging from his handiwork. A man named Gottlieb. An assistant Metro editor. New. He had changed her lead and had moved certain paragraphs around in the body of the text so that to her they no longer scanned. She considered that the story no longer had any emotional impact, barely made sense.

She remembered how long and hard she had worked on it and with what pleasure she had turned it in. Not exposing scoundrels this time, exposing instead the suffering of women much like herself. A story, she imagined, that could be read two hundred years from now as a true picture of the world that women had faced in the next to last decade of this century, how they had thought and felt, a true and special picture of their lives.

As it had made its way through the editorial process no one had touched it. And then this man Gottlieb had come upon it, had told her he thought she should rearrange the top, and had begun to do it himself. From that moment there was little chance the piece would ever run the way she wanted it to, maybe no chance. It had felt as if her throat had been slit. It would be an uphill battle even to get something she didn't like into the paper.

The piece was long. She had put two weeks into it. It would run about two columns, assuming it ever ran at all. She began to study it. She read it through three times from beginning to end, then put back her own lead and the original paragraph order. This was dangerous.

As she worked she kept watching the front of the floor where the editors sat. The Metro editor, Vaughan, had a reputation for coming in early. This was crucial. She had to see him alone, without Gottlieb or one of the others coming over to see what they were doing.

At ten minutes to ten Vaughan appeared. He sat down at his desk and began opening mail, and Jane went forward and told him she needed his help. She rolled a chair over next to his and asked him to call up her story on his terminal. He hesitated a moment, then did as asked, and she began to plead for her vision of what the story was about.

"Every night in homes across the country," she told him, "hundreds of thousands of women change places. The mother comes home from work, and the nanny or mother's helper or whatever you want to call her, leaves. The child often clings to the nanny, not the mother."

Her story detailed the problems of such working mothers,

women who were absolutely dependent on these other women who were their surrogates most of each day, working mothers who worried about much more than whether or not the nannies treated their children properly. They worried about what they would do if the nanny ever quit, they worried about keeping her happy, they didn't even know what to call her, or what to ask to be called themselves.

They were women filled with doubt and with guilt. They were mothers without guidelines. There was no one to ask. Their own mothers hadn't worked. Their role was new. They stood in a new place in the world.

"Yeah," said Vaughan, "but Bill Gottlieb said the whole premise seems to lack, you know, drama."

Jane knew that she had to be careful. Gottlieb was so new in his post that he had nothing to do nights except call up people's stories on his terminal. Two days ago he had come upon Jane's. It was important to get the focus off Gottlieb, but this was hard for her, so great was her anger and frustration. Gottlieb doesn't understand the story and you don't either, she wanted to tell Vaughan. But she couldn't say this or anything like it, lest it be taken as whining. Male reporters used such arguments all the time. It was known as fighting for your story and they were admired for it, especially if successful; they weren't accused of whining. But she was a woman, and women, at least on this paper, were said to whine.

Originally the story had been Jane's idea, but Vaughan had approved it.

"You thought it was dramatic enough when I started on it," she told him.

"I guess I did." He gazed into his terminal studying her lines. "I see what Gottlieb means. If it had a hard lead, it would stand up better."

"It doesn't need a hard lead. We're talking about millions of women who will recognize themselves instantly."

To lose the story would mean to her no reduction in pay. It would be a career setback, of course. However slight, no woman on this paper could afford one of those. Mostly she was fighting for her story because she had worked hard on it, believed in it, even saw herself in it, though she had no children yet and, the way her life was going, might never have any.

Vaughan, who was still staring at his terminal, suddenly remarked brightly: "I think I see what's wrong. And a solution."

Jane waited warily for whatever this brilliant solution turned out to be.

"My mother never worked," Vaughan said, "my wife never worked. It's obvious that women with children should be home taking care of them, not working. The thing to do is to call up some child psychologists, get them to comment on how this is stunting the development of the children." He glanced over at her, grinning broadly. "How's that for a hard lead?"

He had missed the point, but she was in no position to say so. The point was not that the children were being hurt, which could in no way be proved, but that millions of women were struggling to find a solution to their problem. There were women in pain out there.

Instead, unable to meet his eyes, she said carefully, "Very good, you might have found the answer." She hated herself as she spoke, but was determined to save her story. "The trouble is," she continued hesitantly, "no psychologist is going to make such a pronouncement. You know how mealymouthed they all are. They'll hedge, they'll say something bland."

As she saw his face harden, she added hastily: "I'll call up a lot of them. I'll go for the best quote I can coax out of them, and I'll move it as high up in the story as I can. Do you think that will do it?" And she gave him the sweetest smile of which she was at that moment capable.

"That's all this piece needs," said Vaughan. "This is a good piece."

Gottlieb had just come into the newsroom. Jane saw him out of the corner of her eye. He was at his desk.

Now he was gazing at them.

Now he was coming over.

"One other thing," Jane said hurriedly. "A lot of men have edited this piece so far. I can only work for one editor at a time. When I'm finished, can I bring it directly to you? Will you edit it for me?"

Her piece had already disappeared from Vaughan's terminal. Plainly he was anxious to get back to reading his mail. Jane smiled at him several times, just to keep his attention. She despised herself for doing this. I had to do it, she told herself.

Vaughan smiled fondly at her. "Sure," he said. Then: "We'll get this piece on the front page yet."

Jane went back to her desk and for the first time in her life she thought she knew what people meant when they said: I need a drink.

The newsroom was beginning to fill up, and a reporter named Edith Holtz came by and suggested they go up to the cafeteria for a cup of coffee before work.

"Right now all I want to do is get out of this building," Jane said.

Edith understood at once. "A coffee upstairs would choke you."

Jane laughed. "I'll go across the street with you if you like." Across the street was a bar-restaurant named Dorsey's that catered to the paper's employees.

They started out of the building but at the elevators were stopped by two other women whom they coaxed into joining them. The four women went out onto the street. A number of flatbed trucks loaded with great rolls of newsprint were lined up waiting to back into the paper's various loading bays. Dorsey's neon sign was flashing as they approached.

As she came through the door the hot, beery fumes hit Jane in the face. Early as it was, there were already men at the bar drinking heavily, for she caught glimpses of beer glasses standing beside shots of whiskey. Pressmen, mailers, truckers, she supposed, for several of them turned as the women entered, and one called out:

"Here come the cupcakes."

A remark to dismay Jane further. Not that she cared about the boors at the bar. But certain editors, it was reliably reported, used the term too, in private. Not to our faces, she thought, they wouldn't dare. Behind our backs. The rest of the world may have gone beyond that, but to our bosses female reporters are not to be taken seriously.

As the four women waded through fumes to a table in the back, there came additional comments and asides from the bar, which they ignored. A waitress brought them coffee and they sat over it. Jane liked these women whose lives she shared. She supposed that the male reporters were all rivals one with the other, that their relationships were distorted by competition and jealousy; but the women, being underdogs or underprivileged or whatever they were, were more comrades. Jealousy was muted. They were competing against men, not against each other.

Jane had never previously felt warm camaraderie with other women, not in college, not anywhere else before coming to the paper. It still seemed new to her. It still surprised and pleased her. It seemed to prove—each time only temporarily, unfortunately—that the world was not such a bad place and the paper was not such a bad place.

The four women sat in the bar for thirty minutes, at first purveying office gossip and giggling a good deal. Then:

"It's easy to get ahead around here, if you're a woman—"

"Yeah, you put in your ninety hours a week and—"

The conversation had gone in a moment from amusing, slightly salacious, totally inconsequential gossip to the subjects that really interested them: their career future, their future as women.

"I was working late on a story," said Elaine Belden. "It was past ten o'clock and—"

"You looked up and every reporter still in the newsroom was a woman."

"I said to myself, is this what you have to do?"

Although Jane listened and went on smiling, part of her stood to one side studying the others. Elaine Belden was thirty-four, energetic, cute-looking, disciplined, good; she had already worked on four of the most prestigious papers in four of the biggest cities in the country. She was unmarried and had begun to worry about it. She worried about having children. Her biological clock was running. Her career was not going as well as she hoped. Edith Holtz was good too, and had won prizes. She was forty, dowdy, lumpy. Her biological clock had stopped, most likely, though she continued to pretend otherwise. Sue Parker was the oldest of them, forty-two. Her career was important to her, but she was not striving to the extent they were. She had a husband and two children and only worked four days a week. Her career, as Jane saw it, was humming along at about fifteen watts.

All of them were worried about progress, or lack of progress, in their careers.

"I have nightmares about it," Jane confessed.

"Me too—that one day I'll wake up and find myself in one of the soft sections of the paper."

"The Style section, or something."

Style occupied the far corner of the floor down a corridor and behind the paper's morgue, as far removed as possible from the editors' offices along the north wall—the paper's power elite. A Style reporter could work in the building a year and never even be seen by any of the editors. Being women, they couldn't even arrange to run into them in the men's room, as the male reporters could.

"Style makes money—all those grocery ads."

"And all the free food."

"It comes in all day. Have you been back there?"

"They don't know what to do with it. They lay it out on tables."

"The people back there, they spend their whole time grazing."

These three women were Jane's friends. She liked them, even admired them, and she liked and admired most of the other women in the office as well. But she did not want to be any one of them, and she asked herself, as she had many times lately, as she had as a child: What do I want to be when I grow up?

"You should hear Millie Pender on the subject of the paper."

"I know, she's quite bitter."

Millie Pender was assistant national editor, the only woman even close to the paper's hierarchy.

"She goes to the story conferences each day. The men act as if she isn't there."

"She says they're arrogant, overbearing—"

"She told me it was as if they all had their dicks out and were showing off to her. Mine is bigger."

Women, Jane thought, do not usually speak so crudely. To say such a thing Millie must have been really angry.

Jane wanted to be successful, but not if it meant being like Millie Pender. She wanted to win prizes, but not if it meant being like Edith Holtz. She wanted to have babies, but not a fifteen-watt career like Sue Parker—not after having worked this hard to get where she was. And Jane too was worried about her biological clock.

"They ought to give us a course in college called when is the best time to have babies," said Jane.

"Should you have them right after college, you mean?"

"And start your career afterwards?"

"Or wait until you've made it?"

"How do you know when you've made it?" said Jane.

"It's a harder decision when you're older."

"You're lucky, Sue, you've got your children. And Jane is lucky too. At least she's married. She can have a child anytime she wants."

Could she? Could her career survive a six-month maternity leave? Could her marriage?

The four women split the check four ways and went back into the paper's building and upstairs and to work.

At headquarters as Douglas came in the door his clerks and secretaries, men with guns at their belts, desk-bound cops, stood up applauding.

Grinning, he went through into his private bathroom where he stripped, soaped a washcloth, and washed himself all over the way a woman would, the way he had seen his wife do sometimes: after strenuous daytime lovemaking, for instance, when they were courting.

A nice memory. He let his mind dwell on it a moment, then shaved and put on clean underwear, and his chief secretary, a captain, poked his head in to say the PC wanted to see him.

He put on a white shirt and the brown suit and tie he had brought in yesterday, and bounded up the stairs to the four-teenth floor, but as he made his way along the corridor, men came out of their offices to shake his hand.

"Thank you," he kept saying, "thank you." He couldn't stop grinning, though as he entered the PC's office he tried to.

"Good morning," the PC said cordially, and Douglas waited to be praised, but this did not happen.

"Fellow came in here," the PC began. He moved nervously around in front of his desk. "Not more than an hour ago, it was. Take a seat. Put an interesting proposition to us."

The royal we. Douglas had been worried about flattery. He had been ready to fend it off. Instead he was instantly on guard.

"Yes," said the PC. "Herbert Campbell from Drug Enforcement." To track him, as he paced back and forth, Douglas was forced to keep swiveling his head.

He was confused and wary. Had there been a complaint? —the word to a cop had criminal connotations. Was one of his men in trouble? Was he in trouble himself? Or perhaps some cop had stepped on some federal agent's toes? The Feds always thought they were the last word in law enforcement. Cops thought otherwise. And today we proved it, Douglas thought, and for a moment he again swelled up with pleasure and self-importance.

"You know Campbell?" the PC asked.

"Of course." Campbell was the DEA's agent in charge in New York.

"Sat right in that very chair," the PC said. "Suggested his office take over our major cases."

Douglas was shocked.

But the idea was preposterous, and as he realized this, he gave a confident chuckle. "The Feds can't stand the competition," he said, and grinned and waited for the PC to acknowledge last night's seizure.

"He made some strong arguments for it too," the PC said instead. "Suggested I sound you out."

Douglas's grin faded as he tried to understand what the PC was saying.

"Which of course I would have done anyway." There was no eye contact. The PC, pacing, never once looked at him.

He was a man of fifty, rotund, rosy cheeked. He wore rimless glasses. He had the smooth bland face of a priest—of most priests Douglas had known. In any case, it was not a cop's face. Cops were men who dealt with psychopaths, with predators—men who were ruthless or mindless or both. They learned to live with terror, and on the faces of most of them it showed.

Unlike most of his predecessors who had been career cops, this particular PC, whose name was Leo Windsell, had come from the judiciary. Lots of judges were being made police commissioners, a nationwide trend. Even the last two FBI directors had been judges. Everything in America was trendy these days, even law enforcement. One had to get used to it.

Leo Windsell had been an assistant district attorney for eleven years. Then the political parties put him up for judge, having agreed on him and some others in back-room bargaining; he ran on both tickets, was elected to a fourteen-year term and served it. Most of it. Toward the end the mayor offered to appoint him police commissioner. The money would be about the same, the prestige also. But the exposure would be ten times more, a hundred times more. In his new job he would deal with crime not in hushed courtrooms but in headlines and on TV. He would become more famous than any judge—and able to command a job paying real money afterward. For the rest of his life people would wonder whether to call him Judge or Commissioner. What a problem! Windsell promptly resigned from the bench, and who wouldn't?

The commissionership came with only one quite small risk: there was no tenure. The mayor could dismiss him at a moment's notice according to law. But this could happen only to an impulsive or headstrong PC, one who might choose to ignore a mayoral whim.

"Yes," Windsell said now, "the mayor sent him along to me, apparently. He tried his scheme out on His Honor first, you might say."

Douglas—all cops—knew where true power lay.

"I don't need to tell you," Windsell said, "there are good arguments in favor."

In the NYPD, officers did not resist police commissioners, and if asked an opinion, if they valued their careers, were careful to give the one the PC was looking for. But Douglas was in a state of shock and unable to help himself. "There are better arguments against."

Windsell had glanced at him sharply. Then he smiled.

"You can imagine what the arguments in favor might be," Windsell said. "I don't have to tell you."

But he proceeded to enumerate them anyway: 1. Federal drug laws were tougher and broader than New York State laws, particularly the conspiracy statutes; 2. The DEA had nationwide jurisdiction and could pursue a case wherever it led—outside the city, even overseas. "The Feds are the ones with the good labs," Windsell continued. "We don't have labs like they do."

"We have good labs."

The PC ignored the interruption. "And money for buys. They have far more buy money than we do. A hundred-thousand-dollar undercover buy to them is no big deal."

This was true. The city would not put up large amounts.

"And intelligence," said Windsell. "They have intelligence coming in from all over the world. Admit it, we can't match their intelligence network, can we?"

"Last night we seized two tons of cocaine in Queens," said Douglas. He was almost pleading. "Without their buy money and without access to their intelligence."

"Yes, congratulate the men for me."

"We also seized two million bucks."

"The money," the PC said. "That's almost the major problem, isn't it. There's so much money at the end of these major cases as to constitute a serious corruption hazard for our men. Better for us to let the Feds cope with that sort of thing. Let them take the heat, not us."

Douglas was reduced to silence.

"We would keep the street-level enforcement squads. We would still be arresting your friendly neighborhood pusher. Though, frankly, I'd like to get the department out of the drug business entirely."

The PC pushed the button on his intercom. "Send for Chief Conner," he ordered his secretary. "Reach out for him."

From such a man the police jargon—"Reach out for"— sounded odd. Douglas went to the window, stood between heavy drapes and stared out but saw nothing. The drapes were thick velvet. The city did not furnish its police commissioners with thick velvet drapes. The last PC had left these windows bare. His whole office had been bare. There was some kind of Chinese carpet beneath Douglas's shoes, too. And a row of Chinese vases on the sideboard in front of the other window.

Windsell had moved back to his desk. Douglas heard him sit down. In silence the two men waited for Chief Conner, commander of the Organized Crime Control Bureau and the man to whom Douglas reported.

"The Feds can make arrests under the RICO conspiracy laws," the PC said. "RICO is practically indispensable in drug cases, wouldn't you say?"

"Are you telling me it's done, Commissioner?"

"I'm running it by you. See what your thoughts are."

"We just made the biggest seizure in the history of the city."

A part of Douglas stood to one side and was amazed to hear himself resist even to this extent. It was the smoothly political cops who got ahead, he had noted as a young man. Not yes-men exactly, he had told himself as he strove to join them, but men who accepted the authority of those above them in rank. By behaving, for the most part, exactly as they behaved he had in time been invited to headquarters himself, and had prospered there.

"Two tons," he said. "It's a case the Feds never could have made."

"Oh, I wouldn't be too sure about that."

He saw that he had succeeded in making Windsell uncomfortable; the former judge, like all his predecessors, had become used to acquiescent subordinates, and for the moment did not know how to react.

"It would be a terrible thing for our morale." Douglas was choosing his words carefully.

The PC eyed him. "I'm sure you're exaggerating."

The door opened and Chief Conner came in. When he saw Douglas a grin came on and he stepped up and wrung his hand. Probably he thought he had been summoned precisely for that—a ceremonial handshake followed by a few minutes of gloating.

"Brilliant, Ray," he said. "Brilliant."

Conner was ten years older and outranked Douglas three stars to one. A burly, red-faced man, beaming. "Thank you," Douglas said.

"Ray was the one who set it up," said Conner to Windsell. "I never believed in any stash of that size, a whole roomful as I understand it, but he did."

"The whole department thanks you," said Windsell.

Tired, frustrated, angry, and thoroughly disheartened, Douglas moved toward the door.

As the PC realized that Douglas was walking out on him, his first reaction was astonishment. His second was to attempt to save face in front of Conner, so he gave a quick false smile and called out: "Thanks for coming in," to Douglas's departing back.

But the door closed, and as it did so the PC's smile darkened.

Grasping what had happened, Conner quickly apologized. "Ray hasn't been himself lately."

Windsell muttered something under his breath.

"I'll talk to him," said Conner. "He's had a rough time these last couple of months."

"Yeah."

"What would you like me to do?"

"Sit down there a minute." Conner's reaction was more what the PC was used to. He pointed to the chair beside his desk, and Conner did as ordered, waiting in silence while Windsell again got up and paced the rug.

"Fellow made me an interesting proposition," he began. "Not much more than an hour ago, it was. Had already been to see the mayor, it seems. Herbert Campbell from Drug Enforcement. You know him, I believe. Let me give you the arguments he made."

The three-star chief of the Organized Crime Control Bureau, who had been a cop thirty-two years, and a headquarters cop fourteen years, made no interruptions, only nodding from time to time as he listened.

"We would furnish about a hundred elite detectives to this federal task force," the PC concluded. "That narrows down our exposure considerably, which is all to the good, wouldn't you say?"

There was silence.

These were, ultimately, Conner's detectives as much as Douglas's. The entire elite function of the Narcotics Division was to be given away. But Conner had noted the PC's pretense of seeking advice, the falsely jovial tone of voice. He had heard the mayor's name dropped.

"So how does it sound to you?" the PC said.

"Good," Conner said. "I mean, I can see some problems, but on the whole, good."

"You do see the advantages?"

Conner saw them more clearly than the PC might have thought. Particularly the political ones that had not been mentioned. With the police corruption problem eliminated, with police responsibility eliminated, the voters could no longer blame the proliferation of drugs and drug crime on the department and on the mayor. They would have to blame the Feds. From the mayor's point of view, it was a stroke of genius. From Windsell's too.

"You mentioned possible problems," Windsell said.

"Minor things," said Conner. He held up thumb and forefinger half an inch apart.

"Chief Douglas didn't seem to think they were so minor."

"He's not himself at the moment."

"He's got friends in the press."

"Those guys," said Conner.

"They can make trouble if he goes to them."

"Ray Douglas is not that type of cop."

"No?"

"He's very loyal. You'll see."

The two men looked at each other.

"You don't know him like I do," said Conner.

"You're right, I don't."

"Many years."

The PC looked at him until Conner dropped his eyes.

"Leave him to me," Conner said.

The PC said: "Yes."

Douglas was at his desk, staring at nothing, when Conner burst in the door.

"Are you out of your mind?"

Douglas looked up. "What did I do?"

"You left before he gave you permission to leave."

Douglas laughed. "Did I?"

"Jesus, Ray, he's the PC."

Douglas smiled and gave a negligent wave of the hand.

"You act irrational lately. You'll wreck your career."

Then Conner said in a kinder voice: "You've had a tough

break, but people are not going to make allowances for you
much longer.''

"Did he tell you what he's planning?''

"No,'' the older man lied. ''You tell me.''

"He wants to emasculate the Narcotics Divison,'' Douglas
said, the start of a brief impassioned speech. But when it
concluded Conner only nodded.

So Douglas began a second speech. ''We're like hunters,''
he said. ''It will be like sending us out into a woods that's
teeming with big game, but we're only allowed to shoot
squirrels.''

Again Conner only nodded.

"All those detectives out there trying to stumble on a big
case. Finished. All those white shield guys hoping to win a
gold shield. Finished.''

Conner watched him but still said nothing.

"Do you think it's a good idea?'' Douglas asked.

"It doesn't matter what I think.''

"You don't, but you're afraid to say so.''

"He's the boss, Ray.''

"I want to know what you think, Chief.''

"He's the one we work for.''

"It's as if you don't even care,'' Douglas said.

"I care, but if that's what he wants to do, there's nothing
we can do about it.''

"Oh yes there is, Chief.''

"Like what, Ray?''

"Well, we could go over his head.''

"To whom, Ray?''

It was only a vague idea. Douglas was trying it out. ''To
the press. To the mayor.''

"I don't think that would be very wise.''

It was a guaranteed career wrecker, but to Douglas at the
moment it had its appeal.

Conner walked to the window and peered out. Below was
Police Plaza. Beyond was City Hall, its roof poking above
the trees of the park that surrounded it. Conner's own office
on the other side of the building looked out over the East

River, with Brooklyn beyond. It was a more impressive view, but then he had more rank. "You got a nice view here, Ray," he said.

Douglas was silent.

Conner turned from the window. "Why do you think they had so much stashed in one place last night?"

"I've been asking myself."

"And so much money too."

"Maybe they thought they had a leak. Maybe they thought they could plug it if they localized all their stuff. Or maybe they thought all their other stash houses were under surveillance and this one wasn't. You know how paranoiac they are. Maybe they were seeing cops who weren't there."

"And not seeing cops who were there."

The chief of Organized Crime Control had turned back to the view.

"Some of the packages may have entered the country in a shipment of lumber," Douglas said. "They smelled like cedar. Others were stained with what looked like crude oil. Maybe they came in by tanker."

The chief of Organized Crime Control looked at him.

"We still have no idea how the stuff got into the city," Douglas said, "or where they had it stashed before this. That's the next part of the case."

"It's unusual for them to stash money and goods in the same place," said Conner.

"We found no adding machines, no money-counting machines—which means that usually they kept their money somewhere else."

"You're probably right."

"This isn't your usual case, Chief. It's going to go on and on."

"Sure," said Conner. "But it's going to lead out of the city pretty quick, I imagine. The DEA could probably do a better job than we could. From here on in, I mean."

"The markings on the packages indicate they came from the Medellín group. But the Cali group always had a monopoly on New York in the past. Maybe there's a war brewing."

"Like the old Mafia wars."

"My intelligence guys are studying the packages now."

"No they're not."

"What?"

"The PC ordered it all sent over to the DEA on Fifty-seventh Street."

Douglas sat in stunned silence.

Then, despite himself, he started pleading. "We really hurt them today, Chief. They're going to start shooting each other. Medellín versus Cali. Guys are going to get killed over a loss like this."

"Maybe," said Conner.

"You know how they are, Chief. When they kill you they also kill your wife, your children, your mother."

"And other innocent bystanders."

"There'll be corpses turning up all over Queens, Chief," pleaded Douglas.

"Probably."

"It's a great case," pleaded Douglas, for Conner might be able to do something; he himself could not. "Chief, please."

As Conner strode toward the door, he was smiling. "Ray, you worry too much. By the way, the PC is giving a press conference later. He wants you to be there. Three o'clock. He intends to praise you to the skies, I imagine. Your picture will be on all the news shows tonight, I imagine."

Douglas rose from his chair and began stuffing papers into his attaché case. "I'm going home."

"He wants me to be there, too."

"I've been up all night."

"So take a nap and come back."

"Tell him I'm home sleeping it off."

"You know you don't mean that, Ray."

3

AT THAT SAME HOUR twenty-five hundred miles to the south in the boardroom of the Banco Credito Ley, five of the richest men in the world sat down at one end of a conference table. The fluorescent lighting was recessed. It was an interior room, soundless, bright.

Although the men had greeted each other with smiles and handshakes as Latins do, their meeting began without small talk and without jokes. These were not amusing men, and although colleagues, almost partners, they did not trust each other.

The five were the same age, more or less, about forty, but were not dressed alike. The banker, David Ley, wore a conservative business suit. To his right sat a man in riding breeches and boots. The other three wore open-necked polo shirts and corduroy pants. The clothing differences hinted at equivalent social differences, and these existed, though in most other ways—in wealth and stature in particular—these men were equals.

Pencils and yellow pads lay in front of each place because Ley's secretary, who was not present, thought this proper for meetings. But they were not being used. The business of these men was one in which little was written down. They were men with excellent memories, better than excellent, as those who had tried to shortchange them, short-weight them, abuse their confidence, had learned.

The business suit worn by Ley was beautifully cut, dark gray worsted, summer weight. Medellín, a city of two million people, lies close to the equator but at an altitude of five thousand feet; every day is a warm spring day. Ley's shirt was monogrammed, his tie silk, his mustache neatly trimmed. His hair was combed straight back in a pompadour. He sat at the head of the table chairing, he believed, this meeting. He imagined himself senior to the others, the voice of breeding and therefore reason, their leader. He imagined that by sitting below him at his table they acknowledged his preeminence—at least subliminally. They did not. They were blunt men, not subtle ones. They read a man's eyes, not his suit. They had long ago read David Ley, a man born rich, unlike themselves. They thought him careless, lacking in concentration. He did not like to get his hands dirty. They knew him as a womanizer and disapproved on both moral and practical grounds. In bed men talk, and women—when they were not wives or permanent mistresses—talked too much. They thought him a man who only played at a business that was for them all-consuming, a world unto itself.

They did not quite use the word dilettante.

The three men dressed in corduroys and polo shirts looked like rough types, and were. All three had started their careers as thieves and murderers. The man in the riding habit, affecting it almost as a uniform, was from a family of horse breeders that had gone broke. He had begun his adult life working in a short-order restaurant.

The subject of today's meeting was a major installation certain of them wanted to construct in the department of Amazonas in the extreme south of the country. The installation, if they decided to build it, would be expensive and would require the participation of them all. Of course all would benefit as well.

There was no map of Colombia on the table, and no need for one; they knew their country. There were no graphs on easels; they knew their business.

In the south the Amazon served as Colombia's border with Peru. In places the river was so wide one could not see across. On the Colombian side were the many tributaries flowing into it. In between tributaries was the densest jungle on earth. There were no roads; one used the rivers or cut dirt tracks as needed. There were no people anywhere around except maybe a few Indians blowing poisoned darts at monkeys high up in the trees.

For other reasons, too, the proposed site was good. The raw material of their business was not heavy but it was bulky and difficult to transport; it could be floated down the river from Peru. The machinery and the needed precursor chemicals, which were heavy and bulky both, could come upriver by boat from Brazil.

They had been over most of this once before but had adjourned without acting on it. The installation would not actually be on the Amazon but some miles up a tributary called the Paquirri. There was a single town not too close, Leticia, which gave onto the Amazon. The occasional boat tour sometimes stopped there, but otherwise it was accessible only by air. Leticia would be available for ordinary supplies, and in its post office were a few phones—phones that shut down when the post office closed up each day, which was all to the good also. The men who would work the installation would be enlisted in Medellín. Once on the site, they would have to be brought in to the post office once a week and allowed to call home.

They needed a place that was both isolated and accessible, did they not? said Pablo Marzo, the roughest of the rough trio, and their spokesman. What could be better, he said, and stopped, and eyed Ley speculatively.

"That's FARC territory down there," said David Ley from his chair at the head of the table. FARC was the strongest of Colombia's Marxist guerrilla groups.

"I've rented them," said Pablo Marzo.

He was a stocky man with a dark Indio complexion, black hair and mustache, thin lips, big white teeth. A hard face. And, Ley knew, a hard, dangerous man. He had a wife and teenage sons. He had houses all over Colombia, all of which featured gold faucets and life-size shrines to the Virgin. He liked to drive his own trucks. He liked to load shipments onto airplanes with his own hands. Ley looked at him.

"They will permit us to build the installation, and after that will protect it."

"Even against the army?" said David Ley.

"Especially against the army."

"The demand for our product is through the roof," said Antonio Lucientes, the man in the riding habit. He was grinning wolfishly. "We need a big place."

He seemed so pleased that David Ley, who still imagined he chaired this meeting, expected him to start slapping his riding crop on the table.

Their enemies would find and destroy such an installation, Ley suggested. He liked the sound of this argument and so went on with it. It had happened to them before, when a similar, even grander installation in a similar isolated part of the country was laid waste in a matter of hours at enormous financial loss to them all. Bigness attracted talk, and talk attracted enemies. Better to go on as they had been doing, many small places rather than one big one. Why did they wish to repeat past mistakes?

The installation under discussion was a clandestine laboratory capable of processing huge quantities of cocaine per week, but the word *cocaine* was never mentioned, nor the word *laboratory*, out of deference to Ley, who preferred to use circumlocutions: installation, product and the rest. Lucientes's lips never formed the word *cocaine* either. When others spoke it he sometimes laughed. A harmless vice, he would say, one that was making them all rich.

The other three men were less sensitive. They knew their product for what it was.

Ley's arguments had sounded solid to Ley. Seeking support, he glanced around the table from face to face.

This was one of the rare formal meetings of the so-called Medellín Cartel, which was not a cartel at all but these five men loosely associated, each one, for maximum profits and safety, employing from time to time the expertise of the others.

Ley, for instance, considered himself the money expert, and it was on this basis that the others had invited him into their group. They had allowed him to back their laboratories, to back their shipments, and finally to start up an organization of his own. They believed they recognized him for what he was but did not care. They had needed him then. Cocaine, being a cash business, generated truly shocking quantities of small bills. Ley had sent men to America to develop a network of jewelers and bullion salesmen in Miami, Los Angeles, and elsewhere who could deposit hundreds of thousands of dollars in cash in banks without attracting too much attention; after which, he had found other men, some of them already employed in his bank, who knew how to transfer these now vast sums electronically from bank to bank, country to country, until no one could possibly trace them.

In this way Ley had laundered hundreds of millions of dollars for the men in this room, keeping each time a commission, and recently he had made his service available to the two hundred or more smaller organizations that Marzo and the others permitted to operate, for the cartel had never sought absolute exclusivity. They awarded franchises, so to speak. The world was a big place. They practically handed out licenses, why not, and each time at a better price.

At the head of the table Ley smiled benignly. He considered himself indispensable to them, and at the beginning, five years previously, had been. But the others had learned from him and gone off in their own directions. He was by now less needed and more isolated than he knew.

The other men in the room, in addition to their own organizations, all had specialties of use to their colleagues.

Antonio Lucientes, however silly he looked in his riding habit, had built up the original U.S. distribution network, and had showed the way there. Members of the Lucientes family had been small-time cocaine traffickers in the old days because their horse business left them ideally placed for it. They sold horses abroad. They had contacts abroad. They used to send a few kilos of cocaine buried in the feed, and they knew how to hide horse profits and then cocaine profits so the Colombian government couldn't tax them. These attributes weren't enough now, but had been once. Antonio Lucientes had been in America when the crack explosion hit; he had been working in a restaurant at better pay than in

Colombia, as a cover for handling cocaine distribution. He had rushed home and urged his father, brothers, cousins to expand the cocaine sideline as fast as possible, for the demand, he said, was going to be insatiable. It was a big family and its members had employees, some of them even had servants, and Antonio began to send these trusted people, his own relatives and their employees' relatives and their servants' relatives, to America, and to build his distribution network around them.

His people acquired enormous experience. They learned the choke points where shipments were especially vulnerable to U.S. Customs or coast guard or DEA. They learned to send the cocaine down through three intervening levels of Colombians before it reached non-Colombians in the network, thus greatly enhancing security. They came to know procedures that worked and places to buy equipment: the cellular telephones, the money-counting machines, the Uzis and Mac 10s. They learned the names of lawyers who, in the event of arrest and seizure, could go through the court papers and find out where and how a mistake had been made—so that it would not be made again. Sometimes the lawyers were able to discover that someone had sold them out, making it possible for that person to be dealt with. Together, usually, with his entire family.

Antonio Lucientes's people and methods still dominated the distribution in the United States.

Ruben Jiménez, who sat across from him, was not from Medellín at all but from Bogotá. He was the cartel's link with the coca producers in Bolivia and Peru. He knew the terrain there, where the roads ran and the rivers, where clandestine airstrips existed or could be built, where soil and altitude were apt for new coca plantations, and this last was important because the coca bush required three years to reach maturity; in a booming business, future supply had to be assured. In the producing countries Jiménez knew everyone: the growers and their union heads, the middlemen, the politicians and the generals. He knew who to threaten and who to pay off and how much. He had been dealing with these people since the days when cocaine and also Jiménez were small time, when cocaine in America was a recreational drug restricted by its expense to film stars and rock musicians. In short Jiménez knew how to keep the producer countries producing, how to keep the raw material pouring into Colombia, where it would be processed and sent on its way.

Carlos Von Bauzer next to him was a pilot and the cartel's electronics and aviation expert. He was not from Medellín either, but from Armenia, two hundred kilometers to the south. He advised on which aircraft to buy and he equipped them with the latest detection devices and other gadgetry so as to foil those who might wish to intercept them. Also, he was the first to build airstrips on small Bahamian islands for use as staging bases, and it was several years before these bases were discovered and dismantled.

At the same time Von Bauzer had set up the cartel's state-of-the-art communications network, the parabolic discs that bounced radio and telephone transmissions off other people's satellites, the voice scramblers, and coding machines. He kept updating it for them all. He was the son of a Colombian mother and a German immigrant engineer. When he was fourteen his family had emigrated to the United States. His hobbies came to be electronics, flying, and stealing cars. He grew up to be a professional car thief. He exported hot cars back to Colombia, got caught, and did two years in jail in Connecticut, during which he developed a virulent hatred for America and all things American. While in jail he too came to believe that a cocaine explosion was imminent, so when he had served his time he went back to Colombia to get in on it.

Von Bauzer was the only member of the cartel who actually used cocaine, and perhaps he had used it too much. As he had got rich, and in Colombia famous, he built a private zoo on his ranch in Armenia and stocked it with exotic animals. Big ones: elephants, giraffes, rhinos. His hero was Adolf Hitler, and recently he had begun giving speeches glorifying Hitler. He was attempting to start a Nazi party in Colombia. He gave semipublic orgies involving young girls from good families; his own sexual appetites were said to encompass all living creatures. Someone had once machine-gunned Von Bauzer in his car, hitting him five times, killing his driver, leaving them both for dead. Ever since he had sometimes seemed deranged, and the acting out of his derangement sometimes led him to brutalize people who, if they complained to the authorities, then had to be, as the euphemism had it, suppressed.

Pablo Marzo was the dominant member of the cartel, and everyone realized it but David Ley.

Marzo had a zoo too, but it opened onto a public road and he had donated it to the city. The poor saw him as Robin Hood, for he had built over eighty neighborhood soccer stadiums, and free housing for over four hundred poor families. He owned one of Colombia's major soccer teams, and for a time had published his own newspaper whose articles mostly extolled himself. He had run for Congress and been elected as an alternate, but when voices were raised against this he had contemptuously stepped down. He was a man given to excesses. Excessive generosity. Excessive killing as well.

Marzo had started his career stealing tombstones out of cemeteries. He would grind the names off and resell them. Later two detectives arrested him for smuggling cocaine into Colombia from Peru in the spare wheel of one of his trucks. The case never came to trial because he bribed the judge to get out of jail, after which the two detectives, the only witnesses against him, somehow got themselves assassinated. Case closed. Whether he did it personally or not was not known. Today he oversaw cocaine production all over Colombia, knew what the lesser dealers were doing, allowed them access to raw materials, allowed them to contribute to shipments to North America on a quota basis.

He was the one who had made assassination such an integral part of their business. Cops and judges had been assassinated at his orders, prosecutors and jurors, newspaper publishers and reporters, and even, a few years ago, the minister of justice—the minister's murder had of course produced an incredible amount of heat. The entire cartel had had to leave the country for a while. Ley had toured Paris, Venice, and Rome. The others had crossed the border into Panama where, after paying off the necessary Panamanian officials, they had lived in comfort for some weeks. But the furor in Colombia had died down eventually, all of them were back home now and operating on the surface, and Marzo always defended his decision to murder the justice minister. It was essential that they rule by fear, he maintained, and first and foremost of those to be intimidated had to be members of the Colombian government. Apparently he was right. At the moment there were no cases pending against any of them in Colombia—no judge would dare, no government minister would dare—and the extradition treaty with the United States had recently been voided by the Colombian Supreme Court. Obviously Marzo's announced policy had rendered the Colombian government impotent. He had made it clear that anyone who opposed him would be killed instantly. And probably his loved ones with him.

In addition Marzo was understood to have offered a reward of half a million dollars for the murder of any DEA agent in Colombia. He liked grandiose gestures. The DEA's complement was believed to number less than twenty men. However, these twenty were equipped with vast amounts of money with which they could subvert almost anyone, perhaps even someone in Marzo's own entourage. The DEA was the only entity in Colombia which could not be subverted by themselves. The concern of Marzo and all the others was of being kidnapped by the DEA and being transported at once to Florida for trial—kidnapped without possibility of intervention by Colombia's own tame judiciary.

It was Marzo who had started the school for the training of assassins—''sicarios,'' Colombians called them. Assassinations were carried out, for the most part, by fifteen-year-olds riding pillion on motorscooters. They were all mindless at that age, and would do what they were told. In Marzo's school the fifteen-year-olds were instructed in the use of submachine guns, in marksmanship from moving motorscooters. They practiced driving scooters up onto sidewalks and alongside cars, they practiced keeping the machine straight and level during the shooting, and they practiced techniques for escaping afterwards. As part of their graduation exercises they were sent out onto the street to prove themselves by killing someone. Anyone, it didn't matter who.

Marzo's *sicarios* were for rent to any of the others.

But usually it was Marzo personally who would send them against specific targets. Of course some of these targets were his own subordinates. The man feared betrayal naturally, and he seemed to have a sixth sense as far as sniffing it out was concerned. He watched all his subordinates carefully, and usually struck only just before he believed they were about to.

Colombia was a country where only violence, Marzo believed, was understood. David Ley believed this too, up to a point. He believed he saw the need for revenge, reprisals, and retaliations as well as any man. But he thought that Marzo, as wealth and success piled up, had become more and more arrogant, more and more bloodthirsty, though he did not dare tell him so. That his murders had become somewhat indiscriminate. The victims all had relatives and friends, did they not, who now had an excellent motive for killing or trying to kill Marzo. Ley judged there must be two thousand such people by now. Marzo went nowhere without a dozen or more bodyguards, but surely someone would succeed one day soon.

Marzo was the only man at the table of whom Ley himself was afraid. The only man in Colombia, he told himself.

As today's meeting continued, Ley thought he understood why the former gravestone thief favored the big new installation. He saw it as another grandiose gesture, a grandiose thumbing of his nose at their government in Bogotá, and at the Americans, particularly the DEA.

For a time Ley had continued to argue against the idea, but now, seeing that his objections received no support from the others, he decided he did not want to risk antagonizing Marzo further. Besides which he had a date with a woman that afternoon and was anxious to get away.

So he gave a grin and announced brightly, making it unanimous: "It's settled then." The big jungle laboratory would be built and stocked.

Before he could say more a secretary entered and whispered in his ear.

Excusing himself, Ley got up and followed her out. At her desk he picked up her phone.

"*Digame*," he said, and listened.

When he had hung up he stood a few moments beside the desk thinking. Then he went back into the conference room and resumed his place at the head of the table. "There has been a misfortune in New York," he said. Staring straight at Marzo, he began to describe it: two tons of product seized, together with two million dollars in cash.

Marzo's gaze was fixed on the table top and he was muttering curses. He would not meet Ley's eyes. "In trying to enter the New York market," Ley said smugly, "we have perhaps made a mistake." The mistake was Marzo's doing. Today's result was no different from what Ley had expected.

There was a second cartel operating out of Cali to the south. It was smaller, only two or three groups, but until now it alone had operated in New York. To invade Cali's New York territory had been Marzo's idea. He had pushed it. New York was the most lucrative market in the world; they had a right to their share. At a meeting much like this one, the others had backed him—Ley with reluctance and only because the motion was going to carry anyway. Might as well make it unanimous, he had thought, wanting the other men to admire him, even though moving into New York, as he saw it, would lead only to losses and to killing.

The product seized today belonged to each of them, but could be replaced. That was not the point. The money lost, to these men, constituted an insignificant sum. That was not the point either. The point, to David Ley, was Marzo's arrogance.

"Five men arrested," Ley said, still staring at him.

"All of them?" said Lucientes.

"Yes," said Ley. "Five trusted men."

"The DEA," muttered Marzo. "Sons of whores."

"No," said Ley, "the New York Police Department, apparently." He did not give Douglas's name because he did not have it. It wasn't important anyway.

Salvador had not been arrested, but Ley didn't know this. Salvador was the son of Ley's cook. Ley saw him destined to spend the next twenty or thirty years in an American jail. He was about twenty-eight, with a wife and two kids, and the idea upset Ley. His cook would be in tears for a month and his meals would suffer.

"The Cali people are behind this," said Marzo.

"Maybe."

"Somebody should go up to New York and find out."

"Yes," said Ley, and he glanced around the table. He knew no one would volunteer. Certainly Marzo wouldn't. These men lived in terror of being arrested in a place where they did not own the legal system.

"I'll go," said Ley. He liked the way this sounded. It sounded brave. He would find out enough and when he came back he would force Marzo to agree to close down New York as a market.

"Good," Marzo said. "In the meantime, I'll take care of a few Cali people."

How many of them did he plan to kill? Ley asked himself. "Better not," he advised.

"Just to make sure they understand our position on this."

Ley wanted to get out of Medellín for a while—if Marzo was going to send his gunmen to Cali, there could be no better time. Besides, in New York there were some women he knew. The vacation would do him good. He would return a new man.

When the meeting at last broke up Ley remained at his desk to work out the details of his trip to New York.

He owned a brownstone there. He owned property in many places: an apartment in Medellín, hotels in Cartagena on the Caribbean, a stud farm near Barranquilla, and a ranch outside of Medellín on which he raised fighting bulls for the rings of

Colombia, Venezuela, and Peru, fought usually by ma
from Spain. This Medellín ranch was his principal residence,
insofar as he had one. He would leave for New York from
there. The ranch sprawled over several hills and valleys, and
included an airstrip from which small planes often took off
and landed, frequently at night.

So in two days time he would fly to Panama—he would
have to notify his pilot. In Panama he would be met by four
armed men—these bodyguards would have to be notified too.
He would take no chances during this stage of the journey
that someone—he kept the idea vague—might want to in-
terfere with him. His pilot would turn around and go back.
He would spend the night in Panama and the next day fly
commercial first class to New York. He would travel as an
American citizen on an American passport that he had ob-
tained some years previously in Puerto Rico upon presentation
of false documents. That is, the passport was perfectly valid,
could be renewed indefinitely, and had been. His name, on
this passport, was Michael Palacios. Since Ley had gone to
college in the United States, he spoke English without accent,
and could easily pass as an American.

He would land at Kennedy International Airport at dusk
and take a taxi into midtown. He would have a small suitcase
and when the taxi let him off he would stand on the sidewalk
looking around at all the tall buildings, inhaling the city's
bad breath. Once the taxi was out of sight he would walk the
rest of the way to the brownstone off Fifth Avenue. He would
quickly make calls to some women, see what he could line
up on short notice. He would go to the races a few times,
the theater. New York would be fun. He was looking forward
to it.

He had already forgotten his cook's son, and the work he
was supposed to do there.

In the elevator going down Lucientes said: "I wonder what
really happened in New York."

Von Bauzer muttered: "He won't do anything up there.
He'll just party."

"Don't worry," Pablo Marzo said, "I'll take care of it myself."

4

AT TWELVE THIRTY the newsroom emptied out for lunch. Most of the dayside reporters and the few editors working this early trooped upstairs to the cafeteria, though not Jane who went out of the building and walked east on Forty-third Street to a health club she had recently joined. She had begun to worry about her thighs. Skipping lunch every day would help them. Regular workouts would help them even more. She envied men who did not have this problem. At sixty their legs looked the same as at twenty.

As she changed she had the women's locker room to herself. She dragged a black leotard out of the package it had come in, tugged it on, and surveyed herself in the mirror. In a leotard she looked fine. In a bathing suit she would look less fine, she believed, and next week she and George would be spending the weekend with friends who had a house on Fire Island.

She walked out into the Nautilus room where there were women rowing, women on bicycles, and saw that all of them wore designer leotards: stripes, plaids, hot pinks, electric blues. Everyone looked at her. Jane hadn't known that such outfits existed, had supposed basic black was fine. Now she felt conspicuous, slightly mortified. There were some men in designer tights as well, most of them either staring at her or posturing in front of mirrors. The posturing ones showed no interest in her as a woman.

Annoyed with herself, she began to work out on the machines, and even built up a good healthy sweat, but this club was really cramped. She had to wait for a rowing machine, and then stop rowing whenever someone needed to get past. When she was on the bicycle somebody's elbows seemed perpetually in her ribs, and hers in theirs. The place was oversubscribed. The women's shower room turned out to be less clean than it should have been. This club had a terrific reputation and was one of the most expensive in New York, the in place this year. She had bought a six-month membership. Money wasted. She was certainly not coming back here. Why hadn't she checked it out better before buying the membership? She hadn't had time, she told herself. She should have made time.

She went back to the office, and began telephoning psychologists. A little later Vaughan came by and asked her to cover a press conference at Police Headquarters.

"What's it about?"

"The PC's going to announce another drug seizure some cop made."

He gave Douglas's name. Jane had never heard it before. This wasn't her beat and it didn't sound like much of a story. Jane begged off. "I have all these calls in to psychologists."

Vaughan nodded and began peering about the newsroom. Just then her phone rang and as she began talking to a Dr. Freundlich, making careful notes, she was aware that Vaughan had moved off from her desk.

Douglas lived in a house in New Rochelle, north of the city. It was a narrow house with a narrow garden. He made himself scrambled eggs and toast, took a proper shower, and lay naked on the big bed with all the windows open. Outside the windows it was sunny and hot, and the curtains stirred from time to time. He was upset and fidgety and could not sleep and so got up and went to his closet to put a bathrobe on. After a moment's hesitation he opened his wife's closet and pressed a handful of her skirts and dresses to his face. He breathed her in and out. He saw this as weakness. I should get rid of these things, he told himself.

Downstairs he went to the front door to bring the paper

in. The mail had come. It was lying on the floor under the slot. He brought mail and paper to the dinette table. He looked at the mail and read the paper and drank another cup of coffee.

After that he went to his desk in a tiny room off the dining room, threw the junk mail into the basket unopened, and wrote out checks for the newly arrived bills. His house had come to seem huge to him when he was in it alone. It made him feel—and immediately repress—the need to speak to one of his children.

He had two daughters and a son. Two were at college, reachable only via phones in dormitory corridors—not likely at this hour. His older daughter he might catch at work. She was already married. No children yet, though. He could tell her—what? I'm lonely, he might say. I miss your mother. But that was nothing new. The PC's about to give away our major cases, he might say, how can I stop him? She couldn't help there either. There was not much chance she would even understand. His wife might have, but she was dead.

Dead since Easter Sunday. Killed in a car crash. At night. In the rain. To think about it still made his breath catch. On the Cross County Parkway, which is narrow and winding where it goes through New Rochelle. She always drove too fast. It was possibly her own fault.

He went back to bed but again failed to sleep. He was not going to attend that press conference, he told himself, but eventually he got up, got dressed, and went back to headquarters.

In an anteroom waited most of the detectives from the raid. Chief Conner was there too. Presently some other two- and three-star chiefs came in. Douglas glanced into the packed conference room, and saw that he was about to take part in a circus. All the chairs were taken and the TV cameras were packed shoulder to shoulder along the back wall. At either end of the dais stood cops from Emergency Service wearing bulletproof vests and holding shotguns at port arms. They were there to "guard" last night's haul. The ruined attaché case full of money lay open on the table next to a thicket of microphones. Photographers were bending over it clicking off their cameras. Some of the cartons of cocaine had been carried into the room as well, though somebody had "improved" the look of them. Several were open, and the packages overflowed.

Finally the PC himself entered the anteroom, accompanied by Herbert Campbell.

The federal agent's face lit up when he saw Douglas. "Ray, good to see you again, and congratulations."

Campbell's smile looked false to Douglas. He shook hands with him.

"Are we ready?" the PC asked.

The detectives were sent into the press room to stand behind the dais. Windsell waited until they were in position and then, like a star actor, led out his supporting cast.

He sat down behind all the microphones. He placed Chief Conner on one side of him, Herbert Campbell on the other, distributed the other chiefs, directing Douglas to a chair halfway down the dais.

"Some of you," he began, leaning close to the mikes, "may have wondered how big a suitcase you would need to abscond with $2,000,221 in cash, if the opportunity ever arose." He grinned out at the assembled reporters and TV crew—and beyond them to his audience of millions. "You would need one just about this size."

This quip made the newsmen laugh. When the laughter died down the PC said: "The seized contraband, part of which you see before you, is worth even more. Its street value is about three hundred fifty million dollars." This figure having sobered everyone, the PC read a prepared statement that gave a few—very few—details about the case, and he read out the names of the detectives involved. "They were led by Deputy Chief Raymond J. Douglas, commander of the Narcotics Division. Any questions?"

There were many, most of them beyond the ken of the former judge who, ignoring the presence of his own narcotics chief, deferred to Herbert Campbell, pushing the mass of microphones in front of him. Douglas meanwhile stared straight out at the cameras in the back of the room. It seemed to him that this transfer of powers had already gone too far to stop. He felt bad for himself, worse for his men. His men would be crushed.

What did such a huge seizure mean to street prices and availability, Campbell was asked. Would there be shortages? Would prices rise? Would there be war between the Cali and Medellín cartels? Was the case continuing?

Campbell was as evasive but also as long-winded as a politician. He was appropriately solemn. He used the word *we* a lot, as in: "We have hurt them today." The word *my*, as well. "My men are following this up . . . my lab technicians . . . my intelligence section . . ."

Partly because he had not been to sleep and was exhausted, Douglas's frustration turned into a resentment he could not control. "This case," he interrupted loudly—there were no microphones where he sat—"was initiated and carried through to its conclusion by detectives of the New York Police Department." As soon as he heard himself speak he could have cut his tongue off. There goes my career, he thought.

There was a moment of shocked silence.

"That's true," conceded Campbell into the mikes. "Although I would have wished for an opportunity to contribute some of our expertise along the way. The police department did an excellent job, considering its resources. The size of the seizure is truly impressive. The number of traffickers arrested is less so."

Sensing a possible feud, the newsmen were on their feet, and a vast clamor arose. But the PC swept the microphones back under his own nose and ended the press conference. A moment later he and Herbert Campbell were gone.

Now the newsmen crowded around Douglas, who, finding himself forced into a press conference of his own, tried to keep it bland, keep it neutral. He praised his detectives and the NYPD in general. This seemed safe. In response to a question he said that the department was certainly equal and probably superior to any federal agency you might name and this, under the circumstances, seemed less safe.

He then went back to his office. He knew enough about the newsmaking process to realize that he was the one who would dominate tonight's newscasts and tomorrow's head-lines, not the PC and certainly not Herbert Campbell. After a time he decided he had best speak to the PC again, and he phoned his office, got the deputy inspector who was his chief secretary, and asked to be put through.

After a pause the secretary's voice came back on: "I'm afraid he's tied up, Chief."

"When can I have an appointment?"

Another pause.

"Tomorrow's no good either, Chief."

Douglas put down the phone.

Jane at her desk on the telephone spoke to seven psychologists and psychiatrists and got two to say that the working mother's mental health was more at risk than the child's.

It took her all afternoon. She inserted the quotes near the top of her story, put Vaughan's name on it as editor, and punched the button sending it forward. She could do no more, and was by no means sure she had done enough. She left the building.

By 7 P.M. she was at Berlitz practicing Russian, in case the paper should ever decide to send a woman to Moscow. She went three times a week, an hour each time, and on nights when George worked late she would curl up on the sofa and listen to the conversation records as well. Earlier in her career she had spent three years studying French. She already spoke Spanish.

A foreign assignment was what she wanted. However, nobody had offered her one yet, and on nights when she was being honest with herself she reflected that if one ever came, most likely she wouldn't be able to accept it because of her marriage.

When she came out of Berlitz it was dusk, and the streets were nearly empty. The city had cooled down and she walked across town and up the steps into the Stuyvesant Club, and looked around. She had never been here before, and in fact it had only recently, as a result of a class-action lawsuit, been open to women.

It was a hushed kind of place, almost like a law office, though much older. It had fourteen-foot ceilings, parquet flooring, and oak-paneled walls. She identified herself to the porter and was directed to the third floor. There was an elevator but she chose to go up the staircase, which was marble and carpeted, with a brass handrail. It was hung with portraits dating back two hundred years.

In the doorway to the banquet room she stood looking for her husband, for she would know no one else among the guests. Some thirty people milled about, chatting, sipping cocktails. In the middle was a vast table set with the requisite number of places. The chairs set around it were high-backed, ornate.

George appeared beside her, kissed her on the cheek, and introduced her to their host, a middle-aged man named Carl Hawkins. George then disappeared, leaving her with Hawkins, about whom she knew nothing except that he was a senior partner in a law firm that was wooing George.

"And where are you from, Mrs. Fox?"

Jane said she had been born in New York.

"Do you two have any children?"

Jane confessed that they had no children as yet. "We're still hopeful, though," she added, and immediately felt brainless. Why had she said such a thing? A waiter passed. He was in a bolero jacket and striped trousers, and carried a tray of hors d'oeuvres: celery, carrot sticks, olives with pimento inserts, Ritz crackers. Jane took a carrot stick and nibbled on it.

Hawkins was nodding to someone across the room. He seemed to have forgotten her.

"And you, Mr. Hawkins, where are you from?" said Jane hurriedly. She didn't want to lose his attention, for her job was to be a dutiful wife and he might be important to George.

"Chicago," said Hawkins. "Been here thirty years. Never regretted it a minute. Great town, New York, wouldn't you say?"

"Yes it is."

"As a lawyer," said Hawkins, peering across the room, "George is a valuable man."

"Yes he is."

Dinner was announced. They all searched out their name cards and stood over their places. Jane peered down at a great many knives and forks to either side of her plate.

"Well, let's sit down, shall we?" said Hawkins loudly, and she saw she had been seated beside him. The entire table sat down.

In a dining room on the other side of the city, Douglas's beeper sounded, startling everybody. Forks paused in mid-flight.

His hand had jerked to his belt to shut it off. He gave a half-embarrassed smile and got up from the table.

"In the bedroom," said his hostess.

Sitting on the edge of her bed, he spoke with his duty sergeant. Internal Affairs had arrested two detectives from the South Brooklyn field group, the sergeant told him, and read off their names. Douglas didn't know either of them. "What are they supposed to have done?"

He was in the midtown apartment of Paul and Cora Coniff, old friends. This was the evening of the day of the great seizure. He had still not been to bed. His eyes were gritty with fatigue, and he closed them.

The two detectives were accused of stealing money from street dealers they had arrested, according to the sergeant. Not a big case then. Still, he should have been advised in advance. He hadn't been. Why?

He set the phone down and leaned his face into his hands. He dreaded going back to the dining room. He was too tired to concentrate on what the other guests might say to him. In addition there was an unattached woman present whom he had known as a teenager and not seen since. She was a friend of Cora's and had been invited just for him, apparently.

He fished his address book out of his pocket, thumbed

pages, then dialed the unlisted home number of Chief Quinn of Internal Affairs.

Because Quinn outranked him, and because this was a corruption case, he was obliged to approach carefully: "I hope I didn't get you up from dinner, Chief."

"What's on your mind, Ray?"

"Seems like some of your men just arrested some of my men."

"Sorry about that."

"Two of them."

"Couple of thieves."

"Well, is there any more to it, Chief? It's just the two?"

"That's it, as far as we can tell."

Douglas tried to work out what his next words should be, but could not make his head think clearly. "Well, then," he said, "I wonder why I wasn't advised."

"You mean the PC never informed you?"

Warning bells. Sudden alertness. Douglas sat up straight. "I guess he did," he lied, and gave a shallow chuckle. "I guess I just didn't pick up on it." The chuckle was supposed to sound confident. "I've been preoccupied with last night's seizure." Throw it onto that, he thought, and hope for the best.

Quinn let a silence build up. If the PC hadn't informed Douglas at all, was operating behind his back, what did this mean? Was Douglas on the way out? Quinn then gave a false chuckle of his own. It meant he would pretend to believe the lie for now. "I'll bet you have been preoccupied," he said. "And congratulations."

After hanging up, Douglas pondered. Someone was trying to embarrass him. Was it Quinn? Not likely. Quinn was higher ranking and older. Douglas was no threat to him.

There were only two possibilities, Quinn or the PC. The PC, then.

Why? To weaken whatever prestige I may have, he told himself. When he gives our major cases to the DEA I'll be too worried about my job and future to try to stop him.

It made Douglas suddenly unreasonably furious. When that

passed he was exhausted again. He went back to the dinner table.

"I hope you don't have to run off," said Cora.

I should never have come here tonight, Douglas thought. He should have canceled out on Cora this afternoon. But he couldn't have done that to her at the last minute. He couldn't even leave now though he wanted to—there was too much concern on Cora's face.

"Run off?" he said, managing a smile, "I haven't even eaten yet." Cora and Paul had been inviting him to dinner at least once a month since the funeral, at first just him and them, a morose threesome; and then, when Cora felt he was ready for it, she had invited others as well. Including, the last two times, some unattached female to sit beside him. Tonight it was a woman named Gail Beutel, formerly Gail Simpson, who had lived on his street in the Riverdale section of the Bronx when they were children.

And now as he regained his chair Gail informed the table loudly, archly: "I can remember when he got his first bike, and now he's so important he has to have a beeper."

Douglas frowned.

"I'll bet you carry a gun, too."

"He has to," said Cora.

"Let me see it," said Gail, reaching for his waistband.

Douglas jerked away from her. "No," he snapped. Too late he realized she was only clowning. The table—there were ten of them around it—fell suddenly silent. Douglas made himself grin. "I'll let you see my beeper, though, if you like."

He was relieved to watch the smiles come on again, and he plunged his fork into the food on his plate, which was by now cold.

Dessert was served in the living room. Douglas sat down on the sofa. A moment later the cushion beside him sank down with an outrush of air. Gail. He remembered her well. He had nearly asked her for a date once. She was three years younger, meaning that when he was seventeen and between girlfriends, she was only fourteen. She was very pretty—at least as pretty as any of the candidates for Miss Rheingold that year—and already had a plump, prominent bosom. She had a lively, confident way about her that he didn't expect from one so young. She usually wore penny loafers and bangs and was always chewing gum. Finally he had decided she was too much a child. He couldn't ask her: all the other guys would rib him.

There was no baby fat now. She would be forty-one. She had become a blond in a black dress, from whom emanated a faint perfume. She was very nice looking, and she sat beside him on this sofa. She was in the real estate business, and good at it, she told him. She wore nice jewelry and he thought he discerned a knowing look in her eyes. But she exuded nervousness. She had a daughter in college, she told him. A son had died of leukemia years ago, aged three.

She hasn't had such a happy life, Douglas thought.

Her husband's name was Chuck, from whom she had been separated ten months. Divorce was her idea, not Chuck's.

Douglas was trying to track her words, trying not to spill his dessert as well, while his eyes kept wanting to close.

"I asked myself," she was saying, "do I really want to spend the rest of my life watching the back of Chuck's head while he watches television?" There was a pause. "I don't regret leaving him." Another pause. "Even if it turns out that I have to spend the rest of my life alone."

"Did you leave him for another man?" Douglas asked, more to fill the silence than because he wanted to know.

"No."

Another silence. He couldn't remember what he had already asked her, what she had already told him. He was looking for a question to keep her talking, for he was too tired to talk himself. "What was the problem between you and Chuck? Was it sex?"

Unfortunately the entire room had chosen that moment to fall silent, so that Douglas's question came out like a detonation. He glanced from face to face. So did Gail, who wore a sudden too-bright grin.

"Are you going to answer that one, Gail?" said Paul Con-iff.

As the other men in the room picked up the joke, Gail began to blush.

"Let's hear your answer, Gail."

"Don't hold back, Gail."

"We're all friends here, Gail."

Douglas, who had been awake forty-two straight hours, was alert enough to see his question as grotesque. He had one thought only, escape. So apparently did Gail. Both jumped to their feet.

"I've got to be going," said Douglas.

"Yes," cried Gail, "me too."

They fled. They rejected coffee, thanked host and hostess, engaged in handshakes and fast kisses all around, and were gone. The door slammed behind them.

Nonetheless, Douglas was surprised to find himself in the elevator with her. "I embarrassed you," he said.

He embarrassed her still, apparently, for she would not look at him and she made no reply.

"I'm really sorry," he said.

They came out onto the sidewalk. Stepping out between bumpers, arm above her head, Gail attempted to flag down a taxi.

"I have a car," said Douglas, who was anxious to make amends. "Where do you live?"

No answer. But no taxi happened by either.

"I'm parked just across the street," Douglas said to her back. It seemed essential that her opinion of him be changed.

Gail stood with her arm up while Douglas waited glumly on the curb. No cab stopped. Finally she turned to face him. "I live in Chelsea," she said, and gave the address.

The opposite direction. It would take him twenty minutes out of his way. He nodded and gave her a smile. "Come on, then."

He led her to his department car, opened the door on her

side, and remembered to advise her to watch out for the police radio under the glove compartment. "You could ruin your stockings, not to mention your shins."

As he started the engine, the police radio came on, but he reached across her lap to switch it off: "I don't imagine you want to listen to that."

If she was surprised to find herself in an unmarked police car, she gave no sign.

He drove downtown. The blocks passed. He tried to make conversation but she did not answer, so he too fell silent.

Suddenly she said: "Sex was not the problem. He never complained, and I certainly did not."

"Well," said Douglas, "I certainly am awfully glad to get that cleared up."

It made both of them smile and after that it was better. She had met the Coniffs when she sold them their apartment, she said. "And you?" she asked.

The Coniffs seemed a safer subject than her sex life with her husband. "Paul was an assistant district attorney when I was a cop on the street. In those days he was on the side of the angels."

"And now he's not?"

"Now he's a defense lawyer. He defends scoundrels. And he's so good he gets them off."

"And you can't understand that?"

"Good is good and evil is evil. Absolutes do exist in the world, you know."

"That's something taught to you by priests when you were a kid."

He thought this observation perceptive. "Maybe."

"And you wonder how you can still be friends with Paul."

This was true. The whole subject was one he had puzzled over for years, but he was too tired to focus on it now.

He pulled up in front of her building. "I want to apologize for my conduct tonight," he told her, "I'm not usually this stupid. I haven't been to bed since the night before last."

She studied him. "And now you have to drive home to New Rochelle?"

"Yes." At that moment another wave of exhaustion came over him. It was as if he carried something on his back that was too heavy for him, that was pressing him to his knees. Seated behind the wheel he waited for the moment to pass, and fought to keep his eyes open.

"You should have stayed for Cora's coffee," said Gail, watching him. She paused, as if to think out how her words would sound: "If you want to come upstairs, I'll make you coffee and you can sit down and rest for a moment."

Douglas did not answer.

"You don't want to fall asleep on the road."

Douglas had a forty-minute drive ahead of him.

"All right," he said, and got out of the car.

Jane was on Hawkins's right. There were two other women to his left. New York seemed to have more than its share of unattached women, so on occasions of this kind there were often more women than men. Hosts got stuck with gaggles of them. This was probably the way Hawkins saw it. George was across the huge table and down, fifteen feet away at least—too distant to help her.

"Do you have dinners like this often?" Jane asked Hawkins.

"About once a month. Helps the lawyers get to know each other—some of them are women, these days, you know. And the wives, don't forget the wives. It's a big firm. We senior partners take turns running it."

Jane nodded and tried to think of something to say.

"In a year's time," said Hawkins, "I'll have sat between most of the wives. I'll get to know them all."

Was attendance mandatory for husbands and wives both? Jane wondered. What would Hawkins reply if she asked?

The waiters moved around the table with their platters. The service was impeccable but the fare dreary. Jane lifted onto her plate a small portion of mashed potatoes from the first waiter, of pot roast from the second, of what had once been frozen peas from the third. A few minutes later the same three waiters came out carrying bottles of wine wrapped in napkins and they moved around the table dispensing it. Although Jane tried to sneak a look at the label as wine poured down into her glass, this proved impossible.

Hawkins was talking to the woman on his left. "Where are you from originally?" Jane heard him ask. The woman replied something and Hawkins said: "From Chicago. Been here thirty years." Then: "I've never regretted it, no."

The conversation on Jane's other side concerned crack, about which she knew a good deal, and she joined it. The man was a lawyer. The woman was a lawyer too, but they had never met until tonight and were uncomfortable with each other. Their knowledge of crack was meager, apparently, whereas Jane had done stories on it, and they listened with fascination as she described crack houses she had gone into behind police raiders the month before. People stoned out of their minds. Piles of knives and guns. Young men, some of them only boys, in handcuffs. Girls too, some of them pregnant. She began to talk of the crack babies she had seen, the one-year-olds who were still unable to sit up, who shuddered unendingly, who would not cuddle. Heroin had been a benign drug compared to crack, she told them. Heroin addicts were sick, usually almost comatose, and no harm to anyone but themselves. Whereas crack sent men berserk. She had seen some of the murder victims. She had been sent out on one story where a man on crack had tried to rape a four-week-old infant.

Beside her Hawkins was staring out over the table. She sensed both that he was listening, and that he found such subjects inappropriate.

At the far end of the table sat Hawkins's wife. Her name was Bitsy, she was similarly middle-aged, and she wore a black velvet headband. She and her husband had begun sending each other signals. Presently she gave a big smile and wagged her finger in Jane's direction, announcing in a loud voice: "I'm going to have to split you people up down there."

When this didn't work, she rapped on a glass for silence.

"I've been talking here to Bill Judge, who is the husband

of our Marlene," Bitsy Hawkins said. "Bill is on Wall Street, and he has something absolutely enthralling to tell us about a new way of investing. It's called, I think, bundled stocks."

Judge, the stock salesman, wanted nothing better than such an opportunity. He gave a fifteen-minute sales pitch, explaining to the entire table not only the theory of bundled stocks, but also the opportunity it provided to wise investors such as themselves. You might think it was like investing in mutual funds, he said, but it was not. It was splitting up the various components of stocks, or so Jane understood. You sold the stock certificates to one person, the dividend interest to another. Was that what he was saying?

Only the serving of dessert cut him short. Strawberry shortcake. With gobs of whipped cream out of an aerosol can. Almost none of the women ate any of it, Jane noted. Then came coffee. For almost an hour afterward most of the guests stood around sipping liqueurs, talking about client business, the financial scene, possible mergers. Probably lots of people wanted to leave, but didn't feel they could yet. Jane listened with her arm linked through George's.

Upstairs Gail sat him down on her sofa, then attempted with quick nervous movements to tidy the room around him. She stacked up magazines, straightened cushions. All the while she talked. Douglas had to keep blinking to keep his eyes open. She had recently revisited their old neighborhood, she said. It was all changed. He wouldn't recognize it.

Then she was in the kitchen, but talking through the open door. No, her voice said, sex was not the problem between her and Chuck. She herself was a perfectly normal woman with perfectly normal desires. Douglas could smell the coffee brewing, and thought he would put his head back on the sofa and rest his eyes. "We were completely compatible on that score," her voice said. He permitted his eyes to close for a moment. Then he was asleep.

Gail, still talking, came out of the kitchen carrying two steaming cups on a tray. Her mouth closed with a snap. She put the tray down on the coffee table, sat down opposite him, and for a time watched him in silence. Finally she tried to shake him awake.

"Coffee's ready."

But his head didn't come forward and his eyes didn't open. She put milk and sugar into his coffee and her own, then shook him again. He did not awaken.

She became irritated: "Well, you can't stay here," she muttered and shook him roughly. "Wake up," she said. "It's time to go home." She kept shaking him. Once his eyelids parted—his eyes were rolled half up into his head as if he was dead—and then they closed again.

She sat watching him while both coffees grew cold.

She went into her bathroom, took her makeup off, put on a nightgown and bathrobe, and came out and stared down at him. She put the TV on loudly and for a few minutes, standing in the center of the room, stared alternately at it and at him. The noise had no effect on him.

He lay with his head on the armrest and his feet on the floor. She picked up one leg and let it drop. He didn't stir. She tried the other leg, then both at once. Same result. She was so annoyed or perhaps disappointed she was almost crying.

She took his shoes off and lifted his legs onto the sofa, then fetched a pillow from her bed and placed it under his head, for his black hair looked none too clean and she didn't want it soiling her upholstery.

She wondered about loosening his belt. Was it an act of intimacy or compassion? Was it permitted? She chased such thoughts from her head. She was a grown woman, not some silly girl. But when she reached under his clothes her fingers touched his gun, the existence of which she had forgotten, and she jumped backward. She was as shocked as if she had accidentally reached into his fly. She peered down on the grip, the clip-on holster. Finally she removed it and placed it on the coffee table. She unbuttoned his trousers and unzipped his fly partway. She found a light blanket, which she threw over him. He still did not wake up, so she turned the lights off, left him there, and went to bed.

"That was fun," Jane's husband said. They were in their bedroom undressing. "Those are good people."

She was tired but gave him a smile. "I'm glad you enjoyed it." As she got a clean nightdress out of her drawer she thought: Better that one of us spent a pleasant evening than neither. She sat down on the bed to take off her hose. It was just business, she told herself. I mustn't resent him.

"It's a good firm. I may go with them."

"More money?"

George shook his head. "Bigger mergers."

"You're already working on the biggest merger imaginable."

"That's how much you know about mergers."

With the air conditioning on the room was cool and they got into bed under a cotton blanket. Jane reached to turn out the bedside lamp. When she settled back onto her side of the bed in the dark, she landed almost on top of her husband, who was already there. He captured a breast and blew into her ear.

"It's late," she said. "Go to sleep."

But he did not intend to, apparently. She accepted this and tried to will interest in what he was doing to her. Men need sex more than women do, she thought. For men it was the glue that held a marriage together, someone had told her once. She believed it. He had her nightdress hiked up and was massaging her in his rhythmic way. She was unable to concentrate on it. Instead, she reflected that he hadn't even asked whether she had enjoyed the evening. The idea as always had never occurred to him. His hand on her was insistent, but her body did not respond. She began to feel guilty.

"I don't know what's the matter," she murmured.

This caused him to redouble his efforts, but she only got more tense.

He threw a leg over one of hers. Then he was on top of

her. Her guilt was so strong that she did not immediately protest.

What he is trying to do is not going to work, she thought, but she kept silent. Perhaps it would work. It had worked sometimes in the past. She tried to relax and couldn't. She bit down on her lip and kept silent as long as she could.

"You're hurting me," she murmured.

Her husband, who had still not spoken a word, pushed himself off her, moved to his own side of the bed and lay facing away from her.

Now she had a sexually frustrated male on her hands. She put her hand on his hip. He pushed it off. She felt frustrated herself, though in a different way. "I'm sorry," she said to his back. "I don't know what's wrong."

He did not reply.

A woman can't control the way her body reacts down there, she told herself. If true, then why this sense of failure? Why such guilt?

After a while she fell asleep.

Douglas awakened to daylight streaming in the windows of a strange living room, with a strange woman standing over him. He realized he was fully dressed and had been asleep on a sofa. His head felt so thick he imagined he had been drugged and rolled, or assaulted and rolled. If so his wallet would be gone, and his gun of course, and he felt quickly for both. The wallet was where it should be, the gun was not, but as he sprang to his feet his pants fell down and he had to grab for them. Simultaneously he spied his gun on the coffee table and so grabbed for that too. The result was that he lost his balance, and, being caught up in his trousers, could not regain it. He stumbled into the coffee table and then over it, heard the crotch of his pants rip, lost his balance further, and crashed to the floor at the woman's feet.

"Did you sleep well?" she asked.

She was trying to keep from laughing.

Having picked himself up, he hiked up his trousers and buckled his belt. "I guess I fell asleep on your sofa," he

mumbled. He zipped up his fly. He couldn't remember un-
zipping it, so she must have done it. He clipped his holster
on and made for the door.

"I'll make some coffee," Gail said hastily.

"Don't have time," said Douglas. "Sorry about your
sofa." His ears were red he was so embarrassed, and he was
wrenching at the door but was unable to get it unlocked.
There were three locks, because this was New York. The
problem was to get them all functioning at one time. He could
hear Gail approaching behind him, and he worked with increased haste. At last the door opened. Without looking back,
he bolted.

As he came into his own house the phone was ringing. It
was his older daughter. "I called you all last night, Daddy.
I even called at midnight," she accused, "and got no answer.
Naturally I was worried."

He was not going to tell her he had fallen asleep on the
sofa of a woman he barely knew. And crashed over her coffee
table the next morning. He felt his ears get red again. "I
arrived home a bit later than that," he told her. Why had he
gone up to Gail's apartment in the first place? His daughter
would form conclusions. He did not want her to believe
him that kind of man. "I had dinner with the Coniffs actually."

"I really was worried about you."

His children phoned every two or three nights. They took
turns at it. Tomorrow night it would be his other daughter.
Next it would be his son. They must have got together on it.
Their concern was touching and thoughtful and at the beginning it was all that had got him through each day.

But he was all right now, or nearly so, and wished he could
relieve them of the responsibility, but he did not know how
to do it without hurting their feelings. He was not their child,
was not yet ready to hand over to the next generation, and
had become able to hold the past at bay, which was a trick
like any other. But none of this could he say to them without
sounding ungrateful, not to mention unloving.

When he reached headquarters freshly combed and shaved,

the morning papers were on his desk. A sergeant came in with coffee. Douglas's picture was on the front pages of both papers. The accompanying articles were as effusive as last night's news shows had been. The PC was hardly mentioned, and Herbert Campbell was not mentioned at all.

The PC would be livid, Douglas supposed.

His phone rang. The PC wished to see Chief Douglas "forthwith."

"Forthwith," used only by superiors to subordinates, was the strongest command in the police department lexicon. It meant more than "at once." Most often it meant the recipient was in trouble. A man could read how much trouble by the amount of time he was forced to wait before being admitted into the superior's presence. In Douglas's case on this particular morning it meant a wait in the PC's anteroom of more than thirty minutes—while others were shown in and came out again, most of them greeting him, all of them looking at him strangely.

The newspapers were on the PC's desk too, when the deputy inspector at last showed Douglas in. The former judge sat in his swivel chair. He did not look friendly.

"I don't know what you were thinking of when you talked to those reporters yesterday," Windsell began. "You may have compromised your case in court."

Douglas doubted Windsell was worried about the eventual trial.

"I don't think so, Commissioner," said Douglas. "There are guidelines for what our department can tell the press. I made every effort to stay within them."

"May I suggest that I know more about judicial procedure than you do."

In the New York Police Department, if you valued your career, you swallowed reprimands in silence.

The swivel chair came forward. Windsell's short arms came down on the desk.

"It is precisely because of the difficulty of obtaining convictions," he said, "that this department tries to speak with one voice. That voice, normally, is either mine or the man who speaks for me, namely the deputy commissioner for public affairs.''

Suddenly Windsell smiled. It was not a particularly successful smile and it was inappropriate to the time and place. ''Can I speak to you off the record, Chief?'' he began. ''Well, then. There are going to be some changes soon in my official family.'' And he named two assistant chiefs, one ill, the other retiring. ''For the time being this is secret, of course.''

Secret? Douglas had heard the news last week. Most headquarters secrets swept through the building in a matter of minutes. This was especially true of personnel changes. The clerks and secretaries who sat outside every office were all cops, in many cases former detectives. They were alert to unusual comings and goings, they listened to voices through doors, they could read confidential memos upside down. Headquarters gossip waited for no man.

''Certain of my advisers have been offering recommendations as to their replacements,'' the PC said.

Why is he telling me this? Douglas asked himself. Assistant chief was the next rank up. The promotions would go to one or another of the older men of Douglas's rank, not him. He was too new in grade and, especially now, he was out of favor.

But Windsell's smile continued to flicker on and off, which puzzled Douglas and made his eyes narrow. Maybe there is a chance for me after all, he thought.

''I'll be listening very hard to those recommendations over the next few days,'' the PC said, ''I don't mind telling you.''

He's offering me a bribe, Douglas thought. Sort of. Why?

''Have you given any more consideration to that other matter I spoke of?'' the PC said, and again his smile wavered. ''The Herbert Campbell matter.''

''Yes, I have,'' said Douglas and paused. Say it, he told himself.

''I'm very strongly opposed,'' he said.

There was a heavy silence.

''Yes, well,'' the PC said, and he stood up. ''Thanks for coming in.''

Douglas saw that the opening had been minuscule, and that it had already closed. Yet he persisted. "Our Major Case detectives are doing a great job."

"Yes they are."

"Every cop in the department is proud of them." Douglas began to speak quickly, for he was being moved toward the door. "There are over a thousand men in Narcotics. Most of them work on the street. But they're working hard, hoping to make it up into Major Cases. That's their dream, their ambition. They want to be important detectives. They want to work against big-time traffickers."

They had reached the door.

"To give Major Cases to the DEA would be to take that dream, that incentive away from them," pleaded Douglas. "We're better than the DEA, and it's our city, not theirs."

Now he was outside the door, looking back in. "I hope you'll reconsider," he said.

The PC nodded vaguely.

"And we ought to consider its effect on the city," Douglas said hastily. "To give Major Cases to the DEA might seem to the city an evasion of our responsibility."

The PC flashed another partial smile. "I'll certainly keep your views in mind."

The door closed.

There were a series of lights over the PC's door: the green meant that he was free, the red that he was occupied, the amber that he was on the phone. The amber light had just come on, but Douglas, who stood almost underneath it, was too preoccupied to notice.

The PC's phone call was to the mayor, who was already thinking ahead to next year's election. The mayor wanted no police corruption scandals between now and then. He wanted to get out from under the drug problem as much as possible. He was thinking more than a year ahead. He wanted a year with no outcries from the media about lack of police effectiveness against major traffickers. The solution he had found was to unload Major Cases onto the DEA, and his police commissioner had gone along with him on

it. Such a solution seemed to both of them a brilliant political stroke.

"I know it's top priority," the PC was saying to the mayor
now. "But I need another week to smooth things out here."
Windsell was a careful man. One proceeded slowly in cases
like this. "Just a case of some ruffled feathers. No, no problem. None at all."

Meanwhile Douglas still stood outside the door. He stood
as if rooted there, and the deputy inspector who was the PC's
chief secretary glanced up at him. "Something I can do for
you, Chief?"

"No, nothing," said Douglas, "nothing." And he moved
out of the office and down the hall. He wanted to stop Windsell but could not think how to do it. Unless he went to the
mayor. Did he dare? The mayor would stop him if he knew,
Douglas reasoned.

Back in his own office he did not immediately phone City
Hall for an appointment. He would think this out very carefully first. Surely the PC would not make such an important
decision on his own authority overnight. Surely he would
consult with people first. Almost certainly there was still time.

5

FOR SOME MINUTES eleven reporters and editors had
watched the Metropolitan editor, Vaughan, more or less co-
vertly from eleven different desks in the newsroom. When
at one minute past one o'clock he rose from his place and
started for the conference room, which was at the rear of the
floor near the Style section, they did likewise. It made for a
sizable group threading through desks toward a single door,
and at a certain point Jane's path and Vaughan's converged.

"Jane," he said amiably, "do you think there's sexism here on the paper?"

"That's some way to greet somebody." She started to laugh. "Of course I think there's sexism on the paper."

"Really?" Vaughan said, but his face had got very solemn.

Which made Jane realize it was a serious question, and as they reached the conference room door she pondered it. Any question about sexism on the paper, as she saw it, ought to have been how much, how dangerous, how bad, not whether or not it existed. It had never occurred to her anyone could have any doubts.

Lately these lunchtime conferences had taken place each Tuesday. Vaughan invited reporters and editors seven days in advance, different ones each week, and they signaled their acceptance by giving their sandwich orders to his secretary.

Today the twelve people, ten of them men, who filed into the conference room went directly to the corner table where their sandwiches and coffee, which had been sent down from the cafeteria, were stacked up, and there was considerable joking and talking while the orders were sorted out and the sandwiches passed around. But once all had taken their places at the table, the room quieted down, and questions began to be lobbed around.

"Are we covering the city adequately?" Vaughan asked solemnly.

No one answered.

"I've noticed the mayor flying off the handle a lot lately," offered the assistant Metro editor. "Should we be doing something on that?"

This question too drew dead air. People munched as quietly as possible.

Somebody had to speak next. Apparently the assistant assignment editor thought it should be himself. "Some people think the mayor's crazy," he said. "Good idea for a story."

Vaughan had instituted these conferences upon being appointed Metro editor six months previously. He saw them as a morale builder; in addition, ideas for stories were sure to "pop out of them," as he put it. If nothing much had popped out to date, he had been heard to tell the managing editor, it was perhaps because the conferences hadn't got untracked yet.

But in fact many reporters, especially the younger ones, were afraid to speak up, and some of the older ones remained silent as a means of showing their contempt for the paper and its management. Reporters who chose to be heard at all tended to stick to subjects related to foster care, the homeless, public housing, welfare—because these seemed to them safe. In poverty areas Vaughan and the other editors, having no personal knowledge, were less likely to pontificate, criticize, or load on an unwanted assignment. But to talk about a major politician, say, or the Times Square Redevelopment Plan— this was risky. The editors were likely to know one of the important players. A reporter could get caught not knowing something or having failed to talk to someone.

For instance, in last week's meeting Vaughan had mentioned the name of Felix Weber, president of the City Council, with whom he had recently lunched. Felix had been really concerned about his subway station. He had seen some bums in his subway station. Maybe we could write something about that, Vaughan had suggested to the table at large. Felix had talked about a really tight corner in his station and he gets squished up against the rabble when he tries to get home.

Around the table Vaughan's subordinate editors had nodded sagaciously at this. But most of the reporters had stared at their sandwiches in silence. As opposed to Vaughan and most of the other relatively highly paid editors, the reporters actually rode the subway every day. They considered Weber's comments—and Vaughan's too—idiotic.

Seated at the table today was a reporter named Carl Doss, who had recently rejoined the Metro staff after ten years as a foreign correspondent. To the other reporters this meant he had come down in the world. He himself seemed to believe otherwise, however. He wore three-piece suits in the newsroom, his manner was pompous, and he seemed to think his status different from theirs, which it was not.

Now Doss said: "I wonder who those people are out there living in doorways, in the street."

Jane looked at him. Read the paper, she thought.

"When I used to live in this city we didn't have that."

The weekend Metro editor said: "Why don't we have a reporter spend the night in one of those homeless shelters?"

Someone seconded the motion by calling out: "Good story." There was always someone willing to pipe up with "good story!"

To Jane the suggestion proved that none of her colleagues ever read the paper. She had done the exact story not three months previously.

Because the homeless was her beat, all eyes had turned to her.

"We've done stories like that in the past," she said. The object at times like this became to come up with an answer that protected oneself but without alienating anyone else. "Maybe we should wait a little while before we do it again."

Silence fell. Although she said nothing more, Jane fumed. Even the executives didn't bother to read the paper, much less the reporters, which seemed to Jane unforgivable. Sure it took a tremendous amount of time each day. One didn't have time to read it all, they would say if caught out. More likely they just didn't give a damn.

In Vaughan it seemed especially unforgivable. Some weeks previously he had assigned Jane at a meeting like this to a story on the concession businesses at the local beaches now that garbage was washing ashore everywhere. The identical story had run in the paper the previous Sunday and so a total silence had come upon the room. "Talk to the hot dog salesmen, the parking lot attendants," Vaughan had said. "Make a good story."

Finally the assistant assignment editor, having cleared his throat, said politely, "Gee, that's a good idea."

"It's a logical story, a good story," said Vaughan.

"Well," said the assistant assignment editor, "we took a look at that."

"When was that?"

"Yeah, well," the assistant assignment editor had said, "Feldman, the new guy, he came up with something kinda like your idea. Yeah, in fact just like it. Yeah, it was on the front page. Just last Sunday. Two thousand words."

But that was weeks ago. This was today, and suddenly Vaughan turned to Jane. "So, Jane, you think there's sexism on the paper."

Startled, Jane glanced around the table. There were ten men gazing at her and only one other woman, and she wondered what to reply. "Yes, but it's a subtle, complicated kind of sexism—" She stopped.

"Go on," said Vaughan.

She found herself choosing her words with great care. Well, she said, men were more comfortable with other men than with women, male editors were more comfortable with male reporters, and as a result there were opportunities for men that were denied women; also there were all sorts of assumptions made about the women reporters and editors, especially those who had children, that they were not serious about their careers, that they did not want to do big projects, hard projects, involving overtime.

Bill Prince, a middle-aged southern-gentleman type, said with a smile: "I always thought the prejudice around here was against southern males, not women."

"Southern males?" Jane said. "Not women?"

Prince grinned at her. "That's right."

"Oh, would you like to compare salaries?"

Prince had recently been moved back to New York from the prestigious Washington bureau, and possibly did not feel good about himself or his career. He laughed and immediately backed off. So did she.

But Doss, the pompous ex-foreign correspondent, decided to butt in. He knew one or two women reporters, he said, who were doing well in the business. "They are competent."

"Really?" said Jane. "You don't say. I don't see where that has anything to do with prejudice against them, however."

"Yes," Doss persisted, "there are women who can do the job. I've known one or two of them personally."

"Isn't that amazing," said Jane. "I certainly am glad to hear that."

It produced a brief nervous laughter. People shifted in their seats—maybe this meeting would get unpleasant. To Jane, Doss's remarks were worse than condescending. She was not going to let them pass.

Doss still held the floor. "Most of the women I know who are successful have taken on one of two roles. Sex kitten or good old boy."

An insightful enough remark. The trouble was, Doss was presenting a situation that he himself accepted and thought women should be happy with too.

"That's part of the problem," Jane said. "What a choice! Those are the two choices." Judging that she had been too serious up to then, she decided to try to lighten it up, so she laughed and added: "I chose the sex kitten myself."

No one else laughed except the other woman present, her friend Edith Holtz.

Did they think I'd be insulted if they laughed? Jane wondered. Maybe they thought she was serious. Hey, she wanted to cry out, I was just joking. I didn't mean it. It's just that I don't want to sound like some militant feminist, because that's not what I am.

Around the table, silence. The fact that they hadn't laughed seemed to have made a bad situation worse.

"Women of my generation," Jane said, "were kind of shocked to find there was any sexism at all. In college we had been taught there was none, it was over, sexism was history. Women before us had had to struggle with this, but we could come out and get a job, do anything we want. Then we come out and find it's not over by a long shot. In some ways it's worse now than it was."

"Worse?" said Vaughan.

She had decided, feeling herself hung out on the line like this, that the subject was going to be treated seriously.

"Because women like me grew up with men as friends, honest-to-God friends." She paused, then added: "Older men aren't used to that."

Carl Doss, seated beside Bill Prince, elbowed him in the side and in a too-loud voice chortled: "That's what we always wanted, right, Bill, women as friends."

Jane could feel the blush come up. Her whole face felt hot.

Silence. No one knew what to say.

Jane said: "The sarcasm or humor or whatever that remark was meant to be, illustrates the point. That men of a certain generation just don't understand women, they would rather talk to other men, they would rather spend their time with other men, they don't know what to do with women. As a result there's no career path for women. A woman really doesn't know how to move ahead."

Beside her Edith Holtz said nothing. No one did.

"There are no women on the paper's masthead," Jane said. "And when I come to work, I notice that there are no women at the front of the newsroom, and I get the feeling that there's a ceiling for women that men don't live with. For men there is no ceiling." She was not at ease with speeches of this kind, and she felt her syntax get clumsy. "There is no sense of modeling yourself after anybody, no sense of following anybody. That contributes to the sense that things are different for you."

Jane had been eyeing Edith Holtz, silently begging her to speak up, take some of this heat off her, and at last Edith did so, introducing the subject of women with kids. It wasn't as bad for her, Edith said, she was unmarried, as for Jane here who had a husband. And for women who had kids it was even worse. Everyone assumed that a married woman, especially a woman with kids, didn't want to work at night, would refuse a promotion if it meant transferring to another bureau. She stopped, and everyone stared at her. Edith was a big, heavyset woman. She had never married and probably never would.

Jeff Burke, a reporter nearing retirement age, said: "But women with families have made their choice, Edith. Their career comes second."

"Jeff," said Jane, "what choice did I or any other female reporter make except to get married or have a child? Don't assume I made a career choice. Every editor on this paper has a wife and kids. Every man overseas has a wife and kids."

"Overseas," he said, "Jane, you don't want that."

"I never said I didn't want that."

Vaughan interrupted, pointing to the assignment editor at the bottom of the table. "How does Edgar there behave in a sexist manner?"

"I'm not accusing anybody in this room particularly of being sexist," said Jane. "In fact this room is not particularly guilty."

Vaughan said to the assignment editor: "Edgar, do you behave in a sexist manner?"

"Sometimes, maybe. I do think whether to assign a man or a woman to a story. If I'm assigning someone to talk to vagrants in the park at night, I want the biggest, burliest guy I can find. And I do that."

Jane said: "I don't think we can be blind to the size and shape of our reporters. It would be ludicrous to send a black reporter to a Ku Klux Klan meeting, or a white one to a black riot. But going into the park in the dark, if you asked me to do that I'd take a photographer with me, two of us, it could be done. We would need the pics anyway. I don't want you to forget I'm not a man, but there are things we can work with."

Most of the room had been silent until now, watching, saying nothing.

It was making Jane increasingly nervous. She said: "Enough of the conspiratorial smiles, would you please say something down there."

In his pompous, too-loud voice, Doss again took the floor, commenting that some women got huge divorce settlements and this gave them an unfair advantage over men.

Jane could not believe her ears. She said: "What?"

"Sure," said Doss. "Some of these women get a tremendous leg up because they get divorced, they get these tremendous settlements, and then they can take chances that men can't take. They don't need money, they can just go places."

Edith Holtz finally reacted. "Oh, don't be ridiculous."

"Furthermore I don't see what the problem is," said ex-foreign correspondent Doss. "As I see it, women are doing very well on this paper. Why, we've had two of them in Nairobi, one right after the other."

Jane wondered if his manner was as offensive to the others as to her. "Nairobi is a hardship assignment," she commented. She wished Edith Holtz would help out more, not leave this entire thing to her. "Nairobi is a difficult place to report, a difficult place to live, and if we screw up there, who's to notice. I don't consider it a great thing that there have been women in Nairobi."

To which Doss muttered: "Well, it's a place where you have to start off."

"I'm not saying women don't have to start off, and do everything men do, but I don't consider two women in Nairobi as proof that women have made great strides."

"In my day," Doss said pompously, "people weren't so concerned about their careers." He seemed to be suggesting that Jane's discussion of careerism was not appropriate. "A reporter just loved journalism. If you got ahead, that was fine; if you didn't, it didn't matter."

He then had the gall personally to conclude the meeting. Glancing at his watch, he stood up and said: "Let's get back to work, shall we?"

In silence they filed out of the conference room. But only Doss struck out immediately toward his desk. Most of the others approached Jane. They consoled her as if she were a bereft widow at a wake. Doss really was an ass, they told her, he was so outrageous it was almost funny.

Jane turned to Vaughan. "Thanks for putting me on the spot. I didn't ask for this discussion."

He shook his head, patted her on the back, and walked away.

For the next hour reporters not present at the meeting kept stopping at Jane's desk. What happened? some wanted to know. Others came to congratulate her. Doss had not calculated that she had worked in this newsroom a long time; that while maybe there was sexism, maybe no one wanted to send her overseas, nonetheless no one wanted to hurt her either.

In another part of the newsroom, Edith Holtz tried to engage Doss in conversation, for his desk was in front of hers. If he wanted to get along around here he should put away the bat, he couldn't just club people, she told him. Doss responded that he had been brought to New York to straighten out the newsroom from the likes of Edith Holtz.

By the end of the day Edith stood weeping at Jane's desk. Her nose was beet red. Doss had asked her to answer his phone, she blubbered. As he was leaving he said, If my phone rings tell whoever it is I'll be back in an hour. Edith was not a secretary, she told Jane. She wept and blew her nose. Doss did not acknowledge her status at all.

Jane was a little irritated. She would never have let the likes of Carl Doss make her cry. If you cried you proved their point. This thing was getting far too much attention and now here was Edith Holtz standing beside her desk in hysterics, attracting more attention still. Jane was becoming concerned.

The story of the lunchtime sexism conference might already have found its way upstairs. Maybe that's where Doss was headed right now. He would be back in an hour, he had told Edith. What did that mean? He had perhaps been summoned upstairs, and he had a big mouth and was perhaps up there right now describing Jane Hoyt Fox as an "ambitious little so-and-so"—bitch was the word that stuck in Jane's mind. To men, women were always bitches, and that was sexism too, if you thought about it. He might accuse her to the executives of deriding the paper that nurtured them all, of being in no way grateful for the position accorded her by the paper.

He might even accuse her of planning a sex-discrimination lawsuit, which she was not.

There had been one. A group of female reporters and editors had instituted it. It had cost the paper bad publicity, legal fees, and a cash settlement. Jane, though invited to take part, had after much thought declined. Not one of those women, as she saw it, was in the mainstream, whereas she was. They perhaps had nothing to lose, whereas she did. The paper, she knew, did not suffer complainers well. And she had been proved right. Although the women had won their suit, every one of them was now shuffling index cards somewhere in the building, their careers dead.

After Edith had dried her tears and departed, Jane sat at her terminal in her semicubicle in the middle of the newsroom and looked out over all the desks and tried to decide what, if anything, she should do. She had a story to write, and deadline was not far off, but this was more important.

Seven or eight desks away sat a woman named Lilian Goodman. She was wearing a red dress and many bracelets, which to Jane meant she had a date after work. It was probably with the publisher, who had been divorced for a number of years. Lilian and the publisher had been dating for some time. It was rumored they might get married. Jane stared at the back of Lilian's head.

After a while she stood up and walked over there. In the past she had occasionally worked on stories with Lilian, whom she considered a friend.

"Are you on deadline?" Jane asked her.

Lilian said she was not. She smiled and seemed glad for the interruption.

"You won't believe what's happened," Jane said, and described the lunch. She did so with amusement, woman to woman, as gossip, almost giggling. But she was not giggling inside. Even if Lilian didn't take this anywhere, meaning to the publisher, still if it ever became a big enough deal she would be available to give Jane's side. It was a conscious, calculating act, an attempt to protect her career.

She went back to her terminal and her story. When she looked up, there was Doss standing over her. He looked contrite. He had perhaps come to apologize. He was perhaps worried now about his own career.

"Are you on deadline?" he asked.

She might easily have listened to whatever he had to say. But she was in no mood to be friendly.

"Yes I am," she said.

"Well, I just wanted to make sure that you're all right."

"Yes, I'm fine." She gave him a brief, too-sweet smile and resumed studying her terminal. After a moment she heard him move off.

The next morning the assistant managing editor, whose name was Bernstein, walked by her desk and asked if she could spare him fifteen minutes later in the day. She didn't know what he wanted. It could be about a story idea, or going to work on another section. It could be about anything. But she did not want other women reporters to imagine she was operating behind their backs on her own, so she walked over to Edith's desk and asked: "How can we make this useful if sexism is what he wants to talk about?"

But Edith only chortled: "We've got the bastards on the run."

Jane wasn't so sure.

That afternoon Bernstein took her into an empty conference room, where he said in a fatherly voice: "Sit down in that chair right there, Jane. Tell me about it. What happened? You should come to me when these things happen."

His serious, fatherly tone took her somewhat aback, but when she tried a laugh it didn't quite come off.

Doss had made a jerk out of himself, she told him, and had said some very offensive things. But it was nothing to worry about.

Bernstein nodded somberly.

They certainly, Jane thought, were treating this with the

utmost seriousness. "Of course," she added calculatingly, "if anyone had said those things about Jews or blacks, nobody would have remained so silent."

This was the notion that frightened everyone, and Jane knew it.

"Vaughan should never have brought the subject up," Bernstein said.

"Why not?" said Jane, watching him carefully. "We had a very interesting discussion. It's something we ought to talk about more than we do. The only thing that offended me was that not one man in the room opened his mouth to defend us or agreed that there was any kind of sexism."

Bernstein said carefully: "Then you do think there's sexism in the newsroom."

What was she to say to this? What did he suppose she had been talking about so far? She tossed her hair back.

"Yes," she said, "there's some."

"Well, yes," said Bernstein, "I've always agreed there's some."

After leaving Bernstein, Jane went directly to Vaughan. Men were tender, she believed. It was best always to tell them exactly what you were doing or had done. "I've just come from talking to Bernstein," she began.

Vaughan was scarcely cordial. "Oh?" he said. "I thought you had been there already."

"No, five minutes ago." She began to explain what she had told him.

"They called me in about it this morning," the Metro editor interrupted. "I told them it was nothing."

Jane supposed that the publisher or Bernstein or both—perhaps others as well—had come down hard on Vaughan. She laughed, or tried to. "I told them it was fine with me too."

"Did you indeed?"

The women's caucus called a meeting. The notice was posted in the ladies' room as always and the meeting was scheduled for Dorsey's across the street at ten o'clock in the morning. Bernstein found out about it, or someone else did and told him, and he stopped Jane in the hallway and said:

"What's it going to be about?"

"Salaries, I think."

Obviously Bernstein wanted to say more. Obviously also he didn't quite dare.

Jane said: "I'll tell you afterward what was said."

She saw him juggling legalities in his head. "You don't have to do that."

"I won't tell you who said what, just the gist of the meeting. I think you ought to know."

"Well—"

"I think it better for both sides if you know."

Something else was on Bernstein's mind, and Jane waited to see what it was.

"We're having a study made on salaries right now," he said after a moment.

Jane laughed. "I think you'll find that men get paid more."

"If that's what's going on," said Bernstein carefully, "we'd like to correct that. But—" He stopped.

"But what?"

"Women should get paid the same as men—if that's what's going on. But, well, you can't just hand over money to all the women. We would want to do it gradually and on our own timetable."

Jane was a woman who abhorred confrontations. If their intention was to make it right, she thought, then why couldn't it be worked out? "That would be better than nothing," she said.

The women's caucus was made up principally of active Guild members. Today's meeting featured an ex-reporter named Lisa Van Kampel, who had recently quit the paper. She had never been a particularly good reporter and the paper had been glad to get rid of her, but she went out charging sexual discrimination. She had made as much noise about it as possible.

Today, in the back of Dorsey's restaurant, the caucus sat

around a single big table, and Lisa told what she knew about salary discrepancies. She knew of a single case only, but it was a specific one and she had specific facts.

It seemed that three months previously the paper had hired a reporter away from the *Washington Post* who had less experience than she did. The editors agreed to pay him sixty-two thousand dollars a year. She was making only fifty-one thousand, so when she heard this she went in and demanded a raise. They agreed she should have a raise but offered her only three thousand dollars, so she quit.

When the meeting ended and Jane went back to work, she was too disquieted to approach Bernstein and although she caught him eyeing her from time to time, he was leery, apparently, about approaching her.

The afternoon passed. At six thirty the day side was given the goodnight, and as Jane got up from her desk to go home, she saw Bernstein, at the far end of the newsroom, do likewise. She was not surprised, when she came out through the vestibule, to find him waiting there for the elevator. In a newspaper building, she reflected, elevator meetings are not always accidental. She nodded to him but said nothing, and when they had stepped out into the summer evening together she merely turned toward the subway station on the corner. But he took her arm and steered her toward the curb, saying:

"I'll share a cab uptown with you."

He flagged one down and she got into it with him, still without saying a word.

For some blocks they rode in silence. Then she suddenly turned on him. "You just hired a guy from the *Washington Post*," she said.

"Bernie Flack," said Bernstein. "He's going to be good for us."

"You're paying him sixty-two thousand dollars a year."

"Where did you hear that?"

"One of the women at the caucus. She said she had more experience and was only getting fifty-one thousand."

"Lisa Van Kampel," said Bernstein bitterly. "She's a

troublemaker, that woman. She dated Bernie. That's how she found out.''

"You're only paying me fifty-four thousand, and I have more experience than both of them put together.''

"They're getting married next week," said Bernstein bitterly. "That's why he told her. She's pregnant. That's why she quit the paper.''

Jane said: "I think the sexism in this place is just incredible. I feel completely taken advantage of. If I were a man I'd not only be getting more money, I'd be overseas by now. I've won three publishers awards, I've written six series that you've put in for all kinds of awards. I speak another language.''

"I didn't know you spoke another language, Jane," said Bernstein defensively.

"My father worked for Pan Am. I lived in Barcelona until I was eleven. I must have mentioned it to you five times. The only reason I haven't been sent overseas is because I'm a woman.''

The cab was proceeding up Eighth Avenue past all the honky-tonk cafés, the porno moviehouses, the tenements with their iron fire escapes. Bernstein, under attack, stared straight ahead.

"You've just sent Dewey Trevor, who has a year and a half's experience, to Guatemala to study Spanish for six months. I already speak Spanish.''

"You want to go overseas?" said Bernstein, as if the idea had just occurred to him. "What would your husband do?''

"That's not your problem, that's my problem. How do you know my marriage is even going to last? You can't make decisions for me. I make those decisions.''

Jane watched Bernstein's jaw work. Obviously he felt he had to do something because she had a point. The first sexism suit was over, the paper had lost it, and the possibility of another loomed ever large. It was a possibility that terrified them upstairs.

Bernstein said: "Where would you like to go?''

Although she had never expected the conversation to lead in this direction, Jane was ready with her answer.

"Madrid."

"You can't go to Madrid, Winograd is there."

"Latin America, then."

"It's too dangerous for a woman."

"See," said Jane.

They had stopped in front of her building. She got out of the cab.

Bernstein said: "You and I never had this conversation."

"Oh no?"

"I'll see what I can do."

When she came into her apartment, her husband was in the kitchen preparing dinner. She put her handbag down on the sideboard and went in there.

"Hi," he said, "how are you?"

"You'll never guess what happened," she said.

"No, I'm sure I never will." He was moving pots around on the stove.

"I may get an overseas assignment," she said. "What's for dinner?" And she waited.

George was cooking tonight because it was his turn. He wore an apron over a sweat suit, and when he turned to face her he was holding a spatula.

A generation earlier, a husband might have answered: But, Jane, if you leave the country, who's going to iron my shirts?

George gave the modern equivalent. He said: "What about our marriage?"

"I may never get it," said Jane.

"And if it comes through?"

She hesitated.

"Would you go?"

"We'd still be married."

"Me here and you there? What country are we talking about, by the way?"

"I don't know. South America."

"You'll get killed," he said bluntly.

"I don't believe that."

"They kill foreign journalists all the time down there. They're just looking for publicity. The guerrillas, the drug traffickers. They're all the same. You'd be perfect for them. A New York journalist, and a woman besides."

"You're worried about me," said Jane. She was surprised and oddly touched.

"You didn't answer me. What about our marriage?"

Jane stared at the floor. Say it, she ordered herself. "A few months off from each other might do our marriage a world of good."

"Are we having a fight now? If so, please tell me what it's about."

"We're not having a fight. I merely said there's a chance I might get an overseas assignment."

"I see."

"No you don't. Do you realize what an overseas assignment would mean to my career?"

He had been cooking lamb chops. He remembered them only when they began to smoke.

"I realize that if you take such an assignment, this marriage is most probably over."

He scooped the chops out of the frying pan and slapped them down on plates. "Dinner's ready."

"Why?" said Jane. "If it was only a few months?"

"Is that how long they're sending you off for, a few months? I understood the normal tour of a foreign correspondent to be more like three years."

"If it was longer than a few months," said Jane, "we could get together often enough. I could come here. You could come there." She trailed him into the dining room. "Or we could meet halfway. Are we having wine?"

"If you want wine, open it yourself."

Jane decided to forgo the wine. She took her place opposite George. "We could meet in Miami, or somewhere in the Caribbean. The world is not such a big place anymore, haven't you heard? They have airplanes now.'' She served potatoes and broccoli onto his plate, then her own.

"I hate airplanes, and I don't have time to go traipsing all over the world just to meet you."

It was as cruel as anything he might have said and it brought tears to her eyes, which she could not understand. "Plenty of couples do it, these days," she said.

He concentrated on his food. He looked calm enough. Watching him, Jane found she could not eat.

"Are you saying you would divorce me if I took an overseas assignment?"

"No, just that divorce is what would happen. Eventually. Eat your dinner."

"Well," said Jane after a moment, "nobody has offered me anything yet, and I haven't said I'd take it if they did."

"Then why did you bring it up?"

Mostly to prove to herself that she could. To hear how the idea sounded. To find out in advance how he would react. "It's something to think about," she said.

"It's something for you to think about, not me."

6

HIS FIRST MORNING in New York David Ley awoke beside a young woman whose name he could not immediately remember. It came back to him in a moment: Marge. She was a stewardess off yesterday's commercial flight from Panama. She had cost him dinner plus a gold necklace she had seen and admired in a shop window as they strolled through Times Square afterward. He had ducked into the shop and bought it for her. A hundred dollars. Cheap. She had squealed with delight then, and squealed in a different way later.

Ley peeled the sheet back and watched her sleeping. She was lying on her stomach, and the line of her back pleased him, and the rising slope of her firm smooth buttocks seemed to him lovely, and he began to stroke it. She lay with her legs slightly parted and he dropped the side of his hand in there and began to work her. At first she was still asleep, and then she wasn't, and he rolled her over and looked at her. She was a real blond—blond top and bottom—and she smiled sleepily and murmured: "That was nice."

"I know something even nicer."

It made her speak from between clenched teeth. "I'll bet you do."

A moment later, her teeth still clenched, she said: "You know something, Mike, you're really good at this."

"I try," he said.

He liked the noise she made. Women made all kinds of noises. They groaned, panted, wheezed. With this one it was more a series of grunts than anything else. He loved women. He loved the way they looked, the way they smelled and talked, the way their flesh felt to the touch, the way their minds worked, the way their bodies were made—everything about them. He thought they recognized this; he knew he was attractive to women and this was part of the reason why.

"I could stay in bed all day," she said presently, almost calmly. She was sitting up, her face still flushed, blotches of color on her breasts.

He laughed and said he had work to do, unfortunately.

They left the building together. On the sidewalk she kissed him moistly. When she had turned the corner he wiped it off, then stepped into a florist and ordered a dozen roses sent to her address. With luck the flowers would get there before she did. She would be extremely impressed, and he might call her again. Probably he would. He'd have to see what else turned up. He had written out a clever note to go in the box. He had spent more than ten minutes thinking out what to write.

There was a limousine standing double-parked outside his house. He had hired it to wait there around the clock. He went back and got into it and had himself driven down to Times Square, where he visited several ticket brokerages. He paid inflated prices for the theater tickets he wanted, but what was money? He came away with tickets to four shows, which posed problems of course. Who was going to sit beside him on those four nights? But he had begun to feel a sentimental attachment to Marge. Marge would be one. Who else?

From Times Square, Ley had himself driven back uptown to Park Avenue toward the apartment of a wealthy socialite with whom he had made a date for lunch. Her husband was a big mover on Wall Street.

Being early, he got out and strolled up Park with the limousine trailing behind him. He noted again that there were no shops at street level on Park—he had forgotten. Park was an extremely boring street. He walked under all the awnings, peered into the different lobbies, nodded at some of the doormen out front. Also, for a short time, his mind grappled with the problem of his cook's son Salvador, and the seizure of so much merchandise and money. By now he knew that Salvador had not been arrested. How to contact him? Ley certainly couldn't go knock on his door, and although he had a phone number, it would be unwise to use it. It was not one problem but a series of problems. Ley could not concentrate on it. He hadn't unwound enough yet, he told himself. His attention span was too short. He was not yet able to work it out. Besides, a more immediate problem was the woman he was about to meet.

He turned in at 708 Park and gave his name—Mike Palacios—to the head doorman. There were three doormen, two of whom ignored him, and he waited while the third phoned his name upstairs. The lobby was a combination of big mirrors and polished wood. Finally he was allowed to cross it to the elevator. Although it was an automatic elevator, one of the doormen took him upstairs in it—pushed the buttons and then just stood there in silence in the corner. The people who lived on Park Avenue had money, Ley reflected.

Barbara was standing with the door open as he came off. He had met her—and her husband—in the Caribbean a year or so ago and had not seen her since, so he gave her a polite kiss on the cheek. But she held on to him saying: "You can do better than that." And she kissed him on the lips with her mouth open. Ley was a bit surprised, but not too surprised. He was confident that he had read her correctly last year, which was why he had called her up so promptly.

She sent the maid out of the house on some pretext and led the way onto her terrace to show him her view.

"The view here is looking at you," he said gallantly.

They were on the twentieth floor and the view was across lower rooftops, across Central Park, and across more rooftops. She could see most of Manhattan as it huddled under its smog. There were so many plants on the terrace it was like walking through a jungle.

It was a hot day. They made small talk on the terrace and more small talk when they had returned to the air-conditioned living room. All this time Barbara had been looking at him in a certain way that Ley recognized.

Ley had thought that if he played her right during the long, luxurious restaurant lunch, then afterward they might return here to the apartment for coffee, and anything might then happen. But now, watching her tongue play across her lower lip as she looked at him, Ley thought: Why wait? And he took her in his arms and kissed her. She kissed back, all tongue and saliva, so that Ley thought: Oh, one of those.

"You're very handsome," she said. "I suppose you know that." Well, he did know it. Many women had told him so.

"You're a beautiful woman," he murmured in reply.

She took his hand. "In here," she said in a smoky voice.

It was as easy as that.

It was an apartment of ten rooms at least, but the one she led him into was certainly the master bedroom, and again he was a bit surprised, but not too surprised.

"Your bed?" he asked.

She nodded, and began unbuttoning her blouse. He saw she was already breathing hard.

"Your husband's bed too."

"He'll never never know, and if he finds out, he's getting what he deserves."

Ley thought: There are many reasons why a woman might choose to go to bed with a man. This one is mad at her husband. She's getting even. I'm just the instrument. Interesting. There was no telling what women would do, he thought. Or why. Women were fascinating, constantly amazing.

He removed her fingers from her blouse. "Let me do that for you," he said. She was ten years older than Marge, and as he worked on her clothes, he wondered how the two female bodies would compare.

They compared quite well, in fact. In some ways that was the best moment, a woman you did not know very well standing without her clothes, totally vulnerable, totally defenseless, waiting, watching you, wondering what was about to happen to her.

He took her for lunch to the Polo, which was perhaps the most elegant and luxurious of the Upper East Side restaurants, and he distributed money on the way in so that they would be treated with the utmost consideration. Halfway through the meal he wondered why he had bothered. Barbara led a vapid life and had nothing much to say. Because he was bored, his cook's son Salvador came to mind again, which was annoying. It was like homework hanging over his head when he was in school—he would have to address the problem soon. But not now. Today was his day off.

In the meantime the hatcheck girl had caught his eye. She was one of those he had tipped on the way in. She looked younger than Barbara, older than Marge, and prettier than both in a dark sort of way. Since there was not much for her to check on a nonrainy summer afternoon, she stood in the entryway with her hands behind her back looking out over the diners.

Ley had begun to stare at her. Very soon she was aware of this, and her eyes dropped to the floor. He kept staring. Her eyes would rise from time to time, darting this way and that like small animals she could not control, then drop immediately, furtively once again. But she did not withdraw into her little cubbyhole.

Ley, who continued to stare, hardly heard what Barbara was saying to him. He watched the hatcheck girl's eyes come up once more. This time she stared grimly back as if unwilling to let him intimidate her. It became a test of wills. Which would look away first? Ley grinned. He loved a good contest of this nature. He had no intention of losing. Neither did the girl—for a time.

The girl's will cracked first. She not only broke eye contact but seemed to glance wildly about, as if seeking escape.

"Isn't that so, Mike?" said Barbara.

"Excuse me," said Ley, and he got up and walked ostensibly toward the men's room.

When the girl saw him coming she fled to the rear of her cubbyhole.

On the way by he peered into it. It was coatless, empty except for her, almost cowering in the rear. She gazed at him almost truculently.

"I'd love to see you, take you out," he murmured. "Could I take you to dinner some night?"

She said: "No. That wouldn't be possible."

He smiled, and said: "Think about it," and continued on.

When he came out of the men's room he didn't see her at all, and he imagined he had failed. He shrugged it off. More often than not, one failed. Back at the table he continued his inane luncheon with Barbara.

When they had finished and prepared to leave the restaurant, he noted that the girl had returned to her post once more. Going out Ley distributed more money—to the waiter, the maître d'hôtel and also to the girl, and he got back professional smiles from all of them. He and Barbara had reached the door to the street when Ley on a hunch doubled back to the girl's cubbyhole.

"What night are you off?" he asked.

"I'm off tonight," she said, looking at the floor.

"Where will I pick you up?"

"I'll lose my job."

"They won't know."

She gave him an address and apartment number. He suggested a time and she nodded. A moment later he was outside and putting Barbara into a cab.

From there he walked along until he came to another florist; he sent Barbara a dozen roses and was about to send a second dozen to the hatcheck girl when he realized he didn't know her name.

Nonetheless, before midnight she was in bed sitting on him. She kept apologizing for her inexperience. She had the biggest breasts of the three. She had hips like a boy. When he had asked her to get on top she had looked shocked. Her name was Barbara also. He began to think of them as Barbara One and Barbara Two. Too bad Marge's name was not Barbara as well. Three Barbaras in one day. That would have been unusual. As Barbara Two worked him he was feeling extremely impressed with himself. The problem of Salvador had gone from his mind completely.

He called up Marge again and took her out to Belmont to the races. He gave her five hundred dollars and told her it was hers to bet, that she could keep her winnings, if any. She gambled and giggled all afternoon and he watched her and was happy. He raised racehorses himself in Colombia and had had many winners there. He never bet. He liked looking at racehorses almost as much as looking at women.

He took Marge to the theater that night, then to dinner, then back to his house. He didn't want to spend all night with her, though. At three o'clock in the morning he sent her home in his faithful limo.

The following day there were some polo matches out at Blindbrook. As a young man he had played polo himself. He had broken both ankles and his collarbone in various accidents and no longer played. But he loved the game. Marge was flying and Barbara Two could not get the day off, so he was obliged to go with Barbara One, who spent the whole afternoon talking about how much she would like to divorce her husband. Very boring.

What to do about Salvador? From time to time the problem had nagged at him. Finally, posing as a lawyer sent up from Colombia to find out what was happening, he spent an hour in the office of the defense lawyer handling the case. The New York lawyer brought out copies of the indictments, copies of motions he had filed, copies of responses by the district attorney, plus the newspaper reports. All this material Ley scanned or read. He saw at once that Salvador's name was not mentioned.

"Only four arrests?" he asked him.

"Right."

"A sealed indictment? More arrests coming, perhaps?"

"I don't think so."

Ley's cook would be overjoyed. But he ought to make contact with Salvador and somehow get him out of New York.

First he put some important questions to the lawyer. "How did the four men under arrest get caught? What did they do wrong?" The four men were lost. The important thing to someone like Pablo Marzo, and to Ley as well of course, was that it should not happen again.

The lawyer hedged. "The indictments tell very little."

"An informant?" said Ley.

"No informant testified before the grand jury."

"A new police tactic? Did they step into some kind of police trap?"

"We'll know more as the discovery procedure continues."

"My clients can't wait. Find out immediately."

This was what the New York lawyers were paid so much money for—to stay abreast of police techniques, to provide information the cartel could get no other way. The lawyer said he would try to find out.

Barbara One invited him to a dinner party. Her husband was there so he was seated next to a minor actress named Melissa something. The race meeting was to open at Saratoga the following day and he had been wondering who to take.

The answer turned out to be Melissa. With Barbara One staring daggers at him, he left the dinner party with her and the next morning she was seated beside him in the limousine as they started north toward the Adirondacks.

They stayed three days. The scenery was gorgeous, the races exciting, Melissa turned out to be an extremely imaginative woman, and he never thought of Salvador at all.

Upon returning to New York, he dropped Barbaras One and Two, dividing his time between Marge and Melissa. He found himself quite busy. Marge flew to Panama every other day. In between they saw shows together. Melissa was always available. He took her shopping and bought her things. One day on a whim he even revisited Barbara One, telling himself it was only to see if she was still mad at her husband. She was.

As a consequence he did not have much time. He did keep a second appointment with the defense lawyer, who by then had some answers for him. There had been no betrayal, apparently. The Cali people were not involved. No new police techniques were involved. Apparently it was a detective working undercover on something else. He had become aware of five new Colombians in his area and had decided to follow them.

"There are thirty thousand cops out there," the lawyer said apologetically. "They're bound to stumble on something once in a while." The police investigation had lasted some months, apparently.

In one way this was good news. No one would have to be liquidated and Marzo's bloody reprisals against the Cali group, if they had started, could be stopped. And Salvador was in the clear. There was no reason for Marzo or anyone else to move against him.

Ley deplored all the recent violence in Colombia. It was, or soon would be, bad for business. Selling drugs to the arrogant Americans had never bothered most Colombian citizens, who up to now tended to look on certain of the *narcotraficantes*—Marzo for one—almost as folk heroes. But the violence at home was another matter. Violence directed against judges, journalists, and police bordered on terrorism. The cartel might soon be seen as a terrorist group, and might lose public approval. So much violence might provoke national outrage, even turn their own country against them, and once that happened they would have more to worry about than just the Americans.

"By the way," said the lawyer, "someone else was in here yesterday asking these same questions."

Ley said: "Who?"

"A Colombian lawyer like yourself." The lawyer gave a name. Ley didn't recognize it. Probably an alias anyway.

But it made him concentrate for a time on Salvador. How to extricate his cook's son from New York? The man was probably in hiding, but if not he was perhaps being watched by the police. How even to contact him?

But Ley was meeting Marge in an hour and had things to do. She was coming to his flat. He had to bring in some champagne, for one thing. The problem of Salvador had waited this long. It could certainly wait another day. And so it slipped from his mind.

By the next day it was too late.

7

THE TRUCK WAS parked outside 121 Vermilyea Avenue in the Inwood section of Manhattan. Salvador, the loose end, lived at Number 123.

Detective Sullivan, who was driving, gestured at the truck with his chin. "It was there yesterday too."

"Cruise on past," ordered Douglas.

It was a meat market delivery truck with a butcher's name

stenciled on its sides, and it stood out because plainly it did not belong there. Vermilyea was a residential street: six-story apartment buildings on both sides. The buildings were about sixty years old. At sidewalk level there were no stores of any kind. There was certainly no meat market and in fact the address on the truck was Brooklyn.

The truck was parked in full sunlight. The windshield shone like steel and the roof, what they could see of it, like glass. "I don't envy those guys inside," Sullivan said. "It must be over a hundred degrees in there."

"Maybe it's not them inside at all," Douglas said. "Maybe it's a South American hit squad."

"I recognize the truck, Chief. They've used that truck before. I swear to God."

"You think you recognize the truck," said Douglas.

Sullivan steered around the corner into 207th Street.

"It makes you want to go up and bang on the sides, don't it," said Sullivan.

Douglas said nothing.

Sullivan giggled. "Or let the air out of their tires."

Sullivan drove up the hill to Broadway and they waited at the light.

"Over there's the phone booth Salvador likes to use," said Sullivan, pointing. "He's used it only once since we hit them. And that's the other truck."

It was parked at a meter not twenty feet from the phone booth.

"Jesus, they're close," muttered Douglas.

It was a panel truck. Since it was ten or more years old, badly dented, and partially rusted out, it did not look like a surveillance vehicle. Its windows were painted over. No one could see into it. The vent on the roof was turning slowly.

"It's a good truck, isn't it," said Sullivan.

"Go around the corner," said Douglas. "Park in that bus stop."

Sullivan did so, and they sat several minutes. Beside them

the traffic moved up Broadway. Douglas knew this neighborhood, which had once been middle-class Irish but was now heavily Hispanic.

"It's been two weeks since we hit them," Sullivan said. "We haven't gone near the guy."

Douglas stared straight ahead, his fingers drumming on his knee.

"We watched the school," Sullivan said. "Made sure his wife was still bringing the kids. That proved they were still around, right?"

Douglas said nothing.

"And we watched this phone booth from the empty office we been using upstairs above that hardware store. We still have a wire on it. Just in case he starts making a lot of calls. He only made the one I told you about. He comes up the street to the phone booth and there's a guy tailing him. The next day they got the truck parked where you see it now. It's been there ever since."

A bus pulled in behind their car, took on passengers, then surged on past. The car filled up with its fumes.

"Who did he phone?"

"His consulate. It was about his wife's passport. From the phone booth he went down into the subway. We didn't try to follow him. We had a detective watch for him at the consulate, in case it was a code. He showed up there, came out after about twenty minutes, and took a taxi back. They hadn't followed him downtown, but I think when he came out of the consulate it was their taxi he got into."

Douglas got out of the car and walked back to the parked surveillance truck as if he meant to pound on it, order whoever was inside to come out. But up close he only stared at the painted-over windows for a time, eyeball to eyeball with someone he could not see. The truck might even be empty.

Then he went back to the car. "Head downtown," he told Sullivan. "Fifty-seventh Street."

The DEA rented several floors in an office building opposite the CBS television studios on West Fifty-seventh Street. The two groups, painted television stars and armed agents, dominated the neighborhood. At lunch hour each day the nearby restaurants filled up with them. They dined at adjacent tables. The difference was that some of the agents had death threats over their heads, and bodyguards stood watchfully at the bar.

The DEA did not take death threats lightly. The New York Police Department paid special attention to their building. Two uniformed cops, Douglas noted as he climbed out of his car, patrolled the sidewalk outside, and a third wandered around the lobby.

Herbert Campbell's office was on the nineteenth floor. Douglas rode the elevator up, coming out into a reception room. An agent, he found, was on duty there as well, and he eyed Douglas carefully. It was his job to scrutinize those who came and went all day. In between visitors, like a man waiting his turn in a doctor's anteroom, he leafed through magazines. At the end of eight hours he went home. To Douglas this seemed a waste of law-enforcement personnel. On the other hand the new drug lords were capable of almost anything, and back in their own country had assassinated any number of people.

Douglas gave his name to the receptionist. The glass in her window, he noted, was one inch thick. He signed in. The steel door through which he was admitted was as solid as the door to a bank vault. He strode toward Campbell's office in the rear corner of the floor.

Campbell was on the phone. He smiled and waved Douglas to a chair. Douglas did not smile back, nor did he sit down. There was an American flag behind Campbell's chair, and the walls were covered with framed diplomas and citations, and with photos of Campbell shaking hands with the mighty.

When he had hung up, Campbell came around the desk. He was a small, tightly knit man in his fifties. He was highly thought of in Washington. He not only headed the New York office, but also was part of the directorate that ran the entire agency. Lately he had been mentioned as the country's next drug czar.

The two men shook hands and for a moment made small

talk, after which Campbell switched to flattery: "Your men did such a great job the other week, Ray, and—"

"As a matter of fact," Douglas said, "that's why I'm here." And he hesitated. Doubtless this interview would turn into a confrontation, but he would keep it pleasant as long as possible. "You see, Herb, we're still working the case. I would appreciate it if you would take your men off it."

"I didn't know we had men on it, Ray."

Maybe he did, maybe he didn't. "You have surveillance teams in the neighborhood of Vermilyea Avenue and 207th Street. They're working an illegal alien who goes by the name of Salvador."

Campbell gave a brief, acquiescent nod. "I'm not familiar with the details."

"You've flooded the neighborhood."

"My men are experts at surveillance."

"So are mine."

"My men don't get made."

Though Douglas began to get angry, he tried at first to conceal it. "We made them. It took us about five minutes."

"I don't know what I can do for you, Ray."

"Salvador is ours."

"That's an extremely broad statement, I find."

"Let me explain something to you. These people just lost two tons of stuff. They're very touchy."

"Yes, you did a great job. I've said so publicly."

"The mood they're in, they're seeing cops that aren't there."

"We're operating with the greatest of care."

"We pulled way back. You parked a truck right outside the guy's house. Jesus."

"Come on, Ray, come on. We're not amateurs at this."

"You'll get him killed."

Campbell shrugged. "If he gets killed, he gets killed. He's not an informant, Ray. He's part of the conspiracy. We don't owe him anything."

"I don't believe I'm hearing this."

"If his people decide to whack him out, then he gets whacked out. Happens all the time."

"He can take us right to the top."

"Maybe he can, maybe he can't."

"It's certain."

Campbell frowned. "Nothing's certain in law enforcement."

As Douglas saw it, Campbell had one object only: to establish DEA control of the case. He knew better than to move his men up so close so soon, Douglas believed. He was like an animal urinating on every tree as a way of claiming territory.

Douglas's voice took on a pleading tone. "Salvador needs room, which is what we're giving him."

Campbell said quietly: "You really should talk to the PC about this, Ray, not me."

"How did you know about Salvador in the first place?"

When Campbell did not reply, Douglas feared the worst.

"Did Windsell send over our case folder too? Did he give you the entire case? Is that what you're telling me?"

The federal agent made no answer.

Douglas's mouth worked, but no sound came forth, and after a moment he turned on his heel and stalked out of Campbell's office.

About thirty men sat around the table in the fourteenth-floor conference room at police headquarters. There were men from the Secret Service, from the FBI. There were men from the DEA, though not Herbert Campbell. There were men from the fire department and from the Port Authority police who controlled Kennedy Airport. The NYPD was represented by more than ten men, including the chiefs of detectives, patrol, traffic, intelligence, and, in the person of Douglas, narcotics.

The subject of today's conference was the president of the United States. The security of. Plots against the life of.

The president was coming to New York tomorrow night,

and these men were charged with assuring his safety. Douglas was drumming a pencil on his knee, his legs crossed, his mind elsewhere. The president's visit was routine and this was a routine conference. He attended conferences just like it in this same room every time the president, this one or any other, scheduled a trip to New York—several times each year. The conferences lasted two hours and every step the president took was plotted out. *Air Force One* would land at Kennedy Airport at a precise hour and come to a stop at a precise spot. The president, his wife, and members of his immediate staff would transfer to one of the White House helicopters, which would have been ferried up the day before. Assorted White House and Secret Service limousines would have been ferried up also.

The helicopter would rise up immediately, would set down at the Wall Street heliport precisely eight minutes later, and the president and his party would step into a waiting bullet-proof limousine. The helicopter containing the press pool and other aides would arrive moments later. Surrounded by Secret Service cars and preceded and followed by police and detective cars, the cavalcade, sixteen cars, would start uptown at once over streets empty of all other traffic.

All of this scarcely needed to be said, reflected Douglas. It was the same every time.

At present the chief of traffic was at the easel pointing out the cavalcade's route up the East River Drive to the Waldorf-Astoria, where the presidential party would spend the night. Entrance and exit ramps would be blocked off by squads of police, and ordinary traffic stopped some blocks away and rerouted. From the Forty-second Street exit through streets to the Waldorf, same thing. The route had been divided into eight segments, each in charge of a deputy inspector. From the heliport by limousine to the hotel would take twelve minutes. It was unfortunate, the chief of traffic commented, that the president had chosen to land during rush hour—unfortunate, that is, for the rest of the citizenry, who would be outraged and screaming. But his men could handle it.

At the Waldorf the secret service command post would be

set up in suite 33A beginning at noon on the day of arrival, and approximately six hours later the presidential limousine would drive in under the building to the Tower well where two elevators would be kept waiting, in case one should fail.

People would be ringing for elevators on every floor, Douglas thought, but for a while nothing would come.

The purpose of the president's visit this time was to attend a new Broadway musical. He and his party would be given precisely one hour to freshen up in their suites, continued the chief of Traffic, then be taken to the theater. Again side streets would be blocked off. The theater was on Forty-fourth Street, which was one-way. The limousine would drive in against the flow of the now nonexistent traffic and stop directly in front. The Secret Service would have men inside the theater, as would the chief of detectives, seats having been provided by the management.

Other commanders replaced the chief of Traffic at the easel. Other placards went up and other details were decided. There would be four other helicopters in the air over the Wall Street heliport, none closer than a quarter mile from the landing pad, and they would sweep the rooftops of the buildings as the cavalcade moved uptown. The police bomb squad would sweep the Waldorf in advance and also the theater. The bomb squad disposal truck would be standing by outside the hotel.

None of this concerned Douglas, who brooded instead about Salvador, Vermilyea Avenue, and Herbert Campbell. The case had to be saved and Salvador's life had to be saved. He saw no way out but to go to the mayor, whom he had met several times but could not be said to know—who probably would not remember him. Who might even be angered to be approached by a mere deputy chief. Who might simply refuse to see him.

The Secret Service chief moved to the easel. Radio frequencies were specified, and also code words. "Hailstone" meant a bomb threat. "Heartbeat" meant the bomb squad actually had something. Lapel buttons were passed around, green triangles for the Secret Service, tricolor rectangles for the FBI, green and yellow shields for detectives and other plainclothes police personnel. Douglas accepted the lapel button offered him. There was no reason for him to attend the presidential arrival, and he had not intended to do so. But now an idea came to him and he saw that the lapel button could be useful.

The department's chief of intelligence took the floor. Certain protest groups had applied for permits, he said. The Union for Puerto Rican Solidarity would be kept behind barriers on the southwest corner of Forty-ninth Street opposite the hotel. There would be a pro-abortion group on the northwest corner, and an anti-abortion group on the corner of Broadway near the theater. Other groups had not applied for permits but might demonstrate anyway, and an FBI specialist stood up and described who they were and what precautions would be taken.

There had been recent threats against the president's life. There were always threats. None of the men present was surprised by them. The problem was always to decide which might be serious, and which not, and of the serious ones, which demanded special attention.

Scarcely listening, doodling on the yellow pad in front of him, Douglas brooded.

The black militants of the past were no longer a problem, apparently. The Italian and German terrorist groups were not at present active in the U.S., or so it was believed. The Palestinians had calmed down, but not the Libyans. What about the Iranians? What about the South American drug traffickers?

This last question was addressed to Douglas. In terms of presidential safety the problem was a new one, but it was real. The drug lords were violent and they were outrageous. Recently, according to informants, they had sent hit squads to New York to murder Herbert Campbell, and also the mayor: Campbell because he was the most visible drug agent in the country, and the mayor for his virulent antidrug speeches. Some weeks ago two of Douglas's detectives had stopped a car and found detonating devices in the trunk. They arrested the car's occupants, three South Americans, one of them an illegal alien who was later deported. Since the possession of detonating devices was not a crime, the other two had to be released, and they were still here, though being watched—they would be even more closely watched during the president's visit.

Could there be others out there besides these two? Douglas was asked.

Of course there could, he replied, but informants had not reported them and he had no way of knowing.

The DEA agents present were asked the same questions and gave the same answers. They were aware of no overt threats against the president's life.

"The president is so well guarded," Douglas said, "that I don't think we need worry. It's not an ideological thing with drug traffickers. They're violent, not suicidal."

On this note the conference at last broke up, and Douglas went back to his office.

There were a dozen or so cops working at desks in his bullpen, with a captain, who was his chief secretary, at the desk at his door. The captain handed him a sheaf of telephone messages as he went past.

"Get me the mayor's appointments secretary," Douglas told him.

He went through into his own office, shuffled through the messages, and waited.

But the captain buzzed him with a different call. "Woman says her name is Simpson. Says you know her."

Douglas was surprised. But after hesitating a moment he said: "All right, I'll take that.

"Hello," he said into the phone, "how are you?"

Someone had given her tickets to a play, Gail told him. It was the day after tomorrow. She wondered if he'd like to go with her.

He could hear the stiffness in her voice, the fear of rejection. She was of a generation where girls never asked boys for dates. They waited to be asked themselves. To make this phone call must have been hard for her.

When Douglas did not immediately answer, she said: "It's *Tables Turned*. It's supposed to be very good."

Douglas started to say that he was obliged to work very late these days. If he accepted he'd probably have to cancel anyway, he would tell her. So he'd best say no. She would say: Maybe another time. He would say: Yes, maybe another time.

At the very least it would ruin her day. She would feel mortified. He found he did not want to hurt her to this extent. He found himself agreeing to meet her at the theater.

When he had hung up he was annoyed with himself, and he buzzed his captain again. "Where's that call to the mayor's office?"

"On line four, sir."

Douglas punched the button. "How soon can you get me in to see the mayor?" he asked the appointments secretary.

"What's it about?"

"Personal."

The secretary seemed to take this as a personal affront. "Not before next week, I'm afraid."

"I'll only need a minute or two. Or I could meet him somewhere. What's his schedule like today and tomorrow?"

The secretary declined to tell him. "We're keeping that kind of information pretty close, with all these death threats he's been getting."

Douglas, repressing his irritation, decided to try charm. "I wouldn't want to kill the mayor," he said. "You, though, that's another story."

The secretary still declined to tell him.

"Well, will he be at the East Side heliport to greet the president tomorrow night?"

"I really couldn't say."

The heliport was a concrete pier built out into the river. Douglas was there early. He was not the only one. Already several police harbor launches, all named after slain cops, cruised back and forth, and a fireboat twice their size held position in the current. Sixty or eighty yards of fire hoses snaked around the perimeter of the pier, with firemen standing every few feet. The firemen wore firehats, rubber boots, and slickers, though it was a warm evening. Some held axes. One carried a great chain saw. They were ready to cut the president out of the flaming wreckage of his helicopter, if need be.

Also spaced around the perimeter were frogmen in rubber suits and scuba tanks. If the president in his helicopter crashed into the river, they too were ready. At the head of the pier waited a mobile operating room. Two surgeons stood outside it smoking.

The outranging helicopters already hovered not far off, forming the points of a square, and now more cars began to pull into the heliport parking lot, and cops and agents stepped out, came out onto the pier and took up position along its rims. The center of the pier, the landing area, was like an altar, completely bare, surrounded by worshippers.

In the street the tops of the Secret Service cars folded themselves backwards into the trunks and disappeared. The long leather cases came out and were made ready. They contained, Douglas knew, powerful rifles equipped with sniper scopes and would be used, if necessary, for picking would-be assassins off rooftops or out of high windows. The visit of a president to New York—or to anywhere else, if you were aware of the preparations—was a sobering thing. The Secret Service cars were equipped with handrails and running boards. It would be the job of numbers of agents, standing on the running boards and hanging on, to eyeball windows and rooftops all the way uptown—no hardship on an evening like this, though if the weather were rainy or cold they would have to do it just the same.

The mayor's car arrived as Douglas had thought it would, and behind him came cars and vans containing part of the City Hall press corps, reporters, TV crews, photographers, all with press cards dangling on chains from their necks. The press was allowed onto the pier, but herded into one corner and confined behind a barrier. The mayor stood close by. It was the New York press he was interested in, not the president who was of the opposition party and with whom he was feuding.

Douglas waited several minutes for the mayor to step forward into an area where there would be a certain amount of privacy, but this did not happen. The man seemed to have no intention of moving from the press barrier. Finally Douglas approached and introduced himself.

The mayor seemed to know Douglas's name, which was a surprise. "Your guys are doing a great job over there," he said, but he was not looking at Douglas as he spoke. Instead his eyes scanned the skies for the president's helicopter.

"May I speak to you seriously for a moment, sir?" asked Douglas.

The mayor frowned. "Sure, go ahead."

Douglas, as he began to describe his meetings with the PC, the plan to hand over major cases to the DEA, watched the mayor's face darken.

With Douglas still talking, the mayor pointed into the sky: "There it is now."

Douglas started over. The PC's plan ought to be stopped for the following reasons, he said, enumerating them. Meanwhile the helicopter got bigger and bigger, louder and louder, so that at the end Douglas was shouting into the mayor's ear.

The helicopter set down with a rubbery bounce. The rotors blew dust into everyone's eyes, then abruptly shut off.

"The DEA has a couple of hundred men in this city," Douglas said earnestly. "We have nearly thirty thousand. We're not only better than the DEA, there are more of us. We're like a gigantic spiderweb."

The mayor studied the helicopter. The steps were down but the president had not yet appeared. Some men came down the steps onto the concrete and reached back up to lend a hand to the president's wife. In the doorway behind her was the president himself.

"It's nearly impossible for any criminal conspiracy to operate here without at some point somebody getting stuck in our web," said Douglas. He was speaking with increasing haste. "The PC's plan is wrong from every point of view."

"Tell him about it," the mayor said bluntly, 'don't tell me."

"Only you can stop him."

The president and his wife, trailed by aides, had almost reached them.

"Has it ever occurred to you," the mayor said, "that I told him to do it."

Pushing Douglas to one side, the mayor stepped into the president's path, grasped his hand and began to wring it enthusiastically, all the while turning the president in the direction of the City Hall press corps. The cameras were turning. The mayor was smiling. The president at first was not. Presumably he had had no intention of meeting the mayor at all, much less of getting photographed shaking his hand. Meanwhile, the mayor was making a welcoming speech that would appear on TV. The president, managing a half smile, was obliged to wait until it ended, before freeing his hand and making for his car.

The bemused Douglas watched him go. When he turned back, the mayor was gone too. Douglas hurried out but the City Hall cars were rapidly leaving the parking lot. He watched the Secret Service agents jumping onto their running boards, watched the cavalcade start uptown.

The next day there was a brief meeting in the mayor's office at City Hall. It was attended by the mayor, the PC, and Herbert Campbell.

The mayor said to the PC: "I can see now why you wanted to wait ten days or so."

"Yes," said the PC, "he could make trouble."

"Only," said Herbert Campbell, "if he goes to the press before we do."

The mayor said: "What are you trying to say?"

Campbell was worried. For days he had felt himself half a step away from controlling every major drug case in New

York, with the consequent increase to his own power and prestige. Although at the beginning it had seemed to him unbelievable that the mayor and the PC actually meant to give him those cases, still he had come to believe it; he had told his wife, told his superiors. But the official announcement had not come, and now at the last minute he saw it slipping from his grasp.

"I got an idea," he said, and during the next several minutes explained what it was.

The mayor waited until both Campbell and the PC had left the building, then called in the City Hall bureau chief for the *New York Times* and offered to be interviewed. The fellow had been asking for an interview for some days, and in the course of this one the mayor mentioned that a high-level New York cop was to be sent to South America to work with drug enforcement agents there. He would be attached to the DEA but would continue to be paid by the city, much as happened with the various federal-state-municipal task forces that the DEA and other federal agencies had put together throughout the country. He would study the drug situation close up. He would move into each of the countries in turn, and the hope was that when he returned to New York some months hence, he would bring with him new insights into how the drug war in America's largest city was to be fought and won.

"Because, God knows, we're not winning it now," the mayor said piously.

"Who?" said the reporter.

"If what he brings back works in New York," the mayor said piously, "then by extension it ought to work in all major American cities."

"Who?" the reporter said again.

"I can't divulge that," the mayor said. "He hasn't agreed yet. He's thinking it over now. He would come back a new and eloquent spokesman for America's cities."

"You already said that. Who?"

"It might be a good thing for him personally too. Poor fellow recently lost his wife. Change of scenery would probably do him the world of good."

"I think I know who you mean."

"The best narcotics man we have, who else. Look, you didn't get it from me. Ray Douglas."

Douglas and Gail met outside the theater, shook hands, chatted a moment, and went inside. The curtain rose.

Douglas's mind was on his job, he was unable to concentrate on the play, though from time to time, realizing that it was expected of him, he would turn to Gail in the dark and flash her a half smile.

When the play ended, they stood on the sidewalk in the outgoing crowd.

"It was a very good play," Douglas said.

Gail grinned and looked grateful.

Douglas wanted only to get home, but something more, obviously, was expected of him. "Would you like to have supper?" he asked.

Gail looked dubious. "It's very late. You have to go to work tomorrow."

"I'm really quite hungry," said Douglas.

They walked along Forty-sixth Street. Crossing Eighth Avenue, she took his arm. On the other side was a row of restaurants that catered to the after-theater crowd. She still had his arm. Douglas was looking into the restaurants one by one.

"Lattanza's is very good," he said.

So he had heard. They went down the three steps from the sidewalk and were shown to a table. Gail ordered a Cinzano, Douglas a scotch and soda. They studied their menus. The waiter came, recited the day's specials, and took down their orders. He went away. Gail toyed with the stem of her glass. Douglas searched for something to talk about.

She wanted this to be nice, and I'm ruining it, Douglas thought. He had known this woman thirty years but was as uncomfortable as a schoolboy. "When were you last in our old neighborhood?" he asked.

More recently than he. She knew what had become of people he had almost forgotten.

"Remember Father Finnegan?"

"The fastest priest in New York. He could say the old Latin mass in under twenty minutes."

"He's now a delivery man for United Parcel."

"No!"

"One day he simply walked out. It's time to take care of number one, he said, and he was gone."

It made Douglas laugh. How animated she had become; all it took was for him to show a little interest. She wore a black dress with a gold brooch above her left breast. She looked very nice.

"Harry Malkin's candy store is now an off-track betting parlor."

"Is Harry still alive?"

"He died. He ran out of his store chasing some kid who had stolen a comic book, and got a heart attack. He was dead before the kid got around the corner."

"Poor Harry."

"Yes." She was silent a moment. "Isn't it odd as adults to look back at all these people who seemed so stable to us when we were children?"

They lingered talking until the waiters began to yawn. They were the last to leave the restaurant.

Douglas drove her home. In her vestibule she said: "Would you like to come up?"

Douglas hesitated, then took both her hands. "I don't think so, Gail."

"You're thinking of your wife."

"I need more time," he said.

She smiled, kissed him briefly on the lips, and turned toward the elevator. As the doors closed she gave him a wave.

The reporter's story, credited to a "highly placed City Hall source," appeared the next day. Douglas read it. It infuriated him. He phoned the PC's appointments secretary, who told him the schedule was too full, Douglas could not be fitted in. In a rage, he went up to the fourteenth floor two steps at a time and attempted to burst into the PC's office.

"Wait a minute, Chief," expostulated the deputy inspector, "wait a minute." He attempted to bar the PC's door. "You can't go in there."

Douglas pushed past him. The door banged back against the wall.

But the office was empty.

Douglas phoned the mayor's office. The mayor refused to take the call. He phoned Herbert Campbell, same thing. All day his own phone rang—reporters. To avoid them he got into his department car and drove out to the headquarters of his Brooklyn South field group. All day he fumed.

Next morning there were more stories. All of the principals were quoted except Douglas. The mayor "regretted" that the news had somehow leaked out before any decision had been made; the city would certainly profit if Douglas took the job. The PC said the idea had come from "Washington"; he was suitably vague, praising Douglas to the skies, declaring that the idea certainly had merit, he had not talked to him himself. Herbert Campbell said that the addition of such a high-ranking and experienced New York City police officer to DEA field offices in South America would give new emphasis to the nation's determination to wipe out the drug scourge.

Douglas stayed home where reporters could not find him. His phone did not ring. Like most law-enforcement officers, his number was unlisted. He paced his floors. He paced his small garden. He saw exactly what was being done to him. Later he went out food shopping. When he came back he pushed his lawn mower up and down his small lawn. He tried to read a book, but that didn't work.

After supper he watched a baseball game on TV, and then his phone did ring.

It was his night duty sergeant. They were asking for him up on Vermilyea Avenue, the sergeant said. There had been some shooting. It was pretty bloody, apparently.

"One of our guys?" Douglas asked.

"No, one of theirs."

It took Douglas twenty minutes to get there. Radio cars blocked off the street. The dome turrets threw hallucinatory light against the staring faces, the walls of the buildings. Douglas drove on through. The police barriers were already up. The neighbors were standing on stoops, hanging out windows.

Douglas went into the building and at the door to the apartment was met by Detective Sullivan. "Wait till you see this," the detective said.

"Salvador?"

"And family."

The apartment was full of detectives, most of whom Douglas did not know. Sullivan led the way into the kitchen. Salvador lay on his back on the linoleum.

"He's been shot several times in the head," Sullivan said.

"I'm glad you told me," said Douglas. "I wouldn't have guessed otherwise."

The corpse's skull was about two inches thick. The face had collapsed inward and was barely recognizable as Salvador.

The brains had run out over the linoleum. They looked like a pool of mushroom soup. Douglas had seen brains before. These looked no different. Salvador seemed to have been stitched across the chest by machine-gun bullets as well.

"I guess they wanted to be sure he was dead," said Douglas, because a scene like this demanded a response and he could think of no other.

"The bedroom is worse," said Sullivan.

He led the way in there. Douglas stood at the foot of a double bed. It was unmade. A young woman had fallen backward across it. She lay sprawled and grimacing. Her eyes squinted and all her teeth showed. One bullet had caved in her cheek. The rest had hit her in the chest. She was wearing a dark skirt and a blouse that had once been white. Now it was mostly red, and the bedclothes all around her were red and sopping.

Other detectives stood in the room. Douglas said: "Close her eyes, for chrissake."

Sullivan had moved into a second bedroom. "In here, Chief," he said.

The second bedroom contained bunk beds, school desks, and a small TV set. It also contained two small boys, one in each bed.

Douglas turned away. Involuntarily his eyes closed. When he opened them he was facing Herbert Campbell.

"I just heard," Campbell said. "I came as quickly as I could."

"I warned you to stay away from him," Douglas said. "Why didn't you give him room?"

"He wasn't one of ours," Campbell said. "I told you that before."

"Never mind him, what about them?" Douglas, who was almost in tears, jerked his chin in the direction of the two murdered children.

"These things happen."

Douglas began cursing him, cursing the DEA, a stream of obscenities that caused the drug agent's eyes to darken, his mouth to get thinner and thinner.

"I didn't put the bullets in them," Campbell shouted, and left the room.

"Oh yes you did," said Douglas, running after him.

Forensic detectives were already at work and they watched in amazement. "I'm sick of the whole lot of you. Did you look at those two little boys? Did you see the woman in the other room? You don't even care, do you? The PC doesn't care, I know that. The mayor doesn't care." The death of his wife had destabilized Douglas's emotions, and therefore his judgment. "I'll take that job no one has the nerve to offer me to my face. I can't get out of this city fast enough. The enemy isn't them, it's you people. Give me the tickets and I'm gone. Who do I tell? Do I tell you?"

He had second thoughts before he reached New Rochelle, but it was too late at night to act on them, and by morning it was too late altogether: the papers carried the news on page one with his picture. In the war against drugs something new and promising was to be tried. The press, and by extension the city, seemed thrilled with him. They could stop worrying about the drug scourge now. It was up to Raymond Douglas now.

What nonsense, he thought, what can any one man do?

He went to Washington where the DEA put him into language school. A month of eight-hour days of Spanish. It should have been more, but everyone was in a hurry, Douglas included. He wanted to be elsewhere—out of his old life. His children didn't need him and believed he did not need them. The police department didn't want him. It was obvious that he had wrecked his career—he had done it himself, there was no one else to blame. He was bitter nonetheless. The department might have protected him against himself, but had not done so.

After language school came antiterrorism school. The State Department's Diplomatic Security Section ran it. He learned about hostage-taking, assassination. How to converse with your kidnapper. Roadblocks, defensive driving techniques, car bombs. The properties of various weapons and how to recognize them.

How to crash through roadblocks. Never slow down. Blast into the lightest point of the blockage at maximum possible speed.

"Lots of roadblocks where you're going, friends."

If it was a tree lying across the road, smash through the end with the branches. If it was cars or trucks, aim for the end opposite the engine. Of course this required instant recognition of the makes of the cars forming the roadblock. Were their engines mounted front or rear?

"Make sure your seat belts are fastened first."

The instructors made constant jokes. Or at least what sounded like jokes under the circumstances.

What kind of country am I going to? Douglas asked himself.

After lectures and charts, the class went outdoors. First had come the theory, now came the demonstrations. The State Department owned a good many old cars, apparently. Stunt drivers too. How to make high-speed U-turns, frontward and backward.

"Now you fellows try it," the instructor said.

In the classroom Douglas and the other students had learned

what sticks of dynamite, lumps of plastic explosive looked like. Now came a demonstration of what they did. On a windy, sunny afternoon a half pound of dynamite was placed under the seat of a car, and detonated. The entire car rose ten feet in the air. The roof burst open, as did all four doors. The driver's seat went out the roof. It went up and up, tumbling across the sky, and for the longest time did not come down.

"That's you up there," joked the instructor. "The best thing to do when you see someone trying to start a car," he joked, "is to walk to the corner and put your hands over your ears."

The car had hovered in the air like a helicopter. It landed bouncing. The seat bounced down some distance away.

They were eight in the class witnessing this demonstration, including the newly appointed deputy chief of mission to Peru and his wife, a frail slip of a woman. The hulk lay there smoking and she was the last to turn away.

"Actually, bombs are the least of your worries," the instructor said. "What you really have to watch out for is motorscooters." In Colombia this was the favored method of execution, apparently. "They drive up alongside your car, and the guy riding pillion lets you have it in the ear with a machine gun. Or else they drive up onto the sidewalk where you're strolling along, same thing."

The next week came briefings and seminars at State, the CIA, and from the DEA's cocaine desk. Douglas was inoculated against every known tropical disease, including some no one had caught in years. He went up to New York to say goodbye to his children. His arms ached and he had a frightful headache.

There was a one-week course in jungle survival training in Panama on the way south, though he had no intention of going into any jungles.

Then he was in Bogotá.

BOOK II

BOOK II

8

JANE HOYT FOX landed in Bogotá at dusk, took a taxi to the hotel, washed six hours of stale air off her face, and went out onto her balcony. The lights went on for miles. The city was bigger than she had thought, this new job was bigger than she thought, and suddenly her confidence was gone and she could no longer hold off the loneliness that had been tugging at her all day. Emotionally, professionally she was on her own here. In New York she had cultivated her sources, but it had taken years. She knew New York, where to find people and things, ways to check facts. But she did not know this city and she had not a single friend or even acquaintance in it. Her assignment was the normal one, three years, and included the other Andean countries as well, and she knew no one there either. She would be thirty-nine when she went back, still without a child or children, having wrecked her marriage, and unless she excelled her career would be wrecked as well. How do I start? she asked herself. Suppose I fail? I'm a good reporter, she tried to encourage herself. I write well. She missed her own desk in the newsroom, her own apartment, her own kitchen, her own bed, and half wished she had stayed home. How did the men do it? she asked herself. Some awfully klutzy men had made good in places not that different from here.

She remembered the day she was offered this assignment —people kept coming by her desk to congratulate her, shake her hand, wish her luck. There followed a whirlwind of preparations. Getting visas stamped into her passport, getting shots, buying clothes. Telling George—he didn't take it at all well, so that she came to feel thoroughly estranged from him before she ever stepped onto the plane.

For two weeks she had lunched in the executive dining room with editors, a different one every day. One-on-one lunches with the publisher, the executive editor, the foreign editor—with every important editor on the paper. Some she had never met before. All had ideas they tried to force on her, and she had her notebook beside her plate taking them down. In an America paranoid about drugs she had thought drugs would be her focus.

"Coffee," the publisher said. "Colombia's number-one export. As coffee goes, the country goes. That's what I want to read about."

"There's a talk show host running for president of Peru," the executive editor said. "I want to know more."

"Peru is already down the tubes," the foreign editor said. "You can pretty much skip Peru. Bolivia can be saved."

"Money," said the financial editor. "Debt. That's your story."

"Emeralds," said the style editor.

"Archaeology," said the cultural editor.

Bernstein had talked to the State Department about security. As a result he wanted her based in Venezuela or Ecuador. "The last guy who covered Colombia for us used to fly up from Rio."

"Sid," Jane said to him, "Rio is twenty-five hundred miles away, and no direct flights."

"I didn't know it was that far," said Bernstein.

"I might as well cover it from here. The big story is Bogotá," insisted Jane. "That's where I should live."

"If you're determined," said Bernstein, "okay, we'll try it. But I want you to hire an armed security guard to accompany you everywhere you go."

"Sid," said Jane patiently, "I can't do that."

It had all seemed so romantic, so exciting. She was to be a foreign correspondent at last, with half a continent as her beat.

And now she was here, standing on a balcony overlooking the city. There was no one to congratulate her or shake her hand, no one to give her advice or even to talk to, and nothing seemed romantic anymore.

It was chilly on the balcony. She felt half frozen and she came back inside hugging herself and sat down on the edge of the bed and tried to decide what to do first, but couldn't. She would have to find an apartment, get accredited, hire an office assistant, open a bank account, plug in to the embassy, interview government ministers, meet people, meet people, meet people. And write her stories.

And then make trips to the other Andean countries and do most of the same jobs there. And write her stories. She knew no one anywhere. It was too much. She was not strong enough to do it. She had never before been so totally alone.

Sitting on the edge of the bed she tried to force herself to make a start. Do something, anything. She got her address book out. She began to consider telephoning Raymond Douglas at his office. She didn't know Douglas, but he was a possible contact, one of the few names she had. Since he was also from New York, he might be kind to her. While preparing for this assignment she had studied his morgue clips. She knew his age, education, and dates of promotions, but not him. She knew the details of some of the important cases he had worked on. She knew his wife was dead. She knew the names and ages of his children. She could be said to know him well, sort of. But he had never heard of her, most probably.

In New York before leaving she had thought of him as a possible story, and had wormed his phone numbers out of a detective who owed her a favor. Douglas was supposed to have been sent to South America to find answers to the New York drug problem. So what had he found?

Call him, she ordered herself.

Finally she dialed his office number. It turned out to be the embassy number. She waited on the phone until the embassy operator came back on. Señor Douglas had left for the day.

What time was it? If he was not in his office he might be at his apartment, and she stared down at this number. Did she dare call him at home?

But some people did not like phone calls at home after business hours. Especially, in her experience, cops with their unlisted numbers. Most of them seemed to consider any call of whatever kind an intrusion.

She looked at her watch. It was dinnertime. She began to contemplate eating by herself in the hotel restaurant. Sitting alone trying to appear inconspicuous while everybody stared at her, felt sorry for her, wondered why she was alone, something had gone wrong, surely. The waiters being especially solicitous of her. Perhaps even some jerk trying to sit down at her table. She hated eating alone in restaurants. Everybody did, she imagined, but especially women.

She continued to think about Douglas. He had been here a while. No one else had interviewed him yet, probably because no other American news organization had a permanent correspondent in Bogotá. She was the only one. The other news organizations were satisfied to send people flying in and out. If she could interview him, perhaps write a story about him, the future would not look so bleak, and perhaps she could begin to make a life for herself here.

Dial his home number, she ordered herself. The minutes were passing.

Finally she made herself do it.

After identifying herself, she said: "Are you free for dinner by any chance?" And then, because it was important to keep this as professional as possible, she said: "If you are, could I invite you out to a restaurant?"

"Dinner?"

She was smoothing the bedspread over the pillow. "Unless you have something else on for dinner."

"Well—" He sounded both surprised and cautious.

He had a nice voice. "Then how about meeting me in the restaurant at my hotel?"

As she waited, she realized how much she wanted him to say yes. "Unless you know a better place," she said into his silence.

Upon reaching a new foreign post, most reporters took their time getting oriented, settling in. It was weeks before their bylines reappeared in the paper, usually. But she was a woman, and she had been sent out so reluctantly that she could not afford weeks. If she could see Douglas tonight and write the story tomorrow, her byline could be back in the paper the following day. Bernstein, Vaughan, and the others would be impressed, and at the very least she would have bought herself time. And so she waited anxiously for Douglas's reply.

He said cautiously: "I'm not ready to give any interviews yet."

She wanted this interview and she wanted to make contact with another human being. She wanted to do it tonight, prove it could be done, so that she could go to bed and be able to sleep and not be so afraid.

"Well, could we at least get to know each other? I've just arrived, I know nobody." By nature she was not a tenacious woman, she believed. "I'm feeling a bit lost," she said. She had tried to keep the helpless female quality out of her voice, but to her own ears had failed, and she was annoyed at herself.

"Yes," he said, "the day I got here I felt that way too."

He sounded kind, and this registered on her, but she went quickly past it. She had her teeth into something now and the hopeless mood of only a few minutes ago had begun to recede. "Shall we say eight o'clock then?"

"I can't come to your hotel. There isn't time to set it up."

Not knowing what this meant, Jane suggested hastily: "I could come to where you are. There must be a restaurant nearby that I could take you to."

"Hmm. Yes. There isn't time to set that up either."

She was standing at her window now, having carried the

phone to the end of its cord. She could see as far as the mountains that rose up at the back of the city. They were black under the early moon. She believed he had refused her, and did not know what to say next. The mountains looked high, close, somehow ominous.

"You could come here," Douglas said after a moment. Perhaps he is lonely too, she thought. This perception was more accurate than she knew. It had been a long time since he had talked to a woman for an hour—any woman—and the prospect was attractive to him. "I could fix something," he said, "maybe open a bottle of wine." He gave her the address.

Jubilant, she put the phone down. She had an hour and spent it taking a bath. She had been under pressure for weeks—the resistance from the paper, the relentless pulling from George, the work to get ready, and then the bleak loneliness of a while ago, the feeling that in coming here she had ruined her life. Lying out in the water she felt her tension turn itself into a kind of excitement. To be a foreign correspondent was the adventure she had dreamed about, she encouraged herself, and it was about to begin.

She spent some time worrying about what to wear. This was a meeting between two professionals, and whatever she wore must convey that, must give him no other idea. And she didn't have much with her. Most of what she had selected to bring was coming down in boxes by ship and would not arrive for a week or two. Finally she chose a tailored blue suit with a white silk blouse. The blouse was wrinkled and she got her traveling iron out and pressed it and put it on. She put on earrings, stepped into black shoes with three-quarter heels, and surveyed herself in the mirror once more.

He was waiting for her out front, sitting out on the stoop in the night with his arms clasping his knees. Her taxi came through the gate in the high spiked fence and he stood up as she got out and came over and shook hands. When he smiled, his eyes crinkled up. He had exceptionally white teeth. He wore a rose-colored sweater—alpaca, she judged. The pleats in his black trousers were very sharp, and he wore black Italian loafers. He looked very nice.

They rode up in the elevator. The cabin was small, forcing them to stand closer together than she would have liked. Close enough so she could see the stubble of his beard. They invaded each other's space. She could smell him, and he, presumably, could smell her. Nothing she could define specifically—he smelled like a man.

The elevator was slow. He lived on the top floor. They stood together so long she got slightly flustered and began apologizing. "I practically invited myself to your house for dinner, I didn't mean—" Certain modern inventions—the telephone for one and small elevators for another—produced a sensation of intimacy that could be totally disconcerting.

Finally the elevator stopped and they got out. "The reason I couldn't meet you in a restaurant," he said as he led her along the corridor, "is because I gave my bodyguards the night off, would you believe it?"

This stopped her. "Are things as bad as that here?"

He laughed and denied it.

Did even policemen need bodyguards? she wondered. If so, what about herself?

The embassy owned or controlled a good many apartments, he explained as he inserted the key in his door. All were in this "luxury" section of the city, which supposedly was safer than the others, and all were on the fourth floor or above. "We're not allowed to rent low apartments. They don't want snipers picking us off from the street or from the tops of trees." His eyes had crinkled up again. "A car bomb probably couldn't get us above the fourth floor either."

The American embassy had rules, he said, stepping back to let her enter his apartment. They were paranoiac over there. They had placed strictures on the movement of everybody, which made it hard for him or anyone else to get any work done.

She stood inside his apartment glancing around—what did

it tell her about him? She was a working journalist. She wanted to learn about him as quickly and as unobtrusively as possible.

Brooklyn was at least as dangerous as here, he said behind her. She turned and watched him take a gun out of his belt and lay it down on a sideboard. She had never seen that done before. It looked like a big gun to her. It probably weighed a lot. Beginning next week, he said, he was going to pretend he was in Brooklyn, and act accordingly.

This made her smile. She decided he was charming and she began to relax a little.

His apartment was large and comfortable, neat. Glossy hardwood floors. It looked almost unlived in.

"You have a cleaning woman," observed Jane.

Again the crinkly smile. "How did you know?"

His reply made her smile too. Men. To them cleaning women were mysterious. One paid and asked no questions.

"It's not a very big apartment. I don't know what she does all day."

High ceilings. Modern living-room furniture. A glass coffee table. A television. Stereo speakers. The dominant wall decoration was a framed, rather primitive tapestry. A large landscape woven mostly in pastel colors: Andean peasants with burdens on their heads approaching a village, with towering mountains in the background.

"Nice," said Jane.

But he was gazing at her, not the tapestry. Look out, she thought, and she pretended to study the tapestry so as to give herself a few seconds to work out what to do, what to say —how to handle him.

Of course she wanted him to find her attractive, but in a way that threatened neither of them. She wanted him in a mood where he would be willing to open up to her, give her the story she was hoping for. So she decided to keep the conversation as impersonal as possible. Standing in the kitchen doorway, sipping from a glass of Chilean cabernet he had poured, watching him baste the chicken he was roasting, she spoke of the cab she had ridden in coming over here, a vehicle thirty years old at least. The springs were coming through the seats. And the buses in the streets had looked just as old, condemned years ago somewhere else, no doubt, and they were canted sideways from all the people hanging off them. The diesel stench of the trucks and buses reminded her of Spain when she was a child. She had interviewed her cab driver: "All he could talk about was the *narcotraficantes*."

He turned toward her from the stove. "You speak Spanish?"

"Yes, of course." And she told him about her childhood in Barcelona, what it was like for a little girl to start school in Spain in Spanish.

He stood holding the wooden basting spoon, wearing that same wry half smile, his nearly black eyes fixed on her face, on her mouth, so that she decided she had become a bit too personal a bit too soon, and the tale of the little girl in Spain stopped.

"No, tell me more," he insisted. "How was it different from an American school?"

Jane talked on, but nervously. She didn't want him focused on her, but on what he as a policeman would say to her as a journalist.

Now his eyes had dropped to her rings. "You're married," he interrupted.

It was more statement than question, and it surprised her. She hesitated, then said: "Separated."

Not strictly speaking true, except that George was there and she was here. Why did I say that? she asked herself.

"You're getting divorced?"

The question flustered her because it seemed to require another lie. She found herself nodding yes, not an accurate answer by any means. Why was she behaving this way? she wondered. She was certainly not trying to lead him on. Her thoughts had become none too clear, but perhaps only insofar as they mirrored her life, which was a mess.

A silence had fallen between them. She watched him carve up the chicken, begin to ladle out peas, spoon roast potatoes and chicken juice onto the two plates. It seemed to her that a lot was riding on this interview and she didn't want to ruin her chances before it even started.

"Have you always cooked?" she asked.

He glanced up unexpectedly and caught her staring at him. Embarrassed, her eyes dropped to her shoes.

"It's something I've had to learn in the last year or so," he said. Perhaps he was embarrassed too. He sounded it. "I know three dishes," he said. "This is my company dish."

She carried the plates to the table. He carried the wine and the salad bowl. They sat down, and she decided to begin the interview at once.

"Let's talk about what you've been doing with yourself down here," she said crisply. "Where have you been, what have you seen?" She had meant this abrupt switch to seem almost casual, but it didn't.

He had shaken a lot of hands, he answered, met all the correct ministers and narcotics generals, not only in Colombia but in Bolivia and Peru as well—the "host" countries, as he called them. He had met all the American ambassadors and officials, too. Looking for clandestine labs, clandestine landing strips, he had ridden with agents and narcotics police above various jungles in helicopters, had landed sometimes and gone in on raids, had talked to prisoners and peasants— he went into some detail. His descriptions were specific and vivid. He made it all sound charming and amusing.

He was learning as fast as he could, he said. He was trying to form his impressions into ideas. It would be presumptuous to talk about any of these ideas yet, for they were only half formed.

She saw how cautious he was, the result no doubt of much experience in talking to the press.

The drug problem was certainly a good deal more complex than he had once thought, he said. He was even working hard on his Spanish. A woman came in two hours a day. He was getting comfortable in Spanish at last.

Jane had become less nervous. The interview was going well. He served as second in command of the DEA contingent here, he said. The boss was a man named Gallagher, who was somewhat difficult to get along with.

Jane took this to mean impossible to get along with. The DEA group seemed to resent his presence altogether, he admitted. They were hard to be friends with. They didn't understand why he was here. He laughed and said he didn't entirely understand it himself.

They talked all through dinner, then moved back to the living room. When she believed she had enough for the article she would write tomorrow, she fell silent a moment. She would have liked to ask him about himself now. She had begun to sense his loneliness here and his worry about his career was obvious, though nothing had been said.

But personal questions might be perceived as a deliberate shift in their relationship, so she stalled for time while trying to figure it out. She was sitting across from the tapestry she had noted earlier. "That's really very nice," she said, gesturing at it with her chin.

"I bought it in Peru," he said. "I have two others much like it." He sounded both proud of his tapestry and relieved that the interview seemed to be over. He jumped up, and she followed him into a kind of den. He had a desk there and some folders and briefing books. The tapestry that hung over the desk was as impressive as the one in the living room, and she told him so. A moment later she was standing in his bedroom in front of the third of them. His bedroom. A thousand bells went off in her head. How did I let this happen? she asked herself. I've known the guy an hour and I'm in his bedroom. Now both of us are thinking about bed. He was standing not really close, yet much too close. He was watching her, or so she thought. As she backed out of the bedroom she felt heavy footed, clumsy.

Safe again in the hallway she looked up into his wry smile, and could not tell what he was thinking, whether it had happened by accident or not.

He talked about his tapestries. He had bought them in Lima in the street, he said. Thirty-five dollars each. They were spread out on the sidewalk. The peasants wove them, he said, then came down out of the Andes into the cities and squatted on the sidewalks between piles of these gorgeous tapestries, spreading them out for anybody who looked interested. He had enjoyed bargaining for them. The frames had cost him more than what was inside them.

They had sat down again in the living room at either end of the sofa. Yes, she found him attractive, she admitted to herself, and apparently he found her attractive. So what. That bedroom business had put ideas in both their heads that should never have been there. When she went into a bedroom with a man, she wanted it to be on her terms, not his. Not only was she a married woman, but there were rules for reporters. Although the ones she had in mind weren't written down, they did exist, and they made sense. Reporters shouldn't have affairs with their sources. Any more, she told herself, than an executive—male or female—should go to bed with a subordinate. It fogged up relationships that afterward didn't work as well, or in some cases at all. Some things one just didn't do.

Abruptly she stood up, said it was late, she had had a long day, she had best go. Immediately Douglas was on his feet too, but urging her to stay, offering coffee, a liqueur, both of which she declined, asking him to phone for a taxi.

They waited for it mostly in silence.

She went to the window and looked down at the entrance driveway.

"They'll ring from downstairs," he told her.

The silence resumed.

"Dinner was really good," she said.

"Thank you."

"No, I mean it." She peered down on the driveway looking for the taxi. "You're a wonderful cook," she said.

His eyes crinkled up. "My other two dishes are not bad either," he said, "if you'll come again."

The guard at the gate buzzed to announce the taxi.

He accompanied her out to the elevator.

"Shouldn't you have your gun with you?" It was still lying on the sideboard; he hadn't picked it up on the way out.

"It doesn't matter."

She wasn't so sure. If Bogotá was so dangerous, he should never be without it, even in the hallway. Was he showing off for her, trying to prove how brave he was? It was a thought that made him seem, suddenly, much less attractive.

The elevator door opened and to her surprise he got into it with her. The door closed. He was again standing too close. They gave each other what might have been called shy smiles, and neither spoke.

Outside, the night air seemed cool with a threat of rain. She breathed in moist lungfuls. His building was one of four sharing a central garden and parking area, she noted now. The garden and parking area were floodlit. The high steel fence went all the way around. There was only the one gate, apparently, and it was controlled electronically by two guards in a booth. They were both armed.

Douglas opened the cab door for her. He stood there waving after her, and she wished he had not left his gun upstairs. She felt responsible for his safety.

In the taxi she took inventory. She certainly felt much better about her job, herself, about Bogotá. Finding Douglas was a stroke of luck. A reporter lived or died on her sources, and Douglas was an excellent one. He had been here awhile and knew many people. He worked in the embassy on the highest level, and he met regularly with influential Colombians. He was as valuable a source as she could have found, and she would cultivate him carefully.

Perhaps she would not fail here after all. Perhaps she could even hope to be a success.

Next morning she called down for breakfast and the local papers. In the shower she brooded about Douglas, trying to order her ideas for the piece she was about to write. But Douglas the man kept intruding on Douglas the subject. He had fine black hairs on the backs of his hands. Soaping herself, she imagined his hands and felt herself shiver. But she repressed that line of thought.

She dried herself off, put on bra and panties, and sat in

front of her laptop and began to write. She was worried about how the piece would be received by editors on the desk. They had not ordered it, did not know it was coming, and might not want it. The waiter knocked with the breakfast tray. She put a bathrobe on and let him in. When he was gone she poured out coffee, then continued writing. But they just had to print it, didn't they? It was the start of her career here. It was vital to her confidence. It was vital to her cultivation of Douglas too. But it was turning out to be a hard piece to write. It had to be stark enough, newsy enough for the desk to print it, yet she had to protect Douglas, make him sound in command of his life and career here, though she suspected he wasn't. That is, Douglas had to like it too.

When she had finished, she read it over and over again, correcting it, trying to make sure of it. Finally she dialed New York, hooked her modem to the telephone, and punched up the command for transmit. In a few seconds the confirmation—the first line of her story—appeared on her screen. Although it was so early that there was most likely no one in the newsroom yet in New York, nonetheless the piece was now there waiting. It would be late afternoon before she could find out what the desk thought of it, whether it would be printed.

The paper had rented her an office on the sixth floor of the *El Tiempo* building on Avenida El Dorado. She took a taxi over. There were troops with machine guns stationed all around the building. She went through security in the lobby and again as she got off the elevator, then walked down the hall to her new office and claimed it: two rooms, two desks, two telephones, two extra chairs. Nothing on the walls. She stood glancing around, feeling lost again, and *El Tiempo*'s publisher came in, shook her hand, and wished her luck. Then the editor in chief came in and did the same.

At the government press office she was made to wait an hour on a hard chair, breathing in and out the stale air of third world bureaucracies, trying to remain patient, before the minor official in charge came out all smiles and gave her what she had come for, her accreditation and press card. A whole hour wasted.

She walked out of the building and up along Carrera Siete, Bogotá's principal shopping street. It was crowded. There were armed troops every hundred feet. She walked repeatedly in front of the muzzles of guns. She gazed into the windows of a few chic shops, passed a nice park and one or two handsome new skyscrapers. The rest was shabby: the lobbies, the shops, the goods on display. The sidewalks were inlaid with mosaic tiles, a luxury New York had never even considered, but every several steps she had to dodge unrepaired potholes or even small excavations full to the brim with rainwater and cigarette butts, usually with a pile of rubble or sand standing alongside them. People were selling goods from mats on the pavement. For several blocks the sidewalk was almost obscured by mats. The merchants squatted beside them. She walked along, noticing everything, drinking it all in. Her worries and uncertainties were forgotten. She could feel the new country all around her, vibrant, exciting, unknown.

She took a taxi to the U.S. Embassy, for she had an appointment with the press officer there. The embassy grounds were surrounded by armed guards of course and by a high steel fence. Steel bars as thick as the bars of a jail. Big gates that gave access to the parking area. They were chained shut and behind them stood a hydraulically operated steel wall that came up out of the pavement; this was to prevent an unauthorized vehicle from ramming through the gates, she assumed.

There were two entrances, one for Americans, the other for Colombians seeking visas. There were about twenty people in front of her on the American queue. About two hundred waited on the Colombian one.

She was obliged to present her passport at a barred window. This was checked against a list, and she was given a form to fill out and sign. She was directed to join the queue that was funneling slowly down a barred alley. Her passport was not returned.

At the front of the queue, she could see, was a revolving gate like the exit gates on subways. It accepted one passenger at a time. Beyond it was a small barred cell, almost a jail cell, and this held one person at a time too. When her turn came, she passed through the head-high turnstile into the cell, where she was patted down by a matron and her handbag searched. Next she stepped through an airport-type security arch. Finally she was allowed out the steel door into the embassy compound. The sun was shining and she walked across to a reception area where she gave her name and sat down to wait for the press officer. Presently a secretary came out and led her to his office. The entire procedure had taken about thirty minutes.

After welcoming her to Colombia, the press officer handed her several briefing papers, one of them the embassy's travel advisory for visiting Americans. He was cordial and wanted to chat and she half listened while scanning the travel advisory. Most of the country was unsafe for Americans, supposedly. Putumayo, which was infested with hundreds of cocaine labs, was certainly to be avoided, and Caquetá, where much of the Colombian coca was grown, and Boyacá where the emerald mines were, and Nariño with its dangerous Indian tribes, and Arauca where the guerrillas kept blowing up the pipeline and kidnapping people, and Santander because of violent labor unrest. These were vast provinces the size of American states. All rural areas were dangerous as well, not to mention major cities like Medellín and Cali, which were said to be in the grip of the narcotics traffickers.

Once again Jane was forced to consider her personal security. The press attaché was still talking. These people, she thought, are just trying to scare me. She could not do her job scared, and she resolved there and then to take reasonable precautions only, no more. Thirty-two million Colombians moved about normally, and they were not molested and they were not scared. Why should she be?

She decided she would avoid walking down dark streets alone at night, avoid driving alone in isolated places—same as in any country—and that otherwise she would ignore this travel advisory. It would be impossible to do her job otherwise.

The press attaché took her around to the various offices, introducing her to officials, one of them the leader of the DEA contingent whose name was Eddie Gallagher. He was called the "country attaché"—everything was euphemisms and acronyms here. He was a tall skinny man about forty years old. He was also, she remembered, the man with whom Douglas was having so much as yet unspecified trouble.

"I'd like to sit down with you for a half hour or so, when you have time," she said to Gallagher, for she saw the DEA's work here as her major continuing story.

"Fine," he answered. "Whenever you say. Fix it up with Madeleine outside."

"Sorry to disturb you," she said, and her tour of the offices continued. She did not see Douglas.

All this time she had worried about how her article had been received in New York, and as soon as she got back to her office she phoned the desk. The assistant foreign editor, McMichael, took her call. She explained she had been out of the office. Had her piece arrived safely? It was a way of asking what McMichael thought of it. She could not ask directly. One just didn't.

"I said to myself, why am I reading about this guy?" McMichael said bluntly. "In what way is he important? He's just another cop, the way I see it, only he happens to be in South America."

Silence. Jane was not ready for a response as demoralizing as this. It took the heart out of her and for a moment she could not even talk.

But she dredged up the strength, the resolve, from somewhere, or perhaps it was only repressed anger. She began arguing for her piece. Did McMichael not remember the splash when Douglas agreed to take the job here?

No he didn't.

And this was the first piece about him since. "Look at the clips," said Jane, "it was front page in our paper."

McMichael wasn't getting it. "Even so," he said, "where's your news peg?"

In desperation Jane suggested he turn her piece over to the Metro desk. "Maybe it's more a Metro story than a foreign story."

"That might be the place for it, because it's not a foreign story, the way I see it," McMichael said.

"Well turn it over to Metro then. That's fine by me."

By the time she had hung up she was covered with sweat and thoroughly discouraged. If McMichael didn't like this piece, maybe he wouldn't like anything she wrote, and he was one of her bosses.

And if the piece didn't run, what would happen to the relationship with Douglas as a source that she was hoping to build up?

There were three young women waiting outside her office. This too had been arranged from New York. She had come through them a moment ago, asking them to wait a moment longer while she made her call; now she invited them in one after the other. She needed a secretary or assistant and she interviewed them from behind the desk that had nothing on it but dust and her handbag. She kept waiting for the phone to ring, for McMichael or Vaughan or someone to call her back. It was hard to keep her mind on the interviews. All three girls were fresh out of convent school. At least they were not in the employ of the *narcotraficantes*. But they knew nothing about journalism, nor about the functions of a foreign correspondent. They wouldn't do. But she had to have a trustworthy assistant. How was she to find someone?

She waited in her empty office the rest of the afternoon, because surely someone would call her back about her piece, knowing how anxious she must be. But her new phone did not ring, meaning there were not any queries from any desk at all, neither foreign nor Metro, meaning most likely her piece was not going to be used. Finally she went back to her hotel and stared glumly out the window. Unable to face dinner alone in the hotel dining room, she ordered a sandwich from room service. She ate it and the phone still did not ring. Nine thirty came. The first edition would have gone to press. Still nothing, and she gave in to her discouragement.

The phone got her out of the bathtub about an hour after that. Not the desk. Her husband.

George said he hoped she was comfortable there, and would not take any foolish risks. He said he missed her already.

He had gone out to buy tomorrow morning's paper, he said. Her story was on the front page, congratulations.

She became immediately excited. She glowed. She was not discouraged anymore. In an instant her dismay had turned to joy. She wished he would read the piece to her, so she could see what if anything the desk had changed, but he did not volunteer to do this. Read her the lead at least, but he did not have her career on his mind just then, so she did not feel she could ask him.

She remembered how unhappy he had seemed—was it only the day before yesterday?—when he had gone to get the car out of the garage. She had come down with her bags and he was doubleparked in front of their building and he had driven her to the airport. She had waited for angry recriminations all during the drive, but there had been none. He had spoken very little, but each time it was with this terrific sadness that she could hear in his voice even now.

Sadness on his part, and a burgeoning desire on hers to get away from him. She had tried to conceal it of course. She had assured him that the separation would be good for their marriage. At the airport he had wanted to decide on the time and date of their next meeting. It was as if the lawyer in him wanted her to sign a contract. He suggested they meet halfway, on an island in the Caribbean perhaps, but he wanted to fix the day right now. She had protested that for a foreign correspondent this was impossible. They could name a day certainly, but she had no idea what kind of stir the world might have got itself into on that particular day, and almost anything could force her to cancel. But finally, under pressure from him, she had agreed to a date that was eight weeks away.

Tonight he told her he had got reservations on St. Barths for the days they wanted, and he named the hotel. It had cost him money, but he had got them. Jane tried to sound enthusiastic, and at last was able to ring off.

Douglas did not call the next day, which was not surprising, nor the next either, by which time he had surely seen the piece. She became increasingly worried about what he had thought of it. Her paper was delivered to the embassy each day. She had seen copies in offices there.

In her experience, and other journalists often said the same, people usually hated whatever was written about them, even if it wasn't critical. His silence must mean he didn't like it.

She needed him as a source. She couldn't afford to lose him, meaning that sooner or later she would have to confront him, to find out. By the fourth day she was suffering a lesion of confidence. He didn't like the piece and probably didn't like her personally either. She got the piece out and read it again. It seemed harmless to her. It seemed flattering.

9

DOUGLAS SAT ON A LOG in the Amazon jungle and stared into a fire and brooded. It was late and he was the only man, apart from the sentries, not trying to sleep. A few of the sleeping men lay at the extremity of the firelight. He could see them, but not much else, and he could hear them whenever they coughed or moaned in their sleep. There was no order to the spots they had picked. They lay at random. Lumpy bundles. They looked like corpses. Perhaps tomorrow some of them would become corpses. Among them, perhaps, himself.

The night was dark. The edge of the river moved by a few yards away, catching glints of light from the fire and from the stars. The riverbank was wide here, roomy enough for eighty men and seven parked helicopters. During the rainy season, Douglas judged, it would all be under water, but for now it made a good campsite. They had been lucky so far. The laboratory complex they would hit tomorrow was about thirty miles downriver. It was the biggest he had ever heard about, and it was supposedly heavily guarded.

Ten minutes flying time and they would be there. They would jump out of the helicopters into a firefight. He would be in it. A New York cop. Here in the Amazon jungle. It made no sense to him. How had his life got from there to here?

At dawn they would take off. Though the night had only a few hours left, he could not sleep. The jungle was as noisy as a thruway. He listened to the calls of the night birds, the screeching monkeys. He listened to the buzzing insects, to the river tumbling over roots and logs, all these sounds being subject to the irregular punctuations of the sleeping men. He stood up and for a time stared at the river.

The Amazon was about a mile wide here. The helicopters stood on their skids for several hundred yards. Each was surrounded by sentries, the sentries still awake, supposedly. He walked up along the bank. The trees were higher and darker up here. The night was dark, and he could not see the sentries until he was upon them. They were there, and they were awake. He chatted with each of them in turn. They were all boys and it was their country. He was forty-four years old, and it was not. Making small talk in Spanish was hard for him. Above his head the rotors seemed to sigh with every night breeze brushing across them.

When he came to the end he peered up at a billion stars. Since he was below the equator, the southern constellations were unfamiliar to him, something he shrugged off. He would not have recognized many at home. He was a city kid, New

York high school, New York college, New York police academy. To him the stars had been without interest. The city was in his blood, not Colombia, not the Amazon River. What's a New York cop doing in this place? Douglas asked himself. Particularly one his age. How did I get here? But he knew the answer.

When he had reached Bogotá and reported to the DEA office in the embassy, Agent in Charge Gallagher had been barely civil to him, and had interviewed him in Spanish, breaking into English after a few minutes, saying:

"We've established one thing, haven't we? Your Spanish stinks."

The two men were about the same age and were of nearly equivalent rank. Douglas had been preceded by telex messages that Gallagher had found ambivalent. This was Gallagher's first command job and he was not sure of himself. He believed Douglas had been sent to Colombia to spy on him.

"Your Spanish, on the other hand," said Douglas carefully, "sounds very good."

"It's not good, it's perfect."

"Okay, it's perfect. Where'd you learn it?"

Gallagher's father had been an executive with United Fruit. The family had lived in Cuba before Castro, and then in Honduras and Costa Rica. There was no reason why Gallagher could not have explained this to the new arrival, but he chose not to. "I grew up speaking Spanish," he said.

"I grew up in New York."

"Don't get snotty with me, Supercop. What's your mandate?"

"Mandate?"

"Why were you sent here? What am I supposed to do with you?"

"I believe you're supposed to use me as you would any federal agent."

"You're not a federal agent."

"No, I'm not."

"You have no police powers here."

"No I don't," said Douglas coolly, "but that shouldn't matter too much since you don't either."

The two men stared at each other. Finally Douglas said: "My understanding was that I would be your second in command, sort of."

"In a ceremonial sense? Wonderful. I'll tell the men."

Douglas chose not to fight with him. Not then. This is going to be hard, he told himself. He moved into an apartment that the embassy provided and tried to find his way around. He was desperately worried about his career. He knew it was in ruins. His own fault, which made it worse. It seemed to him that nothing he might do here could rehabilitate it or him. He was in exile. Back at police headquarters he was either forgotten, or he was someone men made snide jokes about, all the while moving ahead of him in the queue.

The DEA contingent numbered twenty men. Douglas met the ones attached to the embassy in Bogotá. Taking their lead from Gallagher, they were cool to him. The rest worked out of an office in Barranquilla on the Caribbean coast and presently he went up there and met them, finding them much friendlier. But of course on a daily basis they were outside his orbit. He made his first reconnaissance trips to Bolivia and Peru and was fascinated by what he saw and learned. He met some interesting people and some might have become friends had he stayed. But his job, such as it was, was in Colombia and he went back there.

He formed the habit of writing a report—a kind of newsletter—each week and sending it to Commissioner Windsell. But the reports elicited no response whatever. At the embassy he formed a friendship with the deputy chief of mission, who was also alone. They played gin rummy together, and sometimes went out to restaurants where they could eat dinner and listen to guitar music while sitting with their backs to the wall. But the deputy chief's tour of duty ended and he went back to the States.

Douglas became increasingly lonely. He missed the old police camaraderie. It was not so bad during the day, for the embassy teemed with people—over two hundred of them—

and there was always conversation in the cafeteria and in the halls about sports or politics. But at night it was another story. He missed his wife. There were plenty of women in the embassy. He looked them over but none appealed to him. Like most of the men around them they lived totally within their little American enclave and rarely looked outside it.

At first Gallagher had given him no work to do. When he protested, Gallagher allowed him—grudgingly—to read the cable traffic each day and to study old cases. At length— also grudgingly—Gallagher took him around to meet the minister of defense, and then the commanders of the National Police (CNP), the Judicial Technical Police (JTP), and the Department of Administrative Security (DAS). These were the principal police agencies charged with enforcing the narcotics laws and they were known by their acronyms, which Douglas duly memorized, along with the names of the commanders that went with them. But Gallagher would not allow him to deal with any of these people, reserving this job for himself. He protested, but Gallagher was adamant. Finally Douglas decided to go around him. He began to phone up for appointments with other ministers, other commanders. It was called making contacts. It was called keeping busy. He felt as if he were in jail, trying to get out.

He kept pressing Gallagher to use him as he would any agent.

"You're not any agent."

"Look," said Douglas patiently, "the way things are is a waste of my time and the police department's money." He paused, and his voice got hard. "Let's understand each other. You're either going to stop this horseshit or I'm going over your head to Washington." There was no one in Washington who cared that Douglas existed, nor in New York either. It was an empty threat and he knew it. But Gallagher didn't know it, or so he hoped.

The two men stared at each other.

"There's an informant," Gallagher said. "I'm meeting him tonight. You can come along."

"Good."

"When you hear the details you might think otherwise."

"I've met with informants before, you may be surprised to learn."

They eyed each other coldly.

"Have you now?"

"One or two."

"An electrician," Gallagher said. "He's coming up from Medellín."

"An electrician?"

"So he says. The meet is set for midnight in the Parque de la Independencia, in front of the natural history museum."

"Midnight in the park," said Douglas. He pictured it. "You guys are too much. Jesus."

"That's what he wanted."

"You don't let informants dictate terms to you. You dictate to them."

"If you want to pull out—"

"I'll be there," Douglas snapped.

When people telephoned the Bogotá embassy for whatever purpose, their calls were logged, but if they spoke with an impeccable American accent they were sometimes not put through to the official of their choice. Most members of the foreign service seemed to feel that Americans went abroad just to bother them, and they ignored them and their problems if possible. Bogotá was no exception.

But if the caller asked for the DEA, particularly if he spoke in broken English, or in Spanish, or with the accent of some back-country Indian dialect, his call went forward at once, even in the middle of the night. It was in this way that most potential informants first made contact with the DEA. Eddie Gallagher did not initiate this policy, his predecessor did, but he continued it, even though it was a terrific burden each night on those few of his agents who spoke fluent Spanish.

Yesterday the electrician had phoned from Medellín. It happened that he was put through to Gallagher himself, to whom he spoke cryptically. He would come up to the capital on the Air Bridge, a thirty-minute flight. Gallagher, as he often did, suggested they meet in a room at the Hilton. The informant refused. Probably he had never been in such a hotel before. So Gallagher suggested he come to the embassy—he could pretend he was there for a visa. But nothing could have made him come to the embassy. Midnight in the park, he said, and Gallagher was stuck with it.

At midafternoon he summoned his staff to a meeting in his office. Douglas took a chair against the wall. Gallagher sat behind his desk. The other men stood, or brought chairs in from the other offices.

"All you men and all the cars are to be mobilized tonight," Gallagher told them. "Cancel whatever you have on." This brought a smile; in Bogotá the men rarely had anything on at night.

They would put the park under surveillance from 10 P.M., Gallagher said. The park was the biggest in the city. Even at midnight there would be people in there.

He and Douglas would approach the informant, he said, and he glanced over at him.

Douglas gave a slight nod. The operation seemed to him badly conceived and excessively dangerous. Gallagher was testing his nerve as earlier he had tested his Spanish, and this was galling too. If he passed the test Gallagher might admit him to his elite group. It was childish.

They would interview the informant on the steps of the museum, Gallagher said. If he was alone. If it looked right. If it didn't they would back off, not even approach him. He spread out a map of the park and the others crowded around his desk. The interview should take about twenty minutes. The rest of the staff would be deployed here, here, and here.

To meet with an informant was a ticklish business at any time in any country, but was worse here because the traffickers had penetrated the government, the telephone and telecommunications network, and on some levels the police and the army. The DEA agents were obliged to assume that their movements were known most times almost as soon as they made them. This made any such meeting dangerous not only to themselves and to the informant in question, but also to innocent bystanders, for the traffickers were careless shooters.

At midnight, their hands in their pockets on their guns, Gallagher and Douglas strode across the park toward the museum. They had left their car in the street. It was a long walk in and would be a long walk back. Many times in the past Douglas had met informants in places as dangerous as this: in alleys, under bridges; and often in the middle of the night. It was what cops did. But that was in New York. They were informants he understood in a city he understood. He did not understand Colombia, and he doubted Gallagher did. Supposedly the traffickers had set a half-million-dollar price on the head of any DEA agent who could be gunned down. Tonight's meeting could well be a setup for an assassination. Two assassinations. As they approached the museum, the hairs were standing up on his arms.

But the informant was there, and he told his story. Unfortunately it was a long one. The longer it took, the more nervous Douglas got.

A major new lab was being built in the jungle near Leticia in Amazonas, he told them.

It was on the Paquirri River just before it came into the Amazon. He and a number of other skilled workmen from Medellín were building it. Members of the cartel had rounded them up in the streets like slaves, and forced them onto the plane. No one had refused. The price of refusal, it was understood, was a bullet in the head, or maybe a bomb later under one's truck. He himself was no *narcotraficante*. He wanted out. He had a brother-in-law in Miami. He wanted passage to Miami and an electrician's license when he got there.

Gallagher was purring. "Tell me more," he said.

In Medellín the informant had earned three dollars a day, he said. In the jungle, twenty. So they were well paid. This was supposed to be enough to keep them happy. As entertainment they were furnished with a steady supply of pornographic movies. A kind of outdoor theater had been set up and every night they watched porno movies. Once a month two or three whores were brought in.

Douglas kept glancing nervously around. He could not see any of the backup DEA men. He wasn't supposed to see them, he knew. The strain came from not being sure they were there.

The airstrip had been completed first, using a bulldozer brought up the river by boat. As soon as this was done the rest of the heavy equipment was flown in and they laid down a pipeline to the river, for cocaine processing requires an enormous amount of water. They had built barracks buildings, forty bunks, so that's how many men would work there once the site went into production; and a huge kitchen, a dining hall, a recreation hall. He himself had wired all that. He had also wired the sheds with heat lamps for drying the leaves, drying the paste. Then the word had come down to tear the heat lamps out. The sheds were to be rewired for microwave ovens.

"Does the DEA have devices," the informant asked, "that can detect heat from the air—infrared or something—but not microwave heat?"

"Yes," said Eddie Gallagher.

The informant looked surprised. "That was the rumor. I didn't believe it. It didn't sound right to me."

The microwave ovens had not yet arrived. The construction was being done with the help of local Indians as laborers. The Indians were treated like slaves. They themselves were slaves too, since they couldn't leave. They had been at it two months. In all that time no one had been allowed to leave the site except that once each week they were taken into Leticia by boat and then truck, and allowed a brief phone call to their wives. These calls were monitored. There was no chance to say anything. And some weeks the phones were down and they didn't get even their one call. Then his father had died. He was allowed to go back to Medellín for the funeral. He had buried his father this morning. He had talked to his wife. He had made his decision. He wanted out of the jungle and out of Medellín. Could the DEA help him?

Gallagher began to probe for details about the location of the lab, about when approximately it would go into production. The informant told what he knew, which wasn't much. After only two or three weeks the airstrip had become covered with grass and weeds; it would be difficult to spot from the air, he said.

Douglas kept glancing nervously around.

What about firepower? Gallagher asked. What kind of security was there? That whole area was supposedly controlled by the Marxist guerrilla army known by the acronym FARC. Had the informant seen evidence of guerrilla activity? Was the lab being protected by FARC?

The informant had seen plenty of guns. He was not political. He had asked no questions.

Gallagher began to give instructions. He was counting on the informant to let him know when the lab became operational, when it was in full production, and when a quantity of cocaine—whether as paste, or base, or in its finished form, which was cocaine hydrochloride—was ready for shipment. The informant could forward this information during his weekly phone calls to his wife via a simple code: Getting a cold would mean the lab was operational. A sore throat would mean it was in production. Chest pains meant at least a ton of product on hand.

The informant was to go back to Medellín and brief his wife, then go back into the jungle like a docile employee. His wife was to phone either Gallagher or Señor Douglas once each week. Gallagher slapped the informant on the back. When he came out of the jungle next, Gallagher said, he would personally put him and his wife on a plane to Miami.

The meeting ended there. Nobody shot at anyone. Douglas and Gallagher retired unmolested to their car and returned to the embassy, where Gallagher sat behind his desk rubbing his hands and grinning.

The next day he and Douglas had flown down over the jungle in a DEA Aero Commander. They homed in on Leticia, a town of thirteen thousand, then found the confluence of the

Amazon and the Paquirri. They located the island strewn with driftwood that the informant had mentioned and then what was apparently the airstrip.

"That's it," cried Gallagher, pointing down. He was as gleeful as a kid. "That's got to be it." And he ordered the pilot to punch in the coordinates.

Apart from the rivers, the town, and the airfield, they peered down on triple canopy jungle foliage so thick they could see nothing underneath it.

Thereafter the informant's wife spoke to Gallagher by telephone once each week. Presently her husband felt a cold coming on, she reported. A week later he was suffering from a sore throat.

Then for two weeks the informant did not phone his wife at all.

Douglas overheard Gallagher talking to his deputy, whose name was Bannon. "Something's happened," Gallagher was saying. "Either he's been found out, or else they're working so hard down there that the visits to town have been suspended."

Gallagher was summoned to Washington.

"What about the informant?" asked Douglas as the DEA chief was about to leave. "I'm the only other one who's actually talked to him."

"Take him, he's yours," said Gallagher blithely. "I'll be back before anything happens anyway."

But he wasn't. The very next day the wife had telephoned. Douglas took the call. Her husband had pains in his chest, she said, brought on by working around the clock at something that was not his job. But all that would end in three days time, she continued, and he would be able to laze around for a while.

Douglas took this to mean that (a) a quantity of product was on hand; and (b) it was all to be shipped out in three days.

And Gallagher would not be back by then. With a mounting surge of excitement Douglas decided to take over the case.

He would make something happen. He would be in command again.

How much product was on hand? How could the shipment be stopped? The answer to the first question was several tons at least. They were not going to build such a complex and work around the clock for less. The answer to the second was a good deal more complicated. To stop the shipment required an expedition, and three days was not enough time to mount one. The lab complex was seven hundred fifty miles away, far beyond the three-hundred-mile range of Colombia's U.S.-supplied Bell helicopters. The helicopters would have to proceed south in stages, bringing their own fuel. Since the lab was in FARC territory, troops would be required to secure the perimeter while the lab was destroyed—maybe as many as a hundred men. They would have to be got from the army, which might refuse them. The army was said to be teeming with bribed officers. Just to ask for that many troops would compromise security. He was not in America now. Neither he nor the embassy could order anyone to do anything. They could only request.

Douglas phoned General Nuñez, commander of the DAS, and asked for an immediate appointment. He could not invite Nuñez to the embassy, because getting into the embassy was such a hassle as to be considered an affront to the dignity of any high-ranking Colombian official; several who had attempted it had written letters to the ambassador demanding an official apology.

Nor could so sensitive a subject be discussed over the phone. The traffickers had once managed to tape the private telephone conversations of the president of the republic. They had played the tape to the nation over a radio station they controlled. Thereafter no police or government line was considered secure.

Douglas was obliged to drive over to DAS headquarters. In Bogotá traffic this took forty minutes. Once admitted to Nuñez's office, he explained where the lab was, and that there was very little time.

"That's FARC territory," said Nuñez, staring at the map. "We'll need the support of the military."

"We'll need troops," agreed Douglas.

"A lot of them." The general went to the coat tree in the corner. There was gold braid on the cap that he rammed down onto his head. He was very excited. "I'll go see the minister of defense. Will you come with me?"

In Colombia the National Police came under the jurisdiction of the Defense Ministry, and Nuñez was only a general. He began to deflate outside the minister's door. Douglas should have expected what happened next.

"I worry that he'll refuse us," Nuñez murmured, and got up and began to pace. He did not say so, but he had just seen this request for troops as a serious threat to his career. If refused, he would lose a great deal of face, and never mind the tons of cocaine that would start moving untouched toward the streets of the United States.

By the time they were admitted Nuñez had lost all confidence, Douglas believed. The mere general faced the government minister, and there was no force left in him. He smiled, he agreed with all the minister's remarks, he presented the request for troops as coming from Douglas, rather than himself, and he listened to the minister's reply with a respect bordering on obsequiousness.

The minister was a little man, bald, energetic. He had not stopped moving—had barely stopped talking—since they had entered his office. He spoke fast, staccato Spanish. The proposed operation sounded hastily conceived to him, he said. It was based on flimsy intelligence, and no assault plan had even been developed. It would be very difficult to mount on such short notice, and who was to say that any troops he supplied would not be ambushed by the FARC.

Men possibly killed. Helicopters possibly destroyed. The minister was obliged to refuse their request for troops, he said, moving them toward the door.

Douglas had listened to all this. The Spanish was not too fast for him. He had understood every word. His command of the language was getting better every day. He had perceived almost immediately what would be the result of Nuñez's sick smile, his subservient tone of voice. He ought to have stepped in quickly, taken the focus off Nuñez, who was a subordinate, and onto himself, a representative of the United States of America. There were more and stronger arguments in favor of the proposed raid than against, and he ought to have projected them with confidence and enough underlying power to frighten the minister, if not convince him.

But along with the power he ought to have projected a certain grace and charm also, using the nuances of the language, being careful always to choose the exact correct word, projecting even humor. This was, after all, a negotiation. The minister had to be put in the mood to want to give him the troops. But grace and charm, nuance and humor were beyond Douglas's present command of Spanish, unfortunately. He was pretty much restricted to straight declarative sentences. He was capable of making a blundering, leaden-footed attack on the minister, if he chose. He might have pointed out, for instance, that those were American helicopters the minister was worried about losing, that it was America being wrecked by crack—his command of Spanish was more than good enough for head-on confrontations of this nature. They just wouldn't have worked. The minister would have got angry, then haughty. He would have thrown them out, and Douglas would have failed as miserably as the cringing Nuñez.

In the street outside the ministry, Nuñez said: "Sorry."

With a flash of the same sick smile, he stepped into his car. Douglas got into his own car, which had followed, hurried back to the embassy, and burst in on the ambassador.

Ambassador Thompson was a rich oilman from Texas. He was big, about six-five, and affected a bluff, relaxed style. He met people in his shirtsleeves, often wearing red suspenders.

In English Douglas was able to get out all his arguments. He wanted Ambassador Thompson to ask the president of the republic to instruct the minister of defense to furnish Nuñez with a hundred troops.

Thompson did not want to do it. He was very busy, he

said. He had responsibilities of which Douglas, with his narrow law-enforcement focus—"people like you," was the way he phrased it—was not aware, and he began a lecture about the broad picture. Exxon had coal fields up in the Guajira, did Douglas know that?

"Huge ones. The Florida power companies are almost totally dependent on Exxon's Colombian coal. That's part of the broad picture." In a few minutes he had to leave for the Bureau of Mines and Energy, he said. He would be in meetings about that coal much of the afternoon.

"Colombia wants to renegotiate those leases," the ambassador said. "Exxon doesn't."

After that, the ambassador said, he had a meeting at the Ministry of Agriculture about Colombia's fight against hoof and mouth disease. The Colombians, aided by American experts, were pushing the disease south. "Another hundred miles and Washington may allow Colombian beef into the States again," the ambassador said. "So you can see I have a lot on my mind."

"Phone the president of the republic," Douglas suggested amiably.

"Can't. I'm only the ambassador. He's the president."

"He'll take your call. You're the one he gets his goodies from. Sound him out. See how he feels."

The ambassador was rummaging through papers on his desk, obviously hoping that when he looked up Douglas would be gone. But Douglas stayed.

"I have a Belgian National Day reception to go to at their embassy," the ambassador said, "and a courtesy call on the new minister of transportation—my wife will be eating dinner alone again tonight, I can see that."

"Five minutes," insisted Douglas. "That's all it will take."

"I can't go over the head of the minister of defense. I need him to protect the oil pipeline and—"

"The president is a politician," Douglas interrupted. "He'll know how to keep you out of it. Your hand won't show."

"You probably don't even know about the oil pipeline. The guerrillas keep blowing it up. The people at Occidental Petroleum—"

"This is one of the biggest clandestine labs ever discovered," said Douglas. "There may be tons of cocaine there, just waiting for us."

"—can't get their oil out. They've been on me for weeks to get them more troops and—"

"If we botch a case of this magnitude," said Douglas slowly, carefully, "we'll all look bad." The editorial we. The veiled threat. It did not have to be spoken, and wasn't. Ambassador Thompson could not even be sure Douglas had made it. If we botch this case, Douglas's words suggested, Ambassador Thompson was the one who would look bad. Douglas could and would see to it.

Thompson was biting his lip. The policeman across the desk commanded far more attention from the world's press than he did, or so he imagined. If Douglas accused the ambassador of dereliction of duty—

"I bet you never thought you'd be part of a major narcotics bust," said Douglas encouragingly, "did you?"

The ambassador picked up his phone. When his secretary came on he asked to be put through to the president of the republic. "Sit right there," he said to Douglas.

They waited almost five minutes in near total silence. Five minutes of avoiding eye contact. Thompson rummaged through his papers. Douglas got up and gazed out the bulletproof window.

Then Thompson's phone buzzed and he spoke into it with false conviviality. *"Hola, Señor Presidente, que tal?"*

The result was that they got the troops.

Nuñez and Douglas completed the planning that night. They envisioned the use of over a hundred men.

However, when they visited the airfield they found only seven helicopters to be operational. Sixteen had been donated to Colombia. They dated from the Vietnam war and were cared for by American "field advisers" under contract to the embassy. They had been designed to carry ten American troops at a time, but could take twelve Colombians, who were smaller.

"Basically the helicopter is a machine designed to shake itself to pieces," said the chief field adviser, a man named Dunn. "The Colombians would like us to give them the aircraft, allow them to use them as they like, and fix them when they break." Then he added disgustedly: "Which is about what happens."

With only seven available, the plan would have to be scaled back.

"We'll take eighty men," said Nuñez. "What about support planes?"

Several were available. Nuñez ordered extra fuel bladders loaded aboard. Each bladder would hold five hundred gallons.

Surrounding the ambassador's residence were the same type of high steel bars as surrounded the embassy downtown, and just inside the front gate stood the same type of hydraulically operated steel wall—to penetrate the grounds by crashing through the gate and the steel wall behind it would take a tank. Jane got out of her taxi. In the guard booth, which looked armored to her, were two men armed with machine guns, one of whom came out and reached through the bars for her passport, which he checked against a list.

Her name was not on the list, she was told, and her passport handed back.

She began trying to explain. There was an embassy bridge tournament tonight in the basement of the residence. The press officer had invited her.

The guard went into the booth to telephone to the mansion. As she waited, Jane replayed her conversation with the press officer. In Bogotá at night, he had said, the streets, for an American, were not safe. So most nights a lot of the embassy people gathered at the residence. In the basement there were Ping-Pong tables, card tables, Scrabble boards, television. "We have a satellite dish in the garden," he had said. "We get all the channels, the ball games, the news shows, the works."

And tonight there was a bridge tournament. "Do you play?" he had asked her.

In a generalized sense the embassy would be her major source of news. To meet embassy people socially was a plus. In addition, Douglas might be there, and if he was she hoped to confront him. Better over a card game than in an office. If she wanted him as a source, she was going to have to get past whatever difficulty her piece on him might have caused.

Finally someone in the mansion must have vouched for her, for the gate opened a crack and she was passed inside. The grounds were lit up like a baseball stadium. The bushes and trees along the paths were as sharply outlined as if backlit.

As Jane approached, a woman about her own age came toward her out of the mansion.

"Welcome to our house," the woman said. "I'm Martha Thompson, the ambassador's wife."

Jane began to apologize for the trouble she had evidently put everyone to. But the press attaché had invited her—

"It's nice to have company for a change," Martha Thompson interrupted.

For a change? Jane looked at her.

"If you hate bridge," explained Martha, "there's not much to do around here at night."

Jane's antennae were up.

"Apart from my Spanish lesson every afternoon there's not that much to do in the daytime either."

Jane recognized loneliness when she saw it. They were inside the mansion now, and the ambassador's wife insisted on showing her through the rooms. "After all, it's not my house, is it?" Martha Thompson said, "it's your house too. It's every American's house."

The public rooms were enormous, the walls adorned by quite nice paintings, on which Jane complimented her.

But Martha shrugged the compliment off. "The State Department borrowed them from the storerooms of various museums. All the embassies have them. It's part of a program."

Once every seven years the public rooms could be redecorated, Martha Thompson was saying, and she had funds for that now, but how was she to decorate a room as long as this living room?

Jane studied the problem a moment, then suggested dividing the room in two: two rugs, two groupings of furniture. One grouping could go here—she moved about the room—the other here. It was something she had seen in châteaux in Europe as a girl.

"That's a swell idea," said Martha. "I should get the State Department to hire you as a decorator."

As they moved from room to room, Jane, on the lookout as always for possible stories, began to question her about her role as ambassador's wife. Well, she presided over receptions and banquets here at the residence, and accompanied her husband to receptions and banquets at ministries and other embassies. She had four servants and she and her husband lived in an apartment upstairs.

"I'll show it to you," said Martha Thompson, and she started up the rather grand staircase.

"I don't want to intrude—"

"Don't worry about Arthur. He's never home. Tonight he went to a reception somewhere. For once I refused to go. Those things are not too gay if you don't speak Spanish." Then she added with a grin: "Or even if you do."

They entered the Thompsons' apartment: two bedrooms, a sitting room, a library, and a kitchenette. "This bedroom is for our children, when they're here." Martha stood in the doorway looking at the two beds. "Of course they haven't been allowed here yet. No one's allowed to have their children in Colombia. The men have only recently been allowed to have their wives. Do you have children?"

"Not yet, no."

"My girls are eleven and thirteen. They're in boarding school in Virginia. That's too young to be away from their mother, don't you think?"

"You must miss them."

"I haven't seen them in four months." Then she said cheerfully: "We may be allowed to have them down for Christmas."

"That's nice."

"If the security can be worked out."

In Jane's head an article was taking shape—a strong one: the loneliness of an ambassador's wife, it might be called. The foreign desk might go for it. The Style section would certainly go for it. Of course she would try to write it so this unsuspecting woman would not be in trouble with her husband when it ran, nor with the State Department either.

Jane had the tendency to worry too much about fallout from what she wrote, her editors sometimes chided her. Maybe so, but she didn't see where she had the right to cause her subjects pain or trouble they didn't deserve.

Martha Thompson led the way into the next room. "And this is our bedroom." She pointed to the windows. "You notice that we have glass in the windows now, isn't that great?"

Jane, looking out, saw the lights of a few villas farther up the hillside. The rest of the hillside was woods.

"Until last week," Martha Thompson said, "there were iron shutters bolted over all the windows on this side of the house. Night and day my bedroom was completely dark. Arthur didn't seem to mind. But sometimes it made me want to scream."

She nodded brightly at Jane. "Finally I got him to make security take them off." She rapped on one of the windows. "It's bulletproof glass. It's an inch thick and doesn't open, but at least you can see out."

The tour continued. "This is the door to my terrace. It's a nice terrace, don't you think?" She peered out through the door. "I'm not allowed to go out on it, though." Suddenly she laughed. "But I do go out on it sometimes at night."

Jane nodded. "How did your husband happen to get this post?" she probed.

"Arthur gave a substantial contribution to the president's reelection campaign. He thought he'd get a bigger country than here, but he didn't."

"It's a very important country," Jane said carefully, "the way things are."

"Oh yes."

Her husband, Jane remembered, was fifty. That made her about fifteen years younger. She had nice hair and eyes—a pleasant face—and she was a prisoner in this building. She had a flat stomach, a prominent bosom. She was a very attractive woman, Jane thought, and she was more unhappy here than she thought she was letting on.

"I'm afraid they may be waiting for me downstairs," Jane said. Though she had no interest in cards, she was anxious to get down to the game room. She wanted to see Douglas if he was there, and after that to work the room.

"I shouldn't have kept you so long," Martha apologized. But she seemed reluctant to let Jane go. "Maybe we could have tea together some afternoon. Of course you'd have to come here."

As they descended the basement stairs Jane could hear the beating of Ping-Pong balls, and then the riffle of cards.

The game room contained thirty or more people. There were five bridge tables in use. Jane hurriedly scanned the room but did not see Douglas.

Martha Thompson said: "Or we could play tennis together. Do you play tennis?"

"Sure." Jane, looking for faces she knew, was still scanning the room.

"Sometimes I play with Eddie Gallagher," said Martha. "He's the DEA country attaché."

"We've met," said Jane.

"We have a court out in the garden, you know. Eddie's a fine tennis player. He gives me lessons sometimes."

Jane wondered why she was talking about Gallagher.

"You should come and play on our court before Security closes it down," Martha Thompson said.

"Why would they close it down?"

"There are some new villas going up on the hill above the court. Eddie says over his dead body. Still, it's probably going to happen."

The press attaché came forward, all smiles. "I'm glad you could come," he told Jane.

"You forgot to leave my name at the gate," she accused.

"Well, you're here now, let me see if I can find you a table."

He placed her at a table. Martha stood nearby for a time, then wandered away. Jane saw her going back up the stairs by herself.

By the time the next hand was dealt, Jane realized she was not going to be able to work the room at all. She was going to have to play cards. And Douglas was not here. As she played the hand, she found herself thinking about him, about the piece she had written, and as a result forgot to draw trumps. Two hands later, still not concentrating, she overbid and went down four tricks.

She stuck it out for an hour, then asked the press attaché to call her a cab.

"No need," he said, "I'll have one of our cars take you."

So she rode back to the hotel in an armored four-wheel-drive station wagon so heavy on its bulletproof tires that it labored up all hills. Its windows were inch-thick Plexiglas, none of which opened.

10

AT DAWN THE TROOPS filed into the helicopters. Douglas stood on the tarmac with Bannon watching them board.

"The rule is, only one of us goes on a raid like this," Bannon said.

The troops were carrying field packs and automatic rifles.

"They want to believe they're doing it by themselves," said Bannon. "It's very important to them for national sovereignty reasons."

The sun was coming up over the edge of the airfield.

"Lackeys of the gringos. That sort of thing."

"It's our case," said Douglas.

"It's Gallagher's case. He's the one should be going, not you."

All the rotors were turning. Douglas was eager to board. He was in no mood for a lecture from Gallagher's surrogate.

"Your job is to verify that the raid took place and that they actually seized whatever they're going to claim. And to try to make sure nobody puts anything in his pocket. You're an observer only. Got that?"

"I think you told it to me before."

"If there's shooting, lie on the ground with your fingers in your ears."

"I'll be sure to do that."

"A DEA guy got killed, it would ruin it for them. Prove it was our operation, not theirs. Anybody asks you, you're a geologist making a field study."

The rotors were turning fast. There was so much noise Bannon was shouting.

"If you get killed, that's what they'll say you were, believe me."

Bannon stuck his hand out. Douglas took it, why not? He climbed up into the helicopter.

In a moment the machine rose up. All of them did. The cargo planes took off and the flotilla started south. Nuñez was in the lead helicopter, Douglas in the last. No one else knew where they were going. Even the officers had not been told.

The terrain underneath was grasslands first, then jungle. The intermediate stops were stretches of deserted road that had been picked out on maps. Nuñez wanted to stay away from towns for fear that news of this expedition would precede them south, so they landed on dirt roads leading from nowhere to nowhere. Some were nearly overgrown. They were pot-holed, bumpy, and rough on the fixed-wing aircraft.

No cars or trucks were encountered. At each refueling stop the cargo doors were thrown open and one or more fuel bladders pushed out. Full, they looked like giant hot water bottles, and they were pushed and rolled out of the rickety old planes to land on the ground with a mighty thump. While the helicopters were refueled the men stretched their legs. As each plane was emptied of its bladder it started back until finally those that were left stayed where they were, waiting for the return flight, and the helicopters flew on alone.

By now the towns and roads—all traces of human habitation—had disappeared. They flew over country in which no one lived or had ever lived. There was nothing to see below except their own shadows scooting along on the tops of trees.

At last the Amazon came into view, and on its bare bank the helicopters set down. It was dusk by then. The officers were briefed, and briefed their men. They ate from the cold rations they had brought with them, for no fires were permitted. Darkness came down from one instant to the next, it seemed, and the men slung hammocks or curled up under netting to get what sleep they could, except for Douglas who, unable to sleep, stared for a time into the fire, and then got up and walked up along the bank of the river in the dark, peering ahead at parked helicopters he could barely discern, and wondering what, at his age, he was doing here. To arrest an armed felon at gunpoint was one thing; he knew how to do it and had done it. A pitched battle against a fortified camp in the Amazon jungle was quite another thing. He had not been trained for it, did not know how to do it, and he could not believe he intended to take part.

He watched the sky lighten, then at last fell asleep, to be awakened—only seconds later it seemed—by Nuñez's hand on his shoulder. Some of the men bathed their faces in the river. Many of them pissed in it. Most of them ate what rations they had left. All of them boarded the helicopters.

The rotors began to turn, exploding quickly into near invisibility. The helicopters lifted off. The noise was stupendous. It went cascading down over the jungle, alarming every wild creature for miles around, and some not so wild.

In ten minutes the flotilla was over the clandestine airstrip. All seven helicopters dropped down and the men spilled out, but the lab was still two hundred or more yards off, and there seemed to be only one rather narrow trail leading to it. Down this the men ran, mostly two by two, and as those in the lead erupted into the clearing under the trees they were met by heavy fire, for the defenders had heard the oncoming engine noise long ago and had had several minutes to prepare. Though heavily armed, the troops fell back, blocking the exit from the trail, stumbling into each other and finally going to ground, firing their weapons out into the clearing at whatever they could see or perhaps only imagine. Some had been hit and had begun screaming.

Douglas too had run down the path toward the clearing, but the logjam of men stopped him, and the firing seemed so heavy that he dove to the ground and rolled off into the jungle. In New York the average shoot-out lasted one point three seconds. One intervened in a liquor store stickup, the single perpetrator, perhaps two, scared to death of the sudden blue uniforms. Police .38s against Saturday-night specials, a better than even match. Cop and perpetrator, on the average, stood seven feet apart. This was what Douglas understood. He had been terrified many times, but it was a controlled terror, and it ended quickly. The perpetrator raced for the door and if you were scared enough you shot him. Most times, however scared, you grabbed him, wrestled him down and snapped the cuffs on him. No cop wanted to shoot anybody. The paperwork was awesome, and if the investigation decided that the shooting was unjustified, you could go to jail.

What was happening here was no liquor store shoot-out. He lay on the jungle floor, could not tell where the bullets were coming from, and had no idea what to do next. He lay with his hands over his head while branches were shredded and leaves disappeared from the trees and bushes all around him. Automatic weapons. The shooting went on and on so that he thought: Unless we get off this path we'll all be killed. He heard a whoosh, followed by an explosion—several whooshes, several explosions.

Jesus, he thought, what's that?

There was a tree next to his head. Something hit it four feet off the ground and severed it from its trunk. A tree a foot thick. Severed it so that the stalk dropped down to the dirt beside his hand and the whole thing began to topple.

He tried to roll out from under, got snagged on a root, and imagined he would be crushed. He had been frightened many times in his life—fear was an emotion he knew well—but never as frightened as now. He was terrified. But he wasn't crushed. The surrounding trees held this one upright. It didn't fall.

With that the fear—most of it—left him. He still wanted to be somewhere else, anywhere else, this was not his job; he wanted the bullets to stop, but he was no longer immobilized. He knew that something had to be done, he had to move off this spot, they all did. More than half the troops were behind him, huddling into the ground, trying to bury themselves, making no effort to advance. He looked for Nuñez but did not see him. He looked for an officer of any kind, but there was none. He threw a glance to his left. The jungle was thick, but not that thick. He thought he could get through it, they all could, whoever would follow him, and he raised himself up and began shouting orders. This way. Through the bushes. They were to follow him. He waved his puny gun for emphasis and started slithering through the undergrowth on his elbows and knees.

Some of the men followed, then all of them did. He was leading forty or more men through the jungle on their bellies. He was trying to lead them around the encampment. As near as he could tell all the hostile fire was still directed at the trail to the airstrip and when he had gone a hundred feet he felt safe enough to rise up and run crouched over through jungle that was thinner here. From time to time he caught glimpses of the camp structures through the intervening leaves, and could see where some of the fire was coming from, see the blazing muzzles sticking out of windows, above piles of cordwood, could see men crouched behind trees.

It was not going to be possible to surround the compound. In places the jungle was too thick. It would be enough, he judged, just to spread his men out so that their fire poured in from many places. He was no military man but the plan seemed sound to him, and he began dropping off men five at a time, ordering them to crawl forward until they had a clear enough view to fire at specific targets, himself moving on with the rest. He had to shout his orders to make them heard, for the noise was deafening.

He came to a stream bed that apparently led through the compound, and he waded down into it and then stumbled forward, the water up to his knees. The stream opened out. He took cover as did the men behind him; they crouched under the bank, behind rocks, and began firing into the many structures of the compound. Douglas had his gun out but did not use it. These were guerrillas defending the compound, or else they were workmen. They were certainly not drug traffickers. Marzo, Von Bauzer, and the rest never came near a place like this. He, Douglas, had never shot anyone and he did not intend to start now. This was not his country, not his quarrel. He did not have the right.

The fire out of the compound slackened rapidly, then stopped altogether. Being outnumbered and unwilling, it seemed, to die for someone else's profits, the defenders simply evaporated. One minute they were there firing, the next they had backed up into the jungle, which swallowed them whole. For sixty seconds or so there was no sound at all. This potent silence was interrupted by a few tentative bursts of automatic weapon fire, followed by more silence.

Brandishing their guns, several of the bravest of the troops ran out into the open. When this drew no fire, all the troops began to come forward, and in a few seconds they had overrun the compound, laughing and shouting to each other. They made no effort to follow the men who had escaped into the jungle. They were not interested in arresting anyone with guns. Their officers suddenly appeared, but issued no such orders.

Nor did General Nuñez, who ran over to where Douglas had just got to his feet. Douglas looked at him: a middle-aged man wearing dark glasses and pressed fatigues and giggling with pleasure. "It's a big lab, no?" he said. "We find out what else is here."

The terror hit Douglas now, the weak knees, the inability to catch his breath. It was the normal reaction, he knew it well, the unreasoning fear that came afterward, that could not be held off. He had experienced it beginning as a young cop after every door he had kicked down, after every dangerous arrest. Except that today's residual terror seemed a hundred times worse. You got away with it again, he told himself. How many more times can you get away with it?

"No arrests?" he managed to say after a moment, waving his gun at the surrounding jungle into which so many men had vanished.

"Low-level employees," Nuñez said. *"Lavaperros."*

"Lavaperros?" Douglas did not know the word.

"Dogwashers. Not worth bothering about."

"How do we know?"

"Usually they have boats hidden. By now they're probably across the river."

Not everyone had run, and some of the troops were dragging them forth. One was the electrician from Medellín, the informant. Douglas managed to make eye contact with him, to reassure him with a nod of the head. He was terrifically relieved to find him unhurt.

Other troops were merely milling around, or calling out to each other, making discoveries. If a security perimeter had been set up, Douglas hadn't seen it happen. He was a cop, not a soldier; still, he knew a perimeter should have been formed. He mentioned this to Nuñez, who shrugged it off.

"Don't worry," Nuñez said in English. "You too much worry."

Together they moved through the compound, making the same discoveries as the troops. Larders stocked with enough food staples to feed forty men for a month. Walk-in refrigerators stuffed with hanging quarters of meat. There was a game larder too, if that's what you wanted to call it, a series of tree boughs overhung with dead birds, a jaguar, two boa constrictors, fish from the river, and the skinned carcasses of wild pigs and small jungle deer.

There were two dormitories. In one of them they came upon one bloody corpse, in the other, two. Men who had been firing from the doorways. Douglas looked down on them without emotion. He had seen a great many young men dead from bullets in his career. Both dormitories had windows and were air-conditioned, though some of the windows had been shot out. It was icy cold in both. One contained only slung hammocks, the other, beds. The beds were unmade and girlie magazines lay about. Only the important people slept in beds, Douglas supposed. The generators were still pumping in cold air, for he could hear them, and he could feel the drafts on his bare arms.

There was another bloodsoaked dead man in the doorway to the latrine, which otherwise contained rows of showers, rows of toilets. The floors and walls were of ceramic tile, and the fixtures were of good quality.

The diesel-powered generating plant, when Douglas peered into it, looked important enough to power a town. There was a suite of offices. Even as he watched, soldiers under the direction of an officer were sweeping papers and ledgers off the desk tops into plastic sacks, and dumping the contents of drawers in on top.

In the drying sheds microwave ovens had been installed, big ones. Nearby was an enclosed cinema that also proved to be air-conditioned, and then a machine shop that looked fully equipped, and a garage containing earth-moving equipment. In his head Douglas began to count up the money all this had cost. But the money was nothing compared to the effort required to get it all in here and set up. The traffickers were energetic and thorough, sure. But they were also, it seemed to him, incredibly arrogant. How could they have imagined that an installation of this magnitude could escape notice for long?

He entered an air-conditioned storeroom in which plastic packages were stacked almost to the ceiling. If this much product had been processed in just the first two weeks, then what would have been the output of this place once it got fully operational?

"Two tons in here, more or less," he murmured.

"How do you know?" said Nuñez.

The room was about the same size as the one he had raided in Queens, was stuffed just about as full, and Douglas recognized it. "I know," he said.

Outside were rows of fifty-five-gallon drums: ether, acetone, and kerosene for transforming coca leaves into cocaine; gasoline and diesel fuel for running the compound. The rows were stacked three barrels high, and there were stacks of cartons as well, which contained plastic bottles of sulfuric acid. Farther on were a dozen or more vats ten feet in diameter in which the coca leaves were macerated. Most were full, for Douglas climbed a ladder to see; stuff was stewing in there even now. There were piles of rakes, and rows of orange, blue, lavender, and pink plastic garbage cans, the colors more vivid even than the colors of the jungle's flowers and birds, each garbage can full to the brim with coca paste or base, Douglas wasn't sure which, for the two intermediate stages resembled each other in texture, and he had had little experience with either. In New York the usual cocaine seized was the final stage, ready to be snorted or smoked. He reached a hand in and squeezed. It was like squeezing wet plaster. What it most reminded him of was a handful of Spackle.

Beyond were haymows of used coca leaves, some of them fifty feet in diameter, the leaves brown and desiccated, all their juices sucked out of them. And mounds of empty plastic bottles, plastic tubes, plastic packaging, and a pit for kitchen garbage in which animals had been rooting.

Nuñez's men photographed the entire installation, then began to destroy it. Men were formed up in line like a firing squad and at an officer's order turned their automatic weapons on the stacked fifty-five-gallon drums, on the cartons of sulfuric acid, the gun reports drowning out the sounds of pinging metal, the hissing streams of liquid that spurted out and began to spill down the slope toward the river. When these manmade streams entered the river, its surface boiled. Douglas stood on the bank watching as the water frothed and bubbled. The whole river seemed to be boiling. The fish were in for a bad time for a mile or two downriver, and probably the vegetation as well.

The steeping vats were ruptured by gunfire also. A few of the sheds were pulled apart, and a bonfire started. The flames rose up and up. Onto this blaze was dumped cocaine paste out of the garbage cans, but it was seen to burn poorly, so kerosene was poured on. The flames jumped ten feet in height and the paste was ruined, whether the flames ever consumed it or not. A second bonfire was started for the packages of finished cocaine, which were brought to it in wheelbarrows.

Six soldiers had been wounded, some of them gravely. They had been carried back to the airstrip on improvised litters. Some of the fixed-wing aircraft had been called in by radio to take them out, and the prisoners out.

Now some wounded laborers were found as well. Two soldiers probing down a jungle path had come upon them: three men, all bleeding profusely. They had made it as far as the riverbank, but no farther. Nuñez, who was summoned, stared down on them. So did Douglas.

The wounded men were all Indians. They stared up at him with eyes that burned like coals.

Nuñez made no effort to ease their condition. "Leave them," he decided, and turned away.

"Wait a minute," said Douglas, hurrying after him, "you can't—"

"Their friends will come for them," said Nuñez.

"And if they don't?"

Nuñez shrugged and kept walking.

Men began to move through the compound planting explosive charges, trailed by other men sloshing gasoline over wooden floors, against walls. The wounded Indians were not going to survive the explosions, the fire.

Officers were moving men back to the airstrip. Nuñez himself was hurrying from the compound.

"Listen," Douglas said to his back.

Soldiers had begun throwing blazing rags into doorways.

"Better get out of here," Nuñez said.

Nuñez kept walking but Douglas turned back, gathered a group of soldiers, and ordered them to carry the wounded Indians to the airstrip. They obeyed him. They lifted them by the legs and arms. He led the way along the grassy path out onto the strip.

Nuñez came running forward. He was shouting orders at the troops, who dropped their burdens and stood over them looking confused.

"We can't take them," said Nuñez to Douglas.

"We're taking them."

"No room."

Douglas decided to force Nuñez's hand. He sat down on the ground. "Then I stay with them."

With a whoosh the conflagration started. Flames leaped thirty feet in the air, then sixty. The compound filled up with black smoke shot with flames.

Nuñez jerked his head at the soldiers who stood over the Indians. "Load them aboard."

"Thank you," said Douglas.

The charges, as they began to explode, cleared the smoke in an instant, replacing it with dust. Roofs lifted off, wafted some distance away, and crashed back to earth again. The flames shot higher than the towering trees. Heat rushed out and scorched Douglas's face. He began to run toward the helicopters. Everybody was running, including the soldiers carrying the wounded men.

Some of the helicopters were already up and hovering. The others filled fast. Nuñez's demolition experts, having finished planting shaped charges in the airstrip itself, lit their fuses and ran toward the same helicopter Douglas himself had boarded. This lifted off. When it was about five hundred feet up, the airstrip charges exploded. Gigantic craters appeared in the strip and chunks of earth and stone rose up as high as the hovering flotilla. The helicopters hung there for some minutes, as if unwilling to turn away from such a mighty spectacle, then swung around as one and started north toward home.

Douglas's heart stopped pounding and he sat back and tried to count up the score: the dead men back there, the wounded troops, the wounded Indians who might die. A major lab complex had been destroyed, of course. But how many more were there just like it?

The rotor was thundering overhead. He remembered the roomful of packages in Queens, the pleasure of imagining that he had struck the traffickers a crippling blow. Now he understood that he had not done so. He had more likely given them a kick in the shins that day, and today he and these men around him at great risk and great expense had given them another kick in the shins. The fire back there had been stupendous. The significance was perhaps less so. This country was vast and there were, he had come to realize, too many coca growers, too many processors, packagers, pilots, dealers, labs—traffickers in general. No crippling blow was possible. There are more of them than of us, he thought. Was the struggle hopeless? He didn't know.

It was afternoon. He had been on the move and without food since dawn. He was tired, hungry, discouraged. He was vain enough to believe that almost singlehandedly he had made today's operation happen. Now it would be reduced to a few lines in a report that would go to Washington, not New York. He had risked his life, been shot at, suffered the worst terror of his life, and police headquarters would not hear about that either.

How was he to remain in their minds back there? How was he to get back there himself?

The sunlight up here was overbright. The heat on his face felt searing. The noise and vibration of the machine made his head throb. He remembered Jane Fox and the article she had written profiling him. He had scanned it, then rushed off to meet Nuñez and put today's raid together. He hadn't had time to think of it then, but did now. It had been on the front page. He wondered how that had seemed at police headquarters, and tomorrow he might call up someone to find out—if he could think of any ex-colleague who seemed safe. It would be a delicate call. These men were all his friends, yes, but also his rivals. He was not interested in displaying his weakness for all to see.

He didn't think the one article would influence anybody very much, but repeated ones might. Jane could be his passport back to New York. Certainly he had no other. It was worth trying. He was curious about her. She seemed different from other women he had known. More sophisticated, more—something. He liked looking at her, too.

He had been written about before, and was not in the habit of thanking reporters afterward. But now he decided that as soon as he got back to Bogotá he would call Jane and thank her. She would ask where he had been and he would mention this raid. He would let her worm the details out of him, give her Nuñez's telephone number.

And it would not end there, he decided. In the future he would stick to her like glue. She could keep his name before the only public that mattered to him. He wanted his career back.

The ambassador's wife woke up beside her husband in the big bed in their apartment in the residence and the notion came to her that today she was going to test the length of her tether. Lying there thinking about it she got very excited. This day, unlike all the other days, suddenly seemed to have some purpose.

She and her husband were served breakfast in their sitting room. She watched her husband eat it while studying yesterday's *Washington Post*. She watched him leave for the embassy.

She dressed slowly, carefully, taking pleasure in it. As she applied eyeliner and lipstick she studied herself in her dressing table mirror. I'm still a nice-looking woman, she thought.

She was also thirty-eight years old and buried alive in a luxurious residence that belonged to the United States of America, not her. But today she would change that a bit. She put on her green suit and medium-high heels that were comfortable for walking, and phoned down for a car to be made ready.

About thirty seconds later her phone rang. It was the embassy's security officer, whose name was Brent Evans.

"What's this, Mrs. Thompson, what's this?"

She explained that she wanted to go shopping.

"When were you thinking of going shopping, Mrs. Thompson?"

"About five minutes from now, why?"

"Well, that's a tall order, you might say."

"It seems simple enough to me."

"But the cars are all taken," he said. "The guards are all occupied as well."

"All right," said Martha Thompson. "Then I'll ring for a taxi."

"Clothes shopping, Mrs. Thompson? Then I would need to send a female agent along, too. We only have two and neither is here right now."

"Female agent?"

"To go into the changing room with you."

"I don't require anyone to go into changing rooms with me."

"Mrs. Thompson—"

Martha got sharp with him. "I want that car here in five minutes."

Brent Evans tried to get diplomatic, calling her Mrs. Thompson at least once in every sentence, asking for patience. To leave the residence grounds took time to set up, he said. If she could wait until this afternoon—

But diplomacy was not his specialty and he only sounded patronizing, so that Martha became more and more exasperated. "Just send the car."

There was a moment of silence during which she could feel him become adamant.

"I don't have one to send right now."

"Forget I asked. I'll phone for the taxi."

Evans began to sputter. "Mrs. Thompson, you can't do that—"

"No? Are you physically going to stop me?"

"Of course not, but—"

She hung up on Mr. Brent Evans. This gave her pleasure, but it was only momentary, and she found herself staring at the telephone, waiting with discomfort for it to ring.

Almost at once it did. Her husband. She held the receiver to her ear.

"Brent says he can't take you until this afternoon."

"I don't need Brent."

At first the ambassador tried to cajole her. After that he reduced her to tears. The traffickers would like nothing better than to find her out alone, he told her. They perhaps had men up on the hill watching the residence through binoculars. They would kill her without a qualm, then what? Her children would be without a mother, he said sadly, her husband without his beloved wife.

She did not believe the beloved wife part for a minute.

"But you can have a nice excursion this afternoon. Brent will have the car there for you at two o'clock."

"I'm going out now."

"No you're not going out now and if you keep talking like that you won't go out at all." The false sadness had vanished as completely as if it had never existed. In her husband's changed tone his message was clear. He was a busy man and had no time to waste on neurotic women.

She said: "Try and stop me."

He said: "You are not leaving the grounds. The guards at the gate have been instructed to restrain you by force if necessary."

She felt as if he had hit her.

"Two o'clock," he said and hung up. Having put the phone down, she found she was sobbing and could not understand why. I'm a reasonable woman, she told herself. I'm not a hysterical woman. And she willed the tears to stop but they wouldn't.

By two o'clock she had long since regained her composure and repaired her face. The car was there promptly and she came down the steps and got into it.

The car contained, in addition to the driver, four guards. All were Colombians. The two who sat facing backward had submachine guns. One of the others was a woman who, though middle-aged, wore her black hair in braids. She had a hard, Indian face. She spoke almost no English. None of them did, and Martha's Spanish, even after weeks of practice, was virtually nonexistent. Although at first she tried to talk to the woman, it was hard slow work and she stopped.

Ostensibly she was on her way to buy clothes. In America Martha had summer and winter clothes she hadn't seen in months, and for the one season that existed in Bogotá she had two closets full back at the residence—and no place to wear any of them. She did not need more clothes, and the quality of what was on sale here was poor anyway. She had wanted only to get out on her own. But now she had created such a fuss that she was obliged to buy something, wasn't she, and she gave the driver the address of almost the only shop in Bogotá whose name she knew, and sat back and watched this gloomy city pass by.

It was a smaller, grubbier shop than she had expected. The car waited out front with the engine running. One of the guards stood at the door out on the sidewalk. The other three came inside with her. All were now carrying attaché cases. The submachine guns had vanished from sight, but Martha was conscious of them all the same. Those attaché cases were not innocent, and she was aware of how much they weighed.

Inside the shop one guard stood at the door, one at the cash desk, and the female agent, whose name was Juana, accompanied Martha through the racks. She was as attentive as a salesgirl. The proprietor, a middle-aged woman, remained behind the counter watching with frightened eyes.

Martha picked out two lace blouses to send to her daughters. Colombian lace was quite good. Then for some time she fingered dresses, skirts. They looked cheaply made to her. Finally she took two skirts into the changing room. Juana went with her, but the back of the shop was narrow and cluttered, and the changing room was too small for two grown women: a cubicle with a curtain. Martha asked Juana to give her some room. After checking all the other door handles back there, and even then hesitating, Juana nodded and went back out into the shop.

Immediately Martha put the skirts down and tiptoed through the clutter to the back door. She unlocked it as quietly as she could and stepped out into the afternoon air. She was in an alley. After breathing deeply a few times, she decided to go for a walk. The alley was long and narrow. There were many doors. Suddenly one opened and a man came out. Martha almost stopped breathing. But the man only smiled at her.

"Buenos dias," he said, and emptied a basket into a garbage pail.

Martha walked out of the alley. On the sidewalk she stood looking around. Then her confidence came on strong.

She walked completely around the block. She was free and wore a silly grin. She looked in some shop windows. She looked at the traffic, at the other pedestrians. She had a delightful stroll. Nobody shot her. Nobody molested her in any way.

When she came around in front of the shop again, the guard outside the door went white. She smirked at him and went in.

There was a great commotion going on. Everyone was shouting at everyone else. Then they saw her and stopped.

"Where you go?" asked Juana in English. To Martha the woman looked as if she were about to cry.

Martha paid for the two blouses and went out and got back into the car. She could not help smiling. She knew the guards would not report her little escapade; they could lose their jobs.

But presently her smile faded. She had broken a rule, yes, but a rule no more important than the ones she used to break in college. She longed to break a really big rule. Take a car and go for a drive in the country by herself. Or secretly bring her children down and keep them here and have them with her every day, and just defy the State Department. Or have an affair. But who with? The idea of an affair seemed ridiculous to her. Getting one started with all these bodyguards all around would be a trick, and keeping it quiet would be quite another.

11

A CABLE FROM CRUTCHER, who was the DEA's country attaché in Peru, had come into the embassy overnight. When Douglas reached his office, it was on his desk. A major Peruvian trafficker had been arrested and his address book had given up a phone number in Colombia. Could the Bogotá office find out to whom it belonged?

There was a note from Gallagher's secretary attached to the cable. "Mr. Gallagher asks if you'll take care of this."

Supposedly Douglas was the second-ranking agent in this office—by courtesy if not by actual grade—and checking out phone numbers was a job for a junior man. He thought he knew what was bugging Gallagher and he went down the hall to his office. But it was empty.

"Where is he?" he demanded of the secretary.

"Tied up all morning."

"We'll see," said Douglas, and he went looking for him.

He found him in the conference room standing over a polygraph operator who was adjusting his machine. Lying on the conference table was a copy of Jane's newspaper. It was folded to show her front-page account of the destruction of the jungle lab. The name in the headline was Douglas's.

One of the armored car guards was sitting at the table

already hooked up to the sensors, and others were on line in the corridor outside the room.

"Checking out phone numbers—" Douglas began.

"Do it for me as a favor," Gallagher interrupted blandly. "While I polygraph all these guys."

The embassy guards were Colombians. Those who guarded the DEA agents were ex-cops. In a country where the police forces were known to have been penetrated by the traffickers, they had had to pass polygraph tests before being hired. To make sure they didn't switch sides, Gallagher repolygraphed them every three months, sometimes more often.

"Send Bannon."

"I need him to help me on this," said Gallagher blandly.

"Oh?" said Douglas, "I would have thought you and the operator were enough."

"It's going to take us most of the day," said Gallagher.

The folded newspaper still lay on the table. Both of them eyed it. The headline read: DOUGLAS RAID BLASTS JUNGLE LAB.

"Kilpatrick."

"Gone to Barranquilla," said Gallagher blandly.

The guards would come to work and, with no prior warning, be hooked up to the sensors and subjected to questions. Control questions such as: Is your name José Sanchez, are you a Colombiano, do you smoke? And the questions that counted: Have you taken money from traffickers? Has any trafficker made contact with you, or attempted to make contact with you? If the graphs showed movement, the guard or guards were fired on the spot.

"There's no one else available," said Gallagher blandly.

Maybe there was, maybe there wasn't.

Douglas could refuse, but it would intensify the friction between them. He decided he had best submit. "Well, if there's no one else," he said, "okay." I've got to learn to get along with this guy, he told himself. I've got to win him over.

"Good," said Gallagher. He picked up the newspaper,

glanced at it a moment, then dropped it into the basket beside the chair.

The two men looked at each other. I don't need this, Douglas told himself. I've got to get out of this country.

Gallagher gestured toward the line outside the door. "Take the last two guys on the line as your backup."

Douglas nodded, and left.

In New York, putting a name to a phone number took at most a few minutes. One called telephone company security, and got called back with the information almost immediately.

But this was Colombia. The traffickers were supposed to have bribed even senior telephone officials, it was impossible to tell which ones. One took what precautions one could and hoped for the best. Today Douglas made an appointment with a Señor Maldonado, who was believed to be honest, then got into one of the armored cars and was driven through midtown Bogotá traffic to the Telephone Building on Calle Veintetres.

His guards jumped out with their machine guns and saw him into the building and he took the elevator to the sixth floor, where Maldonado made him wait for some time. Though honest, if he was honest, Maldonado was extremely conscious of his station; generally he made police types cool their heels a good long time in his waiting room.

But finally he came forth, gave Douglas a smile and a handshake, and invited him into his office.

As always in this country, the usual preliminaries were essential. It was only after commenting on the weather, and on last night's soccer scores, that Douglas could hand over his phone number, after which he waited again while Maldonado went down the hall with it. Presently he returned with the appropriate name and address, and Douglas thanked him and left.

This was not the end of the assignment. Name and address meant nothing to him; he had not supposed they would. He got back into the armored car and was driven through the same choked traffic to DAS headquarters, where he went up to see General Nuñez, handed over what he had, then sat with Nuñez while an underling went off to run it through the DAS intelligence files by hand. They had no computers here.

"This may take a little time," said Nuñez.

"No hurry," said Douglas, who was growing more impatient by the minute.

Nuñez ordered an aide to bring in coffee.

"Those wounded Indios we brought back," said Nuñez.

"Yes?"

"Two of them died."

"I'm sorry to hear it."

Nuñez's uniform, Douglas saw, had been cut by an excellent tailor.

"The other is not expected to make it."

They sipped strong Colombian coffee from thin china cups.

"Now we have to bury them."

"Well—"

"If we had left them there the fire would have taken care of it."

"Sorry," said Douglas.

"I'm not blaming you, you understand."

Finally the underling came back into the office, clicked his heels, and handed Nuñez a paper.

"It's a house to the south of here near the village of Fosca," said Nuñez. He pushed the paper across the desk. "A safe house apparently. No one lives there but caretakers. It's owned by Pablo Marzo."

Douglas thanked him and stood up.

"Now we know he's doing business in Peru," Nuñez said. "But we knew that already."

Douglas got back into his armored car and was driven back through the same choking traffic. For thirty minutes he sat among cars that inched forward while sending out noxious fumes. By the time he reached the embassy he had missed lunch. The hot table was closed and the basement cafeteria nearly empty. He carried a sandwich and coffee up to his office and on the scrambler sent the required message to

Crutcher in Peru. It had taken him more than four hours to put a name to Peru's phone number, information that was of no particular importance either there or here.

He looked in on Gallagher. The polygraph operator was gone, as were the guards. "Polygraphing over?" he asked.

"It didn't take as long as I thought," said Gallagher.

Douglas nodded.

"How'd that phone number work out?" inquired Gallagher.

"The phone number is taken care of."

"Good work. Anything I should know?"

"No."

Gallagher dismissed him with a wave of the hand. "Appreciate it," he said.

Douglas went back to his own office where he stood peering out the window. I want to go back to America, he thought. He had conceived a positive ache to go home. It made him remember the way he used to long for things when he was a little boy, and this notion made him laugh at himself. He was not a little boy and he could hang on here for as long as he had to.

"The piece was all right?" inquired Jane.

"I told you it was."

"I sense a hesitation in there somewhere. All right but."

Douglas laughed. "Why would I tell you it was fine if I didn't think so?"

Jane looked at him. "I don't know," she said. "Why would you?"

He had the feeling that she could see his motives clearly enough. He wasn't particularly proud of them. It was never pleasant to use somebody. Then he thought: I got on the front page and she got on the front page. I used her and she used me. We used each other. "Well," he said, "you did embarrass me a little, I guess. I didn't singlehandedly blow up that lab. I wasn't quite that heroic."

"Nuñez said you were."

"He said that?"

"He was very effusive."

Douglas was surprised.

Dressed in tennis whites, they were seated on lawn chairs next to the tennis court at the embassy residence, waiting to play. Jane had smooth tanned legs, Douglas thought.

On the court Gallagher was giving a lesson to Ambassador Thompson's wife.

"He's very good, isn't he?" said Douglas. "He can drop the ball in the same spot every time. That's not easy."

"Suppose I told you I was thinking of going to Medellín," Jane said.

"I'd say you had a death wish."

"Why?"

He had glanced at her sharply. "You know very well why."

"Tell me again."

It was about 6 P.M. on a cool, sunny day.

"You're talking about the headquarters of the cartel," said Douglas. "You're talking about the murder capital of the world. Medellín is—"

"—a good story," said Jane.

On the court Gallagher had moved to Martha's side of the net. He was standing behind her, his chest against her back, his hand over hers on her racquet, his arm moving hers back and forth. As she looked up into his face, a quizzical smile played about her mouth. Supposedly he was trying to teach her a stroke, but Douglas couldn't decide which one.

"Is there something between those two?" said Jane.

"I doubt it." The idea had never occurred to him. "I mean, why should there be?"

"Reporters don't dare go there anymore," said Jane.

"You may not get kidnapped," he told her. "You may only get shot."

"It hasn't been written about in ages. That's why it's a good story."

"Bring plenty of bodyguards."

"You ever been there?"

"Embassy personnel are not allowed to go to Medellín."

Jane resumed her study of Gallagher and Martha. Her brows narrowed, and she said: "I think there is."

"Is what?"

Jane turned to look at him. "You're not embassy personnel. You're the New York Police Department. You don't have to obey embassy rules. You could go there if you wanted."

"The DEA doesn't even dare go there."

"They used to have a Medellín office. They closed it up and bugged out. What about it? Would you go with me?"

"As your bodyguard?"

"Not exactly, no."

It was to him a harebrained scheme. Very likely she could go down there and come back and nothing would happen. But he was certainly not going with her.

Gallagher and Martha Thompson were coming off the court. Martha's face was flushed and sweaty, Douglas noted, and her nipples were showing through her tennis dress.

"We could fly down," said Jane. "What does it take, thirty minutes? We could have lunch, look around and come back."

Gallagher and Martha went into the cabana to change. Gallagher was carrying both racquets. "That ought to be safe enough," said Jane. "What do you say?"

Douglas, who was on his feet, started toward the court. "I say let's play tennis."

He walked out onto the court, and she followed. At the net he said: "Tennis is not a cop's game. You're probably better than I am. If you are, please don't laugh."

Her smile caused his heart to give an unexpected lurch. But he shut off that line of thought. You are not interested in getting involved with her, he told himself. Not her nor anyone else. You are interested in her for one reason only: because she's useful.

When they began to rally Jane was unable to keep the ball in the court, and she came forward to the net and began apologizing. She had been playing tennis since high school, but everything she hit flew into the fence. "I don't know what's the matter, I—"

"It's the altitude," he told her. "Calm down. The balls tend to sail. Bogotá is at eighty-four hundred feet. You'll get the hang of it."

Presently her shots began to stay in, and he saw her relax a little. Douglas himself had learned tennis at thirty-eight when he had made captain and moved to the suburbs. As a result he had relatively few shots that he could stroke cleanly and with power. Jane was a much more schooled player and he saw that it was going to be possible for them to play on more or less equal terms. This was a relief, and he began to have fun. He had been looking for something that would throw them together more, and he believed now he had found it. A total mismatch would have been awkward for them both—awkward while they played, awkward afterward.

They were at the net picking up balls. Jane said: "They've been in there rather a long time, don't you think?" And she pointed her chin in the direction of the cabana.

"What a—nice—idea," Martha Thompson said. She was gasping and it was hard for her to get the words out. "I was beginning—to think—it would never—come into your—head."

She was in the shower stall with Gallagher. She felt as if she were floating or flying, no longer attached to the ground. She was standing on tiptoes on Gallagher's insteps, her arms around his neck, their bodies pressed together, the water sluicing down over them. Ropes of her hair were hanging down his back. He was all the way in her, driving her rump against the wall of the shower stall. In between thrusts she rubbed her breasts all over him.

The cabana had two changing rooms, men's and women's, each with its own shower. This one was on the men's side. The street clothes that hung on the pegs outside were Gallagher's. The sweaty tennis togs piled on top of the sneakers were Gallagher's also. He had been under the shower wondering about Martha on the other side of the wall. He thought he had perceived signals but wasn't sure. Even though he had had no intention of making a move in her direction, the possibilities had given him an erection.

Suddenly Martha had come into his changing room. She had come in almost silently, but he had heard her. His back was to her. He knew he had not bothered to pull the shower curtain closed. He had been facing up into the nozzle, rinsing the soap out of his hair, eyes tightly shut, and at first he had not dared turn or open them. When he did turn she had looked hesitant, he thought, almost demure if a naked woman can look demure under such circumstances, unsure of herself certainly. But then her glance had dropped to the state he was in, and immediately that quick little smile had come on, and from then on she had been all confidence. It took little enough to give women confidence, but that always did it. It gave them a confidence that was absolute. Martha's body was sweaty, but otherwise dry. She had walked straight in under the water into his arms.

Gallagher was appalled at what he was doing. The ambassador's wife—my God. If he was found out, he was ruined, his DEA career over, and just when it was going so well. The entire three-thousand-man DEA was focused on one spot in the world right now, Colombia, and Colombia was him. He received personal messages from the director. The president of the United States had once called him up on the phone. He was at present the fair-haired boy of the entire agency and knew it, but Martha Thompson had just put all of that at peril. He believed he would sooner have got into a gun battle than get involved with Martha Thompson, but it was too late now.

Martha was in the throes of sexual ecstasy, apparently. Women sometimes reached astonishing levels of passion. It was never expected. It was always shocking. She was writhing on him and groaning so loudly he was afraid she could be heard on the tennis court. Gallagher himself was as far removed from passion as a man actually engaged in sexual congress could be. His principal emotion was fear. He was cerebrating as keenly and rapidly as ever before in his life, he believed, maintaining his body and its desires under strict control, all stops on hold. That part of his body, though iron-hard, could be controlled, he had to control it, until he had figured out how this thing had happened. If they were caught, meaning if he was caught, which seemed to him likely, how culpable was he, and could he escape the consequences? Was there any way to save his career? His body was clamoring for release, but he was trying to dominate it until he had had time to think, to decide, to solve all these riddles.

"Did you lock the outer door?" he asked Martha. He himself certainly hadn't, his one concession to what he had perhaps wished to happen. But he had never expected it to. If he had he would have locked it. Or gone back to his apartment in his sweaty tennis clothes and showered there.

"No one—will—come in," Martha panted.

"You didn't lock it?"

"Let them come in, I don't care. Let them see us."

That was passion talking. She couldn't possibly mean it, he hoped, but she had said it, and it could happen. "Jesus," said Gallagher.

He broke loose, ran out through the changing room to the door, and locked it.

When he turned he saw that Martha had run out right behind him. She was giggling and pointing down at him. "If anybody had come in, you would have looked pretty silly sticking out like that." Yes, and even sillier with the naked, dripping-wet Martha only a step behind him. The top half of the door was glass but it was hung with curtains. Gallagher pushed them aside and peered out. Ray Douglas and his girlfriend were still playing tennis. No one else was in sight.

"Let's get back in the shower," said Martha, and she took him in hand and led him where she wanted him to go.

The tall skinny Gallagher was six feet two, about 155 pounds. He wore his brown hair in a crew cut. He had blue eyes, a ruddy Irish complexion, a generous mouth and, now, a mat of soapy chest hair. He was from Notre Dame, where he had captained the tennis team, and had spent several pious months considering becoming a priest. By the time he graduated in the middle of his class he had decided to become an FBI agent instead and he took the test, but they did not select him. He had taken a number of tests, and the U.S. Marshal Service did select him. He joined and thereafter spent what seemed to him an interminable period of time taking prisoners to the toilet on airplanes.

He transferred into the DEA, which was a new agency then, being an amalgamation of most of the smaller, specialized agencies which previously had attempted to cope with the drug scourge, and which wanted him because he spoke Spanish. As the DEA swelled in importance and size, Gallagher rose steadily in rank. He was not a spectacular performer. He was known as a nose-to-the-grindstone type agent. He was assigned to sit for hours on wiretaps of Spanish-speaking suspects. He was good with paper. Other agents came to him to do the affidavits on warrants and Title III telephone intercepts. When he prepared a case for court, his work was impeccable.

He had got one supremely lucky break as far as his career was concerned, and this was appointment to the Office of Professional Responsibility, the DEA's anticorruption squad, where, within a year, he arrested a former partner who had accepted money from a marijuana ring. Gallagher had a Catholic tendency to see the world in black or white. His former partner was guilty of a crime and had betrayed the agency as well, and although the man began to cry as the handcuffs snapped on, Gallagher felt very little compassion and he did not flinch in his duty.

In an agency perpetually worried about internal corruption, this stamped Gallagher as incorruptible, and from then on his rise was rapid. A year ago he had been offered Bogotá, together with promotion to G-16 rank. Of course he wanted to take the job. But he had a wife and two teenaged sons, and his wife got furious and told him to turn it down. He was living and working in Washington at the time. Bogotá was a danger post and he could bring his wife but would not be permitted to bring his sons. On the other hand, like every other civil servant assigned to Bogotá, he would be paid in addition to salary a fifteen percent cost of living differential plus a twenty percent salary increment as danger pay. A thirty-five percent raise! Bogotá seemed to him a place to get rich. And if he had any success at all he would be brought back to the States in two or three years and made agent in charge in Los Angeles or New York, with promotion to G-18.

If he wanted Bogotá, he would have to "volunteer." The DEA maintained the fiction that no agent was ever ordered to serve in such posts against his will.

Gallagher's wife was adamant. She was not abandoning her children, she said. He could go to South America by himself. He argued with her, pleaded with her, pointed out the advantages again and again, but finally, glumly, went off to Bogotá alone.

It was the most demanding and at the same time most exciting assignment he had ever had. But at night he was alone and he began to be tortured by sexual fantasies and desires. Hot flashes came over him for no reason. It was like being a teenage boy all over again. There was no way he could slake these desires. For him there were no women available. Given the security restrictions in force he could not go out into the town looking for one, and in the embassy it was known that he was married. There would have been no way to keep such a liaison quiet. His career came first. He was called to Washington for conferences occasionally. He saw his wife. Between times he sublimated his sexuality the same way he had done in college when contemplating the priesthood—by forcing himself to concentrate hard on something else, usually some tennis match he had won, bringing the match vividly into his head, winning point after point until such time as the sexual urges went away, usually within a few minutes.

Martha and Gallagher, though again conjoined, were resting. Their position in relation to each other was the same as before except that his legs were widely spread so that her feet could

reach the floor—so that she could be more comfortable.
Water still sluiced down. He supposed Martha must have
orgasmed early on, and perhaps several times since. He didn't
know for sure. How was he supposed to know? How could
a man ever tell? He himself had not, and given his anxiety
level wondered if he even could.

Martha gave no sign of wishing to let go of him, but she
seemed to be feeling jolly now instead of passionate, in the
mood to make conversation.

"You know what I wish? I wish we could get dressed and
go out to dinner."

"Well, we can't."

"And after dinner I'd like us to go to a disco and go
dancing."

"We can't do that either." He found this conversation—
or, rather, what it portended—frightening. He did not want
her to want to go out with him in public. He wanted her to
forget him and today entirely.

"Do they have discos here?"

"I think they do."

"I want us to be together out where there are people who
can see us."

"We are together. Can't be much more together than this,
can we?"

"I think I'm in love with you."

"That's nice." Nice? It was terrifying. She was an unstable
woman, he believed. Everything pointed to it, especially the
way she had precipitated herself onto him. He saw her as a
woman who would not be able to keep her mouth shut.

"You at least get to go outside where there are people,"
she said. "I haven't been out alone since I've been here. I'm
surprised they let me walk in the garden alone, let me walk
onto the tennis court alone."

"Playing tennis is nice, isn't it?" He did not know what
else to say to her.

"Fuck tennis," said Martha Thompson.

"I'll play with you any time you like—tennis, that is."
He tried a smile.

Her arms came around his neck and she clung to him. "You know what I'd like? I'd like us to walk in the street hand in hand so everyone could see us together, and we'd pass a shop and go into it and you'd buy me something for being so nice to you and—"

She was beginning to come on again. He could see it happening. The slackness that came over her face. Eyes that began to glaze over.

"You certainly are being nice to me," he said.

By holding himself back he had made this act incomplete, he believed. This was one of the wild thoughts coursing through his head—one among many. He had never wanted anything to do with the ambassador's wife. He saw himself up on charges. But if the act ended here he would have a chance. The act was never consummated, he would argue. If he kept the act incomplete on his side of it, they would only be able to get him on a conspiracy charge—conspiracy to commit fornication with the ambassador's wife—but not for the crime itself, for none had ever taken place. An incomplete act is no act, he would argue. So that even if they convicted him on conspiracy, the sentence when it came down would have to be lenient.

She had begun to moan and groan, and to thrust her wet pelvis against his, to scrape her breasts against the hair on his chest, with the result that all his arguments against taking his pleasure began to seem specious. He was well and truly caught. There was nothing he could do about it. His career was gone, his resolve too, and at last he gave in to what his body wanted to do, couldn't prevent it, couldn't stop himself, couldn't control himself any longer, and he cupped her buttocks and lifted her on tiptoe onto his insteps again.

"We can play—tennis—" he said to her, "—play every—every—oh, oh—day, day, day."

Pursuant to the orders of General Nuñez, Douglas and Jane were held in the airport's VIP lounge until moments before takeoff. Jane, who was becoming increasingly nervous, kept checking her watch. Except for the guard, they were the only two left in the lounge.

She said: "We'll miss the plane."

Her anxiety amused Douglas. "No, we won't." She knew nothing about Nuñez's arrangements, had not recognized these exaggerated security precautions for what they were, and there had seemed no reason to tell her about them. She seemed to believe that the police escort, followed by access to this VIP lounge, had been laid on for her as her paper's representative. It was only her due here—a journalist of her category was no great celebrity in the United States, but this was South America.

Finally one of Nuñez's men led them across the tarmac and up into the airplane via the service steps. As soon as they were aboard the doors closed. Douglas peered down the long, hermetically sealed tube and saw that, with the exception of the two seats that had been held for them, the plane was full.

He dropped into the seat beside Jane. "Hello," he said.

She smiled at last. "I was sure we were going to miss the plane."

In South America the Andes come up the Pacific coast like an arm lying on the edge of a table. At the Colombian border the arm becomes a three-fingered hand. The three fingers run north toward the Caribbean. The middle finger is the highest, a range of eighteen-thousand-foot peaks. Bogotá is on one side of it, Medellín on the other. The two cities are one hundred fifty miles apart by air, more than twice that by road. To drive to Medellín would have taken twelve or more hours. Over much of the road there were precipitous cliffs to one side, ravines to the other. In some places its surface was potholed, even partly disintegrated, and in others it was not under effective government control.

The plane rose into the air. Jane gazed out the porthole at the diminishing capital.

"Let's go over the ground rules once again," Douglas said to her. "We're not going to do anything dangerous, right?"

She smiled. "Right."

It was a Sunday—to him, the quietest as well as the safest

day of the week. "We're going to have lunch, look around, and fly back." Nuñez would have plainclothesmen around them at the airport, and again at the restaurant, and would provide a nondescript taxi for them to drive around in. This had seemed safer than sending them through Medellín in a convoy.

"Well, I do have to get a story out of this," Jane said.

"What does that mean?"

"Otherwise there's no point going," she said defensively.

"What are you trying to tell me?"

"I may go to City Hall and try to interview the mayor."

"It's Sunday, Jane. He won't be there."

"I think he might."

"All right, what have you done?"

"He may be expecting me."

Douglas looked at her.

"At three thirty," she said.

It made Douglas extremely angry, but he hid this. "Jane, we agreed."

"Yes we did, sort of."

"Sort of? An interview with the mayor is not part of our agreement."

Jane gave a smile. "Do you think the mayor might kidnap me?"

"Five minutes after you go into the mayor's office, everyone in Medellín will know you're in town."

"Everyone?" she said.

"The mayor is mayor through the sufferance of the traffickers. If you've made an appointment with him they know already."

This seemed to sober her.

"If anything happens to you it will be an international incident."

"Nothing's going to happen to me."

"The traffickers and the various guerrilla armies have the same object: to destabilize the government. To them, you're a plum. Pick you off and everybody's famous: them, you. You'll have headlines all over the world for a month."

"You're exaggerating."

"Maybe. But it's a risk you're crazy to take."

"No one will bother with me." She blinked her eyes at him, trying to make a joke of it. "I'm just a girl reporter."

"You're your paper."

"My paper okayed it," Jane said stubbornly.

"Sure. If you get kidnapped your editors will be delighted. You think they won't? If you get killed, better yet. It will make them seem important and the paper seem important." He saw this hit home. "You are not going to interview that mayor."

Her jaw set into a grim line. "Indeed I am, though."

General Nuñez had hated the idea of this trip to Medellín. Douglas had said nothing to Gallagher, whom he neither liked nor trusted. But he had sought the advice of Nuñez.

The Colombian government—that part of it not subverted by the traffickers—lived in dread of getting a DEA agent killed. To Nuñez, getting Douglas killed would be equally disastrous.

"You can't go," Nuñez had told him.

"Getting her killed would be even worse," said Douglas.

"Women," Nuñez had said.

"She'll go whether I go with her or not."

Nuñez looked at him.

"If I go, I can control what she does. Give her some protection."

"You won't be able to control her."

Douglas thought Nuñez had misunderstood the relationship. He said carefully: "There is no sentimental attachment between us."

To which Nuñez had replied: "Then you have even less chance to control her. Once you are there, she will do what she wants, you will see."

The plane, having crossed the peaks, descended over green hills, green fields and came in to land. They stepped out onto the staircase and descended to the tarmac. Medellín, being thirty-seven hundred feet lower than Bogotá, was much warmer, and the sunlight was blinding. The air was muggy, hot. The passengers trooped across the concrete into a brand-new terminal that resembled in shape the great train sheds of the 1900s. Built possibly with drug money, it was all glass and girders, much bigger than required, quite beautiful for an airline terminal, and nearly empty.

Outside waited a row of taxis, but when Jane attempted to step into one, Douglas stopped her. He was looking around for Nuñez's man, who came running up.

"Señor Raymond?" he asked.

This was the name in which Douglas's ticket had been issued.

"That's me," he said and followed the man toward a rather battered car.

Jane was hurrying to keep up. "Señor Raymond?" she said.

He chose not to enlighten her. "Isn't Raymond my name?"

The airport was on a plateau above the city. As they drove downhill Jane had her notebook out and was recording her impressions. Douglas was watching out the back window. Presently, satisfied they weren't being followed, he too watched the scenery, though not all the time. Often he watched her profile. He was attracted to her certainly, and he admitted that he needed her if he was to keep getting his name in the paper. For the rest, she represented a problem. Women were always a problem, but this was the first time one had ever risked getting him killed.

Medellín is an industrial city of two million. When it came into sight below, Douglas saw that it was spread out the length of its narrow valley, and that its buildings could barely be seen for the smog. The mountains to either side were very high.

They came down into the center of the city. To Douglas it was just a city: busy, crowded, noisy. Tall office buildings. Bad air. The office buildings were all new and there were handsome sculptures outside. There were many parks. The town was building a metro. Many of the concrete stanchions were already in place, and others were rising. There seemed to be a separate traffic jam around each one. It seemed richer than Bogotá. Not too rich though. The buses were very old. They had protruding noses, roof racks, and ladders up the back. They were painted green, yellow, white. They were as multicolored as carousels, and they were jammed.

As their car passed the Plaza de Toros, Jane asked the driver to stop and as soon as he had pulled to the curb she jumped out. There was traffic in the street and pedestrians moving along the sidewalk. Douglas stepped out after her, his body tense. There were bullfight posters glued to the walls, new ones on top of disintegrating old ones. Jane approached them, studied them, then came back to the car.

"Isn't it a darling little plaza?" said Jane.

"I wouldn't know."

"It only seats about five thousand. In Spain they're much bigger than this."

Douglas was glancing carefully about. He was aware she knew things he didn't know, had lived a life different from his. But he wasn't thinking about that. In theory an assassination or kidnapping took time to set up. Therefore, assuming they got in and out of Medellín quickly, and kept moving while they were here, they were safe enough. "We better get back in the car," Douglas said.

"There's a corrida this afternoon. Let's go to it."

"No, Jane."

"The bullfighters are from Spain. I've seen one of them. He's very good."

"No, Jane."

"The bulls are David Ley bulls."

They looked at each other. Both had been briefed by the same people, according to whom David Ley was one of the four or five top *narcotraficantes*.

"If they're his bulls, he'll be there."

"No, Jane."

"They might all be there. The bullring is where they do their business, I've heard."

Douglas had heard this too.

"Aren't you curious to see what they look like in the flesh?"

"Jane, it's out of the question." Yes, he was curious. The answer was still no.

She got back in the car. "You're missing something," she said. "I bet it would have been a good bullfight," she said wistfully.

The driver began to steer through neighborhoods. In the best of them there were lovely villas with tiled roofs, huge TV saucers in the gardens, and steel bars on all the windows. The streets were all steeply pitched, and in the poor neighborhoods there were places where parts of the hillsides had crumbled in storms. Sometimes the resulting landslide had taken houses down with it, and they could see pieces of them protruding from the mud.

Jane had her notebook out and had begun questioning the driver about the traffickers. He proved to be a talkative young man, and he began to alter their route to include sites particular to certain of them, the city's most famous sons so to speak, starting with the houses in which they lived, or had lived, pointing them out almost with pride. It was like a Hollywood tour of the homes of the stars. Here was David Ley's villa, and Antonio Lucientes had lived in that one there. Here was the barrio Pablo Marzo built and gave to the poor. One day Marzo went in there with a satchel full of bills and began tossing them in all directions while the poor scrambled after them.

Douglas had heard this story. He believed it. Why not, the guy was a billionaire. And he was smart enough to see that in his business popularity was important.

And that building there with the side blown off belonged to Pablo Marzo also, the driver said.

Leaning out the window, Douglas peered up at a six-story apartment building. Nearly the entire wall was gone. All the floors sagged. He could see into the rooms. The villas all around had been flattened too. A lot of innocent people had lost their homes.

Marzo's enemies, the driver said, had parked a car loaded with explosives beside the building. He was living in his penthouse on top at the time. The device went off, and boom!

They tried to kill him, but they missed. The driver sounded glad they had missed.

Who is this driver? Douglas asked himself. Where did Nuñez get him from? Nuñez, when he had opted for making Jane's visit as unobtrusive as possible, hadn't known about the appointment with the mayor.

"See that nightclub?" the driver said, pointing. "That's the one they go to."

Next he took them down a street where Pablo Marzo had been seen jogging one day at dawn, supposedly. Or maybe it was his ghost, Douglas thought. With so many people anxious to kill him, Marzo could not afford to go jogging on this street or any other.

To this driver, and people like him, the traffickers were seen not as murderous gangsters but as folk heroes, the most generous men in the city and the world. Robin Hood and his merry men holding entire governments at bay. This very street, on which Marzo had or had not jogged, had taken on a quality of myth.

It gave Douglas a sinking feeling. How did you fight that sort of thing? The ordinary people of the city had the best interests of the traffickers at heart, not those of the police. Every time the police prepared to move, they warned them if they could, impeded the raid if they could.

Jane was taking it all down in her notebook.

"Take us to the restaurant," Douglas ordered the driver curtly. "Wait outside."

"Sobering, isn't it," said Jane in English.

He was pleased that she had discerned his feelings, and he gave her a small smile.

The restaurant was in a Spanish-colonial-style house. The tables were set up outside under arcades around a small central garden in which a fountain spilled water down into a marble basin. The tablecloths were linen, the silverware heavy. The waiters wore white coats. Douglas chose a table where he could sit with his back in a corner, and as unobtrusively as possible he moved his gun around from the small of his back to his jacket pocket. He felt a bit like Wild Bill Hickok, but to ignore such a basic precaution would be foolish. It was Nuñez who had picked the restaurant, and he looked around for the man or men Nuñez was supposed to have here, but did not see anyone who looked likely. He did not, under the circumstances, like restaurants. He had been in too many in Brooklyn or Little Italy in which Mafia chieftains lay on the floor covered with blood and pasta. For assassinations, a restaurant was ideal. It localized the victim, and you had until the dessert course to get the job set up.

He began studying the menu. "Look," he said to Jane, "they have *bormigas culones*."

"What's that?"

"A famous Colombian delicacy, roasted ants." It was true. He showed her the line on the menu.

"Delicious," he said, "yum, yum."

"I'm tired of them," said Jane. "I think I'll order something else."

Colombian soups were odd and quite marvelous, Douglas told her. And the *lechona* was good: roast suckling pig stuffed with strong spices, rice, and peas. Or the *cabrito*: roast baby goat served with yucca and a cornmeal patty called an *arepa*.

"You're a pretty adventurous eater—for a cop," Jane said.

"Well, I've been in Colombia longer than you."

It was their first time in a restaurant together, and he watched her carefully for whatever her choices might reveal.

The waiter was standing over their table.

"I'll have the pigeon soup, and the *cabrito*," said Jane to him.

"And the corn soup for me," said Douglas, "and *lechona*."

While waiting to be served they sipped a local punch called *canelazo*—rum flavored with cinnamon, sugar, and lemon juice, he explained—and he got her to talk about her career. For the first time in their acquaintanceship it was he who did the interviewing.

She was the only permanent American correspondent based in Bogotá, she said, which he hadn't realized.

She sounded proud. "In other countries, all the correspondents pal around together, as I understand it. I have no one to pal around with.''

''I'm palling around with you right now,'' he joked. And I'm going to stick with you, he thought, even when you pull stunts like this interview with the mayor.

They drank a bottle of wine from Chile, both got a bit high, and as the luncheon progressed Douglas, to his surprise, found himself becoming more and more relaxed in her presence.

''Whose idea was it to come to South America in the first place,'' she asked him. ''Yours or Windsell's?''

''The mayor's, I think.''

Perhaps it was the wine or her slightly flushed cheeks, or the nearness of her across the tablecloth, but he told her exactly what had happened.

One second later he realized he had just placed his career in her control.

''You mustn't print that,'' he said, and to reinforce his point placed his hand over hers. ''You could hurt me if you did.''

Jane's eyes were fixed on the tablecloth. ''I would never hurt you,'' she said.

She did not remove her hand. Did that mean he could trust her? Or was it meant only to keep him in the mood for more confidences? Finally he removed his hand from on top. In some way it seemed dangerous not to.

''I've found an apartment,'' Jane said.

He looked up from his plate.

''It's in your building,'' she said. The embassy's press officer had found it for her, she added. She would move in the first of the month.

''Great,'' said Douglas. Sticking to her like glue would become easier, but it might also put a strain on their relationship. He wondered if she realized he was using her, or trying to use her. Well, she called him constantly for leads and information, so she was certainly using him. She was using him today to facilitate this trip to Medellín.

''We'll be neighbors,'' he said. ''You'll finally get to taste my other two dishes." Apart from making use of him, did she like him at all?

"I want to ask a favor of you," Douglas said as he called for the check. "I want you to cancel your interview with the mayor."

"No," she said, and they stared stubbornly at each other. "Please let me pay that," she said. "It will go on my expense account."

He was so annoyed with her that he let her do it.

They waited in the mayor's outer office.

"When you made your appointment," said Douglas, "what did you say about me?"

"I didn't mention you."

"Are you sure?"

"I don't lie."

He looked at her.

"There was no reason to mention you," she said defensively.

They sat in silence until a male secretary came out and said the mayor would see them now.

"Are you coming in with me?" said Jane.

"I'm not letting you out of my sight."

Jane thought about this. "How shall I introduce you?"

"Introduce me as a famous drug-buster. So they can feel good when they assassinate both of us as we go out the door."

"Is that what you are," she asked mischievously, "a famous drug-buster?"

Douglas said nothing.

"I could introduce you as my boyfriend."

"This is not a joke, Jane."

"Or my husband. How about that?"

"Fine."

"Husband, then. This is a Catholic country. They don't like illicit arrangements in countries like this."

"If I were your husband I'd drag you out of here by the hair."

"Would you?" Jane grinned at him. "That might be fun."

The interview lasted forty minutes. The mayor, who met them at the door to his office, was every inch a politician: warm smile, warm handshake, warm words. He led them into the room by the arms. This excess physical contact put Douglas off.

In English the mayor complimented Jane on her Spanish; she complimented him on his English. She and Douglas took chairs in front of his big desk, the interview began, and from then on Douglas spoke not one word until, when it had come to an end, he told the mayor thank you and goodbye.

As a detective he believed he knew how to interview people. It was one of the things detectives did every day. He watched Jane work and decided she was very good. She began by asking the mayor about his work as mayor, a subject that did not interest her in the slightest, he guessed, but she continued on it for some time while making assiduous notes. But finally, with the mayor feeling ever more confident and cordial, she moved into what Douglas presumed did interest her: the possibility of amnesty for the major traffickers of the so-called Medellín Cartel.

The mayor was in favor of amnesty, he said, and Douglas supposed this would be the headline of the article she would write. It was what the drug lords wanted, the mayor said. In Colombia none of them was under indictment at this time, you understand, but they were worried about possible future prosecutions, and about possible extradition to the States. If amnesty was granted, then in exchange they had promised to give up their businesses, end the violence and murder, and repatriate the billions of dollars Colombia needed so much, which at present they had stashed in banks around the world.

As Jane's questions became ever more sharply focused, the mayor became eloquent. He sounded like a man making a speech. The traffickers would keep their bargain, he said. Why shouldn't they? They had all the money in the world. Now all they wanted was the freedom to spend it, to live like other people, to watch their children and grandchildren grow up. Freedom from fear of the DEA, fear of extradition to the United States. Sure it was galling to grant amnesty to such people, but there was no choice. There was no other way to fight them. No previous criminal conspiracy anywhere in the world had ever been this wealthy or this violent. They were able to offer their adversaries—cops, judges, prosecutors, whoever—a choice, you see, *plomo o oro*, lead or gold. What a choice! Do you want to be killed, or do you want to be rich?

In the car Jane was jubilant. "Did you hear what he was saying? This is a story that will make page one."

Douglas leaned over the seat to speak to the driver. "Take us to the airport, please."

Jane waited about ten seconds, then said: "Let's go to the bullfight."

"That's not possible, Jane."

"Sure it is. You know you want to go."

Annoyed, he said: "I don't want to go and we have a plane to catch."

"There'll be another plane."

"Our reservations are on this one." In truth, the chance of a glimpse of certain of the traffickers up close attracted him. Alone he might have chanced it. But he did not believe he had the right to take risks, however slight, with her life.

In the back of the car she sat beside him and said nothing.

"We probably couldn't get in anyway," he said to humor her. He gave her a patronizing pat on the knee. "Since we don't have tickets."

The Plaza de Toros had come into view ahead. The sidewalk out front was full of people.

"As a matter of fact, we do," said Jane.

"Do what?"

"Have tickets."

"What?"

"I sent for them last week," she said. And then in Spanish: "Stop here please, driver." She was rummaging through her handbag. Her hand came out with two tickets. "Here's yours. Do with it what you want."

She got out of the car and marched through the crowd toward the entry gate.

Douglas jumped out, hurried after her, and managed to grab her arm. "Wait," he said.

"I'm going to the bullfight."

They stared at each other. Short of throwing her over his shoulder, he could not stop her.

"Just let me give instructions to the chauffeur."

And so, having no choice, he attended his first bullfight. He liked the opening parade, the costumes, the pageantry of it all. He liked some of the capework. He liked the atmosphere of the place, the cigar smoke, the noise of the mob in the cheap seats in the sun. He thought the beasts were gorgeous. He enjoyed the power of their snorting, the way their hooves kicked up dust when they stopped short.

Jane beside him explained what was happening and why, making him feel somehow uneducated. She was trying to be pleasant and nice to him, working hard at it. But every time he looked at her he got angry, and he hardly spoke a word in response.

David Ley, Pablo Marzo, and Carlos Von Bauzer were there in a *palco* about ten rows above them. So were several of the others whom Douglas recognized from photos. So were about twenty tough-looking young men with briefcases who crowded the back of the *palco*. Bodyguards, obviously. The briefcases would contain Mac 10s and Uzis. Probably there were additional bodyguards out back on the ramp all eyeing each other suspiciously. The drug lords did not trust bullfight fans, nor each other either. Sometimes, when Douglas glanced their way, they seemed engrossed in the spectacle. Other times their heads had come together and they seemed concentrated on whatever negotiations had brought them here in the first place.

Ley's bulls were behaving very well, apparently. Douglas couldn't tell, but Jane said it was so and when he glanced up into the *palco* Ley seemed pleased with himself, and the others were all congratulating him.

"He's a handsome man, isn't he?" said Jane.

"Is he?"

"I think most women would find him so."

"He's a drug trafficker and murderer."

"He's the most interesting one of the bunch," said Jane.

A dead bull was being dragged out of the ring. "The others were all criminals to start with. He's educated, comes from a good family, he's never been in jail—"

"You should marry him. He has everything."

"Excuse me a moment," said Jane, and before he could stop her she was in the aisle and climbing the steps toward the *palco*.

He was stupefied. From the back of the *palco* he saw bodyguards dart forward, guns having appeared like magic. If Jane saw them, she gave no notice. They were above and behind Ley, and the stone balustrade was in the way, so perhaps she didn't see them.

When she was close enough she called up to Ley. Douglas saw spectators all around crane their necks or stand to get a better view. Then Ley too stood. Reaching down over the balustrade, he shook Jane's hand. They spoke for a few seconds, Ley shook his head no, Jane handed up her business card, and it was over. She turned and started back down.

When she again took her seat beside him, Douglas said nothing, did not even look at her. What could he say? Warn her not to do it? But it was already done.

His resolute silence lasted ten minutes, then was overcome by curiosity. "What did you say to him?" he demanded.

"I asked him for an interview."

"And he said?"

"He said no. He said perhaps another time."

When the bullfight ended it was 7:30 P.M., the airport was an hour away and the Air Bridge was about to close down for the night. The bullring emptied out. They went out with the crowd into the street. Were they in danger? Douglas didn't know. Their presence at the bullfight was a surprise, certainly. Killings took time to set up, presumably. In any case there was nothing he could do about it. He stood with his hand on his gun in his coat waiting for the car to come by to pick them up. They watched the several drug lords climb into what looked like bulletproof cars while their bodyguards held station all around them facing outward. It was exactly in this manner that Douglas, Gallagher, and the other DEA agents got into their cars when moving about Bogotá. So the technique was perfect. Did they learn it from us, or did we learn it from them? Douglas wondered. Maybe we learned it from each other.

Their car pulled up at the curb. "We'll go to the Intercontinental," Jane said. "Is that all right?"

They had no choice but to go to a hotel. Nuñez had been right. He could not control her. It was hopeless.

"I don't even have a toothbrush," he muttered.

"I have one. You can use mine."

"Do you have a razor for me too?"

"No. No razor, I'm afraid."

"I'll buy a razor in the lobby. A toothbrush too."

He half believed she had planned on spending the night here from the beginning, had probably made a hotel reservation in advance, but when he asked her about it she said no.

"You're certain?"

"Of course I'm certain."

"All right. How are we going to register?"

"Any way you like."

"I've been your husband so far today. For your protection and also for mine, I had better stay your husband in the hotel."

"What are you saying?"

"We'll share a room." Was this really necessary, or was he just trying to impose his will on her?

"Now wait a minute, Ray. Wait a minute. If you think you're—"

It annoyed him beyond words. "Oh, for chrissake. Is it your virginity you're worried about? Your 'most precious possession,' as the nuns used to say? Oh, I forgot. You're not, as they say, intact, are you? Your honor, then. You flatter yourself, lady—"

A subdued Jane said: "I'm sorry, Ray."

"—You really flatter yourself. Don't worry, I won't go near you."

"I didn't mean to insinuate—"

"I'll look the other way while you're getting undressed, and I'll sleep on the couch. It will be like those 1930s movies."

"Maybe we can get a suite," Jane said. "You can have one room and I'll take the other. The paper will pay for it. It will be tough explaining it on my expense account but—"

They looked up and they were at the Intercontinental. It was one of the new ones. They went inside and there were people moving back and forth and it was like any hotel lobby in Baltimore or Tampa. Each of them had been in this hotel twenty times before.

They registered, then followed a bellhop—a boy of about twelve—upstairs. Douglas tipped him and the door closed. Douglas double-locked it. He went through one of the bedrooms and glanced into the bathroom. A basket on the sink contained vials of shampoo, bath gel, shaving cream, plastic-wrapped toothbrushes, a razor. He would not have to shop in the lobby.

"Which room do you want?" asked Jane, when he came out.

"They're identical," said Douglas. He picked up a menu from the sideboard.

Perhaps I'm being too harsh on her, he thought. Where's your sense of humor? he asked himself. She's run rings around you all day, nobody has taken shots at us yet, so I ought to be laughing at all this. It's certainly ridiculous enough. Laughing at her and laughing at myself.

"We're not leaving this room until the car comes to take us to the airport tomorrow," he told her. "I'll call Nuñez and get an escort."

"All right, Ray."

He was acutely conscious of being alone with her in this suite. "We'll eat in." He studied the menu. "We'll order dinner from room service."

"All right, Ray."

"It's our first day as husband and wife," he said, and tried to joke. "We'll eat in, and of course we'll be sleeping in the nude. On honeymoons, that's what people do."

Jane went over to the window and glanced out. "On our honeymoon we had a big fight. How was yours?"

It sent Douglas back in time. His honeymoon; two innocents in a hotel room in Jamaica. The fond memory was there in his head and for a moment he fondled it. "No, no fights," he said.

"You're very lucky."

He inclined his head slightly: compliment acknowledged.

"Your wife died," she said.

"Yes," he said, and the memory moved up twenty-two years. It had been a good marriage. It just hadn't lasted.

He waited for her to say something patronizing or silly. A platitude of some kind, so he could keep her at a distance. But all she did was touch him. He felt her hand briefly on his arm.

She said: "Let's order dinner."

She had a way of creeping up on him when he least expected it, of achieving an intimacy before he could ward her off.

During dinner the intimacy only increased, or so Douglas felt. They had no luggage. They had nothing here but each other. When they had finished he pushed the rolling tray out into the hall and again chain-locked the door. There was not much choice about what to do next. They had nothing to read, no chores to perform, they could not escape from each other. They sat down and watched television. American sitcoms translated into Spanish. The programs were so obvious that Douglas had no trouble tracking them, even though he missed many words. It was a calm, almost domestic evening, and again more intimate than he was ready for. He felt almost married to her. He felt almost like reaching across and holding her hand.

This mood was ruptured when she stood up suddenly and said: "I'll see you in the morning."

Douglas too had stood up. "Goodnight," he said to her back.

She was in the doorway by then. She gave him a smile. "Sleep well," she said, and closed the door between them.

He listened but did not hear her lock it. Did this mean anything? Was he supposed to infer something from it?

He certainly did not want to watch television by himself. He turned it off, then stood there for a time.

He went into the other room and began to get undressed.

He took a shower and then got into bed naked. The sheets were cold. He lay there.

He wondered what Jane was doing. She might be taking a bath. She might be lying awake as he was. If so, what was she thinking?

This whole thing felt very peculiar. She had made him think about her all day. He had been without feelings of that kind for a long time, but was not without them at this moment. I could get dressed, he thought, go across to her room on some pretext or other, see what happens.

She would be—how? Perhaps sitting up in bed, studying her notes. She would make him wait while she too got dressed again, before letting him in. Or she might not let him in at all.

If he went forward with this woman or any other, it would be for him serious. He would be thinking about possibly marrying her. Marriage to him was the natural state. He was not a man for one-night stands.

His wife had lived for him and for her children; whereas this woman had no thought not centered around herself and her paper. Was such a woman what he wanted? Or would he prefer to stay the way he was? At present what he was, basically, was numb. But numbness was not such a disagreeable state, was it?

What would his wife say, if he could talk to her at this moment? What would she advise? Loyalty to a dead woman was absurd. It was nonetheless there, and would have to be overridden.

He spent the next hour trying and failing to fall asleep. Once he thought he heard a phone ring nearby.

When she saw there was shampoo in the basket on the sink and a blow dryer on the wall, Jane took a long shower and washed her hair. After toweling herself off, she sat on the stool in front of the mirror and blow-dried her hair while working it into the shape she wanted. She spent a long time on this too, and on studying her face, her shoulders, her breasts. It felt good to spend time totally on herself, and to primp again the way she had so often done when she was a girl.

When she came out she plumped up the pillows on the bed and sat down against the headboard with her knees up and her notebook on her thighs, and reviewed what she had seen and learned today and pondered what she might write. She had the piece on the mayor favoring amnesty for the traffickers. She would have liked a piece on David Ley, but he had refused an interview. But maybe he would change his mind and call her. He knew where she was, because she had told him. She had called up to him: If you change your mind, I'm at the Intercontinental—for she knew she and Douglas were going to have to spend the night somewhere, and the Intercontinental was Medellín's best hotel.

Ley had not looked or talked like a criminal, and she wondered if the police might be wrong about him. The police had been wrong before. She had the New York journalist's normal distrust of the police. The police were people who operated on emotion and prejudice, and who lied to you. Ley was good-looking, and he had responded to her as a woman. She had seen that. She wondered if her phone would ring. She had read up on him. He was supposed to be a mighty womanizer. He might call just on that basis. An interview with him would be a terrific coup, because there had never been one in the American press.

Finally she put the light out and lay in bed in the dark. For Jane too the sheets felt cold on her flesh and she waited for them to warm up. She was full of yearnings that were too vague to act on, or even to understand. Certainly she was lonely. She thought of Ray Douglas in the next room. Did she want him to come through that door and jump on top of her? Of course not. Then what did she want?

To be held tight in the dark by a man who loved her. Was that so much to ask?

Unfortunately there was no such man anywhere. Not Ray certainly, he didn't even like her as near as she could tell; and—she had faced this truth often enough previously and she faced it again now—there might never be. A sexual romp was easy enough to come by, if that's what she wanted, but love was not. Sexual romps she had had in the past, and when she was in love they were joyous. When she was not they had only made her feel used afterward, as if she had bought a dress and then when she got it home didn't like it. Something that had seemed nice wasn't.

The phone rang beside her head. She grabbed it up instantly, knowing who it must be, hoping she had cut off the ringing before Ray could have heard.

It was Ley himself.

He apologized for calling so late. He hoped he hadn't disturbed her. His voice was pitched low, as if he believed in his ability to seduce women with his voice alone.

Jane had sat up, her legs out of the bed. She put the light on.

Would she like to see his *finca* in the morning? he said. If so, he would send his car for her. Except for the word *finca* he spoke English. *Finca* meant farm. There were poor farms and there were luxurious ones. She suspected Ley's was the luxurious kind.

When she answered, her voice too was low, her purpose different from his: that Ray should not hear her through the doors. She would love to see his *finca*, she said, but—

Ley chuckled. "When women say but, watch out."

Jane did not believe in the elaborate security precautions to which people subjected themselves in Colombia. She did not believe Ley represented any threat to her person. To her this whole security business seemed overblown. The guerrillas sometimes kidnapped people, yes, but almost always in isolated areas, not in the cities; and they were terrified of the traffickers. They had never operated in Medellín and were no threat to anyone here. The traffickers on the other hand were certainly a threat, but not to her. They regularly murdered each other and also any government functionaries who got in their way. But so far they had left foreigners mostly alone. There was no reason why they should bother her. None at all.

Above all she wanted an interview with Ley. It seemed safe to her. It was a risk worth taking.

He would have to come for her himself, she told him. She was not stepping into any car with strangers.

"But of course," he said.

And she would have to be back at the hotel by noon.

"I will regret to lose you so soon, but you shall be back in your hotel by noon." His English was perfect. He had no accent she could discern. Certainly he could pass for an American, and perhaps had.

"I was hoping to offer you lunch."

"No," said Jane.

When she had hung up she began to plan the interview she would do. Her editors would be thrilled. She saw herself being put in for prizes.

Again she remembered Ray. Her first impulse was to go across and tell him. She would get dressed and run over there. If he was asleep she would wake him and— The idea made her smile. He would take one look at her in his room and he would misunderstand.

What did she want to tell him for? He would only try to stop her.

But she did want to tell him. Tell him of her upcoming triumph. Tell him not to worry when he found her gone from the room in the morning. In a sense she was experiencing gratitude—that he had come with her this far, that he was so willing to protect her if need be.

The trouble was, when she stood in his room she would

be clothed and he wouldn't be. He would either be dreadfully embarrassed, or leap to the obvious conclusion.

And tomorrow he could physically prevent her from leaving the suite. She was about to have an exclusive interview with a member of the Medellín Cartel. She was not going to risk losing it.

She phoned down and left a wake-up call for six thirty, then put the light out, got back into bed, and waited to fall asleep.

In the morning she started out of her bedroom with her shoes in one hand and a note for Ray in the other, which she propped up against a lamp. It promised she would be back by noon and gave no other information. No need worrying him unduly.

As she stepped out into the hall and into her shoes, she worried that he would worry anyway. But he had no right to worry. He wasn't her husband or lover. She was doing what she had to do, and the sooner he recognized this, the better.

It was not quite 7 A.M., and she had more than an hour to wait before Ley would come for her, but she had wanted to be out of the suite before there was any chance of Ray being awake and trying to stop her. She went downstairs to the coffee shop and ordered breakfast and read the paper, and the time passed exceedingly slowly. Any minute she expected Ray to come storming into the coffee shop to drag her out, but this did not happen, and at 8 A.M. precisely Ley's car pulled up in front.

12

SHE WENT OUTSIDE and down the steps, and he came around the car and bent down over the back of her hand, lips two inches away. A gesture, and not unpleasant. This was the way hand kissing was actually done in the Latin countries, as she had learned as a little girl in Spain.

His car was an open Ferrari. Leather seats over which moved patches of sunlight. Rumbling noises from beneath the long hood. He held open the car door.

The seat was exceedingly low. Ley got in on his side and reached across her chest, startling her, but it was only her seat belt he was reaching for. He fastened it, gave her a warm smile.

"My latest toy," he said, patting the steering wheel. "But don't worry, I'm not going to show you how fast I can drive it."

She smiled back to show she was not alarmed, never had been, was feeling quite relaxed and confident. Which she was—almost.

They left the hotel driveway. No chauffeur, no bodyguards. He must feel as she did: the national fixation on security was exaggerated. Then she noticed that the car ahead of them had started up when they did—there were four men in it—and that the car behind, which contained another four, followed them out of the driveway.

The street began to climb up through villas and then the villas disappeared below. Shortly after that the entire city was gone, and they were in the trees. The road kept climbing and the country changed, got very green as if they were in a rain forest. A stream tumbled along beside the road, or perhaps it was different streams. It disappeared at times. At other times it cascaded over cliffs high above, the road surface was wet, and they drove through a blowing, momentary haze.

On top the road came out onto a vast green plateau, most of which Ley owned, apparently. There was white fencing on both sides of the road, and in the meadows grazed some of his horses, some of his fighting bulls, for he pointed them out. The meadows looked lush. They were interspersed with copses of what looked to her to be cork oaks.

They came to a gate. The guard car stopped, someone

jumped out and opened it, and they rolled forward over steel spikes that flattened out under the tires. Jane had seen such spikes before; always they had faced the other way. Here they seemed to Jane sinister: an intruder could get in over those spikes but he was not going to get out.

The driveway was long. There were men here and there under the trees. Not doing anything. Just standing there.

"More bodyguards?" she asked him.

Another warm smile. "Men who work for me, yes."

She said: "Why should you need so many bodyguards?"

"I own a bank, an insurance company, some other things. My board of directors worries that harm might come to me."

"From the guerrilla armies?"

"Yes."

"Not the drug traffickers?"

The house had come into view ahead. "They tried to buy this place. Offered any price. I said no, and that was the end of it. They don't bother me."

Jane nodded and, for the time being, stopped. She had learned not to hurry interviews. She was to have four hours with this man, more or less. Better to save her questioning for later.

It was a Mediterranean villa. It would not have been out of place on Spain's Costa Brava. White stucco. Orange tile roof. Big. Many arcades, arches, terraces. Gardeners working around it. Flowers everywhere. He parked in front, the guard cars continued around back, and Jane got out and stood looking up at the house.

He showed her through it. Antique furniture, mostly English. He said: "I admire the English, don't you?" She agreed she did, still glancing around, trying to remember everything. Dark polished wood. Nice drapes. Brocaded upholstery that matched. Paintings on the walls, rather good ones, including one Matisse, a Raoul Dufy, two Picassos. Jane had expected luxury, but not subdued luxury. The homes of the drug lords, she had heard, were palatial, but in the most garish sense of the word. They were as garish as harems. No expense spared, ornamentation everywhere, almost all of it in deplorable taste.

"You have a lovely house," she said.

"It lacks a mistress," he said.

His voice was low, resonant as always, seductive, a trifle sad. She looked at him sharply. If she didn't know so much about him, she might imagine him only a lonely man looking for a wife.

His house had about twenty rooms, and he showed Jane through most of them, and as they walked she questioned him about his background, his life, only easy questions so far. She would ask the hard ones last and if he did not answer or lied it would not matter. She could fill in from DEA intelligence reports she would ask Ray to get for her.

He showed her through living rooms, dining rooms, marble bathrooms, a kitchen in which maids worked, a sauna, a basement swimming pool, and a gym stuffed with Nautilus equipment. "I like to stay in top shape," he said.

Jane looked at him. Muscled forearms, flat stomach. "Yes," she said.

There was a music room: antique instruments in a glass case, and a grand piano that worked, for Jane tapped on the keys. There was a game room full of tables: Ping-Pong, billiards, cards. "No bowling alley?" murmured Jane.

He said: "What?"

"Nothing."

There were bedrooms for his two daughters when they should visit him; at present they lived with their mother in the United States.

"It was a college romance," he said, "University of Virginia. She was from there."

The two bedrooms were stuffed with stuffed animals. Girlish things. Chintz curtains and bedspreads.

There was an apartment for his mother, an elderly woman dressed all in black. He knocked on her door. She bowed to Jane, but said nothing.

His father had died of cancer, he said. He had had to quit college and take over the family business. He had found the bank in bad shape, the insurance company too. Both were prosperous now, though.

Yes, thought Jane, and I know what supports them. But she made no comment and the tour continued.

The master bedroom was huge. Mirrors. A dominating bed. Jane had learned something from the last time she had been led into a bedroom by a man she hardly knew. She accorded it half a glance and backed away.

They went outside where there was more, much more: a formal garden full of fountains, another swimming pool, a tennis court, and beyond that stables, a tack room, a small bullring, and assorted corrals and outbuildings. Men had brought horses up close to the house and stood there beside them, their caps respectfully in their hands.

"Can you ride a horse?"

"I'm not sure," said Jane.

Jane wore the same clothes as yesterday: flat shoes, tan slacks, a blue blazer over a silk blouse. In the tack room Ley found boots for her. He also helped her on with them, which she did not find quite necessary. His attempts at seduction, if that's what this was, were so obvious they amused her. She sat on a bench and for moments at a time his hands were on her feet, her legs. A forefinger circled her calf inside the boot to make sure, he said, that it fit properly. This was supposed to feel, she believed, as if his fingers were inside her clothes, which they were not. This man exuded a powerful sexuality. She could scoff at it, but it was there. It was in his voice, in the intense way he looked at her. She had the impression he was used to women responding to him, took it for granted.

She left her purse and blazer on the bench, her shoes beneath it, and went outside with him. The smaller of the two horses was a mare that he promised was docile. He helped her mount it, then climbed up onto a horse that looked half again as high as hers, and they rode out across fields and he began to gallop and she galloped with him. They went over a hill and down into a valley and ahead grazed a herd of fighting bulls and Jane, realizing what they were, became alarmed.

As the bulls got closer, as they looked up and appraised

her, Jane's alarm increased, but Ley, now riding so close to her that their boots sometimes touched, laughed in a gentle way. Bulls in a herd on the open range were harmless, he told her, and she remembered from her childhood that this was true. A bull would charge only if alone. She decided to ride in among the bulls. She felt excited and alive. Also, she was in a mood to impress David Ley. She and her horse waded into the bulls. There were bulls all around her.

Ley came up. He sent six corridas a year to the rings, he said, thirty-six bulls. His seed bulls came from Spain. He was trying to raise the bravest bulls in Colombia, bulls so good that one day he would be able to send a corrida to Madrid.

"I suppose that does not sound like much of an ambition to you."

But to a woman on a horse on the range in Colombia it did, and Jane nodded. Most people didn't care about being the best at anything, she said, and she understood the mystique that existed between Latin men and bulls.

He gave her a smile that could only be called grateful. He was really a very attractive man. She rather liked him, and was surprised.

They crossed a wooden bridge over a small river. She was a foreign correspondent, and in a place no other reporter had got to before her. She was going to have a terrific story to write. The saddle bumped her rhythmically in the rump. Her calves were chafed from the stirrup straps, her thighs were sore from gripping the flanks of the horse. The sky was overcast, the air sultry. She breathed deeply and realized she was as happy as she had ever been.

"According to the DEA," she said, "you are a narcotics trafficker."

He said: "Yes, I know they think that."

They had stopped in a field in which horses grazed.

"One of the biggest," Jane persisted.

He laughed. "It isn't true."

"I saw you with other traffickers yesterday at the bullfight."

He looked at her, then back between the ears of his horse. "They are the richest men in Colombia," he said. "They are depositors in my bank. Perhaps you think I should not accept their money. But it's not that easy. Money is morally neutral, as are drugs, American laws do not apply here, and I have stockholders, and payrolls to meet. Those men you saw me with yesterday are clients and so I am obliged to meet with them. It happens they are more at ease if we meet in public, so we do. And as a result these ugly rumors start, and there seems nothing I can do about them." He frowned.

He began to talk philosophically about the drug trade. It brought into Colombia perhaps four billion dollars a year in foreign exchange that was desperately needed—this amounted to a quarter of the gross national product. It employed perhaps three hundred thousand people, and supported four times that many, a major percentage of whom would otherwise be on the dole. Colombia was a poor country. Stop the drug trade overnight as the Americans wished to do, and Colombia would go broke, there would be revolution, and perhaps the Communists would take over. In Bolivia and Peru the situation was much the same. The drug trade was bad for the United States perhaps, but a godsend to the Andean countries, which might finally be able to feed and employ their poor.

Even if drugs were morally neutral, Jane asked, what about all the murders that went with them?

Colombia was a violent country, he said as they rode slowly on. It always had been. The central government was weak. People carried guns. They bought or dispensed their own justice. There was violence and murder on the highways, people shooting each other over traffic disputes; and in the emerald trade, too. Back in the late forties there had been an election whose outcome was contested. In the ensuing battles two hundred thousand people died. The recent violence and murders could not be blamed entirely on the drug cartels. Most of it would have happened anyway for one reason or another.

"Why did you agree to see me?" Jane asked.

"I have nothing to hide."

Some of the reporters she knew would have laughed in his face, which would have ended the interview, certainly. Showing their contempt for him would be, to them, more important than the work they had come there to do.

Jane chose to give no reaction at all. She only nodded, as if satisfied with his response, which she was not, while at the same time asking the question again inside her head. What was he hoping for? A favorable piece in her paper, of course. But why? Pure vanity? Was there something she hadn't even thought of that could bring in profit in some way?

Was he hoping to humanize himself? Improve his image? Disassociate himself in the public mind from the murderous gangsters who were his colleagues? If she wrote only about his house and his art collection, about his mother, his children, his fields and forests and animals, if she included only his denials, it might tend to have such an effect. But he must know she couldn't and wouldn't do this.

Again, why? It was a puzzle, but not unique in her experience. Lots of people who never should have gone near a journalist eagerly submitted to interviews, as if imagining they could talk their way out of whatever trouble they were in.

In the professional sense he was trying to seduce her; that much seemed obvious.

And in the personal and physical sense also, it seemed increasingly clear. Because at all times his attention was focused wholly on her. He gazed at her as if she were not only the most alluring woman in the world, but also the only one who truly understood him—and he her. They truly understood each other. He had begun sometimes to complete her sentences, as if he could see what she was thinking better than she could. He met her gaze as if he could see inside her. He eyed her body as if she sat astride this horse stark naked and he could see everything.

But the country was beautiful, and to breathe the clean morning air gave pleasure. She was enjoying this ride immensely. They turned around and started back. They climbed a different hill and rode down into a different valley in which whole fields were blue with wildflowers. Sometimes they galloped the horses until the necks out front turned to lather. On a lane under trees they walked them along, and Ley asked her about her background, her husband, her lovers, if any. She was amazed that he could make such personal questions sound so normal, so answerable.

When they came to the small bullring, they got down from their horses and climbed up into a loge and watched young toreros in chaps and boots working calves, testing them for stamina and bravery. Cowboys were sending one female calf at a time into the ring, and a torero would run out with the big crimson and magenta cape and give it passes. Some of the animals were heifers, some nearly full-grown cows. They were smaller and lighter than bulls, but faster, and their horns had sharper points. The animals went skidding by just underneath Jane, and the dust rose up and she could hear the noise they made.

It was exciting to watch. She was beaming, and she knew her cheeks were flushed, and David Ley was looking at her with an intensity she had learned to recognize in men.

She sat on the bench outside the tack room and let him help her tug off her boots, his hands on her once again. She glanced at her watch. "I have to be back at the hotel by twelve," she said.

"Don't go," he said.

"I must." For the first time in hours she made herself remember other obligations, including Ray, who was waiting for her.

"Stay for lunch. There's champagne on ice and I have a wonderful cook."

Jane was terrifically pleased with the work she had done, the story she would write. She felt she owed herself a reward. Something excessive. Something more exciting than anything yet. She realized she didn't want to go at all, she liked it here, she was not afraid of David Ley, and she wanted to stay.

"And afterward," he said, "we can both take a short siesta, and then I'll drive you back." He watched her.

She knew what he was offering. At least it was out in the open. She had not been this aware of her body in years, of her sore thighs and chafed ankles, of her well-thumped rump, of her crotch that felt chafed as well. She was as aware of her body as she knew he was.

She recognized all this at first vaguely, then clearly, and it amazed her. She was shocked and she looked away from him. What's the matter with me? she asked herself. The guy is a dope dealer.

"I have to get back," she said coldly.

He presented his invitation again in a variety of ways, his voice low and resonant, his arguments seductive, but Jane kept repeating:

"I have to get back."

Finally he drove her back to the hotel. He did it with bad grace, but he did it. In the car both of them were nearly silent. Jane did not know what he was thinking, nor did she care. While still managing a polite reply or smile from time to time, she ignored him almost completely, all the while rummaging through her own head and not liking what she found there.

In front of the hotel Ley pressed his sexy smile, his sexy voice on her one last time. She smiled and thanked him for a wonderful time. When she had got out of the car he reached across and thrust his business card at her—his private number. He said: "If you ever need anything—"

She went into the hotel and up to the suite.

Ray, who was pacing, stared at her.

She said: "I hope you didn't worry about me."

"Where have you been?" he demanded.

"I had an interview to do."

"Something terrible might have happened to you."

"Nothing happened to me."

They stared at each other. Ray looked furious, which only made her truculent. She offered no further explanation, and he asked no further questions. But she was in no doubt as to how angry he was. She said: "Is there a plane at one o'clock? Can we make it?" She had got her exclusive story, and that was what counted.

He did not speak to her in the car, nor even after they boarded the plane. When they were airborne he stared out the porthole and would not even look at her. At first she tried to shrug it off. She opened a magazine. But she could not read. Yes, she had her exclusive, but it wasn't enough. If she couldn't talk about her triumph, then it wasn't a triumph. Ray made her feel that she was absolutely alone in this godforsaken country. She needed him on her side. At least professionally she did. She wanted to win him back, but for the moment did not know how to go about it.

She began to think about herself, her life. It was going by fast. She wanted to be a normal woman with children tugging at her skirt. She wanted a man she could fuss over and make happy, but she also wanted him to admire her accomplishments and be proud of her. Her life was a mess and she wanted to talk to somebody about it, talk to Ray about it, since there was nobody else around, but she couldn't.

When the plane began its descent Ray suddenly turned to her. "So when are you moving into our building?" he said.

"You're not mad at me anymore?" said Jane.

It made him smile.

She thought she should probably tell him she had spent the morning with David Ley but she did not want to see that smile vanish. She would put it off until tomorrow—in any case until another time.

Ley had returned to his ranch, where he paced back and forth in his office studying the extent of his discontent. Two accountants came in. They were men who worked off telephone reports, not printed receipts or ledgers, but like all accountants they talked figures: quantities of stock on hand, shipments in transit, disbursals, accounts receivable. Monies supposedly spent on bribes that could not be verified one way or the other. Ley was frustrated and edgy, and could not keep his mind on it.

They were followed by the lawyer who looked after property Ley owned that was in the name of servants. He could barely understand what the man was saying. Above his head he could hear one of the maids vacuuming his bedroom. He wondered which one.

Abruptly he excused himself, left the room and climbed the stairs two at a time.

The maid in his room was the young one. She smiled at him, immediately switched off the machine, and asked if she should come back later.

She was the wife of the young man who took care of his horses. A robust girl in a shapeless housedress, she wore a bandanna to hold back her jet-black hair. She had slightly Indian features.

She was not Jane Fox.

Ley looked at her for more than a minute without speaking. He watched her smile fade, watched her becoming afraid.

"I'll come back later," she said and edged toward the door.

Without taking his eyes off her, Ley reached behind him and swung the door shut.

He heard the woman's breath catch, saw the fear spread up into the space between her eyebrows.

There were rules for seduction. Ley knew what they were and most times followed them. It took time. You had to talk to a woman, listen to her concerns, ask her about herself, tell her about herself. You had to concentrate. You had to let the idea come into her head gradually. You had to let her see the excitement that was there for her if she wanted it. You had to make her want to.

You had to make an investment. But Ley had made one such investment today and it hadn't paid off. He was in no mood to make another.

"Take off your dress," he said.

"My dress, Señor?" She was so frightened her voice was little more than a squeak.

He might have smiled, murmured something to put her somewhat at ease. He chose not to.

She was biting on her lower lip. She said: "My husband—"

He saw the ideas go through her head. Her job was at risk. Her husband's as well.

He felt no guilt in advance and would feel no remorse after. To him his behavior was traditional—no different from that of his ancestors dating back to the days of the conquistadors.

Afterward he had lunch, then was driven to the bank for a series of meetings about a new plant that one of the textile mills wanted to build. The owners of the mill came in at 5 P.M. By then he had the figures and the projections and was ready for them.

He wore a three-piece suit hand-tailored for him on Jermyn Street in London, and hand-stitched Italian shoes, and he gave off a faint scent of French cologne. He exuded a mixture of urbanity and money.

Under certain circumstances, he told the mill owners, the loan they wanted was available. He saw them look relieved.

The circumstances were these.

Given the rapid devaluation of the Colombian peso, firms like Ley's no longer acted like the ordinary commercial banks people were used to. Before lending money they demanded equity in the property they were financing. Inflation was rampant and it was the only way to protect their investment. If the mill owners were to have their loan, Ley's bank would have to become a minority owner of the mill.

The mill owners did not like the sound of this. Ultimately they could lose their mill. Patiently Ley explained it further. Like bankers everywhere there was no give in him. Nothing much changes in the world, he thought: the rich get richer, the poor poorer. Business is business.

At the end the principal mill owner could think of nothing to say except: "It's not drug money, is it?"

What else did they imagine it was? Ley wondered, but he frowned, as if digesting an insult. "Of course not," he said crisply. "If you want to deal with drug traffickers, you are free to do so. If you choose to deal with this bank, those are the terms.

"Good day, gentlemen," he said. And he showed them out.

He knew they would be back because in the doorway they posed more questions. He closed the door on them.

For a time he sat behind his big desk brooding, then reached for his phone and asked for information.

In her office in Bogotá Jane answered.

"This is your friend from the University of Virginia," Ley said.

She could not have sounded more surprised. "Yes," she said.

"I just wanted to make sure you got back safely."

"Sure," said Jane.

"No problems?"

"None."

"Because our country can be risky for a woman traveling alone. All these factions. Drug traffickers and all."

"Yes, I had heard that."

"You must be careful."

"I appreciate your concern."

"Well, I wanted you to know that you have a friend in Medellín now."

"Thank you."

"If I can ever be of help to you—"

"Thank you."

"In your work, perhaps. I'm not without influence. If you have trouble reaching someone, or don't know who to call."

"Probably not, but thank you." Well, what else was she supposed to say?

"From time to time I may come across something of interest to you. Some piece of information, some trend. If so, may I call you up and pass it on?"

"By all means," she said.

He rang off shortly after. He grinned and thought of her

staring at her phone for at least sixty seconds before putting it down.

13

DOUGLAS FLEW TO Peru because an operation was planned against clandestine labs and airstrips in the Upper Huallaga Valley. Bogotá had been asked to supply an extra body. No one else wanted to go. Douglas had not been to Peru in a while. He was still sending weekly reports back to the PC. An updated view of Peru might improve next week's report. A successful operation might get him talked about in the halls. He did not know what the operation was to be. He was not expecting to get shot at.

He arrived in time for a briefing in the Guardia Civil building in Lima that was attended principally by officers from the Guardia and from the Policia Investigative Peruana. Some DEA men from Washington had come down. They were big men with big grins and hard handshakes. They were dressed in military fatigues and wore sidearms. A Guardia general chaired the meeting and was nominally in charge, but it was the DEA's operation, not Peru's. The hardware was American, the planning was American, and the Americans would be in command. The rules were different here than in Colombia, and Douglas was surprised. All that was wanted from Peru were support troops and permission to go in.

The general was a small brown man nearly sixty, about five feet six. Some of the DEA agents, not too many, spoke Spanish. Not too well either. One was an explosives expert. The general's name was Armas. They were supposed to show deference to him and pretended to, but they were cops, not diplomats, so pretense was thin. Deference, Douglas observed, came out almost as contempt. They wanted no problems from Armas or anyone else. The briefing room was full of smoke. There were rows of chairs like a schoolroom. The Peruvians were meant to realize whose operation this was. A blackboard. Maps hanging. They wanted to see Armas admit it. Charts. Men using pointers. Armas could admit it with a nod. Prolonged silence would be even better.

Most of the Peruvians were smoking. Armas smoked cigarette after cigarette and said nothing. Good. The room filled up with tension and with smoke. The DEA had even given a name to the operation: Snowcap. They had not bothered to find one that translated into Spanish, which Snowcap didn't. It sounded elegant in English, though. It was a name to make headlines back home if successful. If not, the name could be omitted from the reports that would be written—and buried —and then be resurrected for some other operation later.

Finally the briefing ended.

In the hotel restaurant Douglas sat down to dinner at a table of agents. Conversation was dominated by an agent named Greg Black, whose reputation was known to Douglas. Most law-enforcement personnel never fired their guns during their whole careers, but Black had shot and killed six men, every shooting investigated, every one legitimate. The man seemed to attract shoot-outs. He was fond of talking about them, and did so during dinner. His gun knew just what to do, he said. When he grinned his back teeth showed. He had a mouth like a wolf. There was sure to be shooting tomorrow, he said. He was older than Douglas, yet avid for action. He had gray hair. He had decided that Douglas was a headquarters cop who had never worked the streets, and spoke to him disparagingly. Probably fifty percent of the world's cocaine originated in the Upper Huallaga Valley, he said. The area was not under government control. The labs and coca plantations were protected by heavily armed elements of the Shining Path guerrilla army. Run into them and they go bang-bang, he said.

Was he trying to scare Douglas, or what? During the past

year 262 soldiers—262—had been killed on operations just like Snowcap, he said. In addition the jungle was full of poisonous snakes; step on one of those babies and you're gone. And tropical diseases. Had Douglas had all his shots? Was he sure he wanted to go with them tomorrow?

"You'll protect me," said Douglas, turning his anger into a joke, "won't you?" It drew smiles all around the table.

Before dawn the DEA contingent and about thirty troops boarded a military transport which brought them to Tingo María at the head of the valley. It was daylight by then and very hot. Four American-built helicopters were waiting. To Douglas they were old and rickety-looking, and the pilots were Peruvian. The machines had been brought up close to Tingo the day before, but not too close, for no one wanted news of their coming to reach the traffickers, or the Shining Path guerrillas either. The men climbed on board, and the rotors lifted them up into the air.

The Huallaga River feeds into the Amazon. Its valley is a hundred fifty miles long, ten to twenty miles wide. The temperature is subtropical and its vegetation used to be thick rain forest. From the air Douglas saw that this was no longer the case. The chain saws had worked overtime. The devastation was almost total. For mile after mile every tree had been cut down, and fires started. Nearly the entire valley had been deforested. The foliage and underbrush had burned, but the trunks most times had not. Trees lay in incredible profusion in the disorder in which they had fallen. They lay half on top of one another pointing in every direction. From the air it looked like someone had upended a box of straws except that in every open space amid the straws coca bushes now grew.

In the last few years, Douglas knew, following the collapse of the international tin market and the closing of the mines, about sixty thousand impoverished peasants and laborers had moved into the valley to grow coca. They didn't care about the misery it would cause in Harlem or Watts. Coca to them meant a job, food, shoes for their children. More of them arrived every day. The chain saws were still working. On the ground or in a glider, Douglas might have heard them. Over the banging rotor racket of course he could not, nor could he see the fall of individual giant trees, but he could see the smoke from the fires, blue plumes that rose up into the humid tropical air, then flattened out into a thin haze. The plumes were all around the tiny flotilla, twenty or more of them all the way to the horizon.

People, even international organizations, were worried about what Brazil's roads and ranches were doing to its jungle, Douglas reflected, but no one even mentioned what the coca plantations were doing to vast sections of that same jungle in Peru, and in Bolivia as well. The ecological cost was staggering, and not only in terms of soil erosion—more than soil was running off into the rivers. The chemical runoff from the processing labs was killing animals and fish, was poisoning the entire Amazon River system. If we were indeed all part of the same world, then somehow it ought to be stopped.

But he looked down from the open-sided helicopter at hundreds, at thousands of lime green patches of coca bushes, and did not see how it could be stopped here. Coca bushes already covered a quarter million acres in this one valley, and if law enforcement, meaning himself and a few others, ever managed to stamp out the plantations here, the growers and processors would merely move someplace else. These people could find no other work and had no choice.

At one time the government had appropriated money to pay growers who shifted to some other crop, Douglas knew, but this money ran out. It was a good program but the government was too poor to support it. Next the government had hired gangs of laborers to go in and rip out coca bushes by hand, but this was slow, the program couldn't keep pace with the new plantations. Furthermore, it drove peasants into the arms of the Shining Path boys, who already controlled much of the country. Anyway, before long that money ran out too. Another solution would be to spray the entire valley with herbicides. The DEA was eager to do this, but the Peruvians were not. The Peruvians were appalled, and Douglas didn't entirely blame them.

Greg Black split his helicopters up and they went searching along the watercourses: labs had to have water. That day and the next, Operation Snowcap found and destroyed about twenty labs, all of them small. Douglas thought of them as Mom and Pop businesses, street-corner delis as opposed to supermarkets. The steeping pits were plastic sheeting laid over stakes, forming the equivalent of a child's wading pool. The houses were shacks. The owners ran off into the jungle or stood around looking distraught, while he and the men with him put them out of business. They ripped the steeping pits to shreds. They burned the structures, such as they were, to the ground.

Four clandestine airstrips were found as well. The DEA demolition expert, an agent named Malloy, was called in from whichever helicopter he was on. He planted his shaped charges in the ground and blew craters down to the water table so that they rapidly filled up with water. This meant that these particular airstrips could not be repaired and used again later. Of course two of them were dirt roads connecting hamlets; which roads became unusable too. Losing their roads was liable to make the local peasants mad, even Greg Black conceded. They were likely to give vent to anti-American feelings, but this could not be helped, he said.

On the third day, which was supposedly the last day of Operation Snowcap, still another lab was spotted from the air. It appeared to be of significant size, well worth hitting, but was in jungle so thick the helicopters could land nowhere near it. It could be approached only on the side that gave onto the river. Greg Black ordered the flotilla back to Tingo María where he decided that Snowcap would continue into the fourth day. A number of the agents broke off at this point—they couldn't stay, had to return to Washington—and one of the helicopters was detached to ferry them back to Lima.

Black ordered three inflatable boats with outboard motors

loaded onto the remaining helicopters, offloading troops to make room. His plan was a simple one. The helicopters would land close to the river on the site of a lab they had previously burned, and from there they would launch the boats. He would leave behind a force to guard the helicopters while he and a handful of men drifted downriver and hit the big lab. When they had destroyed it, they would continue downriver, for there was a second burned lab about two miles farther along, and there the helicopters would alight to pick them up.

Black named Douglas captain of one of the boats, and during the rest of the briefing called him captain. He thought this a great joke. The demolition specialist, Agent Malloy, would captain the second boat, Black said, and he himself the third.

Douglas did not think much of Black's plan. By now the DEA presence was known throughout the valley, he told him. On the river they would be vulnerable to ambush, and it was going to be possible to carry just four soldiers in each of the three boats—not enough to intimidate a force of any size, and units of the Shining Path were known to be in the area.

Black scoffed at these objections.

"Hit some other lab," Douglas suggested. He had worked all these years to achieve a position of command, but was not in command here. It was galling and it was dangerous. "There are plenty of choices, God knows. Save that one for another time."

"If you don't want to be captain," Black said, "you can guard the helicopters."

It was a stupid challenge and he thought Black a stupid man. So what made him respond like a boy whose courage was in question? Training more than instinct, probably. In the police society there was no other way to maintain one's authority.

"No," said Douglas, "we'll do it your way."

The next morning the plan went into operation, and at first it worked perfectly. The helicopters landed. The three rubber boats were launched, and they moved down the river under power until they were close, then drifted the rest of the way in silence. The motors came on again only to turn into shore and beach the boats. As the raiding parties jumped out, they could see men disappearing into the jungle. The soldiers fanned out setting up their scant perimeter, while Douglas and Black scoured the structures for ledgers, records, and the like, and Malloy planted his charges.

In addition to drums of chemicals, they found about five hundred kilos of cocaine paste.

The soldiers were called back to help slosh gasoline and kerosene around. It was a sprawling lab and the sloshing took time. They poured kerosene on the cocaine paste, and Black torched it, but the stuff wouldn't burn. He kept pouring on more kerosene, and the flames and smoke rose up. Finally he pronounced the paste ruined.

Now he sent the soldiers running in and out of the various structures dropping burning rags. When everything seemed to be burning nicely, Malloy set the fuses on his explosive charges, and they all ran for the boats.

As soon as they were on the river, still drifting with the current, Black radioed the helicopters:

"Mission completed. Starting home."

But one of the outboards wouldn't start. The other two boats drove in circles, waiting for it. Behind them the flames were as high as the trees, and one detonation followed another.

Finally the motor caught and all three boats pointed downriver at full throttle. Their wakes surged up onto the roots of trees. Over the noise of the outboards they could hear the helicopters flying toward the pickup site, but they could not see them, for the river had narrowed here, it was moving more swiftly, and above their heads the trees had closed up almost completely.

They had about two miles to cover, about a ten-minute run provided the river remained navigable, provided none of the boats was ripped open by an underwater snag, provided the Shining Path or some angry lab owners had not got into position along the bank. Douglas at the helm of the lead boat was counting the seconds.

He could not see two feet into the jungle on either side. The walls of foliage were impenetrable. The river was winding here, twisting back and forth on itself, and he had to throttle way back to make the turns. A soldier in the prow was standing up, pushing off from overhanging boughs with his rifle, trying to keep the boat centered in the current, and then suddenly he fell down into the canvas floor. A red stain appeared on his shirt and he did not move. Douglas heard the sound of the shots only afterward. Many shots. An unending supply of them, rifles and automatic weapons firing from both banks.

In a moment he was around the following bend, unhurt, his life saved apparently, no shooting here. There was shooting behind him, however, and it did not stop. His impulse was to hold the throttle down and run for it, keep going. He had a man on board wounded, perhaps dead, keep going, the boat was made of rubber, for God's sake.

But he had thrown the engine into neutral, had veered toward shore, and had grabbed a branch to hold himself stationary in the current. It was instinctive. He never thought about it or made a decision. But he was trying to think now, for the next decision was urgent. To abandon the other boats was out of the question, but in what way could he help? What could he do? Go into the jungle? Try to get behind the shooters? But he saw no way to get ashore. There were too many trees on both sides, too many interlaced vines, the foliage was too thick. It was impossible to get out of the river.

Motor back upstream? Impossible also. Against the current the boat would be barely moving, and it was made of rubber. If all the boats were sunk, no one would survive. There was no room for the heroic gesture. He had obligations to the men in his own boat, too.

The decibel level had risen and there were new and different sounds among the reports, which meant the other boats were firing back. Then one of them appeared, still coming fast, though less fast than before. It was partially deflated, low in the water, nose down and plowing. The demolition man, Malloy, was at the tiller, his face white.

"They sank Greg," he shouted. He appeared unhurt, but two of the soldiers with him were obviously wounded, and a third lay on his back athwart the gunwale and half his jaw was missing.

"Go for the helicopters," Douglas shouted.

"I don't know if I can make it."

"Go as far as you can."

"Greg—"

"I'll go back for him."

Yes, but how?

Malloy vanished around the bend. Simultaneously heads appeared upstream: swimmers. Three soldiers. One had another by the chin, keeping him afloat. The third was struggling to stay above water. Their weapons were gone. All appeared to be wounded. They were thrashing about in the current.

Douglas jumped out of the boat and grabbed at clothing. The water was up to his waist. The men were spinning by him and he was trying to grasp them and maintain footing at the same time. He towed one soldier to the boat to hands that reached down to help, then went back and dragged in the other two. He stood hanging onto a branch while the three soldiers were pulled over the hump into the boat. Their uniforms rasped on the rubber and they collapsed into the bottom.

Now what? Upstream the shoot-out continued. Agent Black and one soldier against how many? Douglas lifted a carbine out of the boat and waded upriver. When he came to the bend he moved ever more slowly, trying to peer through the overhanging leaves.

Ahead a body had snagged on a sunken tree: the last remaining soldier. Douglas freed the body and pushed it ahead of him back to the heavily overloaded boat. Only Black remained unaccounted for now.

As he waded upriver a second time, the shooting stopped completely. He pushed forward, the current pounding against his chest. Although he stopped often to listen, the river drowned out all ordinary noise.

He came to a tree that lay almost on its side, blocking his way. To get around it he plodded out into the current, holding the carbine above his head with one hand, hanging on to the branches with the other so as not to be swept downstream, concentrating so fiercely on his footing that he did not see until the final instant the man rounding the same tree from the other direction.

It was Greg Black. He too was carrying his weapon high. Neither man was in position to shoot, otherwise they probably would have—and shot each other.

"They're gone," Black said.

Douglas peered upstream. He saw where the shooters must have been placed. They must have waited until all three boats were visible in this stretch of river.

"This area is lousy with the Shining Path," Black said.

Douglas was studying this portion of the river. When the guerrillas had opened fire his boat, in the lead, had been almost to the bend and safety. How could he have been that lucky?

"I got a couple of the bastards, don't worry," said Black.

His face was covered with soot and mud. There was blood on his hands and his fatigues were splattered with it.

"Let's get out of here before they find us," he said.

They waded back to the boat, and nearly submerged it climbing in. Black started the engine, and they drifted out into the stream until they were pointed downriver. When he opened the throttle, water surged over the gunwale. He had to reduce speed almost to zero.

Douglas kept waiting to be fired on again, but it did not happen.

Finally they came to the spot where the helicopters waited. The corpses were thrown up onto the shore. Douglas helped the wounded out of the boat. The destruction of the lab had cost the Peruvian Guardia two dead and seven wounded.

Black pushed both boats out into the river and sank them with gunfire.

It had cost the DEA three rubber boats and three Evinrudes.

The wounded men lay on the ground moaning while the corpses were lashed to the skids. The helicopters took off.

By dusk the survivors of Operation Snowcap had reached Lima. The Americans boarded a minibus belonging to the Peruvian army and were returned to their hotel. Still dirty and unshaven, Douglas was crossing the lobby when a voice called out to him. He turned and it was Jane Fox.

"There's an operation of some kind planned," she said, "can you tell me anything about it?"

"It's over," he said. He wanted a bath.

"What was it, and what happened?"

The foreign desk had heard about it in New York, she said. It had sent her all this way looking for the story.

He didn't want to talk about it. "That man over there, Greg Black, he was in charge."

Black was at the front desk asking for messages. Jane's head swung around, and for a moment she studied Black.

"I'd like to talk to you too," she said. "If possible."

She was wearing a pink shirt, a dark skirt with a big belt at the waist, and a lot of bracelets on her arms.

"Am I just a news source to you," he said, "or am I someone you'd like to have dinner with?" He wanted to be with a woman. He wanted to be out of the reach of death and the hopelessness of fighting drugs.

It brought a smile to her face, and she nodded.

"Just let me get cleaned up," he said.

He took her in a taxi to a restaurant on the beach in Miraflores. By then he felt better. He was alive, healthy, and in no way responsible for what had happened. And if she was going to write an article about Operation Snowcap, he wanted to be in it.

The beach was dark, and the Pacific was dark except for the crests of the rollers that caught the glow of the moonlight. They sat out on a flagstone terrace and sipped *pisco* sours.

She had interviewed Black while Douglas was upstairs in the shower. "What do you think of him?" she asked.

Candles burned on all the tables. The terrace was not otherwise illuminated.

"Greg Black loves this kind of thing," Douglas said. "To him it's all a game."

The candles burned inside glass funnels but there was a hot wind blowing and the flames flickered nonetheless. It did nice things to her face.

"But to you it's not a game."

"Two boys killed. Another got his hand shot off. What kind of future does he have now in a country like Peru? Does he become a beggar or what?"

He inhaled the salt breeze and for a moment listened to the waves.

"Greg Black would say you're not seeing the big picture."

"Sometimes the big picture is hard to see."

The terrace jutted out into the sea like the prow of a ship. The rollers hit it on three sides and sometimes the spray rose up high enough to catch glints of light from the candles.

"You closed down a lot of labs."

"You should see the size of that valley."

"We can't just give up."

"No."

"So what's the solution?"

"That's what I'm trying to figure out, but—"

"But what?"

"Sometimes I wonder if there is one." He did not want to talk about this, and both fell silent.

"Tell me about your husband," he said after a moment.

"You don't want to talk about drugs anymore?"

"No."

"My husband's a lawyer."

"I think you told me that before."

"Do you hate lawyers?"

"All cops hate lawyers."

"You wouldn't like him, then."

"You liked him," Douglas said.

She hesitated. "He used to be fun. And he represented— stability. Which I needed at the time."

"And now the paper is your stability."

She looked pleased with him. "That's very perceptive of you."

"Not really. What do you think my stability is?"

"The NYPD."

He smiled. "My children too, I suppose."

"Tell me about your wife."

"Well," he said, "she died."

After dinner they walked through the streets of Miraflores. "Were you in love with her?" Jane asked.

"Most of the time. When a wife dies on you as suddenly as she did, all you can remember from the marriage is the good parts."

"Meaning that you miss her constantly."

"Yes."

"And if you're out with another woman that's the one thing you can't say."

"How much I miss her? No, I guess not." He smiled and thought he liked her a great deal at that moment.

"And you constantly compare the woman you're with to your dead wife."

Though he did not answer, it made him want to tell her something. Something about himself that perhaps revealed too much. Nonetheless, after a moment he said it: "I haven't been with any woman. So far."

She looked at him sharply. "No one—" She stopped.

He wondered why he had wanted her to know this. "Well, it hasn't been that long, has it?"

He imagined he had said the wrong thing, and so he gave her an inappropriate smile. The conversation had got out of hand, and as they resumed walking past the shop windows he sought a way to put it back in balance.

"This is a poor country," he said. "You've never been to Peru before, have you?"

"No."

"I can show you Lima tomorrow, if you like."

"I have to write my story in the morning."

"The afternoon, then."

* * *

Their stroll, the next afternoon, was not an edifying one. The sidewalks were dusty, dirty, and crowded, and often broken or potholed. An unwary or unlucky pedestrian could step into some of the holes knee deep. The shops were shabby, and the goods on display of poor quality. The buildings were old and shabby. Here and there were windows broken out, the glass not replaced, as if no one lived there anymore, though people did, for they could be seen moving about inside. Was glass that scarce here or was it, perhaps, too expensive? There were abandoned construction sites surrounded by board fences pasted with bullfight posters, except that many of the boards had been ripped off and stolen; they looked in on rusting steel rods sticking up out of half-finished concrete foundations.

They came to a pedestrian mall that was more crowded yet, both with people and with merchants who had set up stalls or even small tables anywhere they could, and who were hawking Kolynos toothpaste, menstrual pads, chewing gum—whatever they had to sell—while the crowds elbowed and jostled and pushed to get around them. Jane took Douglas's arm. It's only because she doesn't want to get separated, Douglas told himself. It doesn't mean anything.

Men and also women stood with eight or ten packs of cigarettes on a tray, their entire stock. Some of the packs were open, for the cigarettes could be bought singly, or in twos and threes. Lottery ticket salesmen also worked the street, most of them horribly mutilated, or else spastic. Bootblacks sat against building walls reading comic books, waiting for business. There were fortune tellers in homemade booths, and a moviehouse featuring what in Hollywood were called "action" movies. Showing inside, according to the posters, was a film called *Los Destructadores*. *Explosiva! Acción!*

In the Upper Huallaga Valley, Douglas remembered, men and women even poorer than these people were trying to stay alive. What else could they do besides grow or process coca? What was the solution?

The pedestrian mall opened out onto the Plaza de Armas, where stood the cathedral that the Spaniards had built in the middle of the sixteenth century. It was a square of lovely proportions and handsome old buildings that were, however, in poor condition, the cathedral included. The facades facing the square were a faded pastel pink—decades had passed since they were painted last.

A faded pink cathedral. "Let's go into it," he said, so they did.

Inside there was much dark carved wood that was very old, the choir and pulpits were lovely, but the chapels were decorated with garish mosaics that showed the Spaniards arriving in galleons to conquer Peru. The chapel to the right of the entrance held the tomb of Pizarro, one of the most rapacious murderers of history, who had conquered the Incas, founded Lima, brought into the Spanish Empire the vice-royalty of Peru, and been murdered in his turn by his own men.

Douglas said: "If the guy were alive today he'd be a *narcotraficante*."

"He'd be Pablo Marzo," Jane said. They had come out into the warm afternoon and he took her hand.

He liked feeling her hand in his. But after a few steps she released it and they walked for some distance without speaking.

"Tomorrow I have to fly to Bolivia," he said.

After a few paces she said looking up at him: "Can I go with you?"

Their flight was delayed. They sat for hours in Lima Airport waiting for it to take off, and in the coffee shop shared a table with an arms dealer en route to La Paz to sell Chinese-built jet fighters to the Bolivian Air Force. British by nationality, the arms dealer had an estate in southern Spain next to the estates of some famous international film stars with whom he played golf. He was about sixty, wore a rumpled suit, and showed pictures of his grandchildren. He seemed a bland, inoffensive man. He had colored brochures on the jet fighters, which he showed them, reciting as he did so their rate of climb, firepower, and other characteristics. Each fighter was going to cost the Bolivian Air Force hundreds of thousands of dollars, he admitted. The entire order would be worth millions. For all of that, the air force would save money because his planes, being Chinese, were much cheaper than what the competition was offering.

"Competition?" said Douglas.

"There are a lot of jet fighters on the market right now, American, French, Italian—"

"What does the Bolivian Air Force need with jet fighter planes?" asked Douglas.

"I don't know," said the dealer. "But they want them and I've got them."

Douglas looked at Jane, and she at him, and when they were alone later, he said to her: "The mass of Bolivian peasantry is so poor that they must grow coca to stay alive."

"While their government buys a fleet of jet fighter planes."

"The world is crazy."

It was nearly midnight before their own flight took off. It landed in Bolivia at two o'clock in the morning. They found that the La Paz airport was at fourteen thousand feet and that they had to stand out in a winter night waiting for the hotel van to load up. They stood quietly, trying not to shiver, and breathed the rare air slowly and with care.

With twelve people in it the van started down from the airport. After a bend in the road the city became visible two thousand feet below. Presently they drove along a broad avenue with flowers along the divider and monuments in the intersections, usually generals on horseback. The van stopped in front of the hotel, everyone rushed inside, and there was a pile-up at the desk.

In the morning Douglas dialed Jane's room but her line was busy. He had breakfast, then tried again. Still busy. He left her a note and walked from the hotel uphill to the embassy. Because he could not be sure what effect the altitude would have on him, he walked slowly. The American embassy, which in other countries was always a substantial building and usually palatial, here was upstairs over a bank.

Compared to Colombia and Peru, security was minimal. He went in and saw the people he was supposed to see—he had met them all before—and for the next several hours they brought him up to date on the drug situation in Bolivia, particularly the locations where coca plantations had recently proliferated.

Douglas also had to see the ambassador—in some ways this would be his most important briefing. But the ambassador, he was told, was in Cochabamba and would tour the Chaparé the next day. The Chaparé was one of the two principal coca-growing regions of Bolivia.

A call was put through to Cochabamba to the ambassador's aide, who agreed to save Douglas a place in the official car. Douglas thanked him then added, after a moment's thought, that he was not alone. He explained about Jane.

"Two places, then," said the ambassador's aide.

Douglas walked down the street to a travel agency and bought tickets on the evening flight to Cochabamba. Then he went back to the hotel. Jane wasn't there, so he had a late lunch by himself.

She came in about an hour later and he sat with her in the coffee shop as she ate a salad and drank a glass of mineral water—not a very big lunch. She had been at the embassy herself, interviewing the chiefs of the political and economic sections, she said. However, she had missed her most important interview, the ambassador, who had gone to Cochabamba.

"I'm going into the Chaparé with him tomorrow," said Douglas.

"Oh?"

"They're saving me a place in his car."

"How did you arrange that?"

"What's the matter?"

"I'm a bit jealous, that's all."

"I reserved you a place in his car too."

Her voice rose to a high, incredulous note. "You did?"

"I can cancel it," he said, straightfaced.

"Are you crazy? How do I get there?"

He tossed her airline ticket onto the table. "You owe me fifty-four dollars."

After picking up the ticket and looking at it, Jane leaned across the table and kissed him on the mouth. It was perhaps only an impulsive gesture. It perhaps meant no more than thanks. But it shook Douglas more than he would have imagined.

"What about a hotel?" said Jane.

"They're arranging it for us."

He stood up. "We better pack our bags and check out. We don't have much time."

As they started up to the airport, dusk had fallen and it was raining. The taxi was so old that its wipers worked fitfully and, as the road climbed and the rain turned to snow, they hardly worked at all. The road to the airport was steep, but extremely wide, well graded, and lighted—though a poor country, Bolivia had had that much money at least—meaning that they were able to see a good distance ahead. The snow was falling harder and harder, becoming deeper and deeper under their wheels, and then they saw that the traffic ahead had congealed altogether, and that cars were beginning to slide sideways and even backward. Cars were still coming down, but very slowly and carefully, headlights probing. But nothing any longer was going up. Their own taxi was sliding now, its wheels spinning, its rear end slewing sideways. Then they were stopped, immobilized, sitting in a decrepit taxi in a blizzard in what ought to have been the tropics.

After a time the driver turned off his engine, and soon inside the cab it got quite cold. Douglas and Jane moved closer together. Before long they were huddled almost on top of each other under his suit coat and her blazer, each of them giving and receiving warmth. Douglas was aware of each breath she took, of her heart beating close to his, of the scent of her hair, her clothes, of the weight of her body.

The snow fell an hour, then stopped. The moon came out, and every star in the sky became visible overhead. The snow's depth at their level was about eight inches. Their driver got out and cleared off his windshield.

Another hour passed, perhaps longer, before the cars ahead began to find traction. Their own engine came on. Slowly they straightened themselves out. Slowly and without confidence at first they began to claw their way up the mountain.

As he paid off the taxi in front of the terminal, Douglas could see through the fence that plows were working on the runway. The Lloyds of Bolivia Boeings were parked close to the terminal. Mechanics were hosing them down with chemicals to get the snow and ice off them.

The terminal building was small and shabby. All the flights were backed up and the waiting room was packed with three or four hundred people and their baggage. No one could tell them when their flights would take off. People were pounding on the counters demanding information, but there was none.

There was little to do while waiting. The terminal boasted two shops. One sold alpaca sweaters, but it was closed. The other sold newspapers and magazines. A four-day-old *International Herald Tribune* caught Douglas's eye. He bought the last two copies, and gave Jane one; at least it was something to read. There was a kind of cafeteria, but it was jammed and they could not get in. The waiters moved about with their trays over their heads.

Elsewhere there was no place to sit down. It was difficult to move through the waiting room because of the masses of people and the baggage at their feet, which seemed to snatch at toes and ankles like snares.

Finally flights began to go out, though not theirs, and they were able to find a table in the cafeteria. By then it was very late, and they were starving. The waiter brought weak tea and two pastries—all that was left to eat. The tea was so watery that Douglas wondered if it might have been made from reused teabags; perhaps the waiters, having run out, were being forced to use the same ones over and over again.

The moon was on the Andes close under the wings. Then they could see the lights of Cochabamba far below. Their flight came in low over a city of one-story houses and of dimly lighted, empty streets. The air, when they stepped out into it, was balmy. For the second night in a row they had landed somewhere at two o'clock in the morning.

Their taxi stopped in front of a colonial-style hotel. There was a high stone wall around it. In the wall was a stout wooden gate that was locked. They had to ring a long time before anyone came to open it.

14

IT WAS COOL in Cochabamba in the early light, and the high Andes looked cool or cold out the windows of the ambassador's car, but inside it got hot and stuffy almost at once, for the car was a bulletproof, bombproof station wagon with inch-thick windows that did not open, and an air-conditioning system that did not work, a car that was full besides, nine people.

Out of Cochabamba, there were trees and vegetation but the road climbed and was soon above the tree line. The country became smooth and brown and barren. Douglas waited to see high peaks, for the Andes were higher than the Alps and he had been once with his wife to Switzerland, but there were none, no houses, animals or people either, just a series of enormously high plateaus, each one higher than the one before, with bare brown hills to either side cutting off the view.

The altitude increased. The sky was cloudless, every color, every line delineated as sharply as if outlined in black ink. The road became a ledge, with mountain on one side and ravines on the other. Its surface deteriorated, then disappeared completely, and they rolled over gravel or dirt and the dust rose up and came into the ambassador's car. In some sections, finding the road half blocked by landslides, their driver steered within inches of the verge to get by.

Badly engineered, unstable, this was nonetheless the only road connecting the Chaparé, a vast area, to the rest of the country. In places the verge was gone altogether, and most of the road with it. It was as if some giant had taken a bite out of the road, a fifty-foot bite. The road was half missing, a sandwich with a bite out of it. Sometimes Douglas could see the pieces of road far below. The car would hug the cliff face until they were past. According to the ambassador, who was seated up front but who often turned to talk, a bad storm in the mountains could knock this road out completely, and it might stay out for weeks or even months because the government lacked the machines and money to fix it; for weeks or months the people who lived in the Chaparé would be completely cut off, except for those—the traffickers, for instance—who could arrange to be supplied by air.

Douglas nodded. He saw Jane beside him write it down in her notebook. The car bounded on the road and her pen bounded on the page. She was not going to be able to read those notes very well later.

The ambassador was a genial man in his forties who had served in Bolivia in the Peace Corps in his youth and loved the country. He was a career foreign service officer. Career officers were all the State Department could get to come to Bolivia, Douglas supposed; no big campaign contributor was going to consider Bolivia an apt reward for his generosity, for it was a backwater even among backwaters. Though huge—it was the size of Texas and California combined—most of it was ten thousand or more feet in the clouds, and it contained only six million people, the majority of them illiterate Indians. The Americans stationed here did not even get danger pay, as in Colombia and Peru. The Bolivians were peaceful. There were no guerrillas. There were drug lords, but they were minor compared to elsewhere, and this was a country with no history of violence and assassination.

Whatever the number of people who had lived in the Cha-

paré in the past, the ambassador said, fifty thousand more
had rushed in in the last few years to grow and process coca.
Whorehouses were set up. Rackets flourished. There had been
lawlessness and even a few killings.

Well, Douglas knew most of this from yesterday's briefings
and also from previous ones, for he had been in Bolivia—
in the capital—some months before. But this ambassador
was new since then and he was trying to take the measure of
the man. The ambassador was the first line of defense against
drugs in all these countries, but some of them didn't know
it, and there was no overall antidrug policy to guide them.
Each of them—the ones Douglas had met—seemed to be
most interested in, and to concentrate on, the local political
situation, and as far as drugs were concerned, they improvised
from day to day. When they had time. When they got around
to it.

Douglas in South America was without a boss. Or rather
he had many bosses: the mayor of New York, the PC, the
DEA, the State Department, even Eddie Gallagher. One of
his jobs was supposed to be to visit and revisit all the countries
so as to be able to articulate some overall policy later—or
so he had been charged by some rather pompous State Department men before leaving Washington. They would be
interested in hearing from him when he got back, they said.
The mayor, adopting a pious manner, had said much the same
to the press; the PC had even said it to Douglas's face. Sure.
He was under no illusions. None of these people was likely
to listen to the recommendations of a career cop who was in
disfavor in his own city and only a deputy chief besides.
Besides which, he had no notion how much more time must
pass before he would be allowed back, be invited to come
back. In the meantime he would do his supposed job con-
scientiously, study the problems from as close to them as he
could get. He would take his chances in the jungles in Colombia and Peru—study while getting shot at. He would study
the Chaparé today, which was not dangerous at all except for
these terrible roads. His work in South America would be
found stunning on every count, if anyone ever looked. His

recommendations afterward would be detailed, carefully thought out, based on personal observation, whether anyone ever asked for them or not.

One way or another he would get his career back. At the very least he would enjoy the scenery. Today he would learn firsthand about the Chaparé.

The ambassador began to order stops. There was a carload of guards directly ahead and another directly behind—this was a country in which the ambassador was heavily guarded, but no one else was. There were seven cars in the convoy altogether: aides, DEA agents, and various Bolivian officials and politicians. The new ambassador was familiarizing himself with his domain, and when an ambassador traveled, this one or any other, it was likely to be an expedition.

At each stop his guards, little brown men in sports shirts, would fan out and stand facing the mountain, facing the jungle, machine guns pointing at whatever might be out there. The other passengers too would jump out, pass back inside the guards, and crowd around the ambassador to catch any thoughts he might drop.

The first stop was at Paracti, where there was a drug checkpoint manned by Bolivian narcotics police and men from the U.S. Border Patrol. Together with the ambassador's party Douglas looked it over. A cinderblock building. In front of it, a red and white striped pole that could be raised to let vehicles through. Whatever went in or came out of the Chaparé by road—produce, household goods, machinery, merchandise, fuel, people—went through here. The precursor chemicals needed to process cocaine had to go through here too, and so did the cocaine base or paste coming out. Not all of it, of course. The major traffickers had clandestine airstrips and planes, and that was another problem. But the small-timers were obliged to use trucks and cars, and to go past the checkpoint each way, and to hope for the best.

As Douglas watched, a decrepit flatbed truck came up the hill toward them. Apparently it served as a bus. It was full of people. They were mostly Indians in bright serapes, the women wearing bowler hats. They were packed in standing up, they hung over the sides and even off the sides. If it rained they would get soaked. If the truck ever slid off the edge into a ravine, it and they would simply disappear, possibly never to be found again. It would be one of those Third World rural tragedies one read of so often. Douglas, watching, felt the ambassador sidle up behind him. A bus with thirty people aboard had disappeared on this road not long ago, he whispered. Douglas looked at him but did not reply.

The bus had stopped at the barrier. Just then a similarly decrepit old truck loaded with goods came down the hill. Now both trucks were stopped, one on either side of the barrier. The guards had come out of the building and stood around them, and papers were handed down. Douglas studied the drivers, and then the Indians in the truck/bus. The Indians were stompers, perhaps. They stomped on the coca leaves soaking in sulfuric acid, lime, and other chemicals in the vats. They stomped for days or perhaps weeks until such time as fissures developed in the flesh of their feet and ankles, to be followed by gangrene, to be followed by amputation. Meanwhile they would have been replaced by new stompers.

Today this load of stompers, if that's what they were, watched patiently as the Bolivian cops fingered through their meager belongings.

Other cops had climbed on top of the goods truck. Its contents were eight feet deep. Anything could be buried under there, Douglas realized. A complete search was impossible. Now another truck approached on the uphill side. It was loaded with enormous logs. How did one search under logs?

Two of the American border patrolmen were watching carefully, with narrowed eyes. They were in their early twenties, and carried M-16 rifles. They were smooth cheeked but, Douglas noted when he began to interview them, already cynical. One led him into the cinderblock building, their living quarters. A small cinderblock room. Bunk beds, foot lockers. On the walls, centerfold pinups. The boy tossed his rifle onto the bed. Last week the Bolivian cops had waved a truck through, he said. He chased it in a jeep and stopped it. It was carrying seven tons of lime, would you believe that?

The Bolivian cops had waved it through. He confiscated the entire load. The traffickers had so much money and the Bolivian cops so little, he said. They were easy to bribe, it was a shame. You had to watch them like hawks.

He took Douglas into a storeroom and pointed to nine plastic bottles on the floor. Sulfuric acid, forty-five liters, seized yesterday. The bottles were marked cleaning fluid. He knew it was acid because it was so heavy, he said, sounding proud. Go ahead, pick one up, it's heavy, right?

There were always three Americans stationed here at a time, the boy said. Last night someone had dynamited their radio antenna. The explosion was pretty close. Scary. A lot of Bolivians had learned to use dynamite in the tin mines. But the world market collapsed and the mines closed down. The workers scurried in here to grow coca, and guess who was in their way. The American border patrolmen, that's who. In Bolivia dynamite was the method of choice for killing.

These are just boys, Douglas thought, they are two hours or more from the nearest town and not one of them speaks Spanish. To ward off loneliness they stare at naked girls on the walls and talk of sticks of dynamite sailing in the window.

He spoke to some of the Bolivian cops, young Indians who did not have much to say. Neither did their officer, who was older.

All this time he was aware of Jane only a step or two behind him, interviewing the same people. In the car she asked him questions and noted down his answers. Good, he thought, my name will be in her story. In New York they will know I was here.

On the way down from the high country the scenery was the same and the road no better. Then scrub bushes reappeared and a little lower down trees, and then as they continued to descend, gorges in which flowed fast-moving rivers. The rivers got wider and fuller and there began to be now and then a house. In one place a cliff face had fallen down into the river, a sudden new island, the water swirling around it. On top of what was left of the cliff stood a house, still perched there, ready to go in the next storm. Then they were all the way down and to either side of the road was the jungle. In his head Douglas made notes on the geography. It was important to understand the geography of a country, he believed, if you hoped to understand the country itself.

The ambassador stopped again, this time at a coca plantation. Same thing: the guards jumped out and stood with their machine guns pointing into the jungle, everyone else crowding around the ambassador, except for himself and Jane, who moved off amid the scraggly bushes, she plucking a few coca leaves and chewing on them.

"Anything?" he asked her.

"No."

"I think you have to chew ashes at the same time."

"Ashes? Ugh."

"It releases the alkaloid in the leaf. Something like that."

Jane spit out the leaves. "Never mind."

Coca-growing was legal in the Chaparé, Douglas told her, which was part of the problem. The law proscribed only labs. The Bolivian Indians of the high plateaus, because of the rare air, the inhospitable land, and the scarcity of food, had been chewing coca leaves for hundreds of years in order to ward off hunger, fatigue, and cold. They used up lots of leaves, which gave off very little cocaine. It was relatively recently that the world had learned to refine the leaves into cocaine-hydrochloride, and more recently still how to find true euphoria smoking it. And the knowledge and experience of the traditional Bolivian coca-growers, their numbers now swelled many times by failed farmers of other crops, by ex-tin miners, by laborers hired by local landowners, was being sold to the highest bidder, usually the Colombian drug lords.

This particular farmer was part of a program, administered by the ambassador, by which the United States paid coca-growers to rip out their bushes and switch to other crops. He had switched to pineapples, the farmer told Douglas, and he led them to where his new pineapples were growing amid the fallen tree trunks. They were heavy, fine-looking pineapples.

Seeing that the ambassador had started back to his car,

Jane got her money out and asked if she could buy one. The farmer grinned, cut two off, and gave one to each as presents. Douglas insisted he pay, so did Jane, but the farmer refused.

But he hadn't gone entirely to pineapples, the farmer said, as he walked them toward the ambassador's car. His original land, the part he had farmed before he had slashed and burned down the neighboring jungle, was still planted in coca, for it was a cash crop that he knew would sell. He was hedging. The coca-buyers came to his door in trucks. He didn't know about pineapples yet. Maybe there would not be a market for them. And as yet there was no way to transport them in quantity out of this valley.

"There goes that program down the drain," muttered Douglas.

"You'd think there'd be somebody assigned to market the substitute crops," Jane said.

"Would you?"

The others were already in the cars, and they had to hurry to take their seats. The cavalcade moved on.

The final stop was the UMOPAR training base in a place called Tumari. UMOPAR was the acronym for the rural narcotics police. The five or six instructors were Americans, either from the Army's Special Forces branch, or they were DEA agents on temporary duty. They were older than the border patrolmen had been, in their late thirties, early forties. Two of them spoke pidgen Spanish, Douglas learned, because he tried them. The rest, none at all.

The visitors were given a military-style briefing, much of it in military jargon. The officer at the podium spoke of official corruption. He got hot about it. Too often, he said, their targets were being warned of raids ahead of time. There were lots of radios out there. You could hear them warning each other. Security was being compromised before they were out the gate. You'd raid a place and there'd be nothing left but the radio. Radios were hard to come by in the Chaparé. "We've caught a lot of radios," he said triumphantly.

Bolivian officers could get big money for protecting traffickers, according to the briefing officer. Thousands of dollars at a time. The officers got the money, not the men. Not one officer, after being caught, had ever been punished. And corruption caused bad leadership. The briefing officer seemed more offended by the bad leadership than by the corruption. The colonel in charge of UMOPAR was under pressure because he was honest, and in La Paz it was thought that he was pocketing all the money, not sharing it. The DEA had begun to give rewards to UMOPAR cops after big seizures.

After the briefing the ambassador and his group were led through the arsenal. Douglas looked in on the weaponry Washington had supplied. All those guns in a country where shooting was rare.

Then it was lunchtime. In the mess hall they were handed boxes of U.S. Army rations. The boxes had to be ripped open: inside were dehydrated meats and fruits, reconstituted fruit juices. Douglas ate some of it. Mostly he talked to the man at his right, a forty-year-old Mexican-American who was the DEA's station chief in Cochabamba. He worked in a corrupt environment, he said. You have some terrific operation going and some cop sells it out. You find you have to lie to the cops who are supposedly helping you. Or you arrest somebody but the cops tell you he "escaped." You find out later the guy's still living in his house. His house is right next to the police station.

"Anything like that ever happen to you?" the DEA agent asked.

"Yes," said Douglas. He remembered as a young cop kicking in a door in Brooklyn, other men behind him, his gun in his fist, his heart thumping with fear. Inside the apartment was nothing. Some cop had sold the case. Nothing. All that work, all that fear for nothing.

"You're not equipped for disappointments like that."

"No," said Douglas, "you're not."

The Bolivians were beginning to refine their own cocaine, the DEA agent said. They were beginning to bypass the Colombians, to establish their own distribution routes. The Bolivians were becoming major, major traffickers in their own right. He had three agents working for him. It wasn't enough. Every morning all over the Chaparé the planes came in with the first light and loaded up and took off again, he said. You could hear them, and you could do very little about it.

Douglas listened to him. He needed to talk, apparently. All the wives had left prematurely, he said. It wasn't so bad for the agents; they moved in a world they were used to: drugs. But the wives—Cochabamba was depressing all the way around. Sometimes there was no soap on sale in the stores. The meat market stunk of urine, human waste, and flies. So the wives all left. One guy's wife went back home and divorced him. He married a local Indian girl. That's all right here, but what happens when he gets transferred to Washington or New York?

All these men, Douglas reflected, are disheartened. They think they are losing. They think it's hopeless. The ambassador would claim that progress is being made. All the politicians would. But the foot soldiers don't believe it.

Lunch was finished. They carried their torn packets over to the garbage bin.

They could hear the racket of the helicopters starting up on the landing pads. They went outside and trooped over there, and those selected to go climbed aboard. The sun felt ferociously hot on Douglas's face, and the dust was blowing about. Then he was a thousand feet up, strapped into a kind of canvas sling behind a machine gun. The machine gun was not loaded. He was not expected to use it. This was a sightseeing flight laid on for the ambassador and the dignitaries with him.

Douglas peered down between his feet at all that hot, flat jungle. The tops of the trees were mauve, like cauliflower. Then for vast stretches there was no jungle, it had been scalped. Slash and burn. Long trees lay every which way on their sides, and amid them, beside them, grew the new coca bushes. It was exactly what he had seen in Peru. Giant straws strewn over the ground out of a box. He remembered a childhood game called Pick-Up-Stix. The fallen trees reminded him of that too, the stix just dumped there, mile after mile, lying every which way on top of each other.

The U.S. had provided the Bolivian narcotics forces with six helicopters such as the one in which he rode. They were twenty years old—so much for our all-out war on drugs, he thought—and only three were operational today. All three were in the air carrying six to eight people each, Jane was in the one containing the ambassador, and he watched the three shadows moving across the top of the jungle below and tried to spot labs or airstrips, though he wasn't sure what they would look like in this country. These were old gunships from the Vietnam war. They were older than the lifespan of most animals. They had no sides, and he could lean out into the void.

The jungle suddenly ended and they were over marshes or grasslands—impossible to tell from the air. Some dirt roads. Occasional A-frame houses with thatched roofs. No cars. Streams that moved so slowly the water was red. There were rivers everywhere, Douglas saw. Tortuous things doubling back on themselves. He could see every bed they had ever run in.

They stayed up two hours or more, and the wind blew. The DEA agent beside him pointed out an airstrip, and then some steeping pits beside a stream, and shouted in his ear. He nodded back. It was impossible to talk.

For the drive back over the mountains to Cochabamba he and Jane were put in different cars. There was fog in the headlights in the high passes. It was night when Douglas's car came into the streets of Cochabamba. He went up to his room and showered and changed. He was sitting out in the night at a table in the garden sipping a beer with the ambassador's chief of security when the passengers in Jane's car entered the hotel.

She stood beside his table. "I got a great story today."
"Good."
"A day like today is what one becomes a journalist for." Her eyes were shining and she looked exultant.

"I want a bath," she told him.

"Take your time," he said. "I'll wait for you and we'll have dinner."

He sat talking to the security man and the ambassador came down and sat down with them and Douglas asked him about his previous experience, his thoughts, his plans for Bolivia. What kind of man was he? Was he the type you would hope to have here or not?

Presently the ambassador and his security man went into the dining room. Jane had still not come down, and he sipped his beer in the garden in the balmy night.

When he next looked up she was approaching his table. She wore a black dress that molded her body, high heels, earrings, and she carried a small beaded purse. She wore no makeup. Her hair looked very nice, her smile too. He stood up to greet her. He had seen her all day in jeans, a cotton blouse, and flat shoes, carrying a rather battered heavy duty handbag with a shoulder strap. This seemed a different woman now, so that he asked himself: Did she get all dressed up for me?

He saw her take in her effect on him. As she sat down she looked pleased with herself.

"Tonight I didn't want to be a reporter anymore," she said. "I just wanted to be a woman."

He nodded.

"And have dinner with a man who likes me."

He could not take his eyes off her.

"You do like me?"

"Yes."

"A lot?"

"A lot," he conceded.

She slid her hand across the table and as their fingertips touched, all the hairs rose up on his forearms.

Jane had had the same reaction, hairs rising on her arms, one she had sometimes experienced as a teenager, feeling some boy's hands on her, but not since, and she was surprised.

"The ambassador has invited us to join him for dinner," he told her.

"Do you want to?"

"Not particularly, no."

She glanced across at the ambassador and his party. "I don't want to do any more interviewing. Couldn't we just have dinner together?"

"I'll tell him."

She watched him bend over the ambassador, whose head turned in her direction. She smiled and gave a brief wave. Then he had returned and was sitting down again.

They drank a gin and tonic each, then went into the dining room and ordered. They talked about their childhoods. He told of some of the crazy things criminals do. She told some amusing stories about life upon the wicked stage. They shared a bottle of wine. Jane imagined her eyes were too bright. But his were, too.

He thought: My God she can look beautiful.

After dinner they went out the hotel's big wooden doors and strolled through the streets. The shops were closed. It was not a pretty town. It was poor, dirty, and in places it stank. The streetlights were dim. The shop windows were not lighted. They were walking very close together. Their hands were trailing at their sides, and then their fingers caught and intertwined.

Here we go, Jane thought. I don't know if I'm ready for this. I don't know if it's a good idea.

Having started back to the hotel by a different street, they turned a corner to where an outdoor market had stood during the day. There was a pile of garbage there, boxes and bags and ruined produce eight feet high.

Suddenly black shapes hurtled out of the darkness and leaped upon it.

"Oh," she said, and recoiled into him. Into the crook of his arm, as it happened. Which went protectively around her.

It was a pack of wild dogs attacking the garbage—dogs hissing and snarling as they tore into the pile.

The dogs took no notice of them, but they had taken notice of each other.

Both of them hesitated a moment—last chance to back out. At the end of that moment it would be too late. The consequences would be what they would be. Lives would come together that afterward might be untangled only with difficulty, perhaps pain. How much safer just to keep a proper, professional distance apart.

I'm lost, Jane thought.

The moment lasted long enough for both to acknowledge to themselves, and also in some mystical way to each other, that there was risk involved here, and that it was being accepted on both sides; following which their mouths and at least a portion of their futures came together. It's only a kiss, Jane thought. Sure.

It's what I want, thought Douglas. Her. I'm not going to stop now.

Behind them the dogs hissed and snarled, leaped upon the boxes and bags, and upon each other. Garbage was being strewn all over the street.

"Not exactly lovers lane here, is it?" Douglas said.

Jane laughed. "No moonlight on the water, no."

"No violins playing."

"Not romantic at all."

They laughed, backed away, rounded the corner, and stopped to kiss again. Jane had not necked in the street since high school. Neither had he. He felt completely giddy. So did she.

At the hotel they moved past the front desk without stopping, past the terrace where some of the ambassador's people were still drinking, went under the arcade and up the steps. On the landing they embraced still again, and now Douglas's hands moved all over her dress, never pausing in any one place, molding her body in the same way he had sometimes patted men down for weapons, though a thousand times more gentle.

Jane thought she'd die if she had to wait much longer.

His arm around her, feeling the weight of her against him, Douglas thought that something as wondrous as this could not possibly be happening.

On their own landing a guard with a machine gun stood outside the ambassador's door.

"Look," Jane murmured, "a walking do-not-disturb sign."

He could not think of any clever rejoinder.

Then they were inside the room, he had locked the door, and they were together, her arms around his neck, her mouth on his. When she stepped back, her fingers went to the buttons at her back, but he stopped her and began undoing them himself.

She began working at his tie, at the buttons of his shirt. She wanted him to hurry.

He was hurrying as fast as he could, but his fingers were not working properly.

She watched him place his garments on a chair. Man's (or woman's) natural state is clothed, she thought. Nakedness was a temporary stage, a prelude to something else. Usually to getting dressed again. It's not supposed to last, she thought. He had a beautiful back. His back was so beautiful she wanted to press her lips against it, almost wanted him not to turn around. Almost.

And then he did turn around. "If you only knew how much I want you right now," she said.

He laid her down upon the bed, and for a moment only looked at her in the half light.

She was not wearing anything tonight, inside or out, nor was he, she had stopped the pill upon reaching South America, and for a second she worried about becoming pregnant, then that notion was gone, and she tossed and bucked under him, gave into it, didn't care.

A little later, as they lay quietly, half on top of each other, she thought about pregnancy again. If it happened, she would take it as a sign. She wouldn't have to decide about George, about her marriage, it would all be decided for her.

George might put up a fight, though. I should tell Ray the truth about George and me, she thought.

Douglas felt no need to speak. After such an experience what was there to say? There were times when the body expressed emotions that the mind could never articulate.

But Jane desired even more intimacy, wanted to give up all her secrets, wanted him to know everything about her. The urge was almost overpowering, too strong to resist. "There's something I ought to tell you," she said, and stopped.

"Then tell me."

Already she was having second thoughts. She burrowed closer against him, and although he kept coaxing her, she remained silent.

When she was a girl she had usually talked too much in bed, or so she had convinced herself later, and usually she had paid the price. Was she about to do the same thing now?

"It's just that—that I'm in love with you."

He said nothing, only pulled her on top of himself so that her breasts were squashed into the hairs on his chest, and pulled her head down and kissed her.

But she raised herself up on her elbows, saying: "You're not, I suppose."

"Oh yes."

"Then tell me so."

"I've been in love with you I think since the first night I ever saw you."

In the emotion that this brought on she felt him fill her to the brim and she began to rock back and forth.

"Why didn't you say so?" she said.

"I didn't think you even liked me."

"What was I supposed to do, rip your clothes off and do this to you?"

"That would have been—interesting."

"The idea," she said, "did occur to me."

But from the expression on his face he was beginning to have trouble tracking the conversation.

He clasped her to him so that she could no longer move, probably hoping to become calm again so that this exquisite moment would not end, men did that sometimes, in her experience. But she could feel from the throbbing inside her that he was too late, so she kissed him and moved some more and made it happen.

They made love in one way or another most of the night. In between they talked and once they took a shower together, afterward climbing into the other bed, for the first one was a mess. They were determined to be good so as not to mess this bed up too, and to sleep, but permitted themselves a single goodnight kiss. The one kiss became several, their resolve failed, and soon they had started up again, so that the second bed became as moist and tangled as the first.

Her principal reaction was astonishment. He had always seemed so correct to her, so proper, she had scarcely ever seen him without a tie on, one would not believe him capable of such passion. Where were the reserve and propriety that were integral to his character? Then she realized—vaguely because of the state she was in, strongly the next day when she had time to think about it—that for such a man it was a way of making a statement, a profession of love, the profoundest statement of all, that he loved her totally, as much as a man could love a woman. None of these thoughts lasted long that night, her astonishment did not last long, she couldn't concentrate on either, for what he was doing felt so nice, he felt so nice where he was that it made her gasp: "Oh, oh, oh Ray, oh, oh, oh." Her heart was overflowing with love for him, and his for her, she believed, and Cochabamba, Bolivia, was the most enchanted city in the world, and she realized there were problems coming, decisions to be made, but how could she think of that now, she wanted this night with him to endure forever, the most stupendous night of her life so far.

BOOK III

BOOK III

15

DAVID LEY WAS invited to lunch at one of Marzo's ranches—the one on which he had built his zoo. A lion's den in both senses of the term. To Ley, the former gravestone thief was a business genius, which was surprising, and a billionaire which, given the current craving for drugs, was not. He was also a paranoid who saw plots and betrayals before they occurred, called it instinct, and ordered people killed. One went near him therefore at great risk. Even his peers.

Supposedly this was to be a meeting of some kind. Supposedly the others would be there. But there was no way for Ley to check with them in advance. These men were not partners. It sometimes seemed amazing to Ley that they had not turned on each other before now.

Today Marzo had some plan he wished to offer, he said. Perhaps. Or perhaps he had summoned his peers for no reason but to assert his supposed leadership.

Perhaps he had something more sinister in mind.

Ley had no choice but to attend. Lest he seem afraid, for one thing. Weakness was dangerous. Lest he abdicate totally and finally the leadership role he had once counted as his. Lest Marzo propose some murderous nonsense which the others proved unable or unwilling to shout down.

What pose to strike? How many men to bring with him? However many, Marzo on his own turf could have more.

Ley decided to come alone. It was a way of displaying power by disdaining any need for it, Ley believed.

When his long black car came through Marzo's gate, it was unaccompanied by guard cars, and he saw the surprise on the faces of the armed men posted at the gatehouse. A single car. In it a chauffeur and, in the back seat, David Ley. A few minutes later the car came to a stop in front of the ranch house. His chauffeur got out to open the door for him. The chauffeur was extremely nervous. He kept hiking his uniform coat down. Ley was nervous too, but taking care that it did not show. Both men were unarmed.

Marzo had come out of the house to greet him, and Ley saw him glancing around for guard cars, and not finding them. Marzo came up to him all smiles, gave him an *abrazo*, and as he did so, it seemed to Ley, he felt quickly for weapons that were not there. When he stepped back, he looked puzzled. But a dozen or twenty tough-looking young men stood about, eyeing each other, and now the newcomers, suspiciously. Marzo sent the car around to the back, then led Ley into the house and into a big, already smoky room.

The other men, Lucientes, Von Bauzer, and Jiménez, were already present. A servant came through offering *finos* off a silver tray. Another followed with a tray of pseudo-Spanish tapas. Ley could almost have believed himself in Spain. In the last few years Marzo, who much admired Spain and all things Spanish, had attempted to take on the veneer, and also the pretensions, of a Spanish grandee.

Lunch was announced. The five men sat down at the table. There were deer and boar heads on the walls, but the linen was thick, the silverware heavy. Marzo poured out French wine such as was usually unobtainable in Colombia, and bragged about how much it had cost him. On the table, Ley noted, stood bottles of equally unobtainable French cognac to be drunk with the coffee.

The food turned out to be peasant food, good but plain;

the servants moved from shoulder to shoulder serving *frijoles con garra*, red kidney beans with pork, together with *arepas*, cornmeal patties.

As always they talked business. New sources were opening up in Bolivia and Peru, and Jiménez was building new labs, this time in the Guajira peninsula to the north. There was more product coming on line all the time. Therefore more smuggling routes would have to be added, new methods of transportation found. Lucientes complained about the product his planes were airdropping to speedboats off Florida. Too often the packaging was inferior, and the product got wet and then had to be reprocessed in Miami. New packaging was needed. The North Americans were getting more vigilant. Customs and the Coast Guard were now working more closely together; as a result, sending product by ship was riskier than it had been. And of course it took too long. One waited weeks to find out if a shipment had arrived safely.

They discussed the possibility of using submarines. One or several subs would solve all their problems. What happened to the subs that were phased out of the navies of the world? Where could they get one? Could they have one built somewhere? Subs could come close inshore at night and off-load tons of product at a time. The radar screens would be scanning the sky and the sub or subs would come in underneath them. Everybody started laughing except Ley, who only nodded. They got boisterous about it. The joke would be on the gringos.

When the laughter stopped there came a lull. It ended when Marzo began talking with his mouth full. "There's another one of those New York reporters come down here," he said, and paused a moment to chew. "A woman. Here in Colombia. She writes bad things about us. Every day she insults us. I think she should be taught a lesson. What do you think?"

No preliminaries. It was as bald as that, and for a moment no one spoke.

The former gravestone thief grinned and pointed at Ley with his fork. "David knows her. They been together. How was she, David?"

"What kind of lesson were you thinking of?" said David Ley.

"You want to marry her?" Marzo was giggling. "I think David wants to marry her."

"You marry her," said Ley, "I have other things to do." As a rejoinder it was weak, but he was too surprised to think up anything better.

Immediately Marzo's giggling stopped. "We don't want her here. She fires up the North Americans against us. Bogotá too. They all take money from the gringos there."

Jiménez gave a laugh. "The ones that don't take money from us."

Carlos Von Bauzer said humorlessly: "Those people in Bogotá take money from everybody. Bunch of leeches."

"How long can we let her go on insulting us?" said Marzo. "It is a matter of *pundonor*." *Pundonor*, which in Spanish connotes pride and honor both, is a word often heard around bullfights. It is one of the strongest words in the language.

"We're businessmen, not bullfighters," said Ley.

"She hurts our business," complained Marzo.

Lucientes, who was wearing riding breeches again today, had turned to Ley. "You know her, David?" he said.

"I've met her."

"She wrote an article about him," said Marzo. "I have it here." Rising, he went to the sideboard and picked up the press clipping. It began to move around the table. While the others looked at it, Marzo resumed eating.

Ley was still choosing his words with care. "You didn't say," he said to Marzo, "what sort of lesson you wanted to teach her. That you thought might help us, I mean."

Again Marzo waved his fork around. "We pick her up." He used the Spanish verb: *secuestrar*.

The others looked at him. Lucientes, who could read English, looked up from the clipping.

"We hold her awhile," Marzo continued. "If she's nice, maybe we let her go. If not—" He drew his fork across his throat and made a guttural noise.

"I don't think it's a good idea," said Ley.

"Nothing to it," said Marzo. "She waltzes around Bogotá, my people tell me. Not a care in the world. It will be easy."

"Easy?" said Ley.

"David doesn't think it's a good idea," Marzo said to the table at large. "We lock her in a room someplace," he said to Ley. He laughed. "We give you the key. What's wrong with that?"

It occurred to Ley that the subject here was not Jane. Marzo was looking for a way to get at him personally so as to reduce his prestige. And thought he had found it.

"Her paper is extremely powerful," Ley said. "If we sequester her, it will provoke headlines all over the world and bring down heat on all of us."

"We sequester her and give you the key," said Marzo, "you do what you want with her." Evidently he thought this idea hilarious. "What will you do with her, David?"

"It will start a manhunt," said Ley carefully. "We'll all have to go underground."

"You want to get married," said Marzo, "we bring in the priest."

Lucientes said: "We had to go underground when the minister of justice was killed. And again when the presidential candidate got blown away. Three months on the run the first time, even longer the second." Marzo had never publicly taken credit for either assassination, but everyone believed he had ordered them.

"Even my father had to hide out," said Lucientes. "He's old. His ulcer acted up, his heart. It's not good for him."

Believing himself to have an ally, Ley said: "Things are quiet right now. It's in our interest to keep them that way."

Marzo got angry. "You don't have to be responsible. I don't need your agreement."

For a time everyone was silent. Marzo resumed eating, but no one else did. "We are fighting for survival here. We have to keep this country off balance," he said around mouthfuls.

"Terrorized, you mean," said Ley.

Marzo shrugged.

"I fear the world will begin to see us as terrorists," said Ley. He saw that Lucientes across the table was giving him little shakes of the head, as if to warn him to tone down his opposition. He was alone here, he reminded himself. He had best not provoke Marzo too much.

"Let me tell you something," said Marzo. He was no longer giggling, no longer waving his fork. "My way works. And it will go on working. In this country there is not a single man who dares move against us."

"For the moment," said Ley.

"The judges do not dare indict us, the jurors do not dare convict us, the journalists and politicians do not dare speak out against us."

This was true.

"The public does not want us prosecuted," said Marzo. "They don't want us extradited to North America. They hate the North Americans as much as we do."

The *norteamericanos*, thought Ley. The most popular bogeyman in Latin America. But the people we assassinate are not North Americans, they are Colombians.

"And they are afraid of another round of bombings, of killings," said Marzo. "We have to keep them thinking that way. We can't leave things peaceful too long." He nodded vigorously. "Survival," he said again. "When you are fighting for survival you can't worry too much about methods."

"I grant you," said Ley, "that your way has worked—up to a point."

Ignoring the interruption, Marzo said: "And if we keep the pressure on, our government will have no choice but to grant us amnesty for all our alleged crimes, after which we will have nothing to worry about at all."

"If you overdo the pressure, you won't get amnesty," said Ley, "you will outrage the country, you will turn it against us. The North Americans and the world are already against us and will help the government put us down."

"David may be right," said Lucientes.

"There have been enough atrocities," continued Ley. "A

few more and the whole world will come after us.'' Did no one else see it this way? Would the kidnapping of Jane Hoyt Fox be too much?

"The sequestering of one American cunt?'' said Marzo. "You call that an atrocity? Don't be silly.''

"You'll have the American army down here,'' said Ley. At the beginning he had thought Marzo an able man in some ways, but he had become uncontrollable, and as a leader he was dangerous to them all. "What do we do then?'' said Ley. He glanced around looking for support, but found none. Von Bauzer and Jiménez were gazing at Marzo with admiration. Three former street thugs grown arrogant with their billions, thought Ley. Lucientes, who was his only possible ally, was peering down at the table. So what did I expect? thought Ley.

Von Bauzer suddenly spoke up: "I agree with Pablo.''

"Yes,'' said Jiménez, "I also.''

There was a long pause during which Marzo stared at the top of Lucientes's head. Finally, without raising his eyes, Lucientes said: "I have some reservations, but basically I'm ready to go along with it.''

Which left Ley with no choice, it seemed to him, if he wished to leave here alive. "Okay,'' he said, and shrugged. "If you're all agreed, I'll make it unanimous.''

Marzo was grinning with triumph. "The female reporter will be good for us, you'll see,'' he said. "We sequester her and it makes exactly the type statement we want to make.'' And he got up and moved around the table shaking hands. "The only better statement would be to rub out one of the DEA agents here. But they're too well protected.'' And he laughed.

Ley did not laugh. Pablo Marzo, he believed, had just become the undisputed leader of what the press called the Medellín Cartel. Ley had been unable to stop it. And from now on his life was in danger.

For a time all ate in silence.

When the servants had come in, had ladled out the dessert and gone out again, Marzo said: "After lunch you all have to come out to my zoo." He got up and began moving around the table pouring out cognac. "I've got some spectacular new exhibits out there."

Sipping his cognac, Ley thought out what to say next. He held his snifter up to the light streaming in the window. "You serve good cognac, Pablo," he said. Flattery was usually useful, and it bought time. "I'll grant you that much." And he grinned. His voice sounded controlled to him, his grin felt firm. There was something else he wished to clear up, and now was perhaps a good time to do it. "Pablo, I've been meaning to ask you. I had a man in New York named Salvador. The son of my cook. He got suppressed." In Spanish the verb is *suprimar*: a polite word for murder. "His wife and children got suppressed as well."

"It had to be done," Marzo said.

Ley had his answer. He began nodding his head up and down.

"He led the police directly to our merchandise," said Marzo.

"I see."

"Cost us a lot of money."

Ley was still nodding. Marzo, having been confronted by this directly, seemed slightly embarrassed.

"I knew you wouldn't do it. How could you? He was the son of your cook."

Ley lifted his glass to his nose. He breathed the pungent fumes and gazed at Marzo through half-closed eyes.

"So I did you a service," said Marzo.

Ley, watching him narrowly, nodded once more.

Marzo chuckled. "Now you owe me one in return."

He drained his glass and stood up. "The zoo," he said.

Obediently the others went out of the house and strolled over there. The mass of bodyguards who had waited outside had started to follow, but with a wave of his hand Marzo checked them.

Ley strode along under the trees beside Lucientes. The others, who were some distance behind, were laughing and socking each other in the arms like teenagers. Ley said carefully: "I worry that Pablo may become a liability to us all."

"I wouldn't say that."

This was less than encouraging. "May have become one already," Ley pressed on.

Lucientes kept silent.

"With all the enemies he has," Ley said carefully, "it's a wonder someone hasn't killed him."

Lucientes would not meet his eyes. "Maybe it will all work out like he says."

Ley, mulling over several ways to express what he meant, had been about to say something more, but decided not to.

The zoo occupied a corner of Marzo's property close to the road. He had given it to the city but with conditions. On days when the owner was in residence, the zoo was not open to the public. The zoo was partly responsible for the immense popularity Marzo still enjoyed in Colombia. Most days its parking lot filled up with school buses and hordes of children trooped through. He himself was rarely nearby; he had many houses and was careful never to sleep two nights in a row in any of them.

His zoo had one lion, one elephant, one rhino—one of almost everything. They were kept in a row of railroad cages like in a circus. Dispirited-looking beasts, Ley thought with distaste, as he walked by them. All had been imported at great expense, and when one died Marzo ordered another. As a child, he must have had a fixation on jungle stories, or wild animals, Ley thought. There were a couple of keepers around. They stood almost at attention, their caps in their hands. The building had a high ceiling with skylights, and a trench down the middle for hosing out the animal muck. Shafts of dust-filled sunlight bombarded the floor, and Ley walked through them. He breathed in the hot humid zoo stink and found it almost insupportable.

He gazed down at a hippo in a small square pool. Marzo brought these animals in without bothering with import licenses. He had once been indicted for it—over this very hippo, Ley believed. But the brother of the judge who indicted him got shot to death on a dark street. The judge got the message and threw the case out of court. Marzo had not been indicted for anything since. In Colombia, that is. He was under several indictments in Florida and New York.

Ley gazed in at the hippo. "You should breed them," he said to Marzo. He nodded sagely.

"What for?" said Marzo, surprised.

"You gave all that free housing to the poor, right?"

"Of course."

The other men were listening attentively. "Got a lot of good publicity out of it," Ley continued. "You even got elected as an alternate to Congress."

"Yes I did."

"Then don't you see?"

"See what?"

"Hippos would be even better. Breed them, slaughter them, and feed the meat to the poor in your houses. Look how big hippos are. One hippo would take care of a hundred families. You'd be famous all over the world."

"You can't eat hippo meat."

"Of course you can."

"What does it taste like?" asked Marzo suspiciously.

Ley thought this over. "It tastes a bit like elephant meat."

"You've eaten elephant meat?"

Ley, though the laughter was bubbling over inside, managed to keep his face blank. "You cook it in a wok. Very tasty."

Marzo studied Ley's face but it told him nothing. Finally he turned away. "Over here," he said. The other men followed him. "There he is," said Marzo proudly. "What do you think of him?"

They stared at the face of a silverbacked gorilla. The beast was enormous, and stared back. The bars of the cage were thick. So were the animal's canines.

"He came in yesterday," Marzo bragged. "I hired a

Boeing 707. Nobody in it but him and his keeper. Flew them in nonstop from Africa.''

Ley looked at Marzo. The man should be suppressed, he told himself. It was amazing that the others did not see it. It was amazing that no one had done it before now. However, if it was to be done, he would have to do it himself. No one would help. The others might cheer afterward, but in the doing he would be alone.

"Is that not a great-looking gorilla?" demanded Marzo.

The other two billionaire street thugs thought it was, apparently. They enthused over it. They were particularly impressed with its supposed ferocity. If it ever got loose—

"Kick him in the balls and run," said one.

"The only thing you can do," said the other.

Both were laughing.

"You could exhibit that ape anywhere," said Ley to Marzo, "and people would know it was yours."

It made Marzo beam proudly.

"The family resemblance," continued Ley, "is uncanny."

Marzo's whole body stiffened, and there was an instant during which Ley feared he had gone too far. But Von Bauzer was already chortling.

"The family resemblance is—" He broke down laughing and could not continue.

"—amazing," concluded Jiménez. He was laughing too.

Marzo had had no time to react. He spun around and gazed into Ley's bland smile. Since Ley was unarmed and unprotected, obviously it was a joke, not a challenge. Or so he must have told himself. Finally he gave a smile all around.

"I have to get back to the bank," said Ley. All of them left the zoo and started back to the house and the cars.

Once back in the city, inside his own office, safe behind his desk, Ley toyed with a letter opener. From now on he had best increase his personal security. Then he began to think about Jane Fox. He would like to get into bed with her—this idea had never left him.

For some minutes he allowed himself to fantasize. Jane

with her legs spread, Jane begging for it. But she had rejected his overtures. Therefore he did not like her and apart from the sexual had no interest in her personally. He wondered how soon Marzo would abduct her and what the overall impact would be. He was thinking about Marzo, not Jane. He wondered if he himself should—could—do something to thwart him.

Douglas sat with Gallagher on the bench at the tennis court in the garden of the residence. His hair was wet and combed, and he was dressed. His racquet bag lay between his feet. Gallagher, who was waiting to go on, wore fresh tennis whites. He was bouncing his racquet against the heel of his hand and listening for the ping.

"Jane Fox," Douglas said, "the reporter—"

"You don't have to identify her to me, I know who she is."

"I want to talk to you about her."

"I see her in the elevator from time to time."

"Then you know she lives in our building now."

"In your apartment, as I understand it." Gallagher's head had turned; it was almost an accusation.

"No, she doesn't live in my apartment." Douglas tried to smother his annoyance. "That's an exaggeration, I believe."

"What you do on your own time," said Gallagher, "is immaterial to me."

In the last few weeks relations between them had not improved, had perhaps got worse. Douglas was not sure why. Gallagher was under increasing pressure from Washington and perhaps blamed Douglas. Was that the reason? In addition Douglas had the run of South America and Gallagher did not; certainly that galled. "She's got her own apartment, I believe."

"Right." The DEA station chief was looking not at him but straight ahead across the empty court.

"The embassy's press department arranged it. She lives in her own apartment."

Gallagher was nodding his head, and still not looking at him. "As far as the federal government is concerned," Gallagher said, "you now constitute a possible security leak, wouldn't you say?"

"I am not in the habit of leaking information to the press," said Douglas.

"How much longer you going to be attached to my office?"

"I think we ought to offer her some security."

"Us? Why?"

"Because we have it available, and because she needs it."

Douglas knew nothing of any plans of Pablo Marzo. But he was aware that Jane moved through the city without protection, and that she was by Colombian standards an obvious target. He was becoming increasingly worried about her.

"The personal safety of this or that newspaper reporter," said Gallagher, "is not the responsibility of the federal government."

"I'm not so sure."

"Did you ever hear about the First Amendment? Freedom of the press?"

"Freedom of the press does not include us letting her get killed."

"They may not kill her. They may only kidnap her."

"Then you agree her profile is rather high?"

Gallagher had begun glancing over his shoulder down the path, obviously watching for his tennis partner to appear.

"Too high," Douglas persisted.

"She attracts attention to herself," Gallagher conceded.

"Well, then—"

"You haven't thought this out. If we offer her protection, she probably won't take it."

"I'll see that she takes it."

"She'll say it infringes on her objectivity and independence."

"We'll see."

"And if she does take it," Gallagher said, "and if something happens to her while we're supposedly protecting her, she sues the U.S. government. Or her husband does. She does have a husband, doesn't she? It's Mrs. Fox, isn't it? She is married, isn't she?"

Douglas said nothing.

"The answer's no," said Gallagher.

"I think we should drive her to work in the mornings and bring her back at night in one of our cars."

Gallagher looked at him.

"What does it cost us? There's you and me and five clerks and secretaries living in that one building, for chrissake. She simply gets in one of the cars and the driver drops her off."

If Gallagher agreed, Douglas judged, it would be because he didn't know how much power Douglas had and deep down was afraid of him. When it came to political infighting, federal agents who had reached Gallagher's level were no different from high-ranking cops. They were ruled by fear.

"She can ride with you," said Douglas. "You drop her off on your way to the embassy."

"I don't want to ride with her."

"I'll take her then."

Gallagher had begun bouncing the strings off his shoe.

"If anyone is hanging around our building," Douglas said, "we attracted them there, not her. We owe her, you might say."

"We don't owe her shit."

"We move her safely in and out of the building, what's wrong with that?" Douglas said. "In addition we get to control her to some extent, control what she writes about us as well."

"You can't control reporters. How long you been a cop? They don't like us and that's that."

Jane came out of the cabana dressed, carrying a tennis bag. They watched her approach.

"What's the answer to my question?" demanded Gallagher.

"What question?" said Douglas.

"How much longer you going to be here?"

"Until they tell me to come back."

"Hanging around my neck. When will that be?"

Douglas shrugged. Until somebody decides I've done penance enough, he thought. His weekly reports to the police commissioner were still unanswered. He received no orders or instructions, nor even any communications. New York seemed to have forgotten his existence. From time to time he telephoned men in headquarters he thought he could trust. One of them he had gone through the police academy with, another had once been his partner in a radio car. These were difficult calls for him to make, and he had to be extremely careful lest he reveal too much: his uncertain status, his increasing desperation about his career. He could not even ask direct questions. Most of each conversation was spent on unrelated subjects while he waited for them to volunteer whatever they might happen to volunteer.

In executive conferences, Douglas had gathered, his name rarely came up.

Gallagher studied his strings. "It can't be too soon, as far as I'm concerned," he said.

"Yes," Douglas said, "I'm aware of your feelings on the matter."

"The normal tour of duty here is two years. I'm extending."

"You don't have to worry about me," said Douglas. "I'm not."

He supposed he was waiting for the mayor to change. The PC at least.

Jane reached them. She greeted Gallagher with a smile and by name. He nodded back. Her hair was damp and tied in a ponytail. She was wearing jeans, a white blouse, and a blue cardigan sweater. There was color in her cheeks and she looked healthy. When she turned to smile at Douglas, he thought his knees were going to melt. He felt sick with love for her.

Behind them the ambassador's wife had come out of the residence and had started up the path. Gallagher stood up. "I have to give a tennis lesson," he said, and walked out onto the court.

Jane waved to the ambassador's wife. "You didn't have to wait for me," she said to Douglas, as they started along the high path toward the gate. "I could have walked home alone."

"You shouldn't be alone, it isn't safe," he said, and felt her look at him sharply.

Once they were past the guards and outside in the street, she took his hand, which felt comfortable. As they walked along under the trees he told her he had arranged for her to be driven to and from her office each day.

Gallagher had warned him of her possible reaction. Nonetheless he was surprised by it.

"In one of those armored cars?"

"Yes."

"I feel like a prisoner in those things. I hate them."

"At least you'll be safe."

"I'm safe anyway."

"Jane, I don't want you moving about this city alone."

"I'm careful. I don't go out at night. I don't often walk in the streets alone. I don't drive off into the country alone. Our apartment building is guarded. My office building is guarded."

"That's not enough."

"They won't kill me, just kidnap me." It was exactly what Gallagher had said. She was treating the subject with the same lack of importance. "I'll become a legend." The idea made her laugh. "Helen of Troy. One of those medieval queens who was always getting abducted. The paper will have to pay. People will write books about me."

"Jane, it's not a joke in this country. They've murdered scores of journalists, a columnist on *El Tiempo*, the publisher of *El Espectador*. The reporters here don't have bylines anymore, so that the traffickers won't know who they are and won't shoot them. But you do have bylines."

"In New York I do, not here." She disengaged her hand and turned to face him. "I appreciate your concern, Ray. But I don't want to ride to and from work in an armored car."

"Just tell me why."

As they resumed walking she studied the ground. "I can't be beholden to the government, or to any individual representing the government."

"That's crazy."

"Ray, a reporter has to be totally independent. Even if I personally did not feel beholden to anyone, it would look like I was, and I can't permit that, and the paper would never permit that."

Their apartment building was only a short distance down this street, which was blocked off at one end by the embassy residence, and at the other by a police car parked sideways from corner to corner. That is, it was a safe street on which to stroll—for them, one of the few in Bogotá. Several of the buildings on the street had embassy people living in them, and so the police provided a twenty-four-hour police presence.

"Then have the paper hire an armored car and guards for you."

"If I asked them to do that, most likely they'd decide Bogotá's too dangerous for me, and yank me out of here."

Somehow this had developed into an argument. "They have to have someone here," Douglas said.

"Do they? They didn't for years. A guy came in from Rio once in a while. For a day. Two days at most."

They argued while walking. They argued in the elevator.

"Drugs is a much bigger story now," Douglas said.

"You're right. Probably they'd send in a man to replace me."

"I don't believe that."

"It's perfectly all right to risk getting a correspondent killed if it's a man," said Jane with some bitterness. "Not if it's a woman."

The argument continued in Jane's apartment after Douglas had followed her in there.

"You let the embassy find you this apartment."

"That's different."

"I don't see how."

"It's a debt if you like, but not a continuing debt. It's not something I would feel, and the paper would feel, we had to pay off day after day."

Jane's cat had come out of the kitchen and was rubbing against her leg. Jane picked it up. The message light on her answering machine was blinking, and she stared at it a moment.

"Listen to your messages," Douglas said.

Instead, Jane suddenly conceded. "All right, I'll ride with you to the office in the morning and back at night. But that's all. The rest of the day I'm on my own."

"We'll see."

"No, we won't see."

Pleased to have won at least a partial victory, Douglas smiled.

Jane went through into the living room and dropped into a chair. She had the cat in her lap. "It will be cheaper than taking a taxi," she said.

Douglas, following, said: "Aren't you going to listen to your messages?"

"In a minute."

He glanced around him. Bleached wood and overstuffed chairs. Modern. A plain rug. It was a furnished apartment that contained nothing of Jane except her clothes in the closet. He wondered why she chose to live in it, why she refused to move in with him, as he had asked her to.

Sitting in the chair with her cat, she looked gloomy, and he did not know why.

"Did your wife used to do everything you told her?" she asked. "Did she walk one step behind you?"

He saw she did not expect him to answer.

"I don't know what she was like, but it sounds like you want me to be her, and I'm not."

Douglas said nothing.

"Maybe she had no other life than you, but I do."

What was he supposed to answer to this?

"She didn't work, did she?"

"No."

"You can't have the same love twice, Ray. That's one of the rules of life." She came over and stroked his face. "Don't you know that?"

"You get each love once only."

"Right."

"Come upstairs with me," he said. The business of living took place in his flat usually, the eating, drinking, lovemaking—though usually she refused to sleep all night there. "We'll have a drink, then dinner, and then—"

"Then what?"

He gave a comical leer. "Something may occur to us."

She put her arms around him. "I do like you, you know that?"

"Listen to your messages and let's go."

"You go. I'll be up in a few minutes."

"What's on there you don't want me to hear?"

She laughed. "I have no idea."

"All right," he said, "five minutes."

"Well, maybe a little longer."

"Hurry up, I have a surprise for you."

Although he left the apartment smiling, and although he bounded up the service stairs two at a time, still he was disappointed. He wanted there to be no secrets between them. With his wife there had been none, or so he believed. They were young when they married, and afterward they grew in the same direction. This time, he admonished himself, it would obviously have to be different. He and Jane were both already grown. It was not the same and it was wrong of him to expect it to be. Their two lives were different, one from the other, and would stay that way ever after. He could wish it otherwise, but this was wrong too.

By the time she came up he had put the chicken on to roast and had poured out two glasses of chilled Chilean chardonnay. He sat her down on his couch and handed her a tiny velvet box.

She put her glass down to take it. "Ray," she said, sounding alarmed, "what's this?"

"Open it."

Inside was an emerald set in a ring. He saw her bite her lip. She looked almost guilty. She stared at it and did not look up.

"It's beautiful," she said finally.

"You don't like it."

"I love it." She hesitated. "Ray, you're a policeman." She let him put the ring on her finger. "You can't afford to buy me things like this."

"Emeralds are cheap in Colombia. Really, it's a rather cheap present."

They both laughed and she put her arms around him. "Thank you," she said, and kissed him.

Later in his bedroom in the dark they talked about babies, neither of them confronting the subject head on. She would have to start soon, Jane said. "I don't have too much more time."

Douglas said nothing.

"But you've got grown children," she said.

Framed photos of his children stood on his dresser.

"You maybe wouldn't want any more," Jane said.

He hesitated, then joked: "Having a baby at my age would be embarrassing. My kids probably think Dad doesn't do it anymore—if he ever did."

They mulled over this exchange for a while—what exactly had been said. And what left unsaid.

"Do you want me to get up and make us a cup of tea?" Jane asked.

Perhaps it was a way of changing the subject. "No," he said and pulled her down and began caressing her face, her body. This too was a way of changing the subject, none better. Presently he made her moan and gasp and also, to his surprise, speak. Her voice was barely under control, hoarse, guttural, a series of grunts.

"Did you and your wife—have—have a—a good sex life?"

It was Jane he was besotted with at that moment. He wanted to get his whole body inside her, indeed he was trying to, wanted to merge the two of them into one person.

"Yes," he said. It was an emotion he had not felt since the earliest days of his marriage.

"As—as good as—as this?"

He was unwilling to defame his wife's memory, but too much in love with Jane not to tell her what she wanted to hear. "Not like this."

"You think about her a lot."

"I do."

"What do you think about?"

"That I'd like to tell her about you."

"She'd—she'd scratch your—your eyes out."

Later Jane said: "If she were alive, which one of us would you—would you choose?"

"That's some question."

"Never mind, you don't have to answer."

He said with feeling: "I don't know what the answer should be. I never believed I could love anyone again as much as I love you."

They lay nestled quietly against each other. He said: "What went wrong with your marriage? Was the problem sex?"

"One of the problems, I guess."

He wondered how much he could ask. He wanted to know more, and at the same time didn't.

Jane said: "His idea of arousing me was not the same as yours."

"Meaning what?"

She seemed to shrug. "Two kisses, roll on top, come, roll off."

It presented a too-vivid picture, one which, despite himself, he wasn't ready for. "I wasn't really asking for details."

She raised up on one arm and gazed down at him. "I do believe you're jealous." She looked pleased.

"No."

"What do you think married people do?"

"I know what they do."

"There's no point being jealous about what's past, is there?"

"None whatever."

"Eight years of marriage. He was ardent enough. Figuring on three times a week, I fucked him about twelve hundred times."

He wondered if she was trying to get him over his jealousy by being brutal about it.

"I don't like you to use that word," he said.

For a time, both were silent.

"And now you're getting divorced," he said.

"Yes." Had she hesitated a moment before answering? he wondered.

He knew what marriage was, it could not be denied. But he did not know what had gone on in her life before he met her, what went on in her head even now. He could feel the whole length of her against him, could feel the heat her body gave off. He knew he should not ask the next question, but could not help himself. "And how many others before your husband?"

She laughed. "That doesn't concern you." She stirred in his arms then added: "I only said that about my husband because you ought to have been able to figure it out for yourself."

Again both were silent. Then she said: "I may have to go to Florida."

"What for?"

"It's about halfway. My husband wants me to meet him there."

"That was the message on your machine."

"One of them, yes."

"What's there to meet about?"

"Things."

"What things?"

"To talk over."

After a silence she said: "I don't mind going to Florida. It will be nice to go to a restaurant, go to a movie, see the shops. Do you realize I haven't been out of this house at night since we got back from Bolivia."

"Well, it just isn't safe."

"I've scarcely been out of bed, as a matter of fact."

"Is bed so bad?"

She did not answer.

"Why do you have to see the guy?" he asked. "Let your lawyer handle it."

"Well, sooner or later I'm going to have to meet him."

She sounded guilty. Guilty about what? "What's the status of this divorce anyway?" he asked.

"I don't know."

"You don't know?"

"It's one of the things I need to find out."

"I get the impression you don't care if you get divorced or not."

She was silent.

"Jane, time is important."

"Yes, I know."

"You're thirty-six years old."

"You don't have to remind me."

In the bed he thought he could feel even the seconds pass. He could feel the weight of her against his chest and the time passing, second by second, an entire minute, perhaps longer, during which she neither moved nor spoke.

She said: "What do you care? You don't want more children. You don't even want to marry me."

"Who told you I don't want to marry you?"

There was a long pause. Then she said: "Well, do you?" Another long pause. "Yes."

"You don't sound too sure."

"I'm sure."

"You hesitated," she said.

"Jane, we're not teenagers. There is a lot that has to be worked out."

"I see."

"When? How? What country would we live in? You're not even divorced yet. And you don't seem to be in much of a hurry."

"Until I met you I wasn't. I wanted time to think this over. I did not want to be rushed."

"And now?"

A few minutes ago he had felt as close to her as two human beings could get. Now he felt they had moved yards apart. They were in separate rooms and the intervening doors were closed.

She got up and began to dress.

He said: "Don't go."

"Yes. I want to sleep in my own bed."

"Why?"

"The telephone is liable to ring, for one thing. Queries from the desk. They call up any hour of the day or night."

"That's not the reason."

"When I came down here it was years since I had slept alone. I found I liked it."

Well, he wasn't going to beg her. He too got up and began to dress.

"You don't have to accompany me," Jane said.

He got dressed anyway, and in silence walked her down the stairs to her door.

There they paused awkwardly. Jane looked up at him. Probably she felt the distance between them as much as he did. "Would you like to come in for a cup of tea or something?" she asked tentatively.

"All right."

At her stove he watched her boil the water.

Afterward, as she was letting him out the door, she suddenly clung to him.

The result was that they slept the night in Jane's bed.

The next morning when they woke up and realized where they were and what had happened, they began to laugh.

He flew to New York to see his children and his mother. He was mulling over a visit to headquarters as well, trying to decide if it was a good idea just to go there and be seen in the halls.

There was a family dinner at which he presided in a restaurant in Bronxville. His mother had had her hair done for the occasion. His children were pleased enough to see him but he had the impression that being summoned here tonight inconvenienced them.

The next morning he woke up disgruntled and again brooded about headquarters. He visualized the layout of offices. Whom should he speak to? What would he say? How long should he stay? What were the risks?

The more he thought about it, the more the risks seemed to rise. Since he had come twenty-five hundred miles from where they supposed him to be, his appearance in their midst was not going to seem casual. He would be seen for what he was, a supplicant, and therefore weak.

He drove to Macy's in White Plains and bought himself a pair of shoes, a new tennis racquet, and a toaster. By then his thoughts were on Jane. He missed her, was worried about her safety, and wanted to get back.

In the morning the ambassador woke up in bed beside his wife. Sunlight streamed in through the bulletproof glass, and Martha Thompson said: "I'm going back to America to be with my children."

The ambassador picked up the telephone to call downstairs. "What do you want for breakfast?"

"I'm leaving."

"Fine. But not till after breakfast, I assume. What do you want to order?"

"Nothing," said Martha Thompson.

Thompson said into the receiver: *"Dos cafes, dos sumo de naranja. Y para me, huevos rancheros, pan tostado y— hay chorizo? Bien."* He turned to his wife again. "I ordered you coffee and orange juice. You want anything else?"

"No." She was sitting up with her arms crossed on her chest.

"Nada mas," Thompson said into the receiver, and hung up. "The children are in boarding school," he said as he got out of bed. "There's no way you can be with them right now."

He padded across the rug to the bathroom, a big man in rumpled pajamas. The door closed. She heard the toilet flush, then the water running as he shaved.

She put a bathrobe on and opened the door to the waiter. He set the tray down on the table in their small dining room, and began laying out the place mats, the silverware, the napkins.

The ambassador approached the table. He was now wearing trousers and a T-shirt, his feet in slippers, his hair combed.

"I'm going back to America."

He poured coffee into both cups. "You can't right now. I need you here. Drink your orange juice."

"You don't need me."

"Martha, when I'm invited to these receptions and banquets, you're expected to attend. You represent the United States of America."

"Bullshit."

Thompson frowned. "Your attendance at these functions is important."

"Not to me it's not."

"I suppose it's not important for me to attend either."

"I didn't say that."

"Then what did you say?"

"That I'm going back to America to be with my children."

"You're leaving me, is that it?"

Martha said nothing.

"Don't be ridiculous," Thompson said. "The children are in school in Virginia. Where would you live? What would you do?"

"Something. Anything."

His resistance, so bland, so confident, reduced her to tears of impotence, of frustration. She tried to hold them back but couldn't.

Thompson got up and put his arms around her. "I need you, I really need you," he said. He didn't like to grovel, and he convinced himself he wasn't doing it. "Tell you what—" He was thinking fast as he spoke. At diplomatic functions she was usually the youngest woman in the room, and the best-looking, and he was proud of her, even if she didn't speak Spanish. He would be lonely here without her, he believed. No one in the bed, breakfast alone and all that. Worse, it would be a public defeat for him. If she left, everyone would notice.

"Tell you what," he said again. "Give me another month, till after the thing at the French embassy that's coming up. You always enjoy the shindigs they put on. Then we'll take a vacation, go up and see the kids. How's that?"

"You don't understand. I hate it here. I'm a prisoner in this house. I hate it, hate it, hate it."

Thompson saw he would have to concede further. "Stick it out just a little longer," he said. "Please."

"How long?"

"The first of the year."

"You'll resign?"

"Yes." If it didn't seem suitable when the date came, he would put her off month by month. Perhaps he never should have accepted this job, and he was certainly not going to keep it forever. But he hadn't been here long enough yet. If he quit now, or if she left him now, it would be devastating to his prestige.

"Promise?" said Martha.

"Promise," he said. "Now drink your orange juice."

Douglas's first job each morning was to read the cable traffic that had come in during the night. Usually there were about two dozen cables, sixty percent of them out of New York, most of the rest out of Miami. They were reports of arrests and seizures, of coast guard sightings, of intelligence gleaned from informants, from prisoners. They made interesting reading, and sometimes there was something in them that had to be acted on.

Upon reaching the embassy that morning he had gone down to the cafeteria in the basement where he bought a buttered roll and coffee in a Styrofoam cup. He brought these up to his desk on the third floor, hung his suit coat behind the door, and loosened his tie. He sat down, peeled the lid off the cup, and started in on the cables. He was about halfway through the pile when Gallagher's deputy, an agent named Bannon, came in and dropped into the chair facing him.

"I had an interesting call in the middle of the night," Bannon said, and waited.

Bannon had had the duty last night, Douglas remembered. He thought: Whatever it is that he wants to tell me, he's going to milk it first.

"Yes?" Douglas prompted.

"It looks like there's a plot on to kidnap your girlfriend."

Douglas did not ask who he meant. "What?" he said, and was instantly on his feet. "When? How?"

Bannon remained seated, his legs straight out in front, ankles crossed, his weight on the small of his back. He seemed to be enjoying Douglas's reaction, for a slight smile came onto his face. "About three A.M. this guy calls up the embassy. The switchboard operator puts him through to me, no questions asked, like they're supposed to."

"Come on, come on," said Douglas.

"He says there's this plot to kidnap her, and that Pablo Marzo is behind it. According to him."

"What language was he speaking? Who else knows about this? Did he have an accent? Did you believe him?" It was important to get the details straight. Douglas had a dozen questions that Bannon should already have answered.

Instead, Bannon yawned.

"Come on, come on," said Douglas again.

"I'm tired, I've been up all night. So don't push me, okay?"

"By all means take your time. Tomorrow will be soon enough. Next week will be even better."

"Yeah, I believed him. He spoke Spanish. Did he have an accent? I don't know Spanish well enough to tell. Gallagher asked the same question. He's going to listen to the tape. He said he should be able to tell."

"Well, what else for chrissake? What else did he say? He must have said more than that."

"Once he spoke English. He did have an accent there."

"Wonderful."

"He didn't want to talk. What can I tell you? I kept him on the line as long as I could. He said he was a cook. Then he switched to English and asked me if I understood."

Douglas was pacing the floor. "We've got to put a guard on her right away," he said. "We've got to guard her around the clock."

"What I really came in here for was that Gallagher wants to see you," Bannon said, and he yawned again. "He sent me to get you."

Douglas went into Gallagher's office. A technician was setting up the tape. Gallagher waited until all the other agents had trooped into the room, then told the technician to start the machine. Eleven men in shirtsleeves stood listening to a tape that lasted less than sixty seconds. When it ended, Gallagher told the technician to play it again.

They listened to it four times.

"I'll tell you one thing," Gallagher said at last, "that guy is no cook."

An agent named Martínez said: "I agree with you. His Spanish is too good. That's an educated man."

Gallagher and Martínez were the only men in the room who had spoken Spanish from childhood.

"When he switches to English," said Douglas, "there's something wrong. He puts on a thick accent that's fake. It sounds to me like his English is perfect too."

"All right," said Gallagher, "we got a bilingual guy. What else?"

The room was silent. "Anybody recognize the voice?" asked Gallagher.

No one did.

"Maybe we should bring Mrs. Fox in here," Martínez suggested. "She might recognize the voice. Maybe it's somebody she knows."

This was voted down. The voice on the phone had become that of a confidential informant. In the police world a confidential informant was confidential; one did not divulge confidential information to the press. Besides which, the notion that Jane might recognize the voice seemed, to most of the men present, preposterous.

"Next question," said Gallagher, "do we believe this guy?"

Everybody believed him.

Especially Douglas believed him. "Do we guard her ourselves, or do we have General Nuñez do it?" said Douglas.

"We ship her ass back to America is what we do," said Gallagher.

"Suppose she won't go?" said Bannon.

Gallagher punched the button on his intercom. "Ask the ambassador to come down here," he instructed his secretary. "Tell him we want him to listen to something and it's urgent."

He sent all the men back to their offices except for Douglas, Bannon, and the technician. Gallagher went back and sat down behind his desk. The other two men took chairs along the wall. The technician stood beside his machine, and they waited.

"We gotta get somebody on her right away," said Douglas.

"Relax," said Bannon.

"She is not my problem," said Gallagher.

"They could be scooping her up right now."

"Did you deliver her to the *El Tiempo* building this morning?"

"Yes, but—"

"Then she's safe where she is."

"Suppose she decides to go out?"

"Then she's an idiot who deserves whatever she gets," snapped Gallagher.

The ambassador came in. He wore a politician's grin and red suspenders and he shook hands heartily all around. He was still digesting the interview with his wife. It gave to his manner more bluff heartiness than usual. He was overcompensating, and was afraid it showed. "So what's so urgent?" he demanded.

They played the tape for him, and his face got dark. The tape ended and there was silence in the room. The ambassador addressed the technician. "You can go," he said. He was such a big man that the room seemed suddenly too small. He watched the man unplug and pack his machine. The door had scarcely closed before the ambassador said: "I want her out of the country. Today. I want her gone."

"That might not be so easy to do," said Gallagher.

"Today," said Thompson. "They're not snatching that broad on my watch."

"She may not want to go."

The ambassador was pacing. "Do you realize how important her paper is? How important she becomes if she gets kidnapped?"

"Douglas knows her," Gallagher said. "Rather well, in fact. Maybe he can talk to her."

Douglas was getting exceedingly sick of Gallagher's snide remarks.

"I'll phone her publisher," said the ambassador. "He's a friend of mine. He'll pull her out of here within the hour."

This was not what Douglas wanted to happen. He wanted her to remain in Colombia, but protected. "Well," he said carefully, "that would certainly make headlines. From the traffickers' point of view, it would be almost as effective as kidnapping her."

"If he gives me a hard time," Thompson said, "I'll remind him of his stockholders. How much would a ransom be, ten million dollars?" Suddenly he looked at Douglas with suspicion. "What do you mean, as effective as kidnapping her?"

"The traffickers want headlines like that. They want to prove the Colombian government powerless. They want to force the government to abolish the extradition laws and grant them amnesty for their crimes. After that, they'll force the government to kick the DEA out of here. There will be no way for the United States to get at them."

There was a long pause. The ambassador looked thoughtful.

"In addition, we blow open the case. It gives us no time to investigate this information." Then he added, "And it may get the informant killed as well."

Seeing that he had their attention now, Douglas began to argue for an alternate solution. Suppose Mrs. Fox could be induced to leave the country for a week or so, while an investigation got under way? Bolivia. Peru. A week, two weeks from now they would have a clearer picture of where they stood, what to do.

The ambassador had begun nodding. After a long silence he said: "Okay, provided she's out of the country no later than tomorrow. And heavily guarded till then." He nodded at everyone again and left the office.

Douglas rode one of the armored cars out Avenida El Dorado, got out in front of the *El Tiempo* building and went through the security and upstairs. Now comes the hard part, he thought: selling it to Jane.

He found her out in the newsroom joking in Spanish with a group of Colombian newsmen. Looking surprised to see him, she led him into her office and closed the door.

Douglas was surprised to see how small the office was, no more than a cubicle, really.

"What did you want to say to me?" She was smiling and looked fond of him.

But he was at a loss as to how to begin. He was about to frighten her out of her wits and perhaps change the course of her life. Unless of course she got angry or stubborn and refused to listen to him altogether.

It would take working up to. When did she plan her next trip to Bolivia or Peru? he asked. Not for a while, she answered.

"What about going back there tomorrow?"

"Why?"

"Well, suppose I had to go. We could go together."

She shook her head. "I couldn't justify it to the paper. I'd like to, though. You know I would. How long would you be gone?"

"Well, what about a vacation then?"

"When?"

"Tomorrow."

"What's this all about?"

He kept glancing around the cubicle as if looking for help. Finally he just blurted it out: there had been a telephone call, a serious threat—

He saw that she was more shaken than he would have expected.

"A serious threat?"

"We think it's serious, yes."

"You better tell me more. Who? How?"

"I'm sorry, I can't."

"Can I listen to the tape?"

"What point would that serve?" Instead, he told her there had just been a second threat against her by the ambassador that was, in its way, equally serious—the ambassador had threatened to phone her publisher to demand her immediate withdrawal.

This shook her too.

"If you want to stay here, you have to disappear for a week or two."

"Thompson said that?"

"Yes."

She was suddenly furious. "He wouldn't dare pull this on a man. If you're a woman," she muttered, "everybody pushes you around."

For what seemed a judicious length of time he waited. Then he said: "You could fly to the Caribbean, spend a few days in the sun on one of the islands."

"Who with? With you?"

"If you didn't mind."

It made her laugh ruefully, and she paced the room thinking about it. He waited.

Finally she came over and put her arms around him. "All right," she said. "Which one?"

16

FROM JANE'S POINT of view it was less than the ideal solution, for it required her to juggle appointments, assignments, interviews. It required lying too. She hated people who lied, and hated to be forced to lie herself.

She worked for the paper, but more specifically for the foreign desk. The foreign desk had always to know where she was and what she was doing. Must know everything about her. It approved or disapproved her story ideas, her movements, even where she lived and how much she paid for her apartment.

She would have to advise the desk that she intended to travel out of Bogotá. In effect asking permission.

She would have to advise her husband as well. She didn't want him getting frantic and phoning the desk to find out where she was. So far she had been unable to make him believe in any permanent separation. He phoned regularly, still wanting his wife to meet him in the Caribbean or Miami for a weekend or a week, but she had broken their first agreed-upon date, had made him lose his deposit, and now each time he asked again she put him off, saying she was too busy at the moment. Their meeting, when it happened, would be the breaking point, she supposed.

Douglas had said she had to get out of Bogotá, and she believed him. So what would she tell the desk? And George? Where was she going, and why? If she couldn't mention the kidnapping threat for fear of being ordered out of South America altogether, then what reason would she give?

She was owed vacation time, but if she requested it the

desk would want details: which island, the name of the hotel, almost her room number. George might find out, and come flying down on the next plane. It was the sort of thing he might do. Or the news might crush him, even if he never found out about Ray Douglas—that she had taken a vacation not only without him, but without even telling him. Which was no way for this marriage to end; George deserved better than that. If indeed she intended to end it. If she was so sure, what was holding her back? It was a problem she could not put off forever.

What was much more likely, if she asked for vacation time, was that the desk would refuse on the grounds that the story she was on, Bogotá and drugs, was too hot right now, better to wait a few months. Permission not granted.

Then what?

She decided she could not ask for vacation time.

She could not ask to go back to Bolivia or Peru either. It was too soon, too expensive, and the big story was here, not there. The desk would certainly refuse.

She would have to think up something else, and whatever it was would be a lie. There was no way out, she would have to lie. This lie, in the form of a message to the desk, she spent more than an hour in her office concocting. She typed it out, rewrote it several times, kept studying it.

Abel Flores, her Colombian assistant, came in. He was about thirty, a freelance radio journalist. She had hired him at the end of her first week in Bogotá. The people at *El Tiempo* had recommended him. He minded the office, watched the telex machines, shared his sources with her, helped out with his knowledge of the country, and sometimes drove her around in his twenty-year-old car.

She told Flores he would be in charge of the office while she was gone. She would call in for messages.

He nodded, and she resumed studying her message to the desk. It alluded to a confidential informant, a field trip, a possible Caribbean connection, a possible big story. There had been no time for consultation with New York in advance.

it said; she would check regularly with her office for messages; since she would be in the field she would be out of contact, could give no firm coordinates.

She sent this lie, this conglomeration of lies, to New York by telex an hour before she and Ray took off, then sat on the plane for three hours, worrying. The telex wasn't the end of it. One lie always begets many lies and she was caught now in a mesh of them. Upon her return to Bogotá she would have to explain why her "field trip" had not yielded a major story, which would require a long message to the effect that none of her leads had panned out. She would seem to have invested time and money belonging to the paper for no useful result, which showed bad news judgment, and which could —would—hurt her career. The desk would want details. Depending on how much it badgered her for them, she would have to come up with still more lies.

And what about the paper's time and money? To take a week's pay for sitting on a beach was stealing. If she got found out she would lose her job. Once back in Bogotá, to preserve her lie, she would have to put in expense vouchers for her "field trip," stealing still more. She could delay this a long time, but the accounting department would keep after her until she sent something.

She was supposed to sit quietly on a beach and hope no one she knew spotted her sitting there with her lover. If someone saw her and word got back to the desk, same thing, she would get fired.

She sat glumly in the window seat staring out at blue sky and blue sea below, and wondered what she could do about all this. Blue. Not another color anywhere except for her reflection sometimes in the porthole. Nothing. She was caught. From time to time Ray tried to talk to her, but she did not respond, and finally he stopped. He was in an ebullient mood, she could tell, only slightly dimmed by her silence. For him this was a honeymoon, without benefit of marriage, the best kind. She had been on one or two such honeymoons and could read the signs. She worried about disappointing him. She loved him and most often wanted to be whatever it was he wanted her to be, but it was hard at the best of times, and on this island they were headed for likely to be impossible. She knew herself. She was not likely to be good company. She was too worried, and he represented still one more worry—that she would make him unhappy.

Ray had wanted to book a hotel on Curaçao for it was one of the closest islands, and it was the one favored by embassy personnel on regular R&R leave. He had been given the names of the best hotels, the best restaurants. But at Jane's urging he had chosen an island farther up the chain. Though she did not tell him so, she could not afford to be seen by embassy personnel. She could not afford to be seen by anyone, and she wished she could talk to him frankly about how she felt. But she couldn't. To her, lying was such a shameful thing that, like certain aspects of sex, she was simply unable to discuss it.

When the plane door opened and she stepped out onto the landing she was unprepared for the stultifying heat. Bogotá being a place without seasons, the days were always cool, and the nights always chilly. In the rain it became quite chilly. No one had central heating. On rainy days on went the electric grills. This was what she had come from and was used to and she stepped out of the plane and the heat hit her, whack, right in the face. During the walk across the tarmac, the sun on her face felt like an instant sunburn.

Then she was inside the terminal glancing guiltily around, afraid she might spot some face she knew. Leaving Ray to collect the bags, she went out through customs and into the airport shop where she bought sunglasses and a floppy straw hat. The hat came down low on her forehead and the sunglasses were almost black. Staring into the shop's mirror, she imagined herself virtually unrecognizable, and felt a bit better.

She went out onto the sidewalk and when Ray came out with the bags they walked over and rented a car and started across the island toward the hotel. She threw her hat in the back and sat with the map open on her knees giving directions. The island was trees and hills and views of the sea. It resembled all the other islands she had been on. It was lush green and beautiful, though of course poor. The blacks lived in shacks with corrugated iron roofs. The women walked along the edges of the roads carrying loads on their heads. Theirs was the traditional role of women, she reflected, whereas hers was not.

While Ray checked in she walked through the lobby and out the hotel's other side onto the sand. This seemed less compromising than to stand at his elbow while he wrote on the card whatever he would write. In her dark glasses under her big hat she looked around. She didn't know what he wrote and did not want to know. She had her shoes in her hand and could feel the hot sand between her toes. She realized she felt as guilty about betraying her husband as about betraying the paper. What had happened in Bolivia was unplanned. This was planned.

Their room was up one flight. She went out onto the balcony. Below the balcony were the tops of palm trees and then the beach. Across the water, five or ten miles away, she could see another island. The sun was going down. The sea was calm, and as she watched, it turned the color of rosé wine.

She came back into the room as Ray was tipping the porter. He locked the door and came toward her, looking as pleased as a boy, and this disconcerted her, for she was not at all in the mood. So that's the kind of vacation it's going to be, she thought; but what else did I expect? He embraced and kissed her, but after a moment she broke the embrace saying: "So, what do you want to do? Do you want to go swimming?"

It was getting dark fast and the beach was deserted. The water was warm and there was no sound. Afterward she took a shower and then he did. By the time he came out she was dressed and on the balcony. She came back in and picked up her purse.

For dinner they drove down into the village. Well, they had to eat, and the chance of being spotted was the same there as here. They walked along the street peering into restaurants. He let her make the choice. She vetoed the ones that were crowded, choosing the one with the fewest people in it.

Then back to the hotel. They got ready for bed. He watched her undress and his eyes were overbright. As always it amazed her that a man could get so excited watching a woman undress—any woman, she did not flatter herself. She felt compromised. In Bogotá she had had her own flat, and had returned to it every night. They had not been living together. Not by her lights. She had not been celibate, but each time it had been almost by chance—or so she had persuaded herself. Here, casually getting undressed in the same room, it felt as if she had moved in with him—while still married to someone else. In Bogotá, making love had never been taken for granted, at least by her. Whereas tonight what was to happen next was accepted by both as a foregone conclusion. It felt wrong.

In bed in the dark she gave in to him—and also to herself. She did love him, she told herself. She was not immune to him, not immune to the same desires that in him at the moment seemed rather out of control. He fell asleep almost immediately afterward, his head on her shoulder. She lay awake in the dark with her guilt.

Morning came. He wanted to snorkel or stroll to the end of the beach. To avoid being seen, she wanted to sit on the balcony reading. The hat and dark glasses, she had decided, did not disguise her enough. But when he asked her what was the matter, she said she didn't like their beach very much—and was annoyed at him for not understanding her mood without being told.

He coaxed her into the car and they went looking for a beach that might please her. She felt and acted surly. Although she hated herself for the surliness, she did not seem able to help it. There were public beaches and hotel beaches but she rejected them. On the far side of the island they discovered a whole row of small, deserted beaches that were apparently little used. They were separated from the road by a hundred yards of bush. There were paths through the bush, and picnic refuse here and there in the undergrowth—the beaches, though empty today, were well enough known to the locals apparently. The one Ray chose was particularly secluded, hemmed in by high rocks.

They spread towels and smeared suntan oil on each other. This was enough to give Ray ideas. He decided they should swim nude.

She refused. "Someone might come."

"No one will come."

"I don't want to."

Stepping out of his trunks he went running through the shallows and plunged in. Jane sat down on the towel and watched him. The sun on her shoulders was very hot, and as it came off the sea and sand it was blinding. His bottom was very white and she imagined it would be burned and sore tonight.

He came marching toward her out of the low surf. "Come on in, it's great."

He reached the towel and when she only looked up at him quizzically, he grasped her hand and pulled her to her feet. He was smiling and happy and she followed him toward the water, but when they got there his hands went to the ties of her bikini.

She started to protest, but her resistance only amused him. "You don't need that," he said, "or that either." In an instant she was as naked as he was. Nervously she glanced over her shoulder at the low cliff, at the bushes on top of it that screened off the road.

"You can hear the cars," she said.

"You can't see them."

"Suppose one stops."

"They'll feast their eyes on the best-looking naked woman on the island."

Her bikini had become two tiny heaps at her feet, and she touched them with her toe. He had her hand and began pulling her toward the water. The water came up over her feet and he was still pulling her. It was up to her shins, her thighs. Finally she shook her hand loose from his and dove in.

The water felt nice on her bare skin, cool and sleek, almost caressing, but she was too nervous to enjoy it, and she swam out a ways and turned and peered back in. She could not see the road and the bushes looked thick, but she did not feel comfortable even where she was, and to contemplate striding up out of the water toward their towel appalled her.

Though eventually it had to be done. She came out of the water high-stepping, hurrying. In passing she scooped up the pieces of her bikini and she almost ran the rest of the way. At the towel she stood for a moment shaking the water out of her ears. Her hair hung in ropes. She got one sandy foot into the bikini bottom, and then Ray had her in his arms, turning her around, pushing her down onto the blanket. He was kissing her, and she knew what he had in mind without being told. She was reasoning clearly and a bit coldly and could feel his commanding presence against her leg.

"No," she said.

"Haven't you ever made love on a beach?"

"Yes," she said, hoping it would cool him down. She hadn't, and it didn't.

He was grinning at her and trying to wedge his knee between her knees.

"Someone will come."

"No one will come." He was behaving like an adolescent. She was reminded of high-school boys pleading with her in dark cars.

This was more serious.

"I don't want to."

It was bright daylight, hot, the sun was beating down, and this beach was exposed to the world not only on all sides but even above.

"Someone will see us."

"I want to make love to you."

If anyone came through the bushes, she realized, this little scene, two naked people, the erect male trying to get between the female's legs, would be every bit as embarrassing as copulation, and it was lasting longer. Unless she gave in to him it showed no sign of ending.

She relaxed her legs, allowed him to pry her knees apart. Was it such a big thing to do for him?

"Oh, Jane, I love you so much."

"Don't get sand in me," she said.

"I love you, I love you."

"Be quick," she said.

But she was not ready and it hurt.

"Jane, Jane," he said.

Afterward she hurried into her bikini and sat on the towel hugging her knees. She said nothing. Still naked, he sat beside her. He stared silently out to sea. His legs were out straight and his ankles crossed. Confronted by her silence he seemed almost shamed. He did not know what to do or say.

"You're going to get sunburned in all the wrong places," she warned him.

It occurred to her that her period was due about now, and she began counting up the days. They did not add up. She was, she calculated, about six days late. It was too soon to worry about it. She studied Ray's crossed ankles and speculated.

David Ley stood in the doorway looking out at the plane through the rain. It was an ex-military cargo ship. It sat on the dirt strip, bloated and squat, belly and propellors almost touching the ground. It was buttoned up tight. The rain was pounding down, bouncing off the wings, coursing down the camouflage.

"What do you think of her?" said Pablo Marzo.

Ley decided not to say what he thought.

"The tail section is on hinges," said Marzo. "It folds upwards and there's a ramp comes down. You could drive a bus up inside that plane."

"A school bus," commented Ley. "Full of kids. Something of that nature."

The irony went over Marzo's head. "A tank," he said. "Anything."

Ley gave a nod as if he approved. He did not approve.

"So what do you think?" An insurance salesman, Ley thought.

That's what Marzo sounded like. Proud of his product. Confident of making the sale.

It was late afternoon. Ley watched the rain falling. He knew why he had been brought here, knew the sales pitch was coming, and had no intention of buying. "And the pilot?" he said.

"Sleeping."

Ley looked into Marzo's hard smile.

"*Hombre,*" said Marzo defensively. "*Es normal.*"

Ley said nothing.

"Flies only at night," Marzo explained. "He's good, this guy."

Ley turned back to the rain.

"A *norteamericano,*" said Marzo. "Absolutely reliable."

Ley did not believe in most of Marzo's schemes, and he did not believe in the reliability of pilots. "I thought you were going to buy a submarine," he said.

"This is better. This is the perfect plane."

Ley did not believe in perfect planes either. Not when they dropped by accident into one's lap.

"When you meet the pilot I'm sure you'll agree."

The pilot could be CIA, DEA. Ley was not going to meet him if he could help it.

"He brought a suitcase full of cash down from my Florida distributors, plus some radio gear Von Bauzer wanted," said Marzo. "That's how reliable he is."

If the pilot was an agent and part of a setup, then to hand over money and gear at this end was permitted under American law, Ley believed. To distribute drugs at the other end was not. Ley wanted to see the pilot take a load north and put it into circulation. Only then would he believe in his reliability.

"You want to go out and check her over?" said Marzo, gesturing toward the plane.

It was as if the rain was pounding the huge fat plane down into the mud. Parts of the field looked half under water.

"This is close enough."

Ley saw that Marzo's grin had switched off.

"It's raining," said Ley quickly. Though he wanted to distance himself from the ex-tombstone thief, from this latest scheme, he did not necessarily want to say so outright.

Marzo's face wore a cold, speculative expression. For a moment they gazed at each other, but then, warning himself still again to be careful, Ley's eyes dropped.

"It's a dream plane," Marzo said.

Ley slapped him on the back. "Congratulations on your plane."

"That plane can land and take off from a handkerchief."

"A handkerchief," said Ley.

"Fully loaded."

"Wow," said Ley.

"That's the beauty of it."

His voice again sounding proud, Marzo began extolling the plane. No longer would they be dependent on a multitude of small smugglers in single-engine planes, each carrying a hundred or so kilos. This plane could reach North America nonstop with tons at a time. They—the cartel—could put together immense loads of their own, and still carry piggyback loads for the lesser producers for a fee. This would give them extra control over the lesser producers. He paused, waiting for Ley's reaction.

"Interesting," Ley said.

"The submarine idea, we can forget it."

Ley said: "That's good."

"We were having trouble finding one anyway."

The building in whose doorway they stood had once been a stable or a barn. Now it was a largely empty warehouse containing a dolly attached to a tractor, and not much else. The dolly was stacked with packages totaling four or five hundred kilos, no more. That plane out there would hold tons, the pilot was expecting tons, Ley realized, but Marzo had only this much to put into it. The pilot's eyebrows would go up. Marzo was about to be embarrassed in front of the pilot. He did not like being embarrassed. Once, when he was an alternate congressman, a colleague had embarrassed him on the floor of the chamber. A week later that colleague had been found shot to death in his car. Ley knew why Marzo had brought him here and he waited for him to get to the point.

Marzo was still bragging about the plane. It was from the Vietnam war, he said. Ley only half listened. It was designed to land and take off from small unimproved fields—even jungle airstrips. Which meant that when not moving their merchandise to North America, it could be used to supply their labs. No more barge traffic on the rivers. It could carry in everything needed: heavy machinery, barrels and barrels of chemicals.

"Let me ask you something," said Marzo.

Now would come the sales pitch, Ley's own part in Marzo's scheme, and he sought to postpone it. "I'm cold," he interrupted. "Aren't you cold?"

Again he felt himself being scrutinized. Again Marzo did not look friendly.

"It's freezing out here," Ley said quickly, and he gave an exaggerated shiver. "I'm not dressed for this." He was wearing a spring-weight business suit whereas Marzo wore corduroy pants and a leather jacket that was zipped up.

Marzo was immediately solicitous. "Sorry. I didn't realize. Let's go back to the house."

They ran out to the pickup truck and climbed up into the cab. Marzo drove. The dirt lane was bumpy. The windshield wiper moved back and forth. They passed a pasture where fighting bulls grazed. The rain ran down the slick black flanks. Marzo had just bought this place, he said, and had had his fighting stock moved onto it. He had hired scientists to check the soil. "Chemists, agronomists—every goddamn thing," he said. "The grass is good here. They were unanimous." He was expecting great things from his bulls in the future.

Ley kept expecting him to renew the sales pitch. The wait was making him nervous. What is he waiting for? he wondered.

"Good grass," Marzo said. "That's the secret."

He parked in front of the ranch house and they got out and ran inside. The downstairs rooms were full of furniture in cartons. Only the dining room pieces had been unpacked. The other men were at the table sipping coffee. Ley and Marzo sat down. A servant came out of the kitchen and poured coffee into their cups.

"I've got to be getting back to the bank," said Ley.

The others all wanted to know his impression of the plane.

"Big, right?" said Antonio Lucientes.

"Did you go inside her?" said Ruben Jiménez.

"I want you to meet the pilot," said Marzo.

"Well," said Ley, "I've met these pilots before."

Marzo ordered the servant to go wake up the pilot.

"I used him in the past," said Carlos Von Bauzer as they waited. "Never the slightest thing wrong."

"Only problem is, he doesn't speak Spanish," said Lucientes.

Marzo, Ley saw, was watching him over the rim of his cup. "That's no problem for you, is it, David?" Marzo said.

Ley said nothing.

"He's from Louisiana," said Von Bauzer. "Flies the stuff in low over the oil rigs. On the radar they think he's a helicopter. Gets through every time."

"He's full of tricks like that," said Lucientes.

They only have to catch him once to turn him against us, Ley thought. He said: "Who made contact with whom?"

"He called me," said Von Bauzer. "I said come on down."

Ley nodded. No one else said anything.

They heard voices in the hallway and then footsteps. The pilot came into the room.

"Good morning, or good afternoon," the pilot said, "whatever it is."

Another man had shambled in after him, a co-pilot or mechanic or something, for the pilot told him to go out to the plane and wait there. The man went out through the kitchen and they heard the door slam.

The pilot turned to Ley. He was all smiles and his hand was out. "I don't believe I've met you," he said in English.

"David, meet Otis Mullan," said Marzo in Spanish. "Otis, shake hands with David."

The pilot was a short fat man about forty-five years old. He had a pudgy hand to go with his engaging fat man's grin. Air smugglers, Ley had learned, came in all types and shapes, except that none of them were very young. They were, after all, experienced pilots. They were rich enough to own their own planes. It was a profession in which you might expect to meet daredevil youths, but this was not the case. Often such smugglers were conservative types; Ley remembered one who had been a lieutenant commander in the navy. All they had in common was skill with airplanes and the desire to make a great deal of money very fast.

Mullan, which was certainly not his real name, was wearing flying coveralls and was unshaven. He sat down at the table and the servant came out and filled his cup. Ley studied him. Who does he work for? he wondered. The American acronyms were familiar, and he gazed at him and ran them through his head: CIA, FBI, DEA? Or maybe he was legitimate. It was too early to tell.

Marzo said: "Talk to him, David. Ask him about himself."

The pilot, who had looked up from his coffee, glanced from one face to the other. "You speak English?" he said to Ley.

"Si, señor, a leetle," Ley said. He had no wish to engage him in conversation. "What you want?"

Though they nodded politely at each other, the pilot's interest in him had died at once. Ley saw this and was pleased.

Turning to Von Bauzer, who had learned English in America when in jail for car theft, and who had been his interpreter until now, the pilot said: "Two things. One is I want some breakfast. The other is that I take off in—" He checked his watch. "—exactly four hours. Tell them that."

Ley stood up from the table. "I have to get back to the bank."

Marzo accompanied him out onto the veranda. "I thought you could speak English better than that, David."

"Not really."

"I thought I heard you speak it fluently several times."

Ley did not meet his eyes. "I'm out of practice."

"Yes, well," said Marzo, watching him closely, "if you've got some product ready to ship, why don't you come in with us?"

"Well—"

"I thought I could fill the plane by myself," Marzo said, "but there was trouble with my suppliers in Peru. Some goddamn thing."

Ley knew about the disruptions in Peru. His intelligence was as good as anyone's. It would be a while before the pipeline was full again, meaning that stock already on hand must be husbanded.

"So I'm a bit short," Marzo said.

Refuse him, Ley told himself. It's what you've intended to do all along. But he looked into Marzo's eyes and did not like what he saw there. He studied the ground and said nothing.

"By the way," Marzo said, "about that other matter—" He paused.

Ley decided he meant the proposed kidnapping of Jane Fox.

"For the time being that's on the back burner," Marzo said.

He's bribing me, Ley thought. This shipment is important to him. I don't have to say yes.

"In case you were worried about it," Marzo said.

"I wasn't worried about it."

"So if you've got a few hundred kilos," Marzo said, "there's room."

On the average about one shipment in ten to the States got intercepted by the coast guard, Customs, DEA. Somebody informed—whatever. Those were your losses, about ten percent. It was a cost of doing business. You accepted it. At the same time, knowing one in ten would not get through, you kept each shipment to a reasonable level. Now here was Marzo determined to send the equivalent of all ten shipments out in the same aircraft with a pilot who could be an agent —who could be anything. It made no sense.

"The other men are bringing in their share," said Marzo.

"I'll have to see what I have on hand," mumbled Ley.

From the veranda, because the house was set on a rise of land, part of the plane was visible. For all its military drabness it was a flamboyant machine, in keeping with Marzo's flamboyant personality. Everything about Marzo was flamboyant, his ideas, his methods, even his murders.

"Stuff'll be here in an hour or so. A few hundred kilos from you will round it out."

"I may not have that much," Ley said.

"I think we should be in this together, don't you?"

"You may be right."

"Shall we say five hundred kilos as your share?"

Ley's cars had come around the house. His driver had got out of the middle car and had the door open, and he went down the steps. His back felt exposed. Maybe I'll send him something, he thought as he reached the car. Why not? What difference does it make to me?

"Look into it," Marzo said. "Call me."

The next day Ray wanted to go back to that same beach, but Jane refused.

"I don't feel like swimming."

"Well, what do you want to do?"

She shrugged.

He offered suggestions, among them a day trip to the island they could see across the way.

"Whatever you want," she said.

"I think a ferry goes over there."

"Fine."

The ride took about half an hour. The other passengers were all natives, the men in open-necked shirts, the women with kerchiefs on their heads. There were about ten of them. The ferry was a disused fishing trawler. It was rusty, and smelled oily. Its open hold was full of produce: baskets of bananas, of pineapples, crates of live chickens. She stood with Ray at the rail in the hot salty wind and watched the other island come closer.

Once ashore they hired a taxi and were driven all over the island. It was flatter than theirs, less naturally beautiful, less built up as well. The native houses looked poorer. For lunch the driver took them to a restaurant on the beach that was little more than a shack, said he would be back in an hour, and departed.

They sat under a straw umbrella and sipped rosé wine. Jane's big hat was on the table. The wine was cold and there was a hot breeze blowing, and it was very pleasant there. A black boy with a face mask on his head and a spear gun in his hand came wading up out of the water. He had a string bag with two live lobsters in it, and that's what they ate for lunch. The proprietor bought them from the grinning boy, carried them over to the table to show them off, then split them and put them on the grill. They could smell the lobsters grilling for ten minutes before they ate them.

When the taxi returned they were driven back to the wharf, where they boarded the trawler for its return trip. Jane spent the rest of the afternoon on the balcony reading. Ray said he would go for a walk on the beach. The beach on which this hotel and several others fronted was a great horseshoe-shaped thing. Once she looked up and saw him standing alone half a mile away, perhaps more, staring out to sea.

Each morning and evening she tried to call Flores in her office in Bogotá, but was unsuccessful. Were there messages? What word from the desk? Had there been a reaction to her cable? But the island's telephone facilities were less than state-of-the-art, apparently. Try the central post office in town, she was advised, and she did, spending one entire morning there while Ray sat in the car, coming in from time to time to see what was keeping her. But no call ever went through.

It made her almost frantic. She wanted to go back at once, she told him. He talked her out of it, but only barely.

By afternoon of the next day she had made up her mind. When they came back to their room after lunch, she suddenly picked up the phone and asked for the airport. She hung up and as she waited for the operator to call her back, began to pace.

"Jane," he told her, "going back this soon is not a good idea."

"Maybe, maybe not."

He had sat down on the edge of the bed. "The ambassador will call your publisher, and the paper will pull you out."

"How is he going to know I'm back? Are you going to tell him?"

"Gallagher will know you're back. He lives in the same building. He'll tell him."

"I'll make sure he doesn't see me."

"He'll know the minute one of our cars takes you to work."

"I'll take taxis."

"No, Jane."

She hesitated, then said: "I'll compromise with you. We'll stop off at Barranquilla." There were only the two DEA offices in Colombia. She had been meaning to look in at Barranquilla for some time. She would write a piece about it, which would at least partially cover her with the desk for this trip.

The phone rang beside the bed and she picked it up. With her hand over the receiver she said to Ray: "One reservation, or two?"

"Do you think I want to stay here without you?" He took the phone away from her. "I'll do it."

They checked out that afternoon and drove to the airport. By then Ray had grown exceedingly morose. He knew something had gone wrong, and she supposed he had no idea what. He was extremely sensitive to her moods. He had expected so much, obviously. Probably he thought she was being a bitch, and she was sorry, but he had expected more than she had to give.

Once on the plane the pressure was off. In a few hours she would be back in communication with the desk and her job would be safe. Nonetheless she sat brooding. Not about him or about the two of them as a couple, but about herself. About her body, and about what was possibly growing inside it at this moment. She had always imagined that a woman would feel it there, would know instinctively it was true. But she felt nothing. If it was true, what would she do? Would she have the baby? What would become of her career, her life? What would Ray say when—if—she told him? Should she mention it to him now, or wait?

Trying to decide, she took his hand. She sat holding his hand, staring out the porthole.

She decided she wanted to know what his reaction would be, started to speak, then stopped.

"Did you say something?"

"No."

She began to imagine a dialogue she was afraid to initiate. "I'm late," she would say.

His head would shoot around. "What?"

It was possible to imagine the scene in great detail, and she did so. He was a forty-four-year-old man with three grown or almost-grown children. He had been through this moment multiple times before, which she found to her surprise she regretted, for this would be the first time for her. "Six days," she would say. "A week. I'm never late."

A big smile would come onto his face. "Now you'll have to marry me. Like it or not."

"Maybe it's a false alarm."

"Marriage, I see no way out."

"Is that so?"

She would turn back to the porthole to hide her smirk. Whatever they might decide to do later, she would be terrifically pleased with him right now.

If she told him. And if this was what his reaction proved to be.

He had said he wanted to marry her, but did he really? And was she so sure she wanted to marry him? The trouble was that he was forty-four years of age and had those grown or almost-grown children, and it was possible to imagine a quite opposite scenario.

"I think I'm pregnant."

First of all, no smile. "Are you sure?"

"No."

"Why don't we wait till you're sure."

Or else he might say:

"I thought you were doing something."

"No."

"You should have been doing something."

And she would want to die.

Which reaction would it be? She stared out the porthole and brooded. How well did she really know him? He was a responsible man, she believed. He would accept what he saw as his responsibility. Would he? She had been wrong before. Often. Particularly with regard to men. She had never been very good at judging men. Look at her marriage. At the very least Ray would feel biologically trapped, as who wouldn't. She doubted he would receive the news with joy, and anything less would shame her.

She decided she wouldn't think about it anymore. She would tell him nothing. She was in a mess, but it was only a small mess so far. She would go to Barranquilla and do her work and think about it later.

They checked into a hotel and she phoned Bogotá at once and got Flores and asked for her messages: a few queries from the desk, he said, a request from the Weekend section for a thought piece on the cartel, a request from the minister of defense to reschedule an appointment.

Nothing pressing. She hung up the phone but remained seated a moment on the edge of the bed. There would be more messages on the answering machine in her apartment, but they would be personal and even less pressing.

Ray turned from the window. "If you contact the DEA office here," he said, "Gallagher is going to hear about it. He'll know you're back in Colombia."

"I'll contact the DEA last."

"I thought the DEA was your story."

He didn't know much about newspaper work, she realized. She chose not to answer, and they went down to the dining room for dinner.

She began by interviewing local journalists: the head of the local *El Tiempo* bureau, the editor in chief of the *Hora de Barranquilla*. This was the way one oriented oneself quickly in a strange city. What was going on here that was news, whom should she talk to? Barranquilla looked prosperous—what she saw of it out cab windows. Which was normal, she supposed. Cocaine went out of here by the ton, stuffed inside teddy bears, hollowed-out pineapples, and such. Barranquilla was Colombia's busiest port, the cocaine-shipping capital of the world. Sure it was prosperous. Why wouldn't it be?

It was an attractive city. The buildings were low and had orange tile roofs. There were many gardens, and many views of the harbor and of the great Magdalena River pouring through. She interviewed the mayor, and after him officials lower down to whom he sent her, including the local chief of police. She interviewed the owner of a shipping company whose name she had been given months ago in New York. Ray looked bored sometimes, but never left her side. He said he was the only protection she had; though she remonstrated with him, it did no good.

There were two stories here, maybe more, and the other was the city itself. What had drug money done to the city, for the city? There were fewer murders here, less violence. It was almost a sleepy Caribbean town. The drug lords needed it that way, perhaps. If their product was to be shipped out in quantity, the port must be kept calm. Was that the reason?

When not working, she worried about herself. She slept badly and each morning when she woke up the worry was always there, always darker. But she kept her secret from Ray, refused to think about the future. She concentrated on work. She also became increasingly closed in, less and less responsive to him. She did not seem able to help herself.

She did not go near the DEA until the last day, then spent

the afternoon there reading what reports they would let her see, interviewing agents. The agent in charge, whose name was Don Creighton, reported to Gallagher in Bogotá. Barranquilla was the most productive office in Latin America, Creighton told her. He sounded proud. He and his staff provided more information leading to big seizures than any other, he said, and when she asked why this was so, Creighton said: "Because Barranquilla is full of sailors, and sailors talk."

That night, after studying her notes, she told Ray she had enough, tomorrow they could go back to Bogotá.

"I guess you're glad that's over," she said, and gave him a tentative smile.

He only nodded. Sitting down on the hotel bed, he phoned the airline and made their reservations.

In bed in the dark she could not sleep. Finally she dozed. In the morning she woke up feeling hung over, though she had had nothing to drink. Sunlight was streaming in the window. Ray called down for breakfast, then sat back against the headboard waiting for it. She got out of bed, and the flow started. She stood beside the bed with her legs spread, and her nightdress hiked up, peering down at herself, stupefied, dripping blood onto the rug. Her body went hot all over, then cold, and she thought she might faint. She seemed unable to move. She wanted to run for the bathroom, or stuff something between her legs, but did neither.

She saw Ray still in bed become aware that something was happening, saw him raise himself up on his elbows to see what it was. She felt her face begin to scrunch up, to go to pieces even as he bounded out of bed toward her. She felt him embrace her, felt the buttons of his pajamas against her flesh.

"You thought you were pregnant," he said.

She was shaking all over.

"You did, didn't you?"

She stood in his embrace, legs spread, shaking, dripping blood down onto the carpet and onto his feet, then lost all control of her emotions and began to cry.

"Why didn't you tell me?" he said holding her. He said it over and over again. "Why didn't you tell me?"

At the airport in Bogotá they were met by one of Gallagher's cars and driven the rest of the way home. Douglas carried both bags into Jane's apartment, setting his own down just inside the front door, hers in her bedroom on the bed.

She had scooped up her cat and was holding it. She eyed her answering machine. The red light was winking, and she wished Ray would go so she could listen to her messages.

"So now Gallagher knows you're back," Ray said. "What should I tell him?"

"Tell him I'm going out of the country again almost at once."

Ray looked surprised. "And are you?"

She went into the kitchen and opened a can of cat food and put the dish down on the floor. "Maybe. I don't know." In the aftermath of this morning's shock or fright or whatever it was, she had decided to meet her husband in Miami or wherever he suggested. This much she had concluded. She would go to Miami and make the decision that had to be made.

"To meet your husband?" Ray said.

"Yes."

She saw him take this in, not liking it, trying to digest it. The cat was eating fast.

"I wonder if the cleaning woman has been feeding it," she said.

"Do you have to?" said Ray.

"I think so, yes."

The winking red light again caught her eye. She couldn't listen with him there. No telling who was on the tape. A news source, maybe; she didn't want Ray knowing too much about her contacts. Her husband certainly; just his tone of voice might reveal to Ray more than she wanted revealed.

Or the phone might ring right now, with Ray still there.

If she answered, he would hear her side of the conversation. If she didn't, he would hear whatever message the caller recorded.

After a moment she asked: "Would you like me to make tea?"

At the stove, she put the pan of water on, got the cups down, got the tea bags ready. She didn't want tea. She wanted him to go and she wanted to listen to her messages.

She drank the tea quickly, then shooed him out, saying she was on deadline, she had to write the first of her Barranquilla pieces and send it today so that the dateline would be valid. Which was true. He nodded, accepting it.

At the door he turned and said: "See you for dinner."

More a statement than a question, though he seemed for the first time a bit unsure of himself.

She didn't want to meet him for dinner. She had just spent a week with him. Tonight when her piece was finished and sent to New York, she wanted to be alone to try to sort out her life, try to think. In addition, there were sure to be queries from the desk, perhaps inserts to write.

He acted as possessive as if they had already been married twenty years. Probably he had behaved toward his wife exactly like this. Probably it was the only way he knew how to act toward a woman. It was nice to be loved, but he was pushing her too hard.

"Better count on dinner alone tonight," she said gently. "I'll be working until midnight if not later."

He recognized the rejection. He understood her mood well enough. She saw this in his face; he just didn't know what had caused it. He looked confused and a bit glum.

"You have to eat," he said.

"I'll make myself some scrambled eggs. You should do the same." When he looked ready to protest, she added: "I really have to get this piece out."

As soon as the door closed behind him she went to her machine. There was only one message. From her husband. A long monologue. It was tender and in places witty, but the upshot was the same as always. He missed his wife. He wanted his wife back.

She wondered if men ever felt owned the way women did. Men always wanted to own you. All men. She had never met one who didn't.

George had to be in Florida on a case on a specific date —she played back the tape to make sure and wrote it down. Would she meet him there?

The date was a few days off.

She got her laptop out, spread her notes over the kitchen table, and began to write. By the time she finished it was dark outside her windows, but the piece was good. She read it over to be sure. It read so well and she was so pleased with herself that she wanted to run upstairs and show it to Ray, an impulse she resisted. Instead she hooked her modem up and transmitted it to New York.

At the stove she sipped a beer and nibbled on slices of spicy Colombian sausage and cooked a potato omelet. She sat on a stool at the kitchen counter and ate it.

The telephone was on an end table in the hall. She rewound her husband's message, listened to it again, and then on an impulse called him.

They talked for a long time. He said he was delighted to have her on the line, and sounded it. He said she was doing a great job there, everyone said so, and perhaps this was only flattery, though she wanted to believe it. He said everyone was talking not only about her articles, but also about her bravery. The paper was making a big thing about her being the only full-time American correspondent in Colombia. He said he was worried about her. The desk had heard rumors that the traffickers were mounting a plot to kidnap her. He hoped she was being careful.

His concern sounded as genuine as his praise, and warmed her. He said he envied the excitement of her life, he himself was stuck in the same old rut, though the case that was taking him to Florida was interesting, he would be in court for two days. Was there any chance she could meet him in Florida?

She would be safe there, relatively speaking—the traffickers wouldn't kidnap her, though her husband might. Throw her over his shoulder and hold her for ransom for the rest of her life.

It made her smile.

"How about it?" he asked.

She hesitated. If she sent a message to the desk that she had to meet her husband in Miami, that it was urgent, she would not be refused, and she knew this. It came under the heading of conjugal visit, not vacation. She was not the only correspondent separated from spouse or family in some foreign place. Conjugal visits by correspondents trying to cope with marital problems were treated as an occupational imperative, provided they did not occur too often, almost like a death in the family. Under the proper circumstances they took precedence over all but the most important breaking news story.

George sounded as amusing and loving as he used to years ago, and for the moment she almost missed him—a reaction that threw her into a state of confusion. Suddenly she didn't want to go to Florida. She didn't want to meet him at all. She wanted to postpone all decisions a bit longer. She wasn't ready yet. She didn't know what to say to him now, much less do.

"I'll ask the desk," she said finally.

"You will?" he said. "That's terrific."

As soon as she had hung up she knew she had made a mistake. She should simply have told him no. What now? she asked herself. She sat hugging her knees rocking back and forth. What had she done, what should she do? She had to see him eventually, had to decide. She wished the future could be held off indefinitely. The status quo was fine with her. She wished she could just sit here with the status quo but couldn't. She was being forced to go to Florida, where she would be forced to take the future in her two hands and make it happen. Whatever decisions she made from now on would be irrevocable.

* * *

She informed Ray the next morning: she was going to Florida. Her decision had made her truculent. "Tell Gallagher so he won't worry about me."

"When are you going?"

"This weekend."

"For how long?"

"Tell him a month, what do I care."

Ray looked stricken. "A month?"

"He doesn't need to know how long."

"Do I need to know how long?"

They were standing in the vestibule waiting for the armored car. She put her arms around him. "It's just for the weekend."

"All right," said Ray. He was trying to digest the news. "Should I go with you?"

"No."

"Moral support."

"Absolutely not."

That's all I need, she thought, both of them there. I could jump from one bed to the other. That's probably what a man would do. She said: "I need to handle this alone."

"Handle what?"

"This mess." An unfortunate choice of words, she realized.

"Jane, what are you going there for? What do you hope to accomplish?"

She was silent. She pretended to be peering out the door for the armored car.

"Will your lawyer be there?"

"Ray, you're not the only man in my life right now. I can't help that. But you are the only man in my heart."

"You're meeting your husband?"

"My husband, yes."

"From whom you're supposedly getting a divorce?"

"I probably will get a divorce."

"You led me to believe—"

"You believed what you wanted to believe."

"You said—"

"I said we were separated, which we were. My God, twenty-five hundred miles. What more do you want?"

"Then what are you seeing him for?"

"Because I have to."

Just then the armored car entered the turnaround, its appearance cutting off whatever response he might have made. The car stopped in front of the glass doors. There was a guard with a submachine gun sitting beside the driver and two more guards in the rear seat facing backward.

During the drive they were silent. At first Jane thought Ray was only angry, then saw from the lines of his half-averted face that he was in pain, and she was surprised. She had seen such pain in the furrowed brows of teenage boyfriends at times, not since. The sense of losing a girlfriend's love, perhaps irrevocably. It seemed strange to her that a man his age could suffer this much over her. She did not want his pain. He was exaggerating the situation, she believed, but there was no way she could reassure him because she did not know herself what would happen in Florida, what she meant to say and do there.

17

TWO DAYS AFTER returning with Jane from Barranquilla and the Caribbean, Douglas received a phone call from a man named Ocampo, who said he wanted to meet with him. Said he had something to say that might be of interest.

"Do we know each other, Mr. Ocampo?"

"It should be soon," said Ocampo. "Quite soon."

Douglas was trying to puzzle it out, but there were too few clues. "I get the impression you mean immediately."

"It would be best."

Douglas made his decision. "About two hours from now. That okay?" This was not New York. He would need two hours to set it up.

"Where?"

Douglas suggested the Hotel Tequendama on Carrera Siete.

Ocampo said he would take a room. Douglas should come to the hotel and ask for the room number and they could talk.

The call had come late at night when he was alone in the DEA section of the embassy. He assumed Ocampo was an informant, or would-be informant, though not perhaps of the usual type, for on the telephone he was at ease rather than hesitant, even sure of himself, did not sound scared, and he seemed to Douglas's ears to speak good Spanish. The hour of his call was normal. Informants often called at night, often at an even later hour than Ocampo, for most of them seemed to feel safer then.

For some weeks Douglas, at his own request, had been taking his regular turn on night telephone duty. The other agents had been glad to let him do it. If he could earn their acceptance it would make his life among them easier, he reasoned. In addition, as he had told Gallagher, he wanted to understand better who the callers were, and how the office worked.

But his most important reason was something else, and he did not speak of it. The rule was that whoever first made contact with a caller got to take that particular case forward, and he was hoping to stumble on a major one. He was hoping for a caller who would drop one in his lap. A major seizure that would take place in the United States. A case which he in Bogotá would control from a distance to wherever it ended. A case that would be talked about in New York.

Of course he had no idea when he hung up that Ocampo represented just such a case.

Unlike its agents Stateside, the DEA conducted no investigations in Colombia, made no arrests, nor did it get involved in shoot-outs. Its principal occupation—almost its only occupation—was the gathering of information.

Information was a ponderous, almost sacred word in the police business. It was not intelligence exactly. The military relied on intelligence but could go in and blast something without it, and often had to. But in the absence of hard information, the police, in civilized countries, could not act at all.

In Colombia the DEA had its antennae out. Some of its information it got free by haunting the halls of the Bogotá police agencies and of certain government ministries. Its agents picked up, were told, overheard a good deal. This was almost all background information. Interesting. Imprecise. Almost gossip. It went into reports. Some of it Douglas himself contributed.

The hard information, the stuff with numbers attached, came from irregular places and cost money. Sometimes a great deal of money. The DEA was equipped with money for this purpose, and spent it. It bought what it needed to stay in business, and it paid top dollar.

By the time he took that first call from Ocampo, Douglas had come to think of the DEA's two Colombia offices as stores—not stores that sold, but stores that bought. People came in and sold what they had. Stores open twenty-four hours a day. The DEA did no advertising. Nonetheless, throughout Colombia people knew its two stores were there. Particularly those with information to sell knew they were there—people like Ocampo, for instance, assuming that that was the purpose of his phone call. For motives of their own, people came into the stores. Or, more often, they telephoned as Ocampo had done, and meetings were set up. Information changed hands, and money changed hands. When tons of cocaine were seized in Los Angeles or Queens, often the case had been sold to the DEA days before and twenty-five hundred miles away.

Douglas had already dealt with a number of such people. He had learned a few things: that legitimate businessmen sold, and illiterate peasants sold, and so did every category in between. Some sold from principle—not very many. Others sold for a variety of reasons. One with whom Douglas had dealt believed a contract was out on his life and he was trying to earn enough quick money to get out of the country. Another was the brother of a man assassinated by a rival gang. His motive was revenge. He had sold Douglas the location of a warehouse belonging to this gang, which, when raided by Nuñez's men to whom the DEA passed along the information, proved to contain a hundred and two drums of ether on their way to clandestine labs.

But most callers sold purely for the money. They sold the locations of caches, of labs, of landing strips, of coca farms. They sold the arrival of the precursor chemicals needed to process cocaine, principally ether and acetone; or they sold the date, place, and mode of departure of the finished product. Some sold regularly, some only once. Some, the brother of the assassinated man for one, were found out afterward, almost always for the same reason. The brother was in a bar throwing money around that he had never had before, and somebody saw him. Douglas had warned him to be careful, had cited for him previous cases. It didn't take. The brother was murdered promptly enough, and in a way no more gruesome than was usual in such instances. All his fingers were hacked off first, one after the other, followed by his ears, his tongue, and his penis, after which he was beaten to death with an iron bar. He had collected from the DEA five thousand dollars.

Douglas, when he first started taking his turn, had been surprised to find out who the callers were, and that they had motives different from what he was used to. In New York, informants were street people who gave up information to avoid arrest, or for the price of a ten-dollar fix. Or else they were high-level felons under indictment or already convicted who were trying to save themselves. There were other categories too, but these were the principal ones. Money had very little to do with it. Money was used to buy physical evidence, drugs or guns or stolen goods, not information.

It was different here. Almost all the callers he spoke to had information that had to be bought and paid for. Since most were nervous about what they were doing, some being downright terrified, it made the negotiations extremely delicate, and usually his first job was to convince the caller, who was already skittish, not to hang up. He had to try not to frighten him away. Since a meeting was difficult to set up and potentially dangerous, his second job was to worm out of him enough information on which to decide whether or not to proceed. Who was the man? Not his name necessarily, but what was his rank, where was he placed, what was his motive, and what might he have to sell? This much being settled, a meeting place had to be fixed. Someplace where the caller would feel comfortable enough to talk, but which offered security on both sides. The money was not a problem until later: financial negotiations always took place last. By that time the informant was committed and his price could be beaten down.

After hanging up on Ocampo, Douglas phoned Gallagher at home. Someone would have to be assigned to cover the embassy phone, and he needed a backup agent to introduce to Ocampo. Backup agents were always introduced promptly so that if something happened to the original agent the contact was not lost. No one knew yet that Ocampo would turn out to be a major informant. Nonetheless, Gallagher assigned himself to accompany Douglas to the meeting, and a few minutes later the embassy armored car stopped in the street and Gallagher came out of his building and climbed in.

"Your friend is back, I see," Gallagher said as he settled into the seat.

"Friend" was better than "girlfriend" and Douglas was silently grateful. In his relationship with Gallagher progress was perhaps being made.

"I saw her in the elevator earlier tonight," Gallagher said. "Does the ambassador know?"

"If you mean did I tell him, no I didn't tell him yet."

"What about the kidnap threat?" said Douglas.

"I talked to Nuñez this afternoon. His people are still working on it, supposedly."

"And?"

"They got nothing yet."

"Maybe there's nothing in it."

"Maybe."

For a time they rode in silence.

"Are you going to tell the ambassador she's back?" Douglas said.

"If he asks me, I'll tell him."

It took them an hour and a half to get to the Tequendama, for their driver went round and round to shake any tail car that might have attached itself to them. When at last they pulled up in front, the bodyguards jumped down and checked out the lobby. Then Gallagher and Douglas marched straight across to the elevator and up.

Ocampo had taken a suite. He was waiting for them. He was a man of about fifty, tall, bald, with a big black mustache. He wore a dark business suit that was well cut and expensive. He paced and chain-smoked as he talked, obviously not nearly as at ease as he pretended. He said he was in a number of businesses, including the shipping business; he did not name the others. He owned a certain cargo ship that was presently at sea, due to land at a certain East Coast port in a day or two.

To learn the name of the ship and the name of the port was going to cost money, Douglas saw. Well, okay. That's how the game was played. And he waited to hear more.

There was a shipment of furniture on board, Ocampo said. He had reason to believe there was something wrong with it. He was afraid Customs would seize first the furniture, and then his ship. In exchange for informing, he wanted a new ship, plus twenty thousand dollars.

This sum, Douglas knew, was the largest Gallagher could dispense on his own authority. He assumed that Ocampo knew it too, and wondered how.

The negotiations took place in Spanish in the sitting room

of the suite, Ocampo pacing, Douglas leaning forward over the coffee table. Gallagher sat back on the sofa and said nothing. He was being very correct according to the rules, and Douglas was both impressed and pleased. It was Douglas's case, and Gallagher by his conduct was recognizing it as such. Already both men suspected it was a big one. Nonetheless, Gallagher was not going to try to take it over.

Douglas asked the tonnage and age of the ship.

"It's twenty-seven years old," Ocampo said.

"For a ship, that's pretty old," said Douglas, "wouldn't you agree?"

"That ship is a fine ship."

"In fact it's practically ancient."

"Not this ship."

Douglas nodded. He was studying Ocampo, trying to size him up. What did he really want? Why was he here? "And from us you would like a new ship. Which would cost how much?"

Ocampo told him.

"I don't know," said Douglas. "That's a lot of money. Washington would have to approve." He had no intention of recommending a new ship for Ocampo, and knew Gallagher wouldn't.

"There isn't much time."

"How much time is there?"

"Two days."

"Two days?" Douglas gave a whistle. He was play-acting, making difficulties, watching for Ocampo's reactions. "Why didn't you come to us sooner?"

"I just found out about it."

"You just found out about it—how long has the ship been at sea, two weeks?"

"Be that as it may."

"All right, how did you find out? Who told you?"

"That's not important."

"Do you speak English?"

"No."

Douglas was sure he did. Turning to Gallagher he said in English: "How much of what we've been saying did you understand?"

"Very little," said Gallagher. "My Spanish is not too good."

"He's giving us less than two days."

"Not enough time," said Gallagher on cue. "Tell him so and let's go. I got a date, for chrissake."

"I wish you spoke Spanish," said Douglas to Gallagher. "Let me talk to him a bit more."

Watching the play of Ocampo's face, Douglas saw that he had understood perfectly well. "My partner says there's not enough time," he said in Spanish.

"Maybe we can work something out," said Ocampo hastily.

"I don't know if we can or not." He's eager, thought Douglas. Why was he so eager? "How much furniture are we talking about, anyway?"

"A lot."

"What does that mean? One containerload? Two?"

"More."

And why was he holding back information? "How many more?"

"An opportunity like this does not come very often."

Although Douglas continued to probe, Ocampo was not forthcoming.

Finally Douglas stood up, breaking the interview off. "We'll get back to you," he said, and with Gallagher at his heels started for the door.

"When?" said Ocampo.

"Tomorrow, if we can. Otherwise—"

"I'll hear from you tomorrow," said Ocampo decisively, and he closed the door on them.

The car headed back to the embassy. At this hour the traffic was light. The two men were mostly silent. "He's in with them," Gallagher muttered once. "He's not just your simple everyday shipping magnate."

"I'm not so sure," responded Douglas.

A few streets later Gallagher said: "They have so much money they can hire the best. The best lawyers, the best accountants, the best chemists, the best bankers."

"Even the best shipowners," said Douglas.

"The secret of their success. The best brains in the country work for them."

"So what's this guy's motive?"

"Did they stiff him on a payment? Kill one of his relatives? Is he paying off a grudge? You tell me."

"Maybe they forced him to use his own ships and he didn't want to."

"It could be anything."

At the embassy the big gates opened, the hydraulic wall descended, and the car drove over it and inside the compound. They got out and crossed the grass toward the building. Only one or two lights showed. They went upstairs to Gallagher's office, which he entered throwing on light switches.

"Your Spanish is getting really quite good. I was proud of you."

Douglas tried not to beam with pleasure.

"Of course you could have interviewed him in English," Gallagher said. "The guy spoke English perfectly well."

He had sat down behind his desk. "It's your case," he said.

"Thank you."

"So what do you want to do?"

It was late at night and they had very little time. "In Washington who's still working at this hour?" said Douglas. "Can we get through to Customs? How many East Coast ports are there, how many cargo ships out of Colombia are due to dock in the next three days?"

Gallagher was nodding. "What else?"

"Who is this Ocampo? What can Nuñez tell us about him?" The DAS police issued passports and identity cards. "They must have something on him over there. Is the office still open? What can we find out by morning?"

Gallagher sat down at the scrambler. ''Let's start sending cables,'' he said.

They settled in to work most of the night.

The next day Jane rode one of Gallagher's cars to the airport; Douglas had arranged it but did not see her off himself. This upset her, and during the drive she passed through a number of emotions: annoyance, confusion, and finally, by the time the car pulled up in front of the terminal, a kind of contrition. She had hurt him, she would make it up to him. She walked into the terminal with an embassy guard to either side of her, and they stayed with her as she checked in, had her passport stamped, and was ushered into the VIP room. There they left her. She had thirty minutes to wait. She missed Ray already. I'll make it up to you, she silently promised, you'll see.

Once aloft the plane filled up with the light of the brilliant cloudless sky, and her thoughts focused on what was ahead, rather than behind. She would tell her husband she wanted out. She would say hello and then tell him. They would meet wherever—in the cocktail lounge, a room, the lobby—and she would tell him. The marriage was over. She wouldn't wait even that long; she would tell him in the street as soon as his cab pulled up. As he got out of the cab. Divorce. Her resolve hardened. Her resolve had reached Miami already, though she herself had not.

How should she phrase it and what would be his response? She tried to decide the first, imagine the second. She meant to be ready whatever happened. She was determined not to falter.

She knew herself. She hated confrontations.

Or should she work up to it more slowly? That might be better. In the course of dinner, perhaps. As the candles burned down and he ordered dessert.

No, just meet him at the curb: Hello, how are you, I want a divorce. She must not sound tentative. She must not hesitate.

Should she tell him she was in love with someone else? She certainly wouldn't volunteer it. But he would probably ask. Ray Douglas has nothing to do with this divorce, she told herself. But she heard George's voice say: Who are you kidding? Yes, who was she kidding?

In her head she went over and over the confrontation that was to come. It did not get easier. The stewardesses passed around cups of Colombian coffee. Jane drank hers, and almost immediately afterward wanted to throw up. She hurried to the lavatory and stood there a while but nothing happened. The nausea passed.

The plane landed in Miami in the middle of a bright sunny afternoon. By the time she reached the hotel her stomach muscles were hard as a board and sore, and she had a ringing headache.

But George wasn't there yet. The desk clerk handed her a message, which she unfolded. George was delayed, but would arrive before dinner. She felt her stomach muscles begin to unknot.

She was shown to their room, which she studied carefully before tipping and dismissing the bellboy. The room was high up and from the window she could see the ocean, but the view did not interest her. The important thing was that there were two beds, not one. Two double beds. That was good, in case they had to spend the night in the same room. Because she might not get it all said at once. If she did, George might move out. Otherwise, she thought, we sleep here. She didn't know what would happen once George had heard what she believed she intended to tell him.

She went into the bathroom and took two aspirin.

She had about four hours to wait.

Having never been to Miami before she decided to go out for a walk which, she kept reminding herself, was safe here. She took her dress off and hung it in the closet. She put on pants and a loose sweater and flat shoes, and took the elevator down.

As she crossed the lobby she noted a hairdresser's shop. Her hair needed to be washed and cut—in Colombia she had been doing her own hair for months—and so she hesitated. She had the time. However, George when he saw her would think she had got all dolled up for him. It would send him the wrong message. His face would light up. It would make her job even harder. So she decided against the hairdresser.

Outside, she walked along looking into the windows. George, when she told him, might weep. She peered in at a simple black dress. She imagined tears running down George's face. Then she thought: Don't flatter yourself, girlie. But he might. A boy she had jilted at sixteen had wept, and the first man she had ever lived with also; it was only a month. She went into the shop and tried on the dress. She loved the way it fitted her body. She had no idea what George had been feeling these last few months alone. He might plead with her to reconsider. He might break down completely, might beg her to stay with him. She couldn't bear the idea of seeing his tears. Of all his possible reactions, she told herself, this was the one she dreaded most. But it wasn't true, she dreaded all of them. She patted her hips in the mirror and bought the dress. The shop promised to send it around to the hotel.

She went out into the street again and at the corner got into a taxi and on an impulse asked to be driven to Miami Beach.

"Whereabouts, miss?"

"Anywhere. I want to walk on the beach."

The sand was hard and there was a cold wind blowing in from the sea. The sky had clouded over.

Or perhaps George would welcome a divorce. Perhaps he wanted one as much as she did. Or didn't care one way or the other. How will I feel then? she asked herself. There was a freighter going by some distance out. Its plume of smoke was being blown ahead of it, the wind was that strong. Had their eight years together meant nothing to him? Did they mean so little that he could divorce her without regret? Closer to shore a few sailboats were being moved along smartly, heeled well over. She passed a man with a dog and a group of boys scaling a frisbee. Her sweater was thin and she was cold. Maybe he has a girlfriend and is anxious to get rid of me, she thought. How will that make me feel? She studied the sand as if for answers, but it gave none. Shivering with cold she went up the steps to the street, and found a cab.

At the hotel she still had more than two hours to wait and did not know what to do with them. She went into the coffee shop and ordered tea, then decided to get her hair washed and cut after all.

She sat down in the chair lying out over the basin and a big Cuban woman began to work on her. She closed her eyes to concentrate on the sensuous pleasure of the woman's fingers, but her mind would not cooperate; it went off in one direction only. Suppose when she told him, George flew into a rage. She had seen him lose his temper often enough. Suppose he raged at her, abused her, called her terrible names. The idea made her feel nauseated again. Or suppose he threatened her with the law? He was a lawyer. How did the law read in cases of adultery? She had no idea. She and Ray had not been too discreet. Other reporters who had been through Bogotá might have heard the gossip. Adultery against her would not be hard to prove. Could he seal their New York apartment, keep her share of the community property, keep everything she owned—not only her half of the apartment and the car, but her books, her photo albums, her clothes that were there, the paintings she had bought before they were married, her collection of antique inkwells, the silver that had been her mother's? Keep it all or even destroy it?

Her hair having been cut and blow dried, her face a bit flushed from the heat, she came upstairs into the hotel room, and her new dress in its package was on the bed. She put it on and stood in front of the mirror admiring herself in it. Then it went back into its package, and the package into her suitcase. The dress was for Ray, not her husband.

She ran a bath, and as she lay in the tub wondered if George, once she had said to him what she would say, could possibly become violent. Was he likely to get so angry as to slap her around? She didn't think so, but it was possible. Other men did sometimes. Would she fight back, or be immobilized by guilt? She could get a black eye out of it, even lose some teeth. Suppose he decided to rape her to "bring her to her senses." It was a solution that had appealed to some men. If it happened to her, she didn't imagine it would be too nice. Or he might clamp his fingers around her throat and by accident or on purpose kill her.

Not George, she told herself.

But was he so different from men who had done such things? Was she so sure? It would be safer to tell him in a public place.

Nude in a tub was not where or how she wished him to find her. She stepped out dripping, dried herself off, put on pantyhose, bra, and slip, and propped herself against the headboard of the bed farthest from the door, where she thumbed through a magazine, from time to time concentrating, or at least trying to concentrate, on the words on the page. Her shoes were beside the bed. The pink dress she had worn on the plane lay over an armchair, ready to be put on. She waited.

It was early evening in Bogotá as well. Douglas came into Gallagher's office carrying a yellow pad covered with notes, and a sheaf of most of the day's cable traffic between the embassy and Washington. "Customs has narrowed it down to two ships," he told him. "The more likely is a freighter named *Caballo Blanco*. It's got six containers of furniture aboard. It docks in Charleston the day after tomorrow. Of course they'll cover the other ship as well."

"So we don't need Señor Ocampo anymore," said Gallagher.

"That's one way of looking at it." Douglas studied his notes.

"What else?"

"According to Nuñez's people, Ocampo may be legitimate. They've got nothing on him."

"Nothing?"

"No known association with traffickers."

Gallagher looked surprised. "Then what's his motive?"

"Maybe he's just worried about losing his ship."

"He's got to be tied to them in some way. Where'd he get his information from?"

"Stumbled on something, perhaps. A hollow leg broke off a table while they were loading it. Something like that."

"Then why did it take him so long to notify us? The ship's been at sea more than a week."

"Or he ran into some guy tipped him off. I'm not saying he doesn't know somebody who knows somebody. Took him a while to decide what he wanted to do."

Gallagher was silent.

Douglas said: "So now we have to decide what we want to do."

"We're not going to buy him a new ship."

"Of course not."

"They'll seize his ship," said Gallagher.

"I've arranged with Customs that his ship will not be seized. Instead agents will follow the shipment to wherever it goes and seize it there—together with whoever comes to get it."

Gallagher looked thoughtful.

Douglas said: "Do we pay him at all?"

"Why should we?"

"Because he can tell us exactly which ship, and maybe which containers." Douglas paused, then added: "And if he takes the money we have a hook into him."

Gallagher said nothing.

"He's a shipping guy. He hears things. Let's assume he is in fact honest. If people come to get that shipment and are arrested, it proves he didn't warn anybody. It proves he's honest. He's come forward once. If he's honest and we buy his friendship, he may come forward again."

"He's a rich man. To him that much money is chicken feed."

"He's a rich man," said Douglas. "To him money is money. Which is how he got to be rich in the first place."

"All right," Gallagher said after a moment, "give him the twenty thousand."

"No, not twenty, ten. Ten would be about right, I sense."

Gallagher began to laugh. "You are too much."

"If you agree, then it's ten."

"Call him up and tell him."

"No," said Douglas, "let's let him sweat it out overnight. I'll call him in the morning."

George came into the hotel room about 7 P.M. Jane on the bed was half asleep. It was dark out and rain was beating against the windowpanes. Of course she had been expecting him. Nonetheless she jumped up with a start as if frightened, and stood there tugging the slip down on her hips.

He put his bag down, and for a moment only stared. Then a smile came on. It was the biggest and happiest smile imaginable. It was an absolutely open, loving smile. She hadn't seen him smile like that in years.

"You look just gorgeous," he said, and came forward. She felt the sandpaper against her cheek, inhaled the familiar scent of him as he took her in his arms.

She permitted this embrace. She had decided in advance she would have to. He held her at arm's length while gazing raptly into her eyes.

She was prepared if he tried to kiss her to offer only her cheek. But he only hugged her tight once more, as if he couldn't get her close enough, at the same time murmuring: "Oh I've missed you so much," over and over again into her neck.

She thought he might attempt to make love to her at once, so she broke loose, skittering shoeless toward her dress. "Let's go to dinner," she said in a brittle voice. "Aren't you hungry? I'm starving." She threw the dress on over her head, came back, and stepped into her high heels.

"Wait a minute," he said, and handed her a box. "I found this on the plane."

She saw it was a jewelry box. "George—" she said.

"I found it on the plane," he said, and laughed. "Let's see what it is."

It was a gold bracelet with, in its center, a circle of rubies around a diamond.

"George—" she said again.

"The guy that lost it is probably pretty mad, I betcha."

She hadn't wanted to open the package, didn't want to accept the gift. But she had to, had no choice.

He left her staring at it and went into the bathroom, all the time talking to her, not waiting for any answer: "I wanted to bring you a present because I like you, see. But I didn't know what to get, see. It was either that bracelet or a bird feeder." She heard him urinate, and flush, then water ran in the sink as he washed his hands and face. These were homely sounds. He was behaving like a husband, as if this hotel room had become his home—their home. As if there were no secrets between them.

He came out of the bathroom drying his face on a hand towel. "I guess I blew it," he said with a grin; "you would have preferred the bird feeder."

He was relaxed. He suspected nothing. Finally she laughed. She was much abashed, and to her own ears the laugh was not successful. I've got to start this thing right now, she told herself, or it will become impossible. She wet her lips, started to speak, but could not.

"Don't say it," said George. "You never believed you could love me this much."

This time her laugh was a bit better. She said: "There's something I want to say to you—"

"Yes I know," and he mimicked her voice: "I'm hungry, George, let's go down to dinner."

Because of the rain they dined in the hotel. In the elevator descending and during the first course he told her of the case he was on. A defense firm had been indicted for cost overruns that the government deemed fraudulent. But this time the government was mistaken, according to the weeks of research he had put in. "You wouldn't believe the things I found."

He had come to Florida to get the indictment set aside. Tomorrow, for the first time in years, he would be back in court: "Isn't that great?" And from now on that was where he was going to work. He seemed as enthusiastic as a little boy. It was a quality he had had when she first met him. She had found it completely winning at the time, and for the moment did again.

Now he began talking about what her life must be like in South America. He wanted complete details, "stuff you didn't get into your stories." What were the Andes like, and the jungle, and Bogotá, and who were her friends, how did she spend her time?

She began tentatively, trying to hold back. This was not what she had come to Florida to talk about. But his interest seemed so genuine that she responded to it—how could she not? She had been living an adventure and perhaps all along had longed to tell him, tell someone, about it—someone who would be impressed with what she had seen and done, how far she had come in her career in only a few months. She looked across at his rapt face in the candlelight and the words spilled out of her.

But even as she told her tales she was looking for a way to shift this conversation onto the one essential ground, or so she assured herself guiltily. But no opportunity had yet come up.

"When you're not working, who do you spend your time with?"

She tried to dodge this one. "I'm almost always working."

"Nights, Sundays?" He kept pressing for an answer.

"I see the ambassador's wife fairly frequently. And the DEA guys." Then she added, as if trying the idea out, her eyes fixed on the table: "I play tennis with that cop from New York sometimes."

She congratulated herself. She had at last got Ray's name into the conversation. Sort of. But it brought with it only a new onrush of guilt. Guilt toward this husband whom she had betrayed, but who was gazing at her with love, if she had ever seen love; and a different guilt toward Ray Douglas to whom, by responding to her husband's interest, she was being equally unfaithful—Ray was counting on her to confront George, which she was not doing.

"There's a guy who's had a tough break," said George.

"Who?"

"That fellow Douglas."

She was surprised. "I didn't know you were interested in the New York Police Department."

"I'm not. I'm interested in him because of what you wrote about him. He's in exile there."

"I didn't write that." She had been careful to write nothing that might hurt Ray's career.

"No, but it was between the lines. They kicked him out of the mainstream and I doubt he'll ever be able to get back."

She was amazed that George had had this perception, the same one she had had, but from twenty-five hundred miles farther away.

"Who else have you met? What about the drug guy you wrote about, David Ley?"

Dinner was nearly over, and still the important subject had not been broached. Soon she would have to go upstairs with him, and if nothing had been said by then, what did she reasonably expect he would expect? And what would she then do about it?

She tried to take a deep breath but couldn't. "George, we have to talk about the future."

"Yeah, we do."

A grin came onto his face—a grin whose meaning she could not decipher.

Something terrible is coming, she thought.

He said: "There's something I haven't told you."

He's about to tell me he's got a girlfriend, she thought. I go to South America for a few months and— Well, what did I expect, she thought bitterly.

"What haven't you told me?" she said.

"We bought the apartment next door."

"We?"

"I bought it for both of us. It's already paid for. I brought the papers down for you to sign."

She was speechless.

"We knock a door through the wall," he said. "We'll have twice as much room." He hesitated, then added: "In case you decide you want to take a few months off and—"

He put his hand over hers on the tablecloth. She tried to withdraw it, but not in time. ''—have a baby.''

He signaled the waiter for the check. ''I have the architect's drawings in my bag. Let's go upstairs and look at them.''

She followed him out of the restaurant, across the lobby, into and out of the elevator. Down the corridor to their room. Her mind an absolute muddle.

He spread the drawings out on the bed and they leaned over them. In the past they had talked vaguely about this other apartment—that they might consider buying it, if it ever came on the market. Jane had coveted it then and did again. She had had definite ideas about how she would arrange it. Despite herself she got interested now in the architect's ideas as they differed from her own, began to consider his solutions to the same problems she had worried about. She disagreed with him here—with a pencil she pointed out the location of a wall—and with this doorway, and—

As he rolled up the drawings, George said: ''It's been a long day. Let's go to bed.'' He gave a yawn, but the yawn, Jane thought, had a leer in it. ''I'm tired,'' he said. ''Aren't you tired?''

Now he will claim his possession, she thought. His possession is me. She had reached Miami resolved, as the nuns used to tell the little girls, to be pure, whatever happened. Not for religious reasons of course, and only partly out of fidelity to Ray, but for herself. To try to see this thing clearly. She had decisions to make which sex would only make more difficult. Sex, the great mystifier. It was like fog. It blinded everyone who stepped into it. It fogged up the spirit, too.

George had begun to get undressed. Standing with his back to her he prepared to step into his pajamas. What do I do now? she thought. I'm lost, she thought. Probably he had an erection already, that would be like him. She couldn't see around him. If he did have one, he didn't want to flaunt it at her. At least not yet.

She got her nightgown out of her bag, started undoing the buttons of her nice pink dress—all the while making a silent apology to Ray Douglas: This isn't my fault. But she knew it was and she was ashamed: All I do is betray men, she thought. The dress came off over her head, then the slip. She unhooked her bra. On the other side of the room was George, and she no longer knew what stage of dress or undress he might be in, for she too was facing the other way.

If I just lie still and don't respond, perhaps it won't count, she thought. Ray, if he ever found out, almost couldn't object. She had taken part but hadn't taken part—don't you see? Rationalizations of all sorts crowded her head. To strip off her pantyhose she had to sit down on the bed. She wasn't really betraying Ray. A new man—that would be betrayal, whereas one more time with George can't be because it would not change her in any way. She would gain no new knowledge of man, or of this particular man, or of herself. No new intimacy. No new man running about the world who might come up to Ray at a party saying: You don't know about me, but one day I had your wife.

She stood up to let her nightgown fall into place, and turned, and found herself facing George, who lifted it over her head again. What constituted betrayal anyway? Was it betrayal for an actress to press her bare breasts against an actor, as Jane's were somehow squashed flat against George, while twenty technicians looked on? That happens more and more these days. What do the husbands, lovers of such actresses think? Was it betrayal to lie with knees up and as spread as now letting a gynecologist approach with eyes on only one thing? He too could do with you whatever he wanted. At sixteen you imagined that saying I love you to a new boy was betrayal of the old one, and to speak those same words now at her age, now at this minute, could be again. Words can constitute infidelity, whereas sexual intercourse such as what was about to happen, was happening—it made her catch her breath—can be meaningless and not in and of itself necessarily betrayal at all, absolutely not. Words were much more important, George was muttering them, a whole series of endearments in fact, whereas she had said nothing, had pronounced no word at all, was silent except for unintelligible sounds that were coming out of her throat against her will, past her lips against her will, sounds no one could possibly recognize as hers, a voiceprint wouldn't work, sounds she could not help and for which no one could convict her.

The next day she went to court with George and after a long wait heard him argue his case. He was very eloquent, she supposed, but she couldn't keep her mind on it.

Once he came over to her. "You know what that guy just told me?"

She looked up and the judge had left the bench. "Who told you?"

"The prosecutor. Your friend David Ley has been indicted."

"What does that mean?" Immediately she felt stupid. She knew very well what indictment meant, but was having trouble keeping her mind on anything.

George said: "It's a conspiracy case. If the Colombians will extradite him here—"

"They won't."

"Or if he decides to come here to go shopping—"

"He won't."

"He'll go to jail forever. Him, Marzo, Lucientes, the lot of them. They're all in the same indictment."

The judge returned to the bench, George went back into the well, and oral arguments resumed. Another hour passed, and then court adjourned for the day. As they left the courthouse George was elated. He thought he had made some excellent points, and tomorrow he would examine his witnesses.

Jane was thinking: What am I going to tell Ray?

"Let's drive up the coast for dinner," George said. "I know a nice place."

She wondered if she was in love with two men at once. Men were capable of loving two persons at once, she believed; women were not supposed to be. Perhaps she was in love with neither, or only with herself. Her emotions were in a turmoil and she was behaving, she thought, either like a man or like a whore.

* * *

Ocampo came into the embassy, ostensibly to have a visa stamped into his passport. The meeting took place in Douglas's office.

"You made me wait an extra day," Ocampo accused.

"Sorry about that," said Douglas.

"You investigated me. You thought I was a *narcotraficante*."

"Not at all," said Douglas.

"I hate those people. They are ruining this country. Because of them no Colombiano can have any more self-respect."

He was an international polo player, Ocampo explained heatedly. He traveled many times to Miami, to New York, often in the company of other polo players, men of means moving through the world together. "We go to the States, the others walk straight through Customs and out. It takes me two hours, because I am a Colombiano. How do you think that makes me feel? Sometimes the others wait for me while the Customs examines my gear, takes apart my mallets, shoves long probes through my suitcases, ruining them. The humiliation of it. Once they strip-searched my wife."

The two men looked at each other in silence. Ocampo was genuinely fuming, and Douglas believed him. "No, Señor," Ocampo said, "I am not a *narcotraficante*. I am a citizen doing his duty to Colombia."

"I am sorry," said Douglas, "if I ever thought otherwise."

"Also, I do not want to lose my ship."

His ship would not be seized, Douglas promised him. Instead the furniture would be tracked to its destination and seized there. And assuming that the information he was about to disclose was valid, he would be paid ten thousand dollars, not twenty.

With a slight inclination of the head, Ocampo accepted the terms.

"The *Caballo Blanco*," he said. "Charleston. Tomorrow noon."

"And from there?"
"I do not know."

Jane had still not returned, and as the days passed she occupied more and more of Douglas's thoughts. He began to sleep badly. The Ocampo affair was over; the furniture, still aboard two flatbed trailer trucks, had been tracked to a warehouse in New Jersey and there was nothing for Douglas to do except wait to learn what happened to it. He was waiting for that report and he was waiting for Jane. He had never been good at waiting and now he sat at his desk and stared at papers. Often enough he saw her face there on his desk top, unsmiling, her expression as inscrutable as her intentions.

Most times when the phone rang he jumped. Perhaps she was calling from Florida, or better still from the airport. But this did not happen. He would have telephoned her, if he could, and never mind that the husband might answer. But he had no idea where in Miami she might be, or even if she was still there.

Especially in his apartment at night he waited for the phone to ring, which it didn't. He missed her badly. It was the classic case of the lonely widower falling in love, he supposed. Which changed nothing. He had believed he would never be able to love again, she had proven him wrong, and the notion that he might lose her, that he could lose two women within a year, was very unpleasant.

He had expected, or perhaps only hoped, that she'd be back the next day. But she wasn't, nor the day after that either. If divorce was what she had gone to talk about, what could be keeping her? By the fourth morning, more and more aware of her empty apartment below his, he conceived the notion that he had to go in there—the cleaning woman might not realize she was away, might neglect to feed her cat. But he didn't have the key.

He sat in his office in the embassy. If he entered her apartment, he might find a bill, a confirmation, some paper that would tell him where in Miami she might be so that he could try to phone her. It was probable also that he wanted to stand among her things and sense her there all around him, but this seemed to him an adolescent notion and he refused to admit it to himself.

"Look at this."

It was Gallagher leaning over his desk, handing down a cable from Washington. Four men had come to get the furniture out of the warehouse, Douglas read. As they attempted to drive away in the two trucks, they were arrested. So were nine men in the warehouse. In hollowed-out spaces in the furniture had been found eight hundred kilos of a controlled substance, namely cocaine.

"Hey," said Douglas, grinning, "that's terrific."

"We seized the trucks too," Gallagher said. "Not to mention the warehouse itself. That's how you hurt them. You confiscate their toys."

"I'll call Ocampo and tell him."

"Should you?"

"We owe it to him, I think."

Gallagher, who had taken the chair beside Douglas's desk, said: "There's something else I have to mention. What are we going to do about your friend?"

Douglas looked at him.

"The ambassador was on me this morning," Gallagher apologized. "He knows she's back. What do you suggest we do about her?"

"She's in Florida at the moment," Douglas said. "Which reminds me, I have to go in and feed her cat."

"She is coming back, isn't she?"

"Unless she asked you to do it."

"Me? I hardly know her."

"She forgot to leave me the key. It's an embassy apartment, so there must be an extra one around. Who should I ask?"

He let himself in and the cat came and rubbed against his leg. He went through to the kitchen, emptied a can of catfood into the bowl, and placed it on the floor. The cat attacked it immediately. He got milk out of the fridge, poured some into the second bowl, and put it down.

He felt strange, an intruder in Jane's flat, though why? He almost had to force himself to enter the living room, where he peered about. They loved each other, practically lived together, probably would marry, he told himself. It was normal that he should come in in her absence to feed her cat. Although this seemed to him a perfectly good argument he had no confidence in it. She had gone to Florida, taking his confidence with her.

Her telephone on the sideboard caught his eye. The message light was winking.

There was no piece of paper lying about that would tell him where she was. He opened only one or two drawers looking, then stopped. He had no right to search her drawers.

He had looked forward to entering her apartment, as if sure she would become more real to him there. But he was too focused on himself, on his own uneasiness. Besides, the essence of her was missing. The essence of her was woman, and woman to Douglas was mystery, the essential unknowability of another human being, no matter how much loved, and today with so much sunlight streaming in the window nothing was hidden at all. It was as if the mystery of her didn't exist, and if it didn't, she didn't.

He was left with his own profound discomfort, as if he had never before stood alone in this room. He sniffed the air but there was no scent of her. Nothing. This furnished apartment was as sterile as any he had ever seen—more sterile than most. It smelled faintly of cat, strongly of whatever furniture polish the maid used. It carried no scent of Jane. He made a kind of pilgrimage into her bedroom—it had been their bedroom often enough—where he tried to conjure up memories that ought to have been vivid. Instead they were inconclusive, as if he had read them in a book, and of a sudden he felt so dispirited he could not believe they had ever happened, could not believe they would ever happen again.

He prepared to leave the apartment.

The phone rang.

He never intended to answer it but he hesitated at the door because her answering machine clicked on and he wanted to hear her voice even though all it said was "Please leave a message after the beep."

He smiled and again reached for the doorknob, but the caller began to speak, a voice that stopped him in his tracks for he thought he recognized it. It spoke in Spanish, so at first he was not sure. He had stepped back into the apartment. He was leaning over the machine listening intently, and when the caller had hung up he reversed the tape and listened to it again.

"This is your friend from Virginia calling. I saw the article you did on my suggestion about the flower industry. Very good. I have another idea for you."

It was the voice of the man who had called the embassy to warn that Jane would be kidnapped.

"A scandal that I can help you uncover. It's about the oil pipeline."

He copied out a rough translation of the entire message.

"So call me in Medellín either at the bank or at the ranch—you have the numbers. I hope we can get together again soon."

David Ley, Douglas thought. It's his voice. It has to be. There's no one else it could be.

He backed up the tape and played it still again, listening for whatever other information was on there that he might have missed. The tone, for instance. The tone was silky, seductive, carefully modulated. In the course of the message he called Jane *"hija"* once, *"guapa"* twice, and addressed her in the familiar *"tu"* throughout. *Hija* meant daughter and Douglas translated *guapa* as "cutie-pie"—perhaps it sounded better in Spanish. To Douglas, Ley's voice suggested sex, exuded sex. He was out to seduce Jane, and since she wasn't home, he made love to her machine. He was trying to do the next best thing, seduce a machine; Douglas almost laughed. But it wasn't funny. He wondered how far Jane had encouraged him. This was not the first phone call nor, apparently, was it an isolated one. A man bent on seducing a woman usually offered gifts. Jewelry. Flowers at least. But to Jane you offered a story, which Douglas saw as a gift like any other. He gives her gifts, Douglas thought, which she accepts. Gifts from a drug trafficker.

As he realized all this he was both astonished and dismayed. What have I just learned about Jane? he asked himself. The answer: that she had a secret life she had kept from him. But how could you keep secrets from someone you loved? It brought such a heaviness to the pit of his stomach that he was afraid he was going to vomit.

What else don't I know about her? he asked himself. What else is she doing behind my back?

He decided he would play through the entire tape.

There were some things it was better not to know. Especially there were things it was better for a lover not to know. These warnings occurred to Douglas, but he ignored them. He started the tape.

It held nearly thirty minutes of old messages, for this was the type machine that accumulated them, that erased nothing until the very end, when presumably it started over.

Voices one after the other that he did not recognize.

He calmed down, became bored, found his own conduct reprehensible. It was the same as snooping through her diary. Voices left phone numbers. Disembodied voices, as if speaking in code. The New York desk. Secretaries confirming appointments. Some of the voices were awkward, some embarrassed—callers not yet used to conversing with machines. Messages that were never personal, yet somehow were. But he was able to justify listening. He was not spying on Jane. This was not personal at all. It had become a law-enforcement matter now.

The tape went forward while Douglas went back—back in time, he had no idea how much time, through old messages and even old conversations, for Jane's machine, if she answered the phone in the middle of a message, continued to record both voices. It was a weird experience. He felt weird.

"It's me."

Me? Who was me?

He was like a husband rummaging through his wife's hand-bag, searching for evidence he hoped would not be there. Except he wasn't her husband. Her husband, he suddenly realized, was the man on the tape, and he listened to him pleading with her to meet him in Florida. Since the succeeding message was similar, obviously she had said no the first time, and Douglas was briefly elated. Jane had been telling him the truth, she never wanted to go to Florida, she had wanted only to stay in South America with him. But there was nothing to be elated about, was there? Because where was Jane right now, and who with?

Her husband's voice segued into Ley's. An entire conversation. Ley suggesting she write a piece about the problems of the new Colombian export flower industry. Cut flowers to American supermarkets. A thirty-million-dollar industry that promised to lift at least part of the Colombian economy out of abject poverty. Except that routinely now the flowers were being held up so long at American Customs, and probed so brutally for drugs, that the flowers were ruined and never got to market. Ley giving her names and phone numbers to call. The Colombian flower industry was on its knees, Ley said. He wasn't seducing the machine this time but Jane in person. Jane plainly taking notes. Ley sounding fond of her, and she of him. Jane thanking him profusely as she rang off.

She's in that guy's pocket, Douglas told himself. She knows he's a major trafficker, one of the biggest, probably owns a flower company himself, probably ships his own drugs out that way. Yet she lets herself be used by him. Didn't she see that? Or did she not care? Favors always had to be repaid. How was she going to pay him back, had she thought of that?

Jane's husband's voice again—and then Jane's voice answering, giving flight numbers, the two of them talking quite cozily, they would see each other in a few hours. Jane sounded less eager than her husband did, though not all that much. There was a sexual undercurrent in the husband's voice too, different from Ley's but in its own way as strong. He did not sound like a man talking to a woman from whom he would soon be divorced. Nor did she.

They had talked to each other the way, in Douglas's experience, married people do.

He rewound the spool and reset the machine.

On his way past the kitchen he stopped to look in on the cat. The bowls on the floor were empty. The animal lay curled up on the kitchen counter, sound asleep. Douglas switched off all the lights and left the apartment.

Upstairs he stood at his window looking down at the turnaround. When Jane came back, if she came back, she would get out of the car just there.

Douglas had always hated the telephone. It was not the same as seeing, feeling, scenting someone you were talking to. The telephone was a whisper in your ear without any breath behind it. Was he so sure he had grasped what Jane and her husband had been saying to each other? One could never be sure. Telephones tended to obscure one's meanings. As a boy when he had called up scarcely known girls for dates, he had never known how to phrase whatever he wanted to say. Nor was he ever certain he understood what they were saying back to him, those girls whom he could hear but not see. The telephone to him had been a diabolical contraption ever since. If you had anything important to communicate, it could not be done by telephone. The telephone could only announce something, like a birth or death. Like a liaison with a drug dealer. Like the resumption of a marriage. And that's all it could do.

So maybe he was wrong.

He left the window, made himself a cup of coffee, and came back.

He hated telephones and their misinformation, and the answering machines into which they had now transmogrified themselves were even worse. Now we had people holding conversations with machines and even machines speaking to each other. People believed such machines could do what machines could not, relied on them in areas where they were incompetent. Machines that pretended to be what they were not. Machines that lied.

So maybe he was wrong.

He knew what time the afternoon plane from Miami landed, and approximately what time she would reach here, if she were on it and came directly home.

Pretty soon lawyers and prosecutors would start subpoenaing answering machines, if they were not already. It was better than subpoenaing diaries and datebooks. Under certain circumstances it was better than a detective wearing a wire.

The afternoon passed. It became dusk, then night. A taxi pulled into the compound and stopped, and Jane stepped out. He watched her lift her suitcase down, pay the driver, come into the building.

She had been gone five days.

Douglas had an answering machine too. Leaving the window, he walked over and switched it on. In a way these ubiquitous new machines were better than telephones, or at least no worse.

Did they not do all a telephone could reasonably do—pass on messages? Was the one machine any more inhuman than the other? It depended on how it was used. Words spoken into a telephone at least had the decency to disappear. Whereas the answering machine could hold on to them almost forever.

His phone rang. He stood near it, heard his own voice say: "Please leave your message after the beep."

This was followed by Jane's voice. She sounded excited. "It's me. I'm home. I'm dying to see you. I'll try you at the embassy. Anyway, I'm here waiting for you."

He made himself a second cup of tea and went to stand again at the window.

The next morning he went downstairs to the turnaround where he waited with other embassy personnel waiting for the armored cars to come for them. Jane came out of the building, saw him, and looked surprised. A smile came on, but as she reached him it turned tentative.

"Good morning everybody," she said to the others. And then to Douglas: "Didn't you get my message?"

"Yes."

"You didn't call?"

"No," he said.

The first of the armored cars entered the turnaround and stopped in front of them. The guards with their submachine guns got out and stood by the open doors. Those assigned to this car boarded it: Jane, Douglas, and three secretaries. The guards, after peering all around, got in last, two of them in the rear row facing backward. The doors slammed.

Douglas was at the window in the next to last row on the driver's side. Jane was beside him in the middle, half turned toward him, her hip and thigh pressed against him. But she stared straight ahead and said nothing. He liked feeling her there and each time he breathed was aware of the scent of her. But he said nothing either. The others in the car began an animated discussion of television shows, for their apartment building had its own satellite dish, its *parabólico* as it was called here, which brought in dozens of American channels from several cities.

Douglas watched Bogotá pass by outside the inch-thick bulletproof glass.

In front of the *El Tiempo* building stood more guards. Douglas had to step out of the car to let Jane out. For a moment he stood with her on the sidewalk.

She said: "When will I see you?"

"The car will pick you up at six P.M.," he answered.

"Will you be in it?"

"It depends on what the day brings."

"I don't know why you didn't call last night," she said. "Or this morning at least."

"Yes you do."

They looked at each other.

"Tell them not to bother to send the car," she said. "I

won't be riding them anymore." Her mouth, in the moment before she turned toward the building, looked stitched shut.

In the evening the armored car stopped in front of the *El Tiempo* building but Jane sent down word that she was working; she was not yet ready to leave; it was to continue on without her.

Sitting beside the driver, Douglas shrugged.

He had brought home a briefcase full of statistical papers that he had collected in Bolivia, in Peru, and also here, but had not yet had time to study. After supper he was poring over these papers when his doorbell rang.

He knew who it was before he got up from his chair, and despite himself felt a surge of joy. He dampened this as best he could and went to the door. Be realistic, he told himself. There is nothing here for you. He opened the door.

Jane stood looking up at him. She was wearing flat shoes, jeans, and a rose-colored sweater. Her hair was tied back with a rubber band.

She said: "Can I ask what's the matter?"

"You were gone five days, Jane," he said after a moment.

"So?"

He kept silent.

"I went to New York to see my editors, if you must know."

He nodded.

"May I come in?"

"I was just going out."

She said suspiciously: "Where to?"

"I thought I'd go over to the residence."

"I'll go with you."

The upshot was that they played bridge with Gallagher and Martha Thompson for two hours in the basement of the residence. Douglas kept up a bright chatter throughout. Jane seemed to become more and more sullen.

"My husband's up near the Venezuelan border," Martha Thompson said once. She studied her cards. "I pass."

Some embassy people were watching an American sitcom on TV.

"The guerrillas blew up the pipeline again," Martha Thompson added. She threw an ace and drew in the trick. "I don't know what he thinks he can do about it."

They could hear a Ping-Pong ball being batted back and forth in the next room. Only Gallagher was paying much attention to the cards.

"It's late," Jane said. The hand had ended. "I'm going to bed."

"All right," said Douglas, "I'll walk you back."

"I'm quite capable of walking home alone."

Douglas stood up. "Goodnight, everyone."

He glanced behind him as they left. Gallagher and Martha Thompson still sat at the card table. They had their heads together. Gallagher was shuffling the deck over and over while Martha, looking pensive, talked to him in a low voice.

Douglas and Jane came out through the security gate onto the street. Jane did not take his arm or hand. She walked with her head down.

"Nice night," said Douglas brightly, but she did not answer.

Tonight the police car was parked on the sidewalk under the trees. The two cops had the light on inside and were arguing about something. Douglas gave them a wave on the way by.

They went into their building. In the elevator Douglas pushed the button for her floor, then his.

When the doors opened on Jane's floor her head rose and she looked at him. Her face was expressionless.

"Goodnight, Jane," he said.

She went out of the elevator and did not look back. The doors closed.

18

THERE WERE POLICE cars parked broadside across the road with their blue lights turning, and in front of them a line of policemen standing elbow to elbow facing the crowd, letting no one through. Other cops were trying to keep a lane open, but cars kept arriving. There were cars parked on the road and on the verge for a hundred yards or more, and Jane was obliged to get out of her taxi a considerable distance away. She handed her driver a hundred-dollar bill.

"Do you know what this is?"

"*Si, señorita.*"

"It's worth thirty-five thousand pesos. Wait for me. Turn the taxi around and be ready to go. You get another like this when we get back to Bogotá."

The lake was on her right, the walls of the village ahead. She walked forward to the police line and showed her press card. It passed from hand to hand. No one knew what to do. She argued and smiled, smiled and argued. At last they let her pass inside.

She walked very fast. She didn't know this village, had never been out here. The road became a street between white-washed walls. The architecture was Spanish colonial. Balconies hung over the street. She passed a small jewel of a bullring, white with ochre trim, but no people. Where is everybody? she asked herself, but she knew.

She came out onto the village square. Shops, restaurants. Mosaic terraces. No cars. It was a big square. Arches and arcades ran along one side of it, and there were balconies above that. The café tables were out but no one was sitting at them. There were stalls in front of the shops: pottery, paintings, handwoven tapestries and shawls; but there were no customers, nor was anyone tending them.

The crowd was in front of one of the restaurants. A line of cops was trying to move back or at least hold back what seemed like the entire population of the village, plus all the excursionists who had come out here for Sunday lunch. Necks were craning. Children were sitting on shoulders. It had turned out to be a lunch unlike any other. Jane could see nothing.

"*Perdon,*" she cried out, trying to force her way forward. "*Perdon, por favor.*"

She came up against more police. They formed a solid line and would not let her through. She kept thrusting her press card into their faces. They would not even look at it. Fuming and frustrated, she stared past them into the restaurant. There were chairs and tables on their sides, and a group of men peering down on lumps that had been people. The lumps were covered with newspapers or tablecloths. Feet stuck out. Some of the men in there she recognized, Ray Douglas for one, whose help she would never ask again, she was that angry at him. But she could not get through the police line, time was passing, and when he next glanced in her direction she cried out and began waving her handbag to attract his attention.

He came out and drew her inside the police line, but prevented her from going forward. "You don't want to go in there," he said.

"Are you crazy?"

"It's not pretty."

"Stop trying to protect me."

"Suit yourself."

As she entered, the group of men fell silent. They watched as she approached the first bundle on the floor. It was small, which puzzled her, but when she had knelt to move the newspaper slightly she saw it was the body of a boy of about eight. He was wearing long pants. His right arm was nearly severed from his body. There was a pool of nearly coagulated blood under his arm. More blood had leaked out from under his back.

She let the newspaper fall back and stood up blinking.

"The murderous bastards," said Ray at her side.

She almost leaned against him.

"Have you seen enough?" he said.

She moved on to the next bundle, which was close to the door to the kitchen. A middle-aged woman, also half hidden by newspapers. Jane toed the newspaper off her. She wore an apron. A waitress, presumably. There was a shocked expression on her face. She must have run for the kitchen after she was hit. Blood had leaked down her legs. She looked like a woman who had got her period unexpectedly.

Jane stood up and glanced around. She was trying to breathe normally but it was hard. She said to Ray: "How many dead?"

"Just the four."

"Has the ambassador been notified?"

"I think so. He's over in Arauca at the pipeline."

"I know that," Jane snapped. But immediately she tried to force her emotions back under control. Don't let him see you like this, she ordered herself.

"And the others?" she said.

He gestured over toward the group of men.

Jane did not want to go over there. The first two corpses, however much they had upset her, were of people she did not know. The next two she had played bridge with just last night.

They lay partially covered by tablecloths. The group parted to let her through. She gazed down at Gallagher's protruding wingtip shoes, at Martha's high heels, one of them half off. She felt a wave of pity. Not for Gallagher so much; in a sense he had contracted for an end like this on the day he was sworn in as a DEA agent. But Martha had not, and Martha was a woman like herself, driven by the same needs and hungers, the same hopes and disappointments as herself.

Kneeling between them, she peeled back the cloth—Martha first. The DEA agent would wait his turn. I'm a reporter, she told herself, if I'm going to report it, I have to look at it.

Martha's lips were drawn back in a grimace of pain. She had been stitched across her ample chest, which looked deflated, but her blouse was no more stained than if somebody had hit her arm while she was blowing on a spoonful of tomato soup. Her face was silvery. Not pale as if sick, pale as if dead. The waxy look that comes from no blood coursing through under the skin. The undertaker may rouge up those cheeks later, she thought, but in real life this is what a recently dead face looks like. Jane felt tears come to her eyes but they were tears of anger. Why did Martha have to come out from behind her gates? She had been told not to. Was she too in love to remember how dangerous it was? Or was she just kicking up her heels, busting free and to hell with the consequences? Couldn't she wait? She wasn't going to be stationed in Colombia forever. Why didn't she wait? She must have felt like a kid playing hooky from school. What sense of freedom could be worth this?

"Silly lady," she muttered angrily.

Whose idea was it to go out for a Sunday drive? Hers? She glanced at the bundle that had been Gallagher. His? Had Martha done it for a man? She dropped the one cloth back into place and raised the other. Gallagher's face was ruined. A bullet had taken out his left eye. The gore had run down into his ear, and overflowed, and got clotted in his hair as it made its way to the floor. The rest of his face was pale. The two sides didn't match. One half pale as ashes, the other ruined. Jane did not know where else the man might have been hit, did not want to know. She dropped the cloth back onto his face and looked away. After a moment she rose to her feet. Douglas still hovered there at her side.

"What were they doing here?"

"Eating lunch, I imagine." He gestured toward a nearby table on which sat two half-eaten desserts and two cups of cold coffee.

"Who did it?"

"We don't know."

"What do you know?"

"Jane, I haven't been here much longer than you."

During this time the group of men, some from the embassy, others presumably from the Colombian police, had watched her in silence.

"Jane—" said Douglas.

She glanced over at the other men, who might know more. She got her notebook out and, turning away from him, approached them.

During the next week Jane and the police conducted parallel investigations. The police sought facts that would stand up in court. She did too, up to a point. She had a story to write each night and it had to be accurate, but she wanted to know far more than the police cared about, more than she would ever choose to print or be permitted to print, enough to understand exactly what had happened and why. To be a foreign correspondent in Colombia, which had seemed fabulous to her only a short time before, did not seem fabulous anymore. She was a very shaken woman.

She worked from early morning to late at night, never stopped for lunch and rarely even for coffee. She wanted answers, and thought the dead voices could give them, if she could get close enough. She became obsessed, but there were breaks in her obsession. Phone calls from the desk. The need some days to highlight the political side: the intense diplomatic pressure on the government to find and arrest known traffickers who, it was assumed, had ordered the murders; the state of siege declared by the president of the republic in response; the efforts of the police who were supposed to be looking for traffickers but who so far had arrested nobody. A group of Spanish-speaking DEA agents had arrived, together with the director, who stayed only one day but had to be interviewed. The agents were there to help the police, supposedly, though they were not allowed to do much. Plus there were other journalists who flooded into Bogotá and got in Jane's way. Some she had known previously. Many phoned her for help—phone numbers, directions, contacts—and she gave it, was taken out of herself for a time.

But she kept building up the picture. She walked the same ground the victims had walked, saw what they saw, breathed the same air, asked her questions of anyone who could provide even partial answers. She considered the physical evidence too: the mud stains halfway up Martha's spike heels, the ticket stubs in Gallagher's pocket, the uneaten lunches and marked maps in the car, the autopsy report. She went backward and forward in time, constructed and reconstructed scenarios of where they went and what they did, and this she documented; and even of what they said to each other—what Martha must have said, what Gallagher must have said—which, being speculative, was not part of the copy she filed each night. She dug up details that readers would have found titillating or even salacious, and kept these to herself as well. Her reports, which held the front page four straight days, were far more complete and restrained than those of her competitors. They were models of journalistic objectivity.

The bridge table—that was the place to start. Jane remembered, as she and Ray had left the game room, looking back at Martha and Gallagher, who were so soon to become corpses. The condemned couple with their heads together over the table. That's where their plans had been hatched, surely. To go out into the country without guards. Whose decision was it? His? Hers? And why?

Martha had often chafed at security restrictions, Jane discovered, and there had been friction between her and embassy security chief Brent Evans. Martha had done this kind of thing before, according to Evans, had once slipped out the back door of a Bogotá clothing store, had gone for a walk in the city alone. Probably other times as well.

Jane noted it down.

Whereas Gallagher appeared always to have worked by the book. In fifteen years with the agency he had never had to be disciplined, his records showed, had committed no transgressions of any kind. He was brave enough when arresting suspects but a timid bureaucrat the rest of the time, his colleagues told Jane, and they did not understand how such a man could have let himself get involved with an ambassador's wife in the first place.

So the drive was Martha's idea, Jane concluded. The plans were discussed over the bridge table. Gallagher would have refused. Martha would have insisted. She wanted a day in the country. She wanted to live like a normal human being for a few hours, was that so much to ask? She couldn't go alone—she had no access to a car. To get him to agree she would have had to threaten him with something. Sex, most likely. What else did she have? Was Martha a woman given to coarse speech? Jane thought she was and could hear the voices, Gallagher's saying no, absolutely not, followed by the brazen Martha saying: Then no more pussy for you, friend. The traditional woman working from the traditional power base. Traditional because she had no other.

Finally of course Gallagher had conceded. He was a lonely, closed-in man and Martha had become as necessary to him as he was to her. He had brought his car to Colombia at government expense. He kept it in the garage under his apartment building—Jane's building as well. He would sometimes lend it to friends or relatives passing through Bogotá but never used it himself because the book said he was to ride only in the embassy cars behind bulletproof glass.

He got it out, drove it up near the gates of the residence, and waited. Probably he kept his face averted, hoping the guards would not even look out at the unfamiliar car, or recognize the back of his head if they did. Martha, wearing a big sweater and blue jeans, wearing high-heel shoes impractical for the occasion, had simply walked out and climbed in. The surprised guards had come running out after her, but too late.

As he drove away, Gallagher would have worried about the guards; he was a man who worried about nearly everything. Not Martha. Her husband would not be back until the next day, and which guard was going to tell on them? To admit he had let the ambassador's wife slip out the gate would cost him his job. Sure, Brent Evans would inform the ambassador if he ever found out, but which guard was going to tell Brent? So Martha wasn't worried at all.

Of course, Evans had found out everything later.

The lovers started out of the city over the Autopista del Norte, hurrying toward where their assassins would meet them. Gallagher had a short-nosed Smith and Wesson .38, five bullets, in a clip-on holster at his belt, and a Colt .9mm submachine gun in a briefcase lying on the back seat. He watched the mirror constantly, looking for any car or cars that might be tailing them.

Jane's picture of him was less vivid than of Martha. She visualized the ambassador's wife and the DEA agent riding in the car, could hear her denying aloud that any danger existed, while inside herself exulting in the idea of flaunting herself in danger's face.

The police didn't care about any of this, Jane knew. They weren't interested in Martha and Gallagher as live human beings, only as corpses.

It was a Sunday morning and there were many cars. Fields of onions, of potatoes, of wheat stretched back from the road on both sides. But there were stretches of forest too, including stands of eucalyptus trees planted in rows. From time to time Gallagher had to slow down for cows or sheep or goats that had wandered onto the road or were grazing on the verges, or to skirt a half-crushed dog with flies all over it. The farther they got from Bogotá the more the road deteriorated, and soon he was slowing just as often to avoid potholes.

Always off to the right was the distant wall of the high Andes. Gallagher would have had his nerves under better control by this time. No one can stay afraid for very long, and their outing seemed safe enough so far. They passed a bike race—files of bike racers head down, pedaling fast— what could be more prosaic on a Sunday morning, or give a greater sense of safety? There was little chance of being intercepted by traffickers or guerrillas, Gallagher would have reasoned, because no one had known of their plans, and there had been no regular pattern anyone might have observed.

And so he drove on and began to relax a little. In places grew acres and acres of flowers, most of them under canopies of clear plastic. And there were more flowers in the villages in the cemeteries, masses of them on nearly every tomb, for heaping flowers on their dead seemed to be one of the things Colombians did on Sundays.

They went through the villages at reduced speed, with dogs running out at them barking. People made room by pressing back against the village walls. The villages had been old when the Spaniards left, and had not changed since. They were built of brick, with red tile roofs, and in each one stood a cathedral, gray with age, that was too big for it. The villages were all crowded, usually because an open market was in progress in the main square, and in one of them Martha demanded that they stop. Certainly Gallagher didn't want to, but he gave in.

They got out of the car and moved through the crowded market. Merchandise lay out in stalls, or on mats on the pavement. Martha peered down at the fruits and cheeses, at the pottery and wood carvings and woven goods. The merchants were mostly Indians down from the mountains. They wore bright Indian costumes. Gallagher moved carefully behind her, his briefcase half unzipped, and he watched only the faces around them, alert to sudden movement, to undue interest in them of any kind. Martha bought an alpaca sweater in a small size for one of her daughters. It was found later when someone drove Gallagher's car back to the embassy. Gallagher bought nothing.

Their next stop was the Parque de Tunja. The ticket taker handed back the stubs that would be recovered from Gallagher's pocket, and they went in and looked at gigantic boulders marooned there on the grassy plain, boulders the size of galleons. How had they got there? What did they signify? Some bore inscriptions and engravings done who knew when by the Chibcha Indians, and Martha put her hand on the carved stone as any woman would, as Jane herself did two days later, and dragged it along, trying to feel—what?

A woman is a tactile person, Jane thought. Much more than a man is. She had to feel things with her body, with her hands. Martha and herself were the same.

They drove on to the so-called Salt Cathedral. Gallagher had to stand in line to buy tickets—more stubs to be found in his pocket. With eight or ten others they started down the long dark corridor into the former salt mine. The corridor became a tunnel buttressed with logs. Gallagher, who carried his briefcase half unzipped as before, watched the others closely until suddenly the tunnel opened up into a truly vast cavern. The altar far ahead was visible because it was floodlit, but the ceiling was so high it almost could not be perceived. It was higher than any cathedral either of them had ever stood in before.

When they had advanced farther they saw that there were other naves to either side, and hollowed-out chapels and shrines as well. The main altar, carved out of a single block of salt, weighed sixteen tons, according to the folder Martha had been handed, and in front of it was a heavy balustrade of an altar rail that looked like carved and polished marble, same grain, same luster—but was actually salt—carved and polished salt as hard as any marble anywhere. The statuary was carved from blocks of salt as well. The whole cathedral was hard polished salt. Gallagher forgot for a moment the briefcase in his arms and stared with awe around him. They both did.

But it was dank and cold in there, and they soon made their way out into the sunlight again, where Martha spent some minutes at a souvenir stand selecting postcards. Was this when and where their assassins picked them up, or was it only later in the restaurant? Gallagher, who stood close to Martha as she paid for her postcards, was still alert, still scanning faces, ready to protect her if need be, not because he was a sworn law-enforcement agent and it was his duty, but like a husband from love. They were two people who simply needed each other; you could not mock it. Love was love, whatever guise it came in, and you took it where you could.

As they drove on they were looking for a spot to have a picnic. Both had brought bags containing cold chicken, slices of Colombian sausage, bread, beer. They had twice as much food as they needed, though ultimately they didn't eat any of it. They came through Sesquile, bought gasoline, and asked for directions to Lake Guatavita. According to legend, the Chibchas used to celebrate religious ceremonies in this lake. After painting his body with gold dust the cacique, who was both the civil and religious leader, would submerge himself in the lake while his followers threw in gold idols and precious stones as offerings to the gods. Having heard the legend, the Spanish conquerors decided this must be the lost Eldorado, whereupon they behaved as they always did. They began torturing and murdering Indians to find out where the lake was, and where on the lake the ceremonies had taken place, they ransacked the shallows, even drained part of the lake, a huge engineering project for the time. When they found no gold, they decided the lying Indians had put them on a false trail and needed a little more torturing and killing, and they gave it to them. But no gold ever turned up.

To get to the lake they would have to leave the car and hike uphill, the attendant told Gallagher. The trail was not very well marked.

Even in high heels Martha was eager to try it.

They started up, Gallagher carrying both lunches and his briefcase. Martha's heels sank halfway into the soft earth, but she kept laughing about it. She was happier and more animated than Gallagher had ever seen her, her eyes brighter, her conversation as well.

Jane, two days later, climbed the same hill. She followed Martha's heel prints. It was like tracking a deer, or some other sharp-hoofed animal. Her rented car was parked down on the verge and she soon lost sight of it. The solitude frightened her.

At the top Gallagher and Martha were out of breath—so was Jane—but the view over the lake was magnificent. They were alone, though not as alone as Jane, there was not a sound to be heard, and he took her in his arms and they fell to the ground and made love. The autopsy report was definite on that count: recent sexual intercourse by both parties. Who instigated the act? Jane wondered. Probably the man. Most men thought you were a toy. But in this case it could have been totally spontaneous, she was willing to admit. It could have been both of them.

Afterward Gallagher would have brushed the dirt off Martha's sweater, her bare behind. He would have gone to the edge of the lake to wash the dirt off his hands, his elbows, his knees. They got dressed again and a herd of schoolchildren came up the hill hollering. The idyllic moment over, their privacy gone, they decided not to eat their picnic lunches after all, but to go on to the restaurant in Guatavita, which was where the assassins, after searching for them throughout the village, finally found them.

What was it Jane was trying to grasp? That a woman could die for no reason in so outrageous a manner? She was trying to comprehend the incomprehensible, but could not stop. The funerals were today, she realized, Martha's in Houston, Gallagher's in New York. A lot of rich people at the one, a lot of cops and agents at the other.

She went back to Bogotá and again phoned the embassy. What progress toward arrests? Had the investigation turned up anything at all? She talked to Bannon, who had taken over Gallagher's job. It was Marzo, Bannon told her. That was the word on the street. The assassinations had been ordered by Pablo Marzo. American police jargon: word on the street. The Colombian police would have some equivalent phrase, you could count on it, but she did not know what it was. All the informants were saying the same, Bannon told her: Marzo.

But the traffickers were still moving on the surface, Jane said. All of them, including Marzo. The government had done nothing.

"That's true," Bannon conceded.

"What about the so-called heavy diplomatic pressure?"

"It's not working."

This was obvious, and for a moment both brooded about it. The police were badly trained, badly paid, and therefore corrupt. The magistrates, who under Colombian law directed criminal investigations, were also badly paid and their choice was a harsh one. Dozens and dozens of colleagues who had acted against traffickers in past cases had been murdered. Sometimes their wives had been murdered too, even their children. Now they deliberately botched such cases, or threw them out on technicalities. Prosecutors, supreme court justices, and justice ministers were no braver.

Bannon sighed. "Nobody wants to die," he said, "just because two Americans got killed."

"Two Colombians got killed too."

"What can I tell you?"

Jane forced down her emotion. "What hard evidence do you have against Marzo?"

There was none that Bannon knew about.

"You're guessing," Jane told him and phoned a police contact. The Colombians had it as Marzo too, she was told. But they also had nothing hard. The investigation was not going well, her contact told her. He sounded embarrassed.

Jane wanted to know when and where the killers had crossed the trail of their victims, and how the hit had been set up. She had to have something specific. She could not print rumor.

David Ley would know or could find out, she reasoned, but forbore calling him. For all she knew he was behind the murders himself. She did not think this likely, but it was possible. She believed him an evil man, not because the Colombian police or the DEA said so, but because, upon reflection, it fit with what she felt when in his presence. And she did not like to put herself any further in his debt.

She brooded an hour, then dialed the number he had given her.

He came on the line at once, said how glad he was to hear her voice, he had been thinking of her. But she cut him short by explaining what she wanted, what she hoped he would be able to tell her.

He fell silent.

She said nothing, waiting him out.

Finally he said he would ask around, that he would be in Bogotá by evening, that if she would have dinner with him he would tell her then what he had found out.

All right, she thought, I'll pay that price, and she wrote down the address he gave her.

It seemed a restaurant made for assignations, she saw when she entered, very dark, candles on the tables, strolling guitar players singing Andean songs. Ley was alternately amusing and intense, leaning toward her so that the candles threw light upward onto the planes of his face, forcing Jane to sit far back in her chair to avoid having him invade what she counted as her personal space. There were men with briefcases who sat or stood at the bar and watched them all through dinner.

Ley had been all smiles so far, his voice again low and resonant, seductive. An old lady came in selling individual roses wrapped in cellophane; he bought one and presented it to Jane across the table.

He was treating this dinner as a date. As if it could lead anywhere, even to bed. Jane had to be careful. She did not want to alienate him before he had divulged whatever information he might have. But at the same time she was trying as delicately as possible to ward him off. She did not want him to misunderstand.

At first nothing was said about the murders. He asked her about herself, her marriage, her career. He seemed deeply interested. His technique—she was sure it was a technique —seemed to her fascinating. She had to keep reminding herself of who he was, and who she was.

She found herself telling him how much the murders had upset her. "I can't get them out of my head. They have undermined my belief in myself, in my values, even in my career. By the way, did you find—"

But he interrupted her. He offered sympathy, told her it was the first time she had faced violent death close up. She had really led a rather sheltered life, she should have tried growing up in Colombia—

He sounded not so much sardonic as troubled, hurt, almost

likable. But for the moment she was concentrated on herself. Colombia was a dangerous place, she said, trying to articulate her thoughts. She had always known it was, especially for people who made it so, like Gallagher and Martha, like herself probably. She was making it dangerous. She had to, that was her job. But Colombia alone could not account for the sense of dread that so weighed on her.

"You are not safe in this country," he said carefully. "I believe your embassy knows it, and I hope you know it. I hope you are taking precautions."

Jane gave a wry smile and after a brief silence asked him point blank what he had found out, if anything.

He grinned. "I've found out everything."

The grin faded and he became deadly serious. The victims—he did not call them by name—were spotted coming out of the Salt Cathedral by a lawyer who worked for Pablo Marzo. The lawyer had met Gallagher once in some government minister's office; he recognized him, knew who he was. The lawyer was at the cathedral with his two children, aged four and eight.

"He went over to the concession stand and phoned Marzo," Ley said. "Told him there was a DEA guy out without an escort and headed for Guatavita."

Interesting. "How did he know where they were going?"

"It's a dead-end road. It ends at the village. The rest of the road hasn't been built yet."

Jane didn't know whether Ley's word could be relied upon. "How were the killers to identify them?"

"Evidently Gallagher was wearing a green sports coat."

This detail had not been published, as far as Jane knew. Ley's story began to ring true to her.

"He was able to describe the woman's clothing too. He didn't know who she was, nor did the shooters."

Jane nodded. Poor Martha. "Do we know the lawyer's name?"

"Jorge Mata," Ley said. "Fellow signed a few death warrants, then went into the cathedral with his kids."

"Can I use that name?" Without independent corroboration she knew she couldn't, but it was a way to test Ley's confidence in his story.

"Sure."

Jane said: "So once they started down that road they were doomed."

"Not if they turned around and came back fairly quickly. It took Marzo about twenty phone calls to line up the killers. It was Sunday afternoon. He couldn't find anyone."

Gallagher and Martha hadn't come back quickly. They had hiked up to the lake and made love under the tree. If only they had eaten their picnic as planned and got out of there. If only Martha had pushed him off. If only she had been not in the mood, or having her period, or—

"The killers had to come out from Bogotá," Ley said. "They almost didn't get there in time."

Martha had made a mistake, sure, but not on the face of it a fatal one. She shouldn't have had to die for it. Adultery was not that kind of crime. Everybody did it, herself included. Martha, if in fact that was the crime she had been killed for, had done no worse than herself, and if Martha was not safe, then she was not safe either; what had happened to Martha could happen to her.

Jane stood up from the table. "I'm sorry," she said. "I have to go home."

To his credit, Ley was immediately solicitous. "I've upset you," he said, signaling for the check. They left their half-eaten dinners on the table. He helped her into his car and gave instructions to his driver. At her door he offered to see her upstairs.

"That won't be necessary."

In his low seductive voice he began to insist. To see her safely into her apartment would put his mind at ease. He worried about her every day and—

It made her grim-faced. She said: "I think I'm going to vomit."

He backed up and gave a slight bow. "I'll call you again soon," he said, and she stepped into the elevator and left him standing there.

* * *

But the next morning she was back on the story.

The road to Guatavita ran along a reservoir, a vast saucer of water on the valley floor, and according to Gallagher's map it continued to the reservoir's far end where it rejoined the Bogotá highway. But as often happened in Third World countries, funds had run out and at Guatavita the road simply stopped. Gallagher didn't realize this, and of course Martha did not. He would be trapped in there.

Being man-made, the reservoir was not nearly as pretty as the lake they had just left. No trees around it. No houses. As they drove along they argued—not about the dead-end road, but about stopping at a restaurant. In this country, restaurants were not for them, he told her. Why do you think he had stipulated a picnic lunch in the first place? And he told her exactly what Douglas had once told Jane. In a restaurant you were immobilized. You sat in a fixed spot for two hours or more and if anybody sighted you, there was time to organize the hit. Back in the States, where do you think all the Mafia dons got hit? It had happened over and over again. They pitched forward into their pasta. No, picnics were definitely safer.

But Martha would have needed to use the ladies' room—both of their bodies were still working perfectly—and besides, she joked, he owed her now a little sophistication. Because of him she had just behaved in a very unsophisticated manner. Making love under a tree. Imagine it. At her age. She sounded so smug, so pleased with herself and with him, that Gallagher grinned and conceded. He drove into the village and parked.

Martha, as Jane saw it, had thought she was risking one thing but had been punished for another. Capital punishment for a noncapital offense. Jane had always believed in a world where you knew what it was you risked, and could decide whether to accept that risk or not. That was the world she wanted to continue to believe in and live in. But she couldn't.

There were forty tables in the restaurant, all taken, a

hundred or more people. The waiters were moving fast, sweating. Gallagher sat with his briefcase upright between his ankles. He watched the door whenever he thought about it. But with so many people around him, what could happen? The herd instinct in humans. People were no different from cattle or sheep. Pack enough of them together no matter where and they felt safe.

The shooters came through the door in time with the dessert, *mantecada* for Gallagher, *masato* for Martha, bullets for them both. Mantecada is a cake made from corn. Masato is a slightly alcoholic rice sherbet. The shooters were two men about thirty years of age; that is, they were not the fifteen-year-old *sicarios* who did most of Colombia's contract killings. They were mestizos—more Indian than white. They carried Mac 10s. They simply ran in and opened up. They sprayed bullets everywhere. Martha never saw them, or if she did, did not have time to react. Gallagher saw them, but it all happened much too fast. He reached down for his briefcase, with the result that the first bullet, which might have hit him in the shoulder or chest, took out his eye. People started screaming and diving for the floor. The waitress wasn't quick enough, and the little boy was at the other side of the room. After no more than five seconds it was over, the shooters had run out of the restaurant and were gone.

Four people dead, and headlines that went around the world.

Before Jane's first story was in print the foreign editor was on the phone to her. She was to pack up and clear out, orders from upstairs. If the two governments, theirs and ours, couldn't protect the chief DEA agent and the ambassador's wife, there was little chance they could protect her. She should go to one of the neighboring countries, live in Quito or Caracas, cover Colombia from there. In either place she would be safe, take your pick, and for spot news out of Bogotá the paper would rely on the AP wire service.

Or fly some male reporter in over her head, Jane thought with some bitterness. It was the type of thing they would do. She had seen the bodies on the floor. She didn't want to write any more stories about people she knew getting murdered. She didn't want to live and work any longer under the threat of being kidnapped. She was scared and had been hoping they would pull her back. But journalists on dangerous stories were supposed to take their chances, and if she proved herself untrue to this code, what chance was there for her future at the paper? In addition she imagined female colleagues watching her all over the world; she wanted to be true to them as well. So she told the foreign editor—and in the ensuing days editors and executives of even higher rank—that she wanted to stay.

They couldn't give in to this kind of thing, she told them. The paper did not become great by shirking its duty. Other news organizations were pouring people in to cover this story, she told them. Did her own paper want to be scooped when it already had its own man on the scene?

Its own man being a woman, herself.

They would never have pressured a male reporter in this way, she believed. As a result, although she wanted only to be back in New York and safe, she had to stay.

Each day it seemed to her she became more afraid. She was sleeping badly. On the day that she went out to Guatavita alone she was unable to keep food down all day.

Her doorbell rang.

It was nine o'clock at night. She was in the kitchen cooking a hamburger, and went to the door.

It was Ray, and she was so glad to see him she almost told him so.

"I was just fixing dinner," she said. She was in need of company, in need of comfort, but couldn't say that either. "There's enough for two," she suggested.

They looked at each other. Neither knew what this offer implied, what mood the other was in, where it would lead. Jane dropped her eyes before he did.

"I better tell you first why I'm here," Ray said.

He held a copy of her paper folded so as to show her byline and story. He rapped it with his knuckles. "Where did you get this information?"

It was the story about Pablo Marzo ordering Gallagher's murder. Jane hadn't seen it yet. She took the paper from him. In the previous several days the desk's interest in Colombia had begun to wane; there were so many other massacres and murders elsewhere, were there not? But this piece on Marzo, based on what Ley had told her, had perked them up, all right. She was back on the front page, she noted, and was pleased. She thought the piece read very well. The editors had barely touched it. It did not name Ley, nor did it name the lawyer who had fingered the victims. But it was packed with the details Ley had given her, which she had credited to a "usually reliable source with strong ties to the traffickers." That is, the piece was properly qualified. It was not the reporter (herself) attesting to the truth of what she had written, but her source. In this way readers were invited both to consider the information and to beware. The only name she used was Marzo's, and this too was legitimate since the DEA and the Colombian police, in addition to Ley, also believed Marzo responsible.

"We'd like to know where you got this information from."

She looked at him. "You'd like to know who my sources are?"

"Yes."

Here we go again, she thought. "I can't reveal my sources to you, Ray."

"Jane, this article contains information even the police don't have."

"Yes, I know." She grinned with momentary pleasure, but the grin faded and disappointment came on fast. In a moment, since she had no intention of revealing her source, he would get angry and leave, and she would eat dinner by herself. She would be alone with her frustration and her fear. "I hope my editors are as impressed as you seem to be," she said.

She handed the paper back to him. He stood there rapping his knuckles on it while eyeing her thoughtfully.

She began gently to explain to him the ethics of her profession. State and local governments, even the federal government, were always trying to force reporters to reveal their sources. Reporters had gone to jail many times rather than do it—

"Yes, I know," he interrupted. Evidently he decided to try charm. "We're not trying to make you reveal them. We're asking you please." And he tried a smile.

She said nothing.

"Was it David Ley?"

She still said nothing.

"Who is the lawyer who fingered Gallagher? He's not a source. You can tell me that much."

She thought about it, then said: "I'll give you the name if, in return, you agree to give me everything the DEA has in their file about him."

"Agreed."

This was better than she had hoped. There might be another front-page piece in it. "It's not a name you'll recognize," she said. "I don't think you will. Jorge Mata."

"Jorge Mata?"

"What's the matter?" said Jane. Ray's face had gone grim.

"He had an office on Carrera Siete. He was murdered this afternoon as he came out of the building. Two men on a motor scooter drove up onto the sidewalk. The passenger hit him with about fifteen bullets."

He turned and started for the door.

"Stay with me, Ray," Jane said in a small, almost inaudible voice.

"I can't. I have to get back to the embassy."

The door closed behind him.

From then on Jane waited with increasing dread for something terrible to happen to her.

19

DAVID LEY LOOKED across the desk at the man who called himself Buford Short.

"How did my people find you?" he said.

"I don't know," said Short. "You tell me." He was smoking and he squinted at Ley through a haze of cigarette smoke.

Smoking was distasteful to Ley, but he did not say so.

"They found me." Short gave a shrug. "What difference does it make."

David Ley knew very well where and how his men had found him and what his reputation was, and that his name was not Buford Short. He looked at him and thought: So this is the guy.

"You've worked in Lebanon, I'm told. In West Germany—" Before entrusting him with a job as important—and as potentially dangerous—as the one he had in mind, Ley wanted to get some personal sense of the man.

"West Germany, yes. Lebanon, no. I was only there a few months. I conducted a kind of school. I didn't work there."

"Yes," said David Ley. "And was the school successful?"

Short shrugged again.

It depended how you measured success, Ley thought. Every time a car blew up in Beirut, every time a bomb went off in a lobby, Buford Short could probably take some credit. He had taught a generation how to do it. His clients in Germany merely blew up airliners. The man must be ice inside.

He made Ley uncomfortable. There was something predatory about him. He was small, about five-six. He looked wiry. Gray hair. He wore a three-piece suit, blue pinstripes.

Garish. The stripes were too wide, and the suit, bought off the rack somewhere, didn't fit.

David Ley prided himself on being able to sit behind his desk and take the measure of a man.

"The money is satisfactory to you?"

"The numbers, yes. The mode of payment, no."

"Please explain."

"I told your people my terms," said Buford Short. "Half up front in cash. The rest cabled to Switzerland to a number I'll give you."

Buford Short was from Philadelphia. Ley had felt it necessary to search that far afield to get what he wanted. "You don't mind," he probed, "carrying that much cash around?"

"No."

"And the rest to a numbered Swiss account, you say."

"A rich Jew showed me how to do it," said Buford Short. "Jews are best for that sort of thing."

In the banking business you let others structure deals, but before implementing them you examined the structure carefully and you made the key yes or no decision yourself, he reminded himself. If you hoped to stay solvent, that is. The decision now was up to him.

"You're sure the job is something you can do."

"You want a parked car to blow up on a radio signal," said Buford Short. "Nothing to it."

"I see."

"Something I explained to your people," said Buford Short. "My part of the contract is, I put the mechanism in place. Then I leave. Your guys operate it or don't operate it. What they do is immaterial to me. By then I'm out of here."

"I see."

"As long as we understand each other."

"And if the device fails to detonate?"

"Then you don't owe me anything more."

"And you immediately return the down payment," Ley said. It was an attempt at humor, and he grinned at him.

Buford Short peered back through the cigarette smoke and did not reply.

"What would you use?"

"RDX, Pentolite, plastic, amatol. Anything you want. You tell me."

"RDX?"

"Also known as cyclonite or hexogen. RDX is good. It's used in artillery shells. When you mix it with liquid TNT it's called Composition B."

Ley nodded. "People speak about a shaped charge. What's that?"

"You want to blow a hole in the ground or do some damage?"

Ley said nothing.

"You know anything about explosives?" asked Buford Short.

They studied each other across the desk.

"Then why don't you let me worry about that end of it," said Short.

He had beady little eyes, Ley decided.

"Dynamite is still the best," said Short. "The most readily obtainable, the most reliable, the safest. I like working with dynamite. The target will be how far away?"

What had been only a notion suddenly became far too explicit. David Ley gave another inappropriate grin. "About twenty meters at the most."

"Dynamite," said Short. "It does the job, believe me."

"How much would you need?"

"Four or five sticks will take out everything for fifty yards around."

"Maybe less would be sufficient." David Ley considered an area that size—the area he had in mind. How many people would be in it?

"You want to make sure, or don't you?"

Well, maybe no one. In any case, it couldn't be helped. "Sure? Yes, of course."

Buford Short looked at him.

"Unfortunately," said David Ley, "it's necessary." Why am I apologizing to this man, he wondered.

"Or I wouldn't be here," said Buford Short, "right?"

Behind the desk, Ley rose to his feet. The interview was over.

But Short remained seated. "We haven't talked about when."

"You'll be advised. Where do my people have you, my ranch? My villa? Are you comfortable there?"

"I'm at the Intercontinental."

"Oh?" This seemed to Ley a security lapse, and he was surprised.

"When I work, I stay in hotels," stated Short. "A little precautionary measure, you might say."

It was almost a challenge. They stared at each other for a moment.

"Talk about when," said Short. "I don't like to hang around a place. You can understand why."

"A few days," Ley murmured, "a few days."

"And I'll have to have a look at the location."

Ley nodded, and showed Short out.

When the man was gone he opened the window and tried to fan out all the smoke. In Philadelphia Short had been a cop. His name was McCoy. When cops go bad, thought Ley, they are the worst. He did not like it that Short was on his own in a Medellín hotel, but basically he was satisfied. He decided to go ahead with it. Picking up his phone, he gave instructions that the down payment be delivered to Short's hotel in a suitcase, and that whatever gear he required be procured.

That night Ley drove Short past the location. He had been about to order someone else to do it, but changed his mind. The whole idea—what was to happen and why—was making him giddy, but also excited. Besides which, security so far had been lax, he believed. The fewer people who knew anything, the better.

It was past midnight. There was almost no other traffic. He picked Short up in front of the hotel and continued on. They were not alone in the car. A young Colombian whose name was Pepe Caceres sat in the back and did not speak. Ley considered Caceres absolutely trustworthy, and had de-

cided to make him part of this operation. He wanted him to
watch as it was set up.

There were no backup cars. Ley drove around in circles
for a while to make sure he was not being tailed, then steered
into a street off Avenida Bolivar, and pointed out the building
in which Pablo Marzo kept an apartment. Marzo had the entire
penthouse floor. It was where he always stayed when in
Medellín. He was not in residence at the moment, Ley believed, but would be tomorrow, because a summit meeting
of the cartel was scheduled for 7 P.M. in the bank.

Ley drove on by without slowing and without stopping—
nothing should attract the attention of any of Marzo's men
who might be watching. There was a garage ramp that went
underneath the building, and he pointed it out. The target
would come up that ramp, Ley told Short. The car loaded
with explosives would be parked at the curb beside the entrance to the ramp. Since this was a one-way street, the car
coming up the ramp would have to turn to the right onto the
street, and for a moment it would be placed exactly beside
the parked car. The car containing the detonator would be
positioned in the driveway of another building about a block
away.

"A block?" said Short, seated beside him. He had half
turned and was peering behind him. "How far would you
say that is?"

"About eighty meters. Is that far enough?"

"Unless the windshield disintegrates and comes in on
you."

"Will it?"

"Blast waves are hard to figure."

"One has to be close enough to see who's in the car when
it comes up the ramp."

"One does, doesn't one," mimicked Short. "That's your
problem, pal. I don't want to know about it."

They drove by twice. Short had a yellow pad on his lap
on which he made a rough map. They spoke English throughout, and no one translated for Pepe Caceres in the back seat.
Ley drove Short back to the hotel.

Marzo's name had not been mentioned. It was not something Short needed to know. Probably he would not have recognized it anyway, Ley believed. But any local bomber would have—and either become paralyzed with fear or gone straight to Marzo with the news. It was for this reason that Ley's men had had to search so far afield. They had had to find someone with the necessary skills who was both willing to take on such an assignment and unknown in Colombia. They had settled on, and brought back, Buford Short.

The next day Short was driven out to David Ley's ranch to prepare the two cars. One was a ten-year-old Chevrolet. He taped the five sticks of dynamite together, and taped the detonator on top. It made a small neat package. He took the back seat out and laid this package down in the seat well, testing to make sure the seat would fit snugly back in place.

Ley, watching him work, was fascinated.

Now he lifted the floor mats and strung his antenna wire forward until it reached the base of the car's radio aerial, to which he attached it. He attached another wire to the car's cigarette lighter, and brought it back under the floor mats to the back seat, where he tied it loosely to the seat frame.

"The cigarette lighter's where you get your power from," he commented. "Your surge of electricity that sets off the charge."

David Ley nodded.

"You don't want to attach the power to the dynamite until the last minute."

"That makes sense," said Ley.

"When you're ready to move, I'll hook it up."

Ley found an almost sexual excitement in contemplating all this. Marzo's car would come out of the garage onto the street and—

At first Ley had thought he would use Caceres to trigger the explosion. He himself would be far away. Now he was not so sure. The stakes were very, very high. Caceres might panic and fail. In any case, he realized he wanted to do it himself. It made him almost dizzy to think about it.

The second car was a Buick. It was newer, though not so

new as to attract attention. The radio transmitter was the size of a garage door opener, and worked, Short explained, exactly the same way. It would send a signal forward to the detonator in the other car. He showed Ley, and also Pepe Caceres, who was present, how it worked, pressing the lever several times, and making them do it. Ley's hands began to tingle as he handled the little black box. Such a neat little box, in appearance totally innocuous, yet deadlier than a great white shark.

Short bolted it to the underside of the dashboard and when Ley asked why, was told that if it were dropped or jarred it might set off the dynamite prematurely.

Ley nodded. He was thinking about pressing that lever. He had never done anything similar before but was confident he could do it, and afterward everyone would applaud. With Marzo out of the picture, the mindless violence would stop before it was too late.

Short attached the wire from the transmitter's terminals to the Buick's cigarette lighter.

"Extra power, to carry the signal forward," he said. "Flashlight batteries might do it, but it's best to be sure."

The transmitter had an antenna wire too. Short strung it over to the fender well and attached it to the base of the Buick's radio aerial.

He had worked about an hour. "That's all I can do for now," he said, and Ley had him driven back to his hotel.

That same afternoon Caceres drove one of the pickup trucks into the nearest village, ostensibly to buy supplies. Instead he made a phone call from the post office, and then drove on to another village where he was unlikely to meet anyone who worked for Ley and where he waited more than an hour in a bar. Finally a man came in, questioned him briefly, and then drove him in a second truck to an isolated house at the end of a two mile long dirt road. Caceres went inside and found himself face to face with a number of men, one of them Pablo Marzo. He had met Marzo only once before, and he was immediately afraid.

Caceres and his wife both worked for Ley. He took care of Ley's horses and his wife was one of the maids in the big house, and one day Ley had raped her. Had simply walked in while she was vacuuming his bedroom and ordered her to get undressed. After moping around for two days afterward, the woman had been overcome by her shame. Amid many tears she had told her husband.

Caceres's first reaction was what any man's would be. He beat her severely, which she seemed to expect and even perhaps to relish. His second was to make contact through a cousin with Pablo Marzo. His one meeting with Marzo had been brief. He let it be known that he was willing to betray David Ley, but when Marzo asked why, Caceres was so ashamed he was unable to answer. How did he mean to do this? Marzo asked next. Again Caceres had no answer. Quickly losing interest, Marzo told him to keep in touch. An underling paid him thirty thousand pesos. With the money Caceres had bought himself a pair of patent leather shoes. He had not yet worn them. They were in the wardrobe in the outbuilding in which he lived with his faithless wife. He liked to take them out and look at them. They were so shiny he could almost see his reflection.

Today, again face to face with Pablo Marzo, Caceres was again unable to speak. Marzo ordered him served a glass of *aguardiente*, and got him calmed down, and finally Caceres was able to speak about Buford Short. He didn't know Short's name but knew the hotel where he could be found. He explained about the car bomb that was being readied, but he didn't know who it was for. He knew the address where it would be placed, but not who lived there. He mentioned this address, and Marzo's eyebrows went up.

"Is this that I have brought you important?" Caceres asked anxiously.

"No," said Pablo Marzo. He ordered someone to pay Caceres another thirty thousand pesos and to drive him back to his truck.

That night Buford Short's telephone rang in his hotel. It

woke him out of a sound sleep. Short squinted at his watch. It was two o'clock in the morning.

"The boss wants to see you," the caller told him.

Short argued with him, but the caller was insistent. "Get dressed, be downstairs in five minutes. Mr. Ley is waiting for you."

Short was driven through the empty city to Marzo's apartment. He recognized the street when the car came onto it, and then the building, and as the car shot down the ramp into the garage he knew he had a problem.

Short—McCoy at the time—had been corrupt almost from the day he took his oath as a Philadelphia policeman. It was a corrupt department at that time and he saw this and wanted his share. When he intervened in family fights he stole whatever he saw lying around that was of value. He stole money and jewelry off corpses. He stole goods out of shops that had been burglarized, making sure first that the burglar was gone and that the owner had not yet appeared. He stashed the loot in his radio car and took it home with him when his shift ended. He extorted money from shopkeepers for allowing cars to double-park outside, and then from drug dealers and others in exchange for their release. He gave perjured testimony in court for a fee.

When a corruption commission was appointed and began its investigation, McCoy knew enough to lie low for a while, and he asked for and got a transfer to the bomb squad. There was no corruption on the bomb squad, how could there be, and the commission was unlikely to look there. He was sent to a school run by the FBI in Quantico, Virginia, for three months. He learned the properties of the various explosives, which were stable, which volatile, how much of each would do what. He learned about letter bombs, pipe bombs, time bombs, all kinds of bombs, and how to defuse same. He watched bombs detonated. No one ever taught him how to make a bomb or rig one, but it wasn't too hard to figure out.

The bomb squad was good duty. The cops sat around all day like firemen, waiting. Of course when they worked, the sweat tended to run into their eyes. Over the next eight years McCoy defused dozens of bombs. Amateur bombs. Professional bombs. Little bombs. Big bombs. Knowledge and technique was what it took. And steady hands. He became a man of absolute confidence. Once he defused two hundred pounds of dynamite in Penn Station. The station had been evacuated. The bomb was already ticking. He volunteered. There was no one in that whole vast enclosure but him. It took him seven minutes to dismantle the bomb. It was the supreme experience of his life so far, and he had had a weakness for dynamite ever since.

Finally, having concluded that he was worth more than the police department was paying him, he took his pension and went into business for himself. He demanded big fees but gave value and the groups he worked for willingly paid them. His first job was in Belfast. The Irish Republican Army had sympathizers in most of the major police departments in the northeast. They were always looking for contributions, arms, people with specific skills. With a name like McCoy they found him easily enough. He stayed more than a year in Ireland and even acquired a bit of a brogue. When he returned he was held up at Customs. The British government wanted him for questioning. He talked his way out of the airport and became Buford Short. He did other jobs for the IRA later, and his reputation and new name passed along the underground grapevine from country to country, group to group. The work was not particularly dangerous if you knew what you were doing. The people he had to deal with were another story. Most were angry and some were not quite sane. They didn't frighten him. Time after time he faced them down. He was a crook; nobody ever said he wasn't brave.

Now he was shoved into a room containing several men. It was a living room: modern sectionals, a thick glass coffee table, a huge television set, glass doors to a terrace. There were no flowers or plants in the room; Short guessed nobody lived in this place very often. There were no glasses or snacks on the coffee table or end tables. But Short already knew that the men in this room were not there to relax.

The one who seemed to be the leader was short, heavyset, with black hair and a black mustache. Short studied him a moment.

"Who are you?" he said bluntly.

Marzo, who did not speak English, glanced at the man who had been Short's driver.

"Pablo Marzo," the man said to Short.

Short knew the name. It was his business to know such names. He nodded.

"Maybe we can come to an arrangement," said Marzo amiably. He spoke in Spanish, and the driver translated.

Short again nodded.

"Maybe you leave here a rich man," said Marzo.

The cars were moved into position late the next afternoon. Short parked the Chevrolet against the curb at the exit to the garage ramp. David Ley, sitting in the Buick in the driveway as planned, watched him walking back up toward him. The Chevrolet was illegally parked, Ley saw. The tail of it extended into the ramp area.

Short stuck his head into the car window. "That's good enough," he said. "It's not going to be there long, is it?" And he grinned.

Ley wondered how he could grin at such a time. Ley's own mouth was dry. His palms resting on the Buick's steering wheel were so damp they felt stuck there. He was in the same state of heightened excitement as before except that it no longer felt a bit sexual.

Short got into the car beside him. "Who's going to do it, you?"

"We have a proverb here," Ley said, managing a weak smile. He was trying to appear debonair but it was harder than he had expected. "A man is never as well served as by himself."

Short nodded. "Interesting," he said.

Marzo said: "Who's going to do it?" and waited while this was translated.

"Him, I think," said Buford Short.

"He's not that crazy."

"That's the sense I have."

Short leaned under the dashboard to fasten the second wire to the transmitter fixed there. "We don't have such a proverb where I come from," he said, "but I can see what you mean."

His fingers seemed to be working with extreme care. "There," he said, "it's armed. Don't touch it now unless you're serious." He sat back and glanced out the window. There were stores along this street and pedestrians moving in both directions. "What's he for?" he asked, jerking his head in the direction of Caceres in the back seat.

"I might need him," said David Ley.

"How much is supposed to be in that car?" asked Marzo.

Short waited for the translation, then answered: "Five sticks."

"Use the same."

"Jesus," said Short. "One stick will send a man through the roof of a car. Five sticks, the birds'll be eating him off the trees for a year."

Marzo did not wait for the translation. Staring at Short, holding up his hand, he counted off his fingers in Spanish: *"Uno, dos, tres, cuatro, cinco."*

To Short his meaning was clear enough. "He won't be identifiable as human," Short warned.

"Bien," said Marzo. Short knew that word. Good. Marzo wanted such a result. He wanted to insult somebody. He saw it as the ultimate insult.

"Have you considered there's stores in that part of the street? People walking by."

This time Marzo spoke in heavily accented English. He said: "You do it."

"This is as far as I go, pal," Short said.

As he started to get out of the car, Ley thought about

making him wait with him for whatever was to happen; then he decided against it.

"Take it easy," Short said, and left. He walked up and turned the corner into the side street where a car waited to take him to the airport. Ley watched him in the rearview mirror until he disappeared.

Ley had two other cars in the side street as well. Backups. Five men in each who didn't know what they were waiting for. They would be terrified if they knew. Afterward he would stroll back there and they would take him to the bank. Although he saw himself strolling, at the moment it was hard even to swallow. Afterward he would chair the summit meeting while pretending not to know why Marzo was late.

He glanced behind him at Caceres. He had fucked the young man's wife, and it had bothered him. She had wept from beginning to end. Afterward, despite himself, he had felt almost a kind of remorse. As a result he had determined to bring her husband forward in his organization. He would make his career for him. Tonight Caceres would serve as an insurance policy if all went well, or else, though he had been told nothing yet of course, he would undertake his first major assignment. Because Ley was by no means sure Marzo was in the building at this time. If he wasn't, still he might return there after the summit meeting, or late at night to sleep. Ley of course would be gone by then—having given Caceres his instructions and leaving him on post. There would be three cars probably, with Marzo in the middle one, he would tell him. He believed he could trust him to press the transmitter at the proper time. This was a careful young man. He took excellent care of the horses.

It was dusk. The sun was well below the buildings. Ley wore disreputable clothes and dark glasses, with a big fedora pulled low on his forehead. He looked like any workman waiting in a driveway. No one walking by had taken any notice of him. Caceres in the back seat was a small brown man and from the sidewalk could barely be seen at all. He sat there as serenely as if they had come out to buy groceries. As if confident that the device would misfire.

Suppose it did misfire? Suppose Ley pressed the lever and nothing happened?

No harm done. Marzo in his three-car cortege would drive off not knowing how close they had come. Ley would wait a few minutes, then drive away in the Buick. Ley almost wished this was what would happen. But a lot of nervousness, a lot of sweaty palms would have been wasted. He would have to notify the police anonymously to come and defuse the bomb before somebody with a cellular telephone or CB radio set it off by accident.

Beside him on the seat lay a pair of binoculars. But he couldn't afford to be seen peering through them at the ramp. Besides, he could see it well enough. Marzo always moved in the middle of three cars, all black Cadillacs. When he saw the first Cadillac come up the ramp, he would know it was now only a matter of seconds. Then, as soon as the nose of the second appeared he would press the lever. He reached toward it now, touched it, almost caressed it. He had a tremendous urge to press it, see what would happen. It was akin to the urge one felt on top of a tall building. The urge to jump that always made one step quickly back. But in this case Ley did not step back immediately. Instead, his finger stroked the lever. There would be nothing to do after he pressed it, but duck. Ley's mouth had grown increasingly dry. His lips felt dry and chapped. He was thirsty and needed to go to the bathroom.

Just then a man walked up the ramp. He stood there glancing around. One of Marzo's men. Ley recognized him. Get ready, he thought, and was gripped by sudden panic. He reached his fingers toward the lever and saw in the uncertain light that his hand trembled. Don't try to caress that thing now, he told himself, you'll set it off for sure.

Apparently satisfied with what he had seen, the man had disappeared. Gone back down the ramp, Ley supposed, though he hadn't seen it happen. Where had he been looking that he had lost sight of the man? He listened hard and thought he could hear car motors coming up that ramp. Impossible. He was too far away.

The first car came up the ramp, five men inside it. One of them was Marzo, but Ley didn't know this. The light was worse than he had expected. He couldn't identify anyone. With a squeal of tires the car burst out of the ramp, veered right, and vanished. It had been in sight only an instant. It didn't even stop at the stop sign on the corner. This might have been a warning to Ley, but wasn't. The adrenaline was surging through him. He was no longer thinking clearly. Taking no chances on a re-double-cross, Marzo was already safe, even as Ley reached for the lever. It was the second car he wanted. The second car was coming. He saw its head-light beams first, then its nose. Another Cadillac. He didn't even wait for it to turn out of the ramp onto the street. Fifty yards, Short had said. Close enough. He pressed the lever.

"Is there some way to build a delay into that thing?" asked Marzo.

Short waited for the translation, and then a bit longer to think about it. He nodded.

"A delay that makes a noise, so he'll know about it?"

"Some clicks," said Short. "Yes."

"Say three seconds," said Marzo. "Do it that way."

Short nodded.

"He should think about it," said Marzo. "I want him to have some last thoughts. He won't have time for any last words."

David Ley pressed the lever but it failed to send its signal forward to the Chevrolet loaded with dynamite, or if it did the detonator up there malfunctioned, because nothing happened. What he assumed to be Marzo's car came up the ramp at a hundred kilometers an hour or so it seemed, and its driver threw it into a ninety-degree turn, hard right, brakes and tires screeching, and it was gone, though Ley pressed the lever again and again. Through the stop sign without even hesitating. Marzo was getting away, he was gone. Ley was angry, disappointed, frustrated. He was outraged. He couldn't believe it. The third car came up the ramp right on its tail, same thing, the wrenching turn, the punished tires. The lever that Ley kept pressing seemed to have no effect this time either. None whatever. On anything.

And then he became conscious of the clicking noise under his seat, click, click, click, the noise that ought not to have been there, that could mean only one thing, and he knew instantly what had been done to him—he entertained exactly the final thought Marzo had wished him—and there was only enough time for him to whisper, or perhaps only think: Oh, my God; and to throw the door open and attempt to dive out of the car, as if that might save him.

The explosion caught him there, half in, half out. He heard only the start of the noise, felt only the start of the blast. That part of him still in the car disintegrated, along with Caceres and the car itself. The part outside got plastered to the wall of the building, as if cans of various colors of paint, red obviously but some other colors too, had been slung up there. When the police arrived they found nothing of the car but the engine block and one axle. All the rest had become shrapnel. Had anyone been in it? There was no way to tell. Other cars were burning in the street and along the curbs, as were some storefronts, and there were a great many dead. It was some days before anyone in an official capacity thought to associate the stains on the wall with a human being, and no one ever associated it with David Ley.

20

"HOW ARE YOU?" asked the voice on the phone. "Everything all right there?"

Bland words, the blandest, but they threw Douglas into an immediate panic. It was early evening and he had just come into his apartment. The voice belonged to Bannon, to whom he had said goodnight at the embassy not twenty minutes before.

What has he called to tell me? Douglas thought. But he knew with sudden premonition that it concerned Jane.

"It looks like your girlfriend's been kidnapped," Bannon said.

Douglas stood with the phone at his ear.

"Yeah," said Bannon. "Abducted. Snatched."

Douglas stood there.

"Yeah," said Bannon.

"When?" said Douglas.

"I've sent a car for you," said Bannon. "We'll know a little more by the time you get here." He rang off.

His wife buried, his children still in boarding school, Ambassador Thompson had returned to Colombia some days before—and had been lauded for his sense of duty in much of the American press.

The conference was held in Thompson's corner office. About ten men were present: the embassy's CIA and FBI attachés, a colonel sent over by General Nuñez, Bannon's senior agents, Douglas, and the deputy chief of mission, who was Thompson's second in command.

Most of the men were in shirtsleeves. All remained standing, as did the ambassador. Behind the big desk he paced, nibbled on his thumbnail, blinked too often.

Abel Flores, Jane's assistant, had been brought to the embassy by armored car. After being offered coffee which he accepted and a chair which he didn't, he was asked to describe what he had seen.

Flores was about thirty, Douglas judged, heavyset, dark complexion. He had been coming into the *El Tiempo* building just as Jane came out, he said. She had stopped to speak to him. She was on her way to an interview with the defense minister that she had been waiting weeks to get, she told Flores. She had phoned for a taxi, she said. As they spoke it drew up, and she got into it.

He paused and looked dramatically around.

"Come on, come on," said Douglas.

"The driver had her name," Flores said. "He spoke her name. I distinctly heard it."

"Maybe she wasn't kidnapped," said Douglas. "Maybe we're overreacting."

"I warned you all," the ambassador muttered. "I wanted her out of here. I warned you all."

"She got into the taxi."

"They'll blame me again," the ambassador muttered. "It's my watch." His office proved how rich he was: Persian carpets, Impressionist paintings from his personal collection. He was agitated and near tears.

As the taxi pulled out, Flores noticed that it did not have Bogotá plates. Not fifty yards farther on it stopped with a jerk, and two men ran out of a doorway and jumped in, one on either side of Jane. The taxi then sped off.

"It was ten o'clock in the morning," Flores said. "The light was good." He nodded several times. "I got the plate number."

He had run into the *El Tiempo* building with the news. Editors crowded around him. When Jane did not show up for her appointment with the defense minister, nor for a subsequent appointment with the minister of mines and energy, two things happened simultaneously: the police were notified and *El Tiempo*'s editor in chief decided he was sure and would go with the story. He ordered tomorrow's front page ripped out and remade. It was by then late afternoon. The U.S. embassy was notified even as the news went out to the world on the AP wire.

Flores's narrative was interrupted several times because the ambassador's phone rang with calls he was obliged to take, the first of them from the president of the republic, offering condolences, the next from Jane's publisher.

"He's sending in some reporters and editors," commented the ambassador, as he hung up. "He said I should feel free to call on them if we need them."

"Just what we wanted," said Bannon, "more reporters."

The phone rang again. It was the secretary of state, who was in *Air Force One* somewhere over the Rocky Mountains. When the call had ended the ambassador said: "He said we were to leave no stone unturned."

Finally Nuñez called from DAS headquarters.

"They've found the taxi," said the ambassador. He put the phone back. "At a construction site. Abandoned." He sat down in his chair and put his face in his hands.

He looked across at Flores. "Thank you. You can go. We appreciate your coming in."

With Flores gone the Americans in the room discussed what they could do. Not much, it seemed. They had no police powers here, and no street informants they might contact. Although they had enlisted a number of high-level informants, they could not reach them quickly without compromising them. They would all try, but—

"That's not good enough," stated Douglas. "We've got to shake every one of them. We've got to keep the pressure on them, on Nuñez, the judicial police, the Defense Department—everyone."

The ambassador looked at him with surprise. The colonel from Nuñez's office jumped up, shook hands with everyone, and went out. The others watched the door close behind him.

The ambassador said to Douglas: "Well. You certainly chased him out of the room."

Bannon said: "If we find an informant knows something but he wants money, who pays him?"

Everyone looked at everyone else.

The CIA man said: "It's not coming out of my money."

"We'll decide that later," said Douglas.

"We don't even know who took her," said the ambassador.

"We know for a fact that Pablo Marzo put a contract out on her. That's where we start looking."

"You're right," said Bannon to the ambassador. "Traffickers, guerrillas. It could be anybody."

"For chrissake," said Douglas, "there are things we can do and we have to do them."

"Let's see what the cops turn up," suggested Bannon.

"I thought they were all corrupt," said the ambassador.

"Maybe not on something like this," said the FBI agent, who was listed on the embassy roster as legal attaché.

"We have to give the cops something to make them work," said Douglas. "Ideas, starting points, keep the pressure on."

"You're talking about cops who may be on the traffickers' payroll," the ambassador said. "If the traffickers kidnapped her, and if they work for the traffickers, they're not going to help us."

"Let's see if any group takes credit," suggested Bannon, "or asks for ransom."

"What else?" demanded the ambassador. "I got Washington on my back, her publisher on my back. It's a paper with a lot of clout. For all I know the president himself will start calling."

"We wait," said Bannon.

"No," said Douglas, "we start to work."

The others stared at him.

"It's late," said Bannon. "We'll take it up in the morning."

"She may be dead by morning."

Bannon shrugged.

The ambassador went back to the residence. Bannon and the others went home to their apartments. Douglas alone stayed on. One by one the embassy lights went off until only a skeleton staff remained on duty.

By day the DEA occupied offices in a secure section of an already secure building. By night these offices were empty. No one disturbed Douglas there, and he worked all night, poring over files. He had some ideas. He needed a plan.

He blamed himself. He had not made Jane see the danger. It was because of him that she was still moving through the streets in taxis. It was for this reason he had to find her, not because he was in love with her. He refused to see the search as hopeless, even though Bannon was right, it was not certain Pablo Marzo was responsible, and Jane could be anywhere by now, even across the border, a prisoner in some uninhabited corner of Brazil, Venezuela, Peru, Panama. At the beginning all investigations looked hopeless. This one, he told himself, was no worse than most. The cops here would work, if you gave them direction, same as the cops in New York. Otherwise they would flail around and accomplish nothing. He wanted to be in position to give them this direction.

There were two hundred or more groups of traffickers. The files made great piles on his desk. Who was in league with whom? Who was in contact with whom? Even if Pablo Marzo was responsible, he might have farmed the job out to another. Alliances were constantly being formed or broken.

Too many of the files interlocked with Marzo's.

Douglas discarded some files, started through others. He paged backward and forward, studying movements, habits, personalities, associates, trying to form a picture of where and how these people had operated in the past and where, if they were in any way involved in the kidnapping, they might be holding Jane.

He realized he could not ignore the guerrilla groups, so at a certain hour of the night he went through those folders too. He was going to have to convince Bannon, convince General Nuñez—others too, no doubt—that guerrillas were not involved, if he was to have any hope of focusing their attention on Marzo, on traffickers. He was sure it was Marzo. A hunch. Instinct. David Ley's warning phone call. But the others would not be sure. They didn't know it was Ley's voice they had on the tape. Douglas knew only because he had heard that voice again on Jane's answering machine, something he had not mentioned heretofore for fear of compromising her.

The guerrilla files were thinner. The DEA was not in the guerrilla business and the files contained notes only where guerrillas and traffickers overlapped—for instance where guerrillas had furnished protection for jungle labs. For the most part each guerrilla group controlled a specific area of the country, with bases in or near a specific village, and he stuck pins in the map on his wall to denote them.

When he moved back to the traffickers, he used different-colored pins to represent what the most important and dangerous of them owned: not only their villas, apartments, ranches, zoos, but also their safe houses, of which there seemed to be a great many. Because once Marzo or whoever had kidnapped Jane, they had to stash her somewhere; and as he worked a plan began to form in his head. He saw distinct possibilities for it.

There was a leather couch in his office. On it, as the dawn rose outside his window, he fell into a troubled sleep. Bannon found him there as he came to work. Files littered the floor, the desk top, the windowsill. Douglas sat up stupid with sleep.

"When you finish with those," said Bannon curtly, "see that you put them back where you found them." He went on into what had been Gallagher's office and closed the door.

Douglas sat a moment on the couch contemplating Bannon. It was not enough to bring forth a viable plan. He would need Bannon's cooperation to have any hope of implementing it. But his relations with Bannon, which had never been close, had lately got frosty. It was obvious why. Bannon was only temporarily in charge and now saw Douglas as Gallagher had at first. An intruder. A man whose duties and responsibilities were indeterminate. Whose influence was indeterminate. Even the value of his rank was not clear. He was suddenly a threat to Bannon's career.

Douglas went down the hall to the men's room and washed his bristly face; and then downstairs to the basement cafeteria, which was already crowded, where he waited on line to buy a buttered roll and two containers of coffee.

He carried the containers and the roll up to Bannon's office, went in and offered one across the desk.

"No thank you," said Bannon. He watched Douglas carefully.

"I got a roll here I'll share with you," Douglas said.

"I'm not thirsty and I'm not hungry."

Douglas sat down, put one container on the desk, unpeeled the top of the other, and began drinking it.

Bannon was a short, tightly knit, baldish man, older than Gallagher had been. He wore a white button-down shirt and a brown knit tie. If he were confirmed as Gallagher's replacement, it would be his first command, and Douglas was aware of this. Bannon was worried about Douglas, whom he knew he did not control, and Douglas was aware of this as well.

"I did some work during the night," Douglas began. "I've got some ideas I'd like to try out on you."

Bannon, still appraising him carefully, said: "Any ideas by you would be premature at this point."

Douglas gave a pseudo-confident chuckle. "You're probably right. Still, we should talk about them, shouldn't we?"

"I don't see why."

Douglas put his container down and briefly rubbed his stubble. "You don't have a razor by any chance, do you?"

Bannon lifted a small plastic box out of his drawer and slid it across the desk.

"Thanks," said Douglas. Then: "I need help going through these files. I'll ask Kilpatrick, if you don't mind."

"He's busy."

"Martínez then."

"They're all busy."

"Alone, it will take me days."

Bannon shrugged.

"The longer they have her, the harder it will be to find her."

"As I see it," said Bannon, "this woman is just another kidnap victim. She may be important to you personally—"

"Never mind me personally. You heard the ambassador."

"And to the ambassador," conceded Bannon. "But this crime has nothing to do with drug enforcement."

"Of course it does. It's the traffickers who took her."

"We don't know that. Why don't you wait until we get a ransom note? Something. Anything."

"Let me tell you what I've worked out."

"We've just had an agent killed," Bannon said, and paused. Figuratively speaking, he bowed his head over Gallagher. "And the woman with him. I didn't want to say anything last night in front of the ambassador. Didn't want to upset him. But that's the case we're working on. That's our priority. And we're stretched too thin to worry about this other thing at present."

The two men stared at each other. Then Douglas nodded and stood up. "I'll get back to you," he said, and returned to his own office and resumed poring over files. And now for the first time he saw that there were too many of them. Even if he could come up with a plan, it would have to be more than carefully thought out, more than complete. Before he could ask others for their cooperation, for manpower and hardware, for permission to implement it, it would have to be unassailable, overwhelming. And that was impossible. Being a policeman in a foreign country was impossible.

Jane in the taxi had been terrified. It was not akin to the terror felt after losing control of her car, when skidding on ice, for instance, the worst terror she had previously known. That kind of terror was always resolved in an instant. This kind went on and on. That kind was almost intellectual in nature. This kind was physical, visceral, an absolute weakness, a loss of control over her body. Her bowels loosened until she thought she could not contain them. Hot and cold flashes began. She couldn't hear or even see, and she thought she would faint.

The two men who had jumped into her cab neither spoke nor looked at her. They did not have to, and this only added to her terror. Her breakfast rose up until it seemed she must vomit, could not help herself. The driver, as he steered down one side street and then another, moving crabwise across the city, neither spoke nor turned around. So he was in on it too. No one to help her. They had knowledge of what they would do to her, and she did not. She was in control of nothing, not of her sweat glands, not of her heartbeat, not even of her breathing.

She had been sitting relaxed and confident in the taxi, perhaps even smiling, already preparing her questions for the minister of defense, when suddenly the doors had been ripped open and the two men were in the cab, pressed against her

on either side. She couldn't comprehend even where they
had come from. One moment they were not there, and then
they were. Without a word of any kind. No explanation. No
command to the driver. They neither spoke to nor even looked
at her. She understood what had happened, no one had to
tell her. What she had feared, even expected for so long, had
taken place. She was a prisoner. Tears came to her eyes.
Kidnapped. Such a weak word to describe it. No word would
be adequate. It could not be described. Control over her
person had been taken from her, over the direction this day
might take, over the rest of her life. However long that might
be. She tried to think all this out, as if honest reflection was
the thing that might help her.

She had begun sweating at once and by now her clothes
were soaked and she was trembling so hard her teeth rattled
in her head. She tried to control her teeth, make them stop,
but could not. Again her vision swam, grew faint. She could
not suck in enough breath.

The taxi was outside the city moving along an open road.
From time to time Jane tried to speak, but no sound came
out. Get a dialogue going, she told herself, but she couldn't.
Finally she managed to cough. Terror is a high plateau, the
Everest of emotions. She was coming down off it. If she
couldn't speak she would cough, and she tried to again and
did. A choked-off cough but definitely a cough. She had been
held, had held herself, at an extreme pitch for what already
seemed an eternity of time, all those miles from there to here,
and nothing had happened to her, except that she had ridden
in a car with two men she didn't know in a direction she had
not chosen, and although this in itself was serious, it was not
necessarily irreversible, and it did not in itself constitute pain.
The only pain so far was the pain of terror, and that was her
own fault, she had caused it herself. Or so she tried to believe
to give herself courage.

She tried her voice again. "Where are you—" She ran
out of air. Then came a fit of coughing. When it stopped she
at last finished the sentence. "—taking me?"

Although there had been a quaver in it, her voice had sounded to her less frightened than she was. Good.

She waited, but no one answered. She tried again. "Who do you work for?"

Still no answer. Her voice was getting stronger. "Guerrillas? Are you FARC? M-19?"

The ride continued. The mountains were to her left; therefore they were heading south. They drove through villages. Dirty, whitewashed walls. No sidewalks. Women dressed in black. She kept trying to question the two men but they remained silent.

"Driver, where are we?" I'll try him, she thought.

But the driver didn't answer either. She watched the countryside pass. Farmland mostly. Some forests. The steep-sided mountains.

Another hour passed. The road seemed to be descending to a lower altitude. Finally the car turned off the highway and they ran along a dirt road for some time. There was a gate. The driver got out to open it, and he got out again to close it after them. The two men beside her stared straight ahead.

The dirt road wound through trees. Then there were pastures in which horses grazed. At length they came to a house and the car stopped. Its two back doors opened and she was pulled out. Her knees were weak, but they supported her. As soon as she was out the car doors were slammed shut, and it turned and started back the way it had come.

"In the house," said one of the guards.

"Well, well. You can talk." She was trying to sound brave but had to clear her throat to go on. "I had begun to think you and your friend were deaf mutes."

It was a Spanish-style house with a red tile roof. There were outbuildings, and meadows with horses. She was not in the hands of the guerrillas. They didn't live in places like this. One of the traffickers, then. Marzo most likely. At least she was able to make one thought follow another. She wondered what would be done with her. She wondered how she looked. Gray with fear, probably, the clothes she had sweated into creased and frowsy. She would need an iron. There was more fear coming, perhaps pain, perhaps worse, but nothing to be afraid of at this moment, she tried to convince herself. She told herself she was angry. She wanted some answers. She had been made to blow two important appointments, had been brought here against her will. She had a right to some answers and nobody was giving her any.

"Who are you? What—" They glanced at her with what seemed total disinterest, so that she began to stutter and could not complete her question.

She was dragged into the house and down a flight of stairs. At the base of it, a small room. A chair, a cot. As she was pushed into it, the man pushing managed to caress a breast, and a new terror rose up in her. She recoiled to the far wall and almost cringed there while he stood in the doorway leering at her. They're going to rape me, she thought. His colleague had gone back upstairs and she could hear that he was telephoning. The man in the doorway made a circle of thumb and forefinger, and thrust the other forefinger through it, in and out, while grinning. If they tried to rape her she would fight and scream. They would rape her anyway, she believed, then kill her.

The second man came back. He had a Colombian sausage and a round loaf of bread. He dropped them on the cot.

"You stay here," he said. With a jerk of his chin he sent the other man out of the room, then followed. She heard the key turn in the lock.

She sat down on the bed and started to sob. They were dry sobs and she was racked by them. She was soaked in sweat but had no saliva left in her mouth, no moisture left to make proper tears. She kept listening for the men to come back. When night came she was still listening for them, too afraid to sleep.

She was kept there three days. There was a toilet and sink. On the sink was a bar of soap, used, the size of a butter patty. On the morning of the second day she stripped and washed herself all over, hurrying in case they should come back now and walk in on her. She washed out her underwear and hoped it would be dry enough by night to sleep in. That was the end of the soap. She sat naked inside her dress and tried to eat the sausage and the bread, carving off pieces with a nail scissors. The air in the room grew fetid. She sat huddled in a blanket on the bed in what was almost a fetal position. From time to time she wept.

She was moved twice, the first time by air to a jungle laboratory where she was kept in a storage room that was made of boards and that was without light, except for what came through the cracks. There was a hammock to sleep in. There were flies and mosquitoes, and great heat. From time to time men—she thought they were workers, not jailers—put their faces up to the boards and peered in at her. From time to time she was led to an open latrine.

She lost track of the days. She was moved out of the shack and tied to a tree. There was activity all around her. She had the impression a police raid was due that day or the next. They had been warned by some officer or government minister and so the lab was being abandoned. They hurried her down a jungle trail to a grass airstrip and pushed her up into a light plane. One of them managed to put his hands all over her. It was almost dark by then and full dark by the time the plane lifted into the air. She believed they were headed south. Some hours passed before the plane landed on another grass strip. The weather seemed warmer than Bogotá, cooler than the jungle. The altitude might have been five thousand feet, a guess—what did she know? She was thrust into a car and driven a short distance to another house. She couldn't see much about it. She was locked into another basement room. Her hair was snarled, her dress ruined, she was dirty, hungry, had no idea where she was, and was racked by terror and despair. No one would know where to look. No one would ever find her.

No communication had been received from the kidnappers. No attempt had been made to extort a ransom. No group had taken credit. There was a special phone number and tips from the public had been coming in, but the police detectives seemed to be checking them out in no particular order and without haste. Apart from the phone tips, they had no clues with which to work.

No one was driving the detectives forward.

As the tips dwindled, the number of cops assigned to the case was reduced. In a country where horrendous crimes took place every day, this one, apart from the diplomatic aspects of it, seemed of little importance. It was unable to hold public attention. There was no proof that Jane had even been kidnapped. She was simply gone, disappeared, vanished.

The government did declare a state of siege, arrogating certain emergency powers to itself. But it seemed in a mood to do nothing with these powers. Finally, after much pressure from the United States, warrants were issued for the arrests of Marzo, Von Bauzer, Jiménez, and Lucientes, but not David Ley. They were old warrants. Marzo's, for instance, was the one about illegally importing animals for his zoo. All four of the wanted men went underground while their lawyers went into court to have the warrants quashed or, failing that, to find out who had signed them.

If anything is going to be done, Douglas thought, we are going to have to do it ourselves.

He had been through what seemed to him the key intelligence files twenty times, had stared at his pin map for hours, had spoken to those DEA agents who would listen to him, invading their offices apparently casually, chatting them up. They were interested in his ideas, but not sold.

Every few days he went over to DAS headquarters and studied the tips that had come in from the public—the ones that had been checked out as well as the ones that hadn't.

He drove to Jane's office and went through her desk. On another day he went into her apartment again. He was looking for her address book and finally found it. He dug out David Ley's private number. Maybe Ley knew something, or could find out. One thing else: he should be able to tell from his voice if Ley himself was involved.

Douglas dialed the number, and waited.

He might have telephoned the bank, but the private number was better, because unexpected. It would catch him off guard. It was the subtlest of threats: Douglas had tracked him down. It had menace to it.

A voice came on the line. It was guarded. Señor Ley was out. It was impossible to say when he would return. Douglas hung up.

He called Ley twice more. Same response. Finally he left his name and phone numbers and the word *urgent*.

At the next staff meeting Bannon announced that there was a rumor that Ley was dead. According to Nuñez, a number of informants were reporting it. Ley's group seemed to be in disarray, and this was being cited as proof. So it might be true.

"Nuñez and his crowd seem to believe it," said Bannon.

"Dead how? Dead since when?" said Douglas.

"They're saying he got blown up in that bomb explosion in Medellín."

The explosion had happened two days before Jane was taken.

"If it's true," said Douglas, "then we know he's not involved in the kidnapping."

"No we don't," said Bannon. "He could well have ordered it, and the plan went forward by itself."

Still looking for help from somewhere, anywhere, Douglas phoned the shipping magnate Ocampo, whose office was in Barranquilla, and flew down and back the same day.

The office overlooked the Magdalena River. Had he received the ten thousand dollars? Douglas asked him nervously, attempting to make small talk.

Ocampo nodded, all the while studying him with black eyes.

Did Ocampo know where Jane was being held, Douglas said, could he find out?

Ocampo was outraged. "I don't know these people. I have nothing to do with them. Why do you ask me such things?" And he attempted to show him to the door.

Douglas stood his ground. "It's important to me on—" He hesitated. "—on a personal level."

"You could have saved the trip," Ocampo said, and the interview ended there.

On the plane flying back, Douglas brooded. Who else could he go to? The answer was nobody. He had dealt with few enough informants here, and of the others, apart from Ocampo, one was dead, and the rest had demanded and been accorded, in exchange for their information, new lives in America.

In New York there was much more he might have done, people he might have leaned on, chits he might have called in. There were detectives who worked for him, informants whose loyalty was to him personally. There was his intimate knowledge of the streets, his only slightly less intimate knowledge of the underworld. There were twenty-two years of experience. But in this place he had almost reached what were for him the limits of the possible.

In Bogotá he went back to work. He began to formulate his plan. It began with a series of arguments.

The guerrillas didn't have Jane, he would argue. They would have demanded ransom by now. They always had in the past. That was how they financed their "revolution." If they had her, they would have tried to sell her. They hadn't, therefore they didn't.

If the guerrillas did not have her, then the traffickers did.

So far so good, apart from the obvious possible flaw, that she might already be dead. Perhaps the guerrillas had killed her by accident and so had nothing to sell. Or the traffickers had, either deliberately or by accident.

The men who had her had not taken her far. A too-prominent victim like Jane would have been got out of sight fast. Therefore she was not in some other country. She was close and could be found. She was not being held in some isolated corner of the jungle.

This was a fragile premise also, but he went forward.

So which traffickers had her, when there were more than two hundred groups?

And why had they taken her? Bannon would ask why, and so would everyone else.

The top seven or eight groups—two in Cali, the rest in Medellín—controlled all two hundred others, more or less, Douglas would argue, and to kidnap an American reporter figured to bring so much heat down on them all, that none of the lesser groups would have dared do it except on a contract.

So only those top seven or eight could be considered as possibly responsible.

Working on yellow legal pads, Douglas was writing all these arguments down. He was trying to think objectively, impersonally—never mind that the reporter in question was Jane. Which of the traffickers was at the same time arrogant enough and also careless enough to kidnap an American reporter? Because from their point of view it was a risky thing to do.

The Cali groups were the ones who operated in New York. They were the ones he knew most about. They were shrewd businessmen who avoided violence, avoided any sort of spotlight if they could. The violence in New York was from the street dealers they sold to. They themselves took their money and got out. If one of the Medellín groups invaded their territory, in New York or anywhere else, they were more likely to get word to the police, secretly of course, than to kill anyone and thus start a gang war. Arrests and seizures discouraged competition; corpses made people mad.

Douglas was willing to discount the Cali group. A kidnapping of this kind was not like them.

Medellín, then. The cartel. Who in the cartel? Not Antonio Lucientes, who was from an old and rather large family. He took advice from his father, who was old and sick and who would be unwilling to bring additional problems down on the family unless there was substantial profit in it for them all. Ruben Jiménez, the cartel's principal connection with Bolivia and Peru, was an important trafficker, yes, and as an ex-street criminal he might applaud such a kidnapping; but he had shown no previous evidence of imagination. How would he think up such a crime, much less carry it out? Carlos Von Bauzer was more of a possibility, and in the past had behaved like a crazed thug often enough. But Von Bauzer liked notoriety, and would certainly have claimed credit. And David Ley, it seemed, was dead. So who else was there except—

Pablo Marzo.

And Marzo was the one man who would not have claimed credit, believing that in this way the impact would be all the stronger. It was either Marzo, or someone to whom he had given the contract. But whoever had Jane, it would be Marzo who would control where she was kept and what would be done with her.

David Ley had warned them of the plot and named Marzo weeks ago. There was no reason for him to lie, and he had given the warning at some risk to himself. Perhaps in the end it was what had killed him, if he was in fact dead.

Such a kidnapping was the type of outrageous act Marzo liked, had done before, without ever taking credit for it, like the murders of Gallagher and Martha Thompson. He liked spectacular gestures that called attention to himself without calling attention to himself. The former gravestone thief was exactly the right personality and the other chieftains were not.

Marzo. A perpetrator of atrocities. Number one in his world.

Who else was even remotely equivalent to him in malevolence, in cunning?

It had to be Marzo because it could not be anyone else.

Which left the question: Why?

It was an act of terrorism, proof that these men did what they liked in Colombia, that no one dared move against them. It was an act of arrogance as well, a thumbing of the nose at the equally powerless United States of America.

The world was well used to political terrorism, the hijacking of airliners and such. The cartel's kind was criminal terrorism. But to be effective the murders and kidnappings had to be increasingly shocking. The terrorism had to be constantly renewed. By kidnapping Jane they had merely renewed it.

Was such reasoning sufficient to explain Marzo's motivation? It was to Douglas. Would others agree?

What did Marzo plan to do with Jane? Would he release her after a time, imagining this would enhance his image as Robin Hood?

Or would he kill her and dispose of her body? Let the mystery hang there forever. Add to the mysterious power he exerted over this country. For him this might seem a worthwhile accomplishment. Perhaps he had done it already.

Or he might kill her and dump her body in some public place, a threat and a warning in what had been until only a short time ago living color.

Douglas began removing pins from the map, all except those relating to Marzo and to several small groups who had been allied to him on occasion in the past, and he studied what was left. Marzo owned all these apartments, ranches, villas, and was known to do so. There had been photos in the papers of their gold faucets, their giant television sets, their shrines to the Virgin. Would he hold Jane at one of them? Was he that arrogant?

Possible. Not probable.

He also owned a multitude of safe houses, some under other names. Some had become known to law enforcement because of a single wiretapped phone conversation, a single reference in a ledger or logbook seized in a raid on a warehouse or lab. This was information Marzo did not know law enforcement had. Which of them would he imagine safer or more secret than which others?

It was on these locations that Douglas began to concentrate. He went back through the files. He plotted where they were, which in towns or villages, which isolated. He made up a short list.

He went around to DAS headquarters, and after that to the judicial police, checking their telephone tips from the public—the old ones as well as the recent ones—against the locations he had short-listed. One of his locations had been denounced to the police only two days ago; it had not yet been checked out. The usual amorphous kind of tip. An A-frame house in a piney woods, a bunch of men sitting around outside playing loud music even at night. A house that had previously been empty for months.

Beside this location on his short list Douglas placed a checkmark.

At both police agencies he went through the intelligence files as well, looking for additional data on the locations on his list. You could not raid potentially hostile places without some knowledge of the layout you would find there. No one asked what he wanted. They were polite to him and let him look.

Finally he narrowed his choices, one by one removing from his map all but sixteen pins, sixteen being the number of helicopters owned by the national police air wing. He liked the A-frame house. He liked a certain ranch as well. It was near enough to the capital, there were fighting bulls on it, and there was an airstrip. Marzo liked fighting bulls, and an airstrip meant he could come and go quickly.

Well, all sixteen locations were possibles.

Douglas's plan became secure in his head. He envisioned a descent by police or troops on sixteen locations simultaneously. It could be done. Because of the government's state of siege, warrants would not be needed. The sixteen simultaneous raids promised the seizure of important quantities of drugs, even if Jane was not found—a valuable fallback argument. It might result in the arrest of one or several of the wanted men.

But could he persuade the police or the army to act on his plan? Could he even persuade his own people?

He prepared a briefing book twenty pages long and went to Bannon and requested a meeting with him and his staff. He said he had a plan, and that he wanted to outline it and get reactions. Bannon at his desk made a show of checking his appointments book, then said he wouldn't be able to fit it in until tomorrow or the next day, perhaps not until Friday.

Douglas was ready for just such a reply. "I'm seeing Ambassador Thompson in an hour," he said. "I thought you might want to be brought into the picture first."

There was a long hostile silence. "In case he wants to talk to you about it," said Douglas.

The two men eyed each other across the desk.

"Shall we have our meeting right away?" said Douglas.

There were fourteen men in the conference room when he handed out his briefing books and began his presentation. As he spoke he tried to read Bannon's reactions, but the DEA chief only tapped a pencil on his knee throughout. He looked skeptical, uninvolved. Most of the men seemed to listen intently, however, and some at the end seemed in favor.

But he was watching Bannon. "How does it sound to you, Nick?"

"You'll never get the Colombians to agree to put sixteen helicopters in the air at once," said Bannon. "It's not their problem."

"That depends," said Douglas.

"On what?"

"On how much pressure the ambassador is willing to put on the president of the republic."

This stopped Bannon, though not long. "Even if Thompson agrees to call the president, and even if the president agrees to the plan, it still won't work because you'll never get sixteen helicopters operational at one time."

"He's right," said Kilpatrick. "A helicopter is a delicate piece of machinery."

"The Colombians take lousy care of the equipment we give them," said Martínez.

"Then we scale the plan back slightly," said Douglas. "Say they have only twelve or thirteen operational—"

"Eight or ten is more like it," interrupted Bannon.

"Well," said Douglas, "we haven't got to that point yet, so let's wait and see, shall we?"

"What about security?" said Kilpatrick.

"If you think you can get sixteen helicopters and a hundred and fifty men into the air without a leak—" Bannon gave a raw kind of laugh.

"Or even half that many," said Kilpatrick.

"—On any airfield that has a tower—"

"At least one air controller in every tower is on their payroll," said Kilpatrick. "Every time one of our planes or helicopters takes off, the traffickers get a phone call. They have advance warning of every raid."

But Douglas had thought this out too. The helicopters would be dispersed to outlying fields, he said. The troops would be brought out in trucks. The final briefings would be held at the foot of the ladders.

"And one of us will be sitting beside the pilots to make sure they don't use the radio." He glanced from face to face around the room. Heads were nodding thoughtfully.

The men filed out until only Bannon and Douglas were left. Bannon behind the desk drummed his pencil on his knee and eyed Douglas, who ostentatiously checked his watch.

"Time for my appointment with the ambassador. You coming?"

But they continued to gaze at each other, and Douglas did not move from his chair. Bannon had a decision to make, and Douglas watched the calculations move through his head. If the plan were accepted by others up the line, if it went forward and Bannon were not a part of it, his career could be damaged.

Finally the DEA agent sighed. "All right, I'll go with you."

In the ambassador's corner office, Douglas made the same presentation a second time. The ambassador seemed attentive. "We can't bring back your wife," Douglas concluded. "We can't bring back Eddie Gallagher. But with your help maybe, just maybe, we can bring back this kidnap victim."

"With my help," said Thompson. He recognized what that help would have to be. He would be asked to strongarm Colombian officials, perhaps including the president.

Thompson was silent a long time. Then he turned to Bannon. "How do you see this thing, Nick?"

"Kidnapping is not the DEA's ball game," said Bannon. "On the other hand, it could be justified as a series of drug raids."

A reply, Douglas thought, as noncommittal as possible under the circumstances.

The ambassador turned back to the author of the plan. "Ten men to hit each location, is that enough?"

"The locations are mostly safe houses, not fortified camps. We'd be going in at dawn, with complete surprise—"

"With a DEA agent aboard each helicopter. I don't want any more DEA guys killed on my watch."

All three men fell silent. Douglas looked from one to the other, but neither met his eyes.

"Will it work, Nick?" asked Thompson.

"It might work, Mr. Ambassador. I haven't had much chance to study it, as a matter of fact."

This too was less than solid support.

"If it is Marzo," mused Thompson, "there's a good chance he's killed her already."

"That may be why we haven't heard anything," agreed Bannon.

"I don't think so," said Douglas with pretended confidence. "He's a cold-blooded murderer, sure. But he's also careful. That's how he's stayed alive so long. She's a trump card that he might want to use at some point. He will have kept her alive this long, I'm sure. How much longer is the question. As I see it, we have to act fast."

"Will the Colombians go for it?" Thompson asked. He was not convinced, and after only momentary contact his eyes dropped and he began busily straightening papers on his desk.

"We don't know," said Bannon.

"With your help, they'll go for it," said Douglas with the same pretended confidence. It wasn't Thompson's help he wanted, it was pressure from the U.S. government. And he was not sure Thompson could or would provide it. "How long does it take you to get an audience with the president of the republic?" he asked him.

"Same day," said Thompson.

"Good," said Douglas, rising. "We'll go forward with it.

We'll come back to you if we hit any snags, and of course we'll keep you informed." Act confident enough and others would believe you. The leader's job was to lead, and not look back to see if anyone followed.

Having returned to his own office, he phoned General Nuñez and made an appointment. But when he asked Bannon to accompany him there, the DEA chief refused.

"I have to work with Nuñez on a daily basis," Bannon said. "I'm not going to try to force him to do something he doesn't want to do."

In situations of this kind bureaucrats—and generals were only bureaucrats with stars on their shoulders—tended to respond according to the number of people who were willing to come in person to press for a project's acceptance. If Douglas stood alone before Nuñez's desk, the project would look thin. Bannon knew this. He was, however, adamant.

So Douglas went alone.

While Nuñez sat smoking his pipe, Douglas outlined his plan. Ambassador Thompson, he stated, was behind the plan, and Bannon as well. But Nuñez looked unconvinced. If they were behind it, why weren't they here?

"Sixteen locations," Nuñez said, smiling politely. "You don't want much, do you?"

"Then you like the idea," said Douglas, though he could tell Nuñez didn't.

An aide came in with a pot of strong Colombian coffee and biscuits on a tray.

He didn't like to mount large-scale operations, Nuñez said, unless chances of success were almost a hundred percent. He lifted the china pot. He poured the cups full. But this operation, Nuñez said, seemed to him marginal.

As they sipped their coffee they began to speak idly of their children and of world events far removed from Colombia, and half an hour went by, perhaps more. It was as if the decision on Douglas's plan had already been made—the decision was no. If Nuñez had other pressing work, it did not show. His boots were shiny. He seemed relaxed and expansive, the gracious host. In Colombia, officers of Nuñez's rank came from the upper classes. They were educated men and their manners were perfect. Douglas noted Nuñez's manners and not much else. What to say next? Nuñez was not a New York police type. He was not even an American. How to move him? Argument or muscle? Douglas lacked experience. Should he coax, cajole, beg, or just threaten? Whatever he decided, was his command of Spanish good enough to bring it off?

"At any one time," Nuñez said, "these people operate fifty or a hundred clandestine labs that we can't find. To imagine that a single strike could find this woman, even assuming we could get all sixteen helicopters into the air at one time, seems to me presumptuous."

"I see your point," said Douglas.

"And the risks are quite high. The helicopter is a dangerous machine, especially in the case of dawn takeoffs from unfamiliar fields. Suppose one of them went down and killed a dozen men?"

Douglas nodded.

"Suppose Marzo or one of the others is there. Maybe they have ground-to-air missiles. We think maybe they do. They shoot the helicopter down. Or we land and there is a pitched battle."

Douglas nodded again.

"We've done jungle operations together," Nuñez said. "I shall always treasure such evidence of our friendship."

"They were dangerous operations," said Douglas.

"*Es verdad,*" conceded Nuñez. "*Pero—*" True, but.

"But what?" said Douglas.

"Jungle laboratories are part of my job. No problem. But what you're suggesting is these people's houses."

A new notion struck Douglas. Were both sides, traffickers and police, playing according to tacitly accepted rules? Were labs considered part of the game, whereas houses were not? Was Nuñez afraid that if he invaded their personal turf the traffickers, considering this an outrage, would come after Nuñez himself?

It was a legitimate worry. They knew where he lived, what his wife looked like, where his children went to school. And even though bodyguards ferried him to and from work, they knew how the cortege of cars and motorcycles was constituted each day, and they had the weapons and men to attack it—the same persons who had killed the justice minister, the public prosecutor, and so many other public officials.

Perhaps this general in the shiny boots, this otherwise honest man, was afraid to get the traffickers, particularly Marzo, mad at him personally.

Nuñez rang for his aide, who came in and took the tray and empty cups away.

It was Douglas's turn to speak. He would have the opportunity for only one attitude, only one line of argument, he well knew. He had best pick the one that would work or his plan would go no farther than this room, and no attempt to find and rescue Jane would be made by anyone.

"Our ambassador is seeing your president tomorrow," Douglas began. Not true, but he would make it true as soon as he got back to the embassy. "He will tell him about this plan and ask his cooperation. At the same time your president will receive telephone calls from certain high officials in Washington—" Douglas did not pretend to know which officials, but the secretary of state would be one, if he could arrange it. "These officials will ask him to consider the plan as favorably as he can."

Douglas paused. Nuñez, he saw, had begun to frown.

"Out of friendship I thought you should know this in advance. I did not tell you at first because I was afraid it would sound like a threat. I do not mean it to be, believe me."

Nuñez said dryly: "I believe you."

"You report not to the minister of defense like the other police agencies, but directly to the president."

"Well," said Nuñez, "in actual practice to one of his aides."

"Possibly the president will call you in for consultation. If that should happen I did not want you to be surprised."

Nuñez's manner was cold: "I appreciate your courtesy."

Douglas wondered whether he had gone too far or not far enough. He wondered if the words sounded as hard in Spanish as they did in his head in English.

"I have been authorized," he said, "to invite you to accompany me and my ambassador to his meeting with your president."

"Thank you, I shall attend." Nuñez had turned and was staring out the window.

"Well," said Douglas after a pause, "perhaps we should go over the plan one more time to get it straight in our minds."

When he left Nuñez he stopped at the Bogotá Hilton where there were public phones, and put through a call to Jane's publisher. This was an open phone line too, but it was less likely to be monitored as it passed through the telephone exchange than was a call from the embassy.

He told the publisher, once he had come on the line, that the police investigation into Jane's kidnapping was inactive, but that the Bogotá DEA office had come up with a plan to rescue her that could work; in any case it was the only plan so far developed. But it had hit snags that were of a diplomatic nature. The ambassador was leery of trying to pressure the president of the republic, and the Colombian police were leery of committing important resources just to return an American reporter to the bosom of her American newspaper.

What was needed, Douglas continued, was pressure from the State Department on Ambassador Thompson, ordering him to go forward with all due prudence; and similar pressure on the president of Colombia, suggesting that he give the embassy's plan every consideration. Would the publisher be willing to ask the secretary of state to lean on both men—

"The secretary of state?" the publisher interrupted. "I'll do better than that. I'll go right to the Oval Office."

Did a New York newspaper publisher have that kind of access?

All Douglas was asking, he reiterated, was for the plan to be considered at the highest level and, if adopted, implemented as quickly as possible. In any case, he said, the plan had been developed by the personnel of the Bogotá DEA office, and no special credit should go to himself or anyone else if it should succeed.

"You want your name kept out of it?" guessed the publisher.

"Yes."

"I'd better start making those calls," said the publisher after a pause, and he rang off.

When he had got back to the embassy, Douglas went in to see Ambassador Thompson. He asked him to schedule a meeting for tomorrow with the president of the republic to push for action on his plan.

"I'll take your request under consideration," the ambassador said, and once again he began fiddling with the papers on his desk.

"You may be getting a call from your boss on this," Douglas told him.

Thompson looked up sharply. "From the secretary of state?"

"I've just talked to Jane's publisher by phone," Douglas said. He did not say who had initiated the call. Thompson did not ask, but his face began to get dark.

In the course of giving the publisher a progress report on efforts to find Jane, Douglas continued, the subject of his plan had happened to come up. The publisher had got very excited and had urged that it receive every consideration. He said he would call Washington to urge that Ambassador Thompson be asked to move forward on it.

"I told him that probably you were meeting with the president of the republic tomorrow anyway," Douglas said.

He and the ambassador eyed each other.

"He said he'd go direct to the Oval Office," Douglas said. "Does he have that kind of access?"

Ambassador Thompson did not answer.

Douglas started out of the ambassador's office but stopped in the doorway. "Shall I ask your secretary to set up that meeting for you with the president of the republic? How does ten o'clock in the morning sound?"

* * *

The room itself resembled every high public official's office Douglas had ever been in: plaques on the walls, flags beside the man's head. General Nuñez sat silent and servile in one corner of the office, and the equally silent Bannon occupied another. Douglas and Thompson sat in front of the desk, and it was Douglas who did most of the talking—in English fortunately, for the president had graduated from Yale.

The president himself was a big white-haired man with a booming laugh. He had already had his phone calls from Washington apparently, for he could not have been more accommodating, nor found more to laugh about.

Ambassador Thompson had received his own phone calls, but was not laughing.

The president asked Nuñez if he had any objections to the plan, and when Nuñez said he did not, gave a wave of his hand and said: "Let's do it, then." He gave another big laugh and showed them out. The meeting had not lasted ten minutes.

"Can we mount this thing for tomorrow?" Douglas asked in the hall.

General Nuñez said: "No."

"All right," said Douglas, "then the day after."

And it was so agreed.

21

THE HELICOPTERS waited in the dark on soccer fields on the outskirts of Bogotá and Medellín. The troops were brought up in trucks. In Bogotá, where Douglas was, the night was windy and cold. There were some bleachers on one side of the field. The wind whistled on its way through the planks. The pilots took their final coordinates off maps spread on the hoods of cars and illuminated by flashlights, after the men were already aboard. The wind kept getting under the maps, making them flap.

Only eleven of the sixteen helicopters had been found operational, and of these Nuñez had insisted on keeping back two in reserve fully loaded, one here, one in Medellín. Douglas's original plan had had to be scaled way back. He had continued to fight for all of it, or at least more of it. He had been trained as a policeman, not a soldier. In the police world you didn't worry about reserves, he said, you kicked doors down and went in with everything you had.

"But these men are heavily armed," said Nuñez. He mentioned again the possibility of ground-to-air missiles, and Douglas was forced to acquiesce. In the end Nuñez had agreed to hit two of the projected locations with men in trucks, and if all went well the reserve helicopters could hit two more later in the morning, although by then the bird, if any, would probably have flown.

The raids were to be made as close to dawn as possible—normal police thinking all over the world. Targets groggy with sleep were less likely to resist. Aggression was down. It was a time of passivity. They were coming out of the womb. They would not react quickly enough. Besides which, even under state-of-siege measures, it was against the law to enter a domicile before 6 A.M.

Helicopters with the farthest to go took off first, for the raids were to be made simultaneously, or nearly so. The dawn had just begun to come up. In Douglas's helicopter the door was shut, he was closed in with ten other men, waiting. He looked out at strobe lights blinking, at rotors turning so slowly it might have been the wind doing it; and at the circle of trucks, at the small group left to guard them, at the van containing radio gear that would serve as the operation's command post. Nuñez had provided them with a special frequency which the traffickers' men at this hour and in that part of the band were perhaps not monitoring. In any case, orders were to stay off the radio unless absolutely necessary. As the sky at last turned gray, Douglas's machine began to vibrate hard, the decibel level went up and up until the thing was screaming as if in pain. Then it seemed to lurch up and forward at the same time, mostly forward. There was a gap in the trees at the end of the playing field in which the top curve of the sun had just begun to show. The pilot headed straight for it. The trees to either side were higher than the machine. Douglas had the impression they would snag on branches, or else on power lines. He felt himself trying to retract his feet. Then they were through the gap and skidding along just above the rooftops at what felt like terrific speed.

As they left the city they picked up the Autopista del Sur, which they followed, flying faster than the few cars on it this early, but not much. They were navigating by the road map folded open on Douglas's lap. They had about a hundred kilometers to go. The light was getting stronger and then the sun seemed to pop free altogether. It was red this morning and as it rose higher it looked as fat and red as a cross-section of watermelon.

The targets, except Douglas's own, had been assigned at random. Douglas had hesitated a long time between the A-frame house in the pine woods and the bull ranch with the landing strip. These seemed the most likely locations. Well, they seemed more likely than the others, the sixteen later scaled down to thirteen, that he had selected. But the A-frame did not seem to Douglas to be Marzo's type of safe house. It backed up against a ravine, there were other similar vacation houses fairly close, and access even by helicopter would be difficult. Ultimately in fact it was one of the two targets that would be assaulted by troops in trucks coming in by road.

Douglas had opted for the bull ranch with the airstrip, and it was toward this location that his helicopter was speeding. During the past hour he had managed to convince himself that Jane was there and he would find her. In a few minutes he might find her.

The helicopter came up on the ranch over meadows that were still in shadow and wet with dew, with here and there the black shapes of grazing animals, horses or cattle. It came over them too fast for more than a glimpse, lifting to clear the trees, and then dropping back down again. It came over the airstrip on which no plane was parked, a bad sign probably, then lifted again to clear more trees. Suddenly the house was there, a low, Spanish-style house, ocher walls and a red tile roof, stables and other outbuildings all around it, some farm machinery, some cars. The sun, rising slowly all this time, took this particular moment to burst up above the trees.

The pilot set the helicopter down in a meadow next to the house. The rotors blew up a rainstorm of dew and the men jumped down into it—rain that fell upward. There were cattle in this meadow—at the last moment Douglas realized they were not cows but bulls. For the moment they had all scampered to a far corner where they stood with rumps together looking back. But they might return.

Douglas, before he jumped down, pointed to the bulls and shouted to the pilot to lift off again and find a better place to park. Then he was on the grass, and running with the men toward the house.

When they reached the front door, they kicked it in, then spilled out into the rooms inside. The main room had big windows. It was empty except for crates that probably contained furniture. Next to it was a game room: an enormous television, a Ping-Pong table. Glass door to a sauna. The men were ripping open all the closets and cupboards. Good. Douglas went on. Indoor swimming pool, showers, empty locker rooms. Jane, where are you? Be here somewhere, Jane, please be here. He ran up uncarpeted stairs. Some men followed and they ransacked bedrooms that were without beds. They went through the attic, the basement, the larder. No one home. Nothing.

Carrying their submachine guns and their frustration, they went out onto the front stoop. A group of peasants, caps in hand, stood looking up at them.

"The North American woman?" said Douglas. "Where is she?"

They answered that she had been there, but was gone. She was only there two days. Some men brought her. She stayed in the big house and did not come out. Then she left. Where she went nobody knew. Douglas asked many more questions, but they had no answers. They were respectful, they shrugged. Foreigners were strange. What more could one say?

Douglas's shoulders had sagged, along with his hopes. This was Marzo's house and targeting it had been correct. His instinct had been correct: Marzo was their man. It had represented their best chance to find Jane, but they had missed her.

One by one he and his men went through the outbuildings. Still nothing, not even a cache of drugs. The farm workers stood watching this activity. They were mystified by it. So were their wives, their children.

After a fruitless hour Douglas climbed back up into the helicopter. He had left men there to continue the interrogations. Perhaps something more could be learned. He and the rest of the men flew away as noisily as they had come. The children on the ground waved to them. Some of the men waved back. The children waved till they were out of sight.

When they landed back at the soccer field, Douglas hurried over to the communications truck and climbed into it. Nuñez and a radio operator were inside. Nuñez was seated on a canvas chair, a yellow pad on his knee. He glanced up questioningly.

"She had been there, General," said Douglas, shaking his head. "She was there two days. We just—missed her."

Douglas's tone was disappointed, almost tragic. Nuñez's reaction was to make a notation on his pad.

Douglas looked down at the pad, trying to make sense of Nuñez's notes. "Who else has called in?"

Nuñez handed up the pad. The helicopters had been numbered one to eleven. Numbers three, four, and five had all called in. They had found nothing and were returning to base.

The radio crackled: "Number nine returning to base. Results negative." It was one of the DEA agents speaking in English.

"Send out the two reserve choppers, General," suggested Douglas.

"Not yet," said Nuñez, doodling on the margin of his pad.

There were two more reports in the next ten minutes. Nothing. And then another one, the voice of DEA Agent Kilpatrick, who had gone in with the truck to hit the A-frame house: "Request that ground transportation be sent out here as soon as possible. We have some friends who want a ride into town, and we'll need a good-sized truck for some merchandise that's ready to be shipped. We're working on our inventory now."

The code was obvious enough. Nuñez jumped up grinning and began rubbing his hands together. From his point of view, it was the best news possible. Prisoners in custody, drugs seized. The "merchandise" sounded like a seizure of major importance. Realizing that today's raids were now justified from any point of view—whether or not Jane was found— even Douglas smiled. His plan was a success, and he himself could play the hero if he so wished.

He didn't wish. He wanted Jane. She had a husband and if she were found it would be for another man. Never mind. He wanted to see her smile, hear her laugh, and if this could be made to happen, it was all he would ask. Or so he told himself.

The radio crackled once more and they heard Bannon's voice on a high, excited note say: "You can call off the search, we've got her, we've got her."

"Ole," said Nuñez softly, *"ole."*

Douglas's lunge for the transmit lever nearly knocked the operator out of his chair. "Is she all right?" he cried.

There was no answer except static. In his anxiety Douglas transmitted the same message a second time.

Finally, after considerable crackling, came Bannon's voice. "She appears to be able to walk. She can't talk for the moment because she's crying. Tears of joy, I would say."

Douglas went outside the truck. All the tension of the past days rose up. His throat got thick, his eyes misted over, and then he found to his astonishment that he was shaking and could not stop.

Nuñez ordered all incoming helicopters to divert to the military side of El Dorado Airport, where total security could be maintained. Those that were on the ground already took off again, the remaining troops and officers drove away in trucks, and the soccer field was abandoned.

At the military base Douglas paced the tarmac. Nuñez had summoned an ambulance and it pulled up and parked. The ambassador's bulletproof Cadillac, the pennant flying on its fender, came in through the gate and parked close to the wall of hangars. The ambassador strode over to Douglas.

"Your plan worked, I see. Congratulations."

"You made it work," said Douglas. "You were part of it."

Ambassador Thompson looked pleased. "That's true," he said.

Douglas went back to his pacing. It was a warm morning. The sun was fully up and shining. He paced and paced.

Most of an hour passed before Bannon's helicopter appeared in the sky. The machine got larger and larger, louder and louder, and then it set down. Ducking under the rotor, holding his hair down, squinting into the wind, Douglas waited at the door as it was flung back.

Bannon jumped down, then reached up into the doorway for Jane. Douglas reached for her too. She took his hand, stepped down the ladder, and then she was in his arms, her body against him, her face in his neck, and he held her.

When she stepped back and looked at him, she tried to smile, but it was a smile that came and went, that showed her teeth and then didn't, that quivered on her mouth, so that it looked as if she might burst into tears.

He tried to think of words that might sound comforting but all he could say was: "Nice to see you again."

Her hair was matted. The heels were missing from her shoes. Her dress was torn under one arm and she was clutching her purse because the shoulder strap had torn loose at one end.

Her hand went to her hair. "I must look a sight," she said.

He said: "You look beautiful."

She looked to him on the edge of hysteria, as if she might start wailing any second.

She said: "I need a toothbrush. Do you have a toothbrush by any chance?"

She said: "And a bath if you can arrange it."

He held her close. "You're safe now, Jane. You're safe."

"And something to eat."

"Didn't they feed you?"

"When they remembered."

"Oh, Jane."

Even in his arms her head, her eyes would not be still. "What's the ambulance for?"

"For you, I imagine."

"For me? Who said I was sick? I'm fine. I'm not sick. I don't want to be in an ambulance. I don't."

Nuñez and Ambassador Thompson had come forward together. Bannon, who had backed off a step, also came into what was now a rather tight circle.

Nuñez said in Spanish: "We'll get you to the hospital, young lady."

"I'm hungry," she said to Douglas. "I'm really hungry."

The rotors had been turned off. The wind and noise had stopped.

"And after that the debriefing," said Nuñez in Spanish. "But not until the doctors say you're strong enough. Did you recognize any of them, Marzo, Jiménez, Lucientes?"

"I want to go to a restaurant," said Jane. She looked almost beseechingly at Douglas. "Not a hospital. Don't let them put me in the hospital."

"To the government of Colombia," said Nuñez with a pretense at humor, "you represent valuable merchandise. We have to take good care of you."

"She doesn't want to go to a hospital," said Douglas.

"She'll go home with me," said the ambassador decisively. "She'll be safe at the residence."

"Do you have a bathtub there?" said Jane. She was still huddled against Douglas, had still not let go of his hand.

There's no bravery left in her, he thought.

"Do you have any food there?"

In the embassy's Cadillac she sat between him and the ambassador. She had her arm through Douglas's and was hugging it to her, but did not seem to realize she was doing it. She did not speak, and the two men, whenever the silence became acute, made small talk around her.

With guard cars front and back, the drive took almost an hour, much of it through city streets. Finally the gates opened and the cortege entered the residence grounds.

They got out of the car. Jane had hold of his arm again and was glancing around, rapid movements of her head as if she had never seen the mansion before or the grounds either, as if she was too frightened to let go. "She'll be all right now," Thompson said to Douglas. "You might as well go back to the embassy."

Douglas disengaged his arm. He no longer knew what role to play. He stood with her a moment until she seemed to calm down, then said: "I'll leave you here."

"Leave me?"

She looked at him and then down at herself. She began to frown. "I need some clothes. Could you go into my apartment and get me some clothes? I need some clothes, don't you see?"

"Sure," he said, "no problem." The prospect pleased him. He wanted to do things for her, and it was an excuse to see her again in an hour.

He watched Ambassador Thompson lead her into the residence.

He let himself into her apartment. He went into her bedroom and opened her closet. In it were clothes he had never seen on her, did not know she owned, and he was surprised. The scent they gave off was the scent of her body next to his in the night.

But all of that was over. He did not regret that it had happened, and he relinquished it with a sigh. She was back, she was safe, and that was all that mattered. He was a grown man, not a moonstruck teenager. He would not die of a lost love, and in a month or two he would be over it, and could look around for someone else.

In another closet he found her suitcases and he pulled one out and laid it open on the bed. Not knowing precisely what she might want, he began to fill it: the black cocktail dress he had always liked, and some tweed skirts, and the sweaters to go with them of course, and some slacks and blouses and a blazer. She owned about ten pairs of shoes. He dropped most of them into the suitcase, along with her slippers, a bathrobe, and a clean nightgown. He found and opened the drawer in which she kept her underwear, and this stopped him for a moment for it seemed such an intimate thing to do. He picked up handfuls of bras, of panties and let them fall through his fingers like sand, and remembered the first time he had ever seen her underwear, with her in it, and what had followed. But even as hot flashes ran up and down his back he shook this image out of his head. A selection of underthings went into the suitcase and he closed the drawer.

She would need toiletries. He went into the bathroom and collected toothbrush and toothpaste, then made his selection from a rather bewildering assortment of creams and rinses and shampoos. Back at the bed he closed and hefted the suitcase, and carried it out into the hall and let himself out of the apartment and locked the door behind him.

By the time he got back to the residence she had had lunch and bathed. She had already washed and blow-dried her hair. She wore what had been one of Martha Thompson's bathrobes. She was in a guest suite upstairs. He set the suitcase down on the rack at the foot of the bed and looked at her. There was some color in her cheeks now, and she opened the suitcase and began lifting out the things she needed.

"The paper called," she said. She paused, as if what came

next was hard for her. "The publisher and the executive editor were both on the line. I've been ordered back to New York immediately."

Douglas was not surprised.

"They tried to recall me once before," she said.

He watched her.

"I put up a terrific fight," she said. "And I won. This time—no fight." Her voice broke but she recovered. "This time I didn't put up a fight. None at all."

"How soon will you be leaving?"

"Tomorrow."

Douglas nodded. Tomorrow she would be gone out of his life. He could think of nothing to say.

Having separated out a small pile of clothes, she went through into the bathroom, but continued to speak to him through the open door as she dressed. "I had a lot of calls. Everyone thinks they should come down here to get me. The publisher. My husband. A whole delegation in fact. To take me home. They want to come down here together. I told them absolutely not."

"No," said Douglas.

"I refused absolutely. I told them I was a big girl, and could get home by myself. I told them I knew how to get on an airplane."

"Yes, of course," said Douglas.

She came out of the bathroom wearing flat shoes, a tweed skirt, and a pale blue sweater. At first glance she looked like any competent young businesswoman. One who didn't need him anymore.

She said: "I want to go home by myself, don't you see?" And for a moment her face broke down and again he thought she would cry. But again she recovered.

"I'll miss you," Douglas said.

She said with excessive brightness: "Should we have a cup of tea together?" She picked up the phone and when the maid came on ordered what she wanted, and hung up. "You have no idea," she said brightly, "how much pleasure it gives me to be able to order a cup of tea."

It seemed to Douglas that she was like a vase with cracks in it. Any stress and it would fall to pieces. The slamming of a door could do it. She was that fragile.

"We compromised," Jane said. "The delegation and I. I have to change planes in Miami. That's where they'll meet me."

They waited for the knock on the door that would be the maid with the tea.

"I'm allowed to go as far as Miami by myself," Jane said. "That's the compromise."

Douglas watched her.

"I don't want to leave here," she said. "I want to stay. But I'm too afraid."

She turned away from him and he realized from her shoulders she was sobbing.

He went to her, put his arms around her. But after a few seconds she broke the embrace, walked to the window, and stared out through the bulletproof glass. Her shoulders stopped shaking and she dried her eyes on her sleeve.

"I'm afraid even to get on that plane alone," she said. "Could I ask a favor of you? Would you come with me as far as Miami?"

"Yes," said Douglas. "Of course I will."

When he reached the residence the next afternoon she was waiting for him just inside the front door, standing between her two big suitcases. Her laptop computer leaned against one of them. She was wearing a wool suit and high-heel shoes and carried a topcoat over her arm.

"Time to go," she told him brightly.

They drove to the airport in the ambassador's car, which he had loaned for the occasion. They were the middle car of a three-car convoy. For most of the ride Jane was silent. "This morning the press officer sent people to clean the rest of my things out of my apartment," she said once. And then a little later: "That was nice of him, don't you think?"

They were led out to the plane from the VIP waiting lounge.

They went up the staircase into the cabin and it was still empty. Jane took the seat in the first row on the inside next to the porthole. Douglas, sitting beside her, eyed the other passengers as they began to file on board.

The plane taxied into position for takeoff. As it started down the runway, she took his hand. She held it and peered out the porthole at the ground whizzing by.

When they were in the air she said: "Two of Nuñez's men came over to the residence."

He waited.

"They had photo albums," she said. "Then they interviewed me."

He waited again.

"I didn't recognize anybody." She turned back to the porthole.

He had decided to let her talk when she wanted to, but not to press her.

When the flight attendant came by, she refused the snack being offered, asking only for a glass of water.

"The paper sent down Joe Crowley to replace me," she said. "He's been here since I got—got kidnapped. He came over and interviewed me too."

Outside the plane the light faded. Then it was dark. Jane took his hand again, holding on to it and staring out at the night.

In Miami a Customs agent led them into a special room where the publisher, the executive editor, and Jane's husband were waiting, together with two U.S. marshals and a photographer from the paper.

One of the marshals dismissed Douglas, saying: "We'll take care of her from here on, so you're free to go."

Go? "All right," said Douglas. "Just let me say goodbye."

Jane was being hugged by her husband and by the two men from the paper. They seemed to be taking turns at it. The photographer was snapping away. When Douglas approached, Jane took his arm and introduced him all around.

The publisher wrung Douglas's hand, saying: "Am I glad to meet you!" Jane's husband was going bald. It was odd to think of her with a bald husband.

The publisher turned to Jane. "This is the guy who put it together for you. He's the reason you're standing here now."

"You're exaggerating," said Douglas with a smile. "The whole office had a hand in it."

"Listen," said the publisher to Jane, "I checked up on this guy and—"

Douglas interrupted him. "I have to go now," he said. And then to Jane: "You'll be all right the rest of the way."

Her face had crumpled at once, and he saw she did not want him to go. But she recovered quickly enough. "I'm very pleased to have met you," she said.

He wanted to grab her and run away with her. "Well," he said, "I'm pleased to have met you too." The inane things people say to each other, he thought.

He put his hand out to her, but she did not take it. Instead her arms came around him and he felt her face against his, probably for the last time. Then she kissed him beside the mouth so that he thought with a rush of emotion: If there is nothing else but this moment, it's reward enough.

"Goodbye, Ray," she said. "And—and thank you."

Ninety minutes later he boarded the same plane, or perhaps another, and flew back to Bogotá.

When Jane landed at La Guardia there was a press conference which her paper had arranged. The marshals didn't like it but were stuck with it, forced to stand beside her, their eyes roving constantly as she fielded the barrage of questions under the bright TV lights. Mercifully, the publisher cut the press conference short after about ten minutes. She could not have stood much more.

"Take a few days off," the executive editor said to her outside the terminal. They stood together at the curbside. "Then come in and write us a first-person account of your experiences. Will you do that? No hurry of course. Relax, take your time. Let us have it by the end of the week."

The end of the week was three days off.

The publisher and executive editor got into the paper's limousine. Jane and her husband were driven home by the marshals. In the back seat George Fox said enthusiastically: "Did you see how many newsmen were at that press conference? You're a heroine."

"No, I'm not."

"You're a famous heroine. And I'm the husband of a famous heroine."

"I didn't do anything," said Jane. "What did I do? I got kidnapped."

"No, you're a heroine."

He didn't seem to understand what had happened to her, or how she might be feeling.

When they reached their building the marshals went with them into the elevator, and then made them wait in the hall while they took their guns out and went in and checked out the apartment.

"It's all right to enter, miss," one of them said when they had come back.

"Was that really necessary?" asked Jane.

"Yes it was, I'm afraid."

She tried to thank them for their help and to dismiss them, but was informed that they would be on duty outside her door all night. They and the men who would relieve them would be responsible for her safety for the foreseeable future.

She closed the door on them.

"Those two guys out there have got to go," Jane said to her husband. He sat on their bed watching as she emptied her suitcases into her closet, into her drawers.

"If they think you need bodyguards," said George, "then you need them."

"Am I supposed to take those two goons with me everywhere I go? I won't. I just won't."

"The prudent thing, Jane—"

"It's impossible. Don't you see that?" Tears came to her eyes, and began to run down her face.

She snatched a tissue out of the box on her dresser and

dried her eyes. Suddenly exhausted, she began undoing the buttons on her dress.

"Let me do that for you," said George, bounding up off the bed. His hands, reaching for her buttons, molded her breasts. He nuzzled her neck, turned her around and tried to kiss her.

She shook him off, at the same time trying to smother the sudden rush of anger. "Not tonight, George. I can't. Don't you see? I can't. I—I need time."

BOOK IV

22

WITH JANE GONE, the country seemed to Douglas half empty.

He talked to his children by phone more and more often. He wanted to know about their grades, their love affairs if any. His son was on the baseball team at college, and he liked to call him up after games. Who won and how many hits had the boy got? His older daughter received a promotion and a raise, and he called her three times in the first week to find out how she liked her new job.

He missed his house too, and often asked about it, suggesting specific repairs and then sending money to pay for them.

He missed Jane.

Three Mondays in a row he phoned the police commissioner, then waited all week for his call to be returned, but it never was. Finally he phoned the chief of personnel and asked how much longer he was expected to stay down here. The man said he would try to find out, and again Douglas waited for the call-back that did not come.

Each day the newspapers arrived from New York and Washington, and he would page through Jane's paper at once, looking for her byline. He liked to see her name. He had read her story describing her kidnapping and captivity. The prose was detached and flat, almost boring. She had kept herself out of it. There was no terror, no relief—as if she had been unable to confront her memories of how it had been. But her later stories were better. Most seemed to be about drug treatment centers, drug conferences, politicians spouting off about drugs, and he supposed this was now her beat. But he did not phone her about it, and she did not phone him.

Elsewhere in her paper and others he read the political news. The mayor was running hard for reelection. The polls had him favored by a wide margin. There did not seem to be any viable opposition. Leo Windsell was still PC, and if the mayor were reelected so easily, was likely to remain so.

But perhaps he was misreading the signs. Perhaps the mayor was not satisfied with Windsell at all. Perhaps he should phone Jane and ask her what the feeling was in the city. Reporters always seemed able to read the future, or at least they so pretended. But he didn't do it.

Day by day he went about his duties, which were less than satisfying. He had learned to care deeply about this country, and to pity it, the way one pitied a loved one in a hospital. He wanted to help in some important way, but could do little, not much more than the equivalent of holding the patient's hand beside the bed. The climate of fear and instability that hung over Colombia was the same as always. Nothing, as far as he could see, appeared to change that, and the flow of drugs into America was not being reduced significantly either.

Thompson departed and was replaced by a career foreign service officer named Malloy. He was about sixty and had a little wisp of a wife. Bannon flew to Washington for a briefing or a debriefing, and by the time he returned had been promoted to a G-16, whatever that was, and had been confirmed as the DEA's country attaché, the bureau chief for Colombia. He seemed much more relaxed as a result, almost but not quite friendly.

For a while Jane's successor, Joe Crowley, was there, and Douglas played tennis with him a few times. Then a group of men tried to wrestle him into a car as he strolled by along the sidewalk. He fought them off and started running. When he glanced back over his shoulder, one of them was pointing a gun at him, but the gun did not fire and he was not pursued. Were they just trying to scare him, or what? The next day he received a death threat in the mail. The day after that he moved to Venezuela. He still came into Colombia on specific stories once in a while, in and out in a day, but Douglas rarely saw him.

A car loaded with explosives rolled down the hill toward the gates of the ambassador's residence but struck the curb before it got there and exploded. It blew the leaves off the trees all along the street, it shattered lower-floor windows in the surrounding buildings, and it blew itself to smithereens. There was almost nothing left of it, Douglas saw when he got there. Ambassador Malloy ordered all the wives back to America, his own included, and put embassy personnel on what he called flex-time—the armored cars started bringing people to and from work at still odder hours along still more randomly selected routes. It made it difficult to work inside the embassy: too often the person you wanted to talk to hadn't got there yet, or had already been taken home.

Each morning, whether he reached the embassy early or late, Douglas bought himself a coffee and roll downstairs in the cafeteria, then came up to his desk and read the overnight cable traffic.

Most mornings a staff meeting in Bannon's office followed, during which the day's tasks were parceled out: phone numbers to track down, informants to try to contact, visits to Nuñez or one of his aides to find out the details of a trial in progress somewhere, or the identity of a victim or perpetrator of a crime. One day a man named Marzo was assassinated at El Dorado Airport. Was he related to Pablo Marzo or not? Accompanied by a bodyguard, he had been about to get on a plane to Medellín but stopped to buy a newspaper first. Someone came up and opened fire. Marzo went down with six bullets in him, and another dozen in the walls of the shop. His bodyguard was late getting his own machine pistol out, but made up for it. He killed the assassin, the owner of the shop, an eighteen-year-old girl bending over the magazine counter, and a ticket clerk across the hall. Douglas spent two hours in traffic getting over to DAS headquarters to find out who the dead Marzo might be and why he was killed. A cousin of Pablo's, it turned out. An underboss in his organization. Nuñez laughed and said that if this were followed by a spate of murders, it meant that one of the other cartel bosses was behind it; if not, it meant that Marzo was suspicious of his cousin for some reason and had ordered it himself.

Reports were sent regularly to the cocaine desk at DEA headquarters in Washington, and Douglas was required to contribute to these.

Everyone was responsible for liaison with one government agency or another. Since in Colombia the national police came under the minister of defense, this was considered the most important ministry, and Douglas and Bannon handled it together. It meant going over there several times a week to drop in on the minister if he was available, and then working the halls, talking to whoever's door was open, picking up information or perhaps only gossip—most times it was impossible to determine which was which—trying at the least to encourage all these people, to convince them that the war against the traffickers could be won, and that America —the DEA at least—was there to help. The object was to try to put backbone into them. Usually the defense minister only begged for more American hardware. He always mentioned helicopters first, machines with enough range to overfly the jungles looking for labs. But what he really wanted was armored cars for ferrying his people to and from work, and submachine guns for the police who served as his own bodyguards, even though he was not sure, he said, whether the cops around him were guarding him or following him. His home phone number was unlisted and his daughter's as well, he said, but his wife and daughter had both received threatening calls, and of course he himself had. They kept changing their numbers, but the calls kept coming. Well, he said philosophically, other cabinet ministers had been assassinated, but no defense ministers yet. And he knocked on wood.

Douglas felt sorry for him, the guy was scared stiff, but there was nothing any American could do for him, no American aid that would help. A request for more aid in the form he wanted did go forward to Washington, and Douglas was one of those whose signature was on it, but Washington seemed to swallow this piece of paper, as it swallowed so much other paper every day, and nothing happened.

One day Bannon said to him: "We can never eliminate the Colombian drug traffic completely, but if we could cut it down by fifty percent I'd consider that a victory."

Douglas had been a cop a long time. Reality had smothered his idealism long ago. Nonetheless he still believed in absolutes. There was good on one side and evil on the other, and these traffickers at the top of the Medellín Cartel, disseminating their killings and intimidations along with their poisonous merchandise not only throughout Colombia but throughout the world, using their vast fortunes to corrupt policemen, judges, government functionaries and officials both at home and abroad, beginning to move their factories into Bolivia and Peru and Brazil and Panama, spreading now fear and murder into the emerald trade as well—these few men represented the most monstrous evil he had ever encountered. And the world seemed powerless to do much about it. For Douglas, fifty percent would not be enough. But even fifty percent he was beginning to believe impossible. Nonetheless they had to be fought. He never gave up on that idea. But fought how? Fought where?

Ocampo called. It was nearly midnight. In the embassy Douglas was again taking his turn on night telephone duty.

"Do you know who this is?"

"Yes," said Douglas into the receiver.

"North of Honda about two kilometers there's a road to the right. At the end of it is a banana plantation. Got that?"

"Yes," said Douglas.

"Marzo."

"Thank you," said Douglas. But Ocampo had already hung up.

He stared at the dead phone for a moment, puzzled, then went to the wall map and found Honda. It was down in the valley of the Magdalena River. It was less than fifty miles away.

Bannon ought to be notified. General Nuñez as well. The information ought to be considered and a plan devised. He went back to the telephone, lifted it, and even began to dial. But then he put the receiver back. He stared down at it for some time, but did not pick it up again.

The next day he took a taxi over to the Hilton and rented a car. The sun was shining as he drove out of the city. It was the first time since he had been in Colombia that he had driven a car, or been in one by himself.

It was Sunday and there was other traffic all around him. The road plunged down off the Bogotá plateau. It went down five thousand feet, perhaps more. One moment he was driving along in autumn weather, the next it had become a hot day in summer—and getting hotter. The hot steamy air came into the car and his shirt stuck to the seat.

He found Honda, and then what must be the plantation, but from the car could see nothing. Row after row of head-high banana plants. Could Marzo be in there? There was a dirt lane that presumably led to the house. He drove past and when the road had risen a bit he stopped and got out and looked back. Now he could glimpse the roof of the house, together with some sophisticated-looking radio antennas. He knew he was in the right place. No banana-planter needed antennas like that.

Ahead was a grove of trees on the edge of the river and he pulled into it and parked among other cars. People were eating picnics beside the river. Some were eating at bridge tables they had set up there. Most sat on blankets under the trees.

He walked back the way he had come, waited until the road was clear, then hurdled the drainage ditch and disappeared among the banana plants. The leaves were big and dry. The buzz of insects was the loudest he had ever heard. In places the rows were laced together with spiderwebs, which he broke with his hands or waded through. As he moved forward, he worried about snakes. In Colombia they were big and lethal and in here he would never see one until its fangs were in his leg.

Slowly, carefully so as not to rustle the tops of the plants, crouched over so his head would not be visible from the upper windows, he worked his way toward the house. When he could hear voices he knew he was close and he stopped, but he could see nothing yet, nor could he distinguish words, so he moved closer. And then closer still. Finally, by parting the leaves, he could see men on a veranda. He counted seven, none of them Marzo. The ones sitting down had Uzis, or something similar, on their laps. He himself had his off-duty revolver, five shots. If there was a shootout he would lose.

There could be sentries making regular rounds. He was only half hidden. To anyone peering down his row of plants he was plainly visible. The heat was suffocating. He lay down in the dirt, peering between the stalks of the plants. He could see the door to the house and a small part of the veranda, and he composed himself to watch and to wait.

The men on the veranda came and went. There were about fifteen of them. He still did not recognize anyone. The Uzis stayed with whoever was sitting down.

He waited an hour, then most of a second. Then the front door opened and Marzo came out. Douglas had seen him once in person at the bullfights, many times in photos. His face was more familiar in Colombia than any film star's. He stood yawning, scratching his crotch, staring straight at Douglas. Finally he turned away, said something that made some of the men laugh, and went back into the house.

Douglas stood up and, moving as slowly and carefully as before, worked his way back to the road, then walked along the verge to the grove beside the river and his car.

When he reached Bogotá he phoned Nuñez at home and they met that night. Nuñez's apartment house was fortified like a bunker. Guards took Douglas up in the elevator.

"You're sure it was him?" said Nuñez.

"I saw him. With a squad of men you can take him easily."

And once you have him, he thought, we put pressure on you to extradite him to us.

They eyed each other. Both knew what the stakes were.

"Importing animals without a license," Nuñez said. "It's not much of a case."

"A guy like that," Douglas said, "you arrest him, you get a judge to hold him on high bail or no bail, and you put your case together afterward."

Marzo, in custody, would know what the stakes were too.

"Holding him," said Nuñez, "that's the problem. Our judges don't like to do it. They have wives, husbands, small children, you see."

"You've got to do something, man."

"I'll send a memo to the president, see what he wants to do."

"Jesus," said Douglas under his breath. Aloud he said nothing, but glumly left the apartment.

The next day he phoned Nuñez. "Our technicians tell me an unusual amount of radio traffic goes in and out of that place," Nuñez said, "so you may be right. Marzo may be there."

"I saw him," Douglas said. "Don't you believe me?"

On the third day, Douglas phoned again. "Do you at least have guys watching the place?"

"The president has decreed that it is a police matter. So now I must decide what to do."

"If you wait much longer, he may be gone."

Finally Nuñez invited him to a briefing. About a dozen officers were present. On the easel was a diagram of the banana plantation. Nuñez at the easel explained how his men would be deployed. His initial attack would be made by a dozen men on foot coming up the lane behind an armor-plated assault car.

The plan looked flawed to Douglas and he took Nuñez off to one side: "It looks to me as if he could escape out the back."

"I don't think he will try it," said Nuñez.

"You have nobody covering on that side."

"You worry too much," said Nuñez.

He himself would be aboard the command helicopter, he said, and he invited Douglas to accompany him. The arrest was to be made at 6 A.M. the following morning.

When the sun rose the helicopter was hovering at about two thousand feet, the accepted limit of small arms fire, and well to the far side of the river from where the action, if any, would take place. The machine was a U.S.-built Huey with open sides such as Douglas was familiar with from Bolivia and Peru. His feet hung over the void. Beside him was a machine gun with a boy behind it whose uniform didn't fit and who looked about eighteen. Nuñez sat strapped in on the other side of the boy, farther toward the front of the machine, close enough to shout orders to the pilots. He had a microphone at his mouth, and he must have given the troops orders to advance, for Douglas saw the assault car start up the lane, the troops walking slowly behind it.

When the assault force had almost reached the house, Nuñez shouted more orders at the pilot, and the helicopter moved up closer, though still very high, and Douglas, peering downward, noted that no troops at all had been ordered to the rear of the house, it had not been cordoned off, an escape route was wide open, for a second dirt lane led out through more banana groves toward a paved road a mile or so distant. With an emotion akin to outrage he began shouting and gesticulating at Nuñez, who pretended to be unable to hear him over the engine noise, or to understand. Any moment Douglas expected to see Marzo, if in fact he was still there, run out the back of the house where cars and trucks were parked. He would jump into one and drive away. And apparently Nuñez meant to let him go, to be satisfied with arresting the dog-washers who would be left behind.

There came a burst of fire from the assault car. The troops were still behind it, hadn't even fanned out. In the racket the helicopter was making Douglas couldn't hear the fire, but he could see it, and it was followed by answering flashes from the front windows of the house.

Then occurred exactly—up to a point—what he had expected. Here came Marzo out the back door, two other men running with him. He was still tucking his shirt into his pants, hobbling on shoes that were not quite on, and then he had leaped up into a pickup truck, the two men were in it with him, and he was speeding away down the back lane.

Douglas saw all this clearly and only then realized how much altitude the helicopter had lost, how close it was to the ground, only then with a flash of intuition realized what he was about to witness.

The helicopter swooped low over the house and began chasing the truck up the lane. The lane was narrow, banana plants coming up to the edge on both sides so that in places the fronds were brushing the doors. There was no room for the truck to maneuver. It was not close to the paved road beyond, and never would be.

Now the helicopter was directly above it and had lifted slightly. Now it had drifted slightly off to one side. It was perhaps two hundred feet up and Douglas peered down through his shoes at the truck, at its roof bounding and tossing on the dirt lane.

He threw a glance at Nuñez, and saw him nod at the boy between them, who stood up in his sling and fired a burst of about thirty rounds straight down into the roof of the truck. The noise beside Douglas's ear was stupendous. Below him the roof opened up like a sardine tin.

The truck went off the road, flattened a number of banana plants, and stopped. No doors were thrown open. No one climbed out. The helicopter was still making its normal racket, its normal vibration. Nonetheless, the image that filled Douglas's mind was one of silence. An empty, eerie silence. He was totally unprepared for the second burst of fire, which shocked him in some respects more than the first. The helicopter had drifted around in front of the motionless truck and for a moment only hung there. The dawn sunlight reflected up at them off the windshield, a rose-colored glare. After another signal from Nuñez, the boy again jumped up in his sling, and the former thunderous noise reoccurred, the excessive vibration as if the helicopter would be shaken out of the sky. Below them the glare of windshield disappeared, the glass as well, shattered into a million fragments. The boy was shooting directly into the cab in which nothing moved except for the lumps that had been men that were shuddering and jumping under the impact of the bullets.

Douglas looked at Nuñez and saw him, rather than heard him, mutter the words: "Fire with fire."

When the helicopter again came up over the house, the assault car was parked up close with a soldier in the turret pointing his machine gun in the direction of the front door, and the troops had fanned out, with more appearing now from out of the banana rows and surrounding the house, and the dogwashers had begun to trickle out one by one with their hands raised. In a moment an officer led his men forward and the house was invaded.

The helicopter set down in the parking area. Officers kept coming up to Nuñez and saluting, calling him "*mi general*." All was secure, they said.

A number of them gathered around him, Douglas included, and all trekked down the lane to the riddled truck. Junior officers hauled the bodies out of the cab and lay them on the ground, and they looked at them.

"Pablo Marzo," Nuñez said with contempt, and he nudged the body with his shoe.

He turned to Douglas. "Killed trying to escape," he said. "You of all people ought to be willing to testify to that."

Douglas looked at him. He had expected to witness an arrest and had taken part instead in an assassination. He nodded and said nothing. What was there to say?

The bodies were carried up to the house where they were stripped and the blood hosed off them, after which they were laid out naked side by side close to the wall. The house was scoured for white cardboard, the tops to boxes mostly, three placards were prepared, and Nuñez wrote out the three names and placed the appropriate placard on each dead chest. Then the press was notified.

That afternoon a public relations officer brought about fifty newsmen to the plantation in a bus. No one involved in the assault was there to pose with the bodies. Men had been left as a guard of course, but no one higher in rank than sergeant was still on the premises, and the official communiqué which the public relations man handed around credited the death of Pablo Marzo only to "units of the Colombian armed forces," mentioning no names at all.

23

SOME WEEKS PASSED. As he made his rounds, as he studied the cable traffic, Douglas searched for evidence that the demise of Marzo, following so closely on that of David Ley, had had some effect. He failed to find it. In Colombia all the other traffickers had simply moved up a rung or two. On the streets of America there were still no shortages of supply. The price still did not rise. The federal agencies, the big-city police departments were better than they had been, the seizures being made were bigger than ever, but this seemed to have no effect either.

With all the dependents sent home, few women were left inside the embassy. These had the pick of the men who were there and Douglas, watching closely, came to believe that a great deal of casual sex went on. What else was there to do?

He kept himself apart, perhaps only because none of the secretaries and clerks, the one or two female section heads, appealed to him very much. But as a result he got exceedingly edgy and sometimes caught himself snapping at people for no reason. He had lived with one woman for many years, and then in his grief had been numb to all that, and then Jane had come along and had reawakened in him the ability and the desire to fall in love again. But Jane was gone, and not just gone from Colombia. Gone back to her husband. He was not grief-stricken this time, but he was just as alone.

That the Bogotá newspapers had color capability continued to impress Douglas. One day guerrillas entered a village in Antioquia and massacred forty-three surprised and defenseless peasants. This was of course the lead story in both *El Tiempo* and *El Espectador*. But there was another big story that day, namely the election of Miss Colombia. As far as the newspapers were concerned, this curious juxtaposition made for a nice balance, the massacre occupying the top third of the two front pages, the beauty contest the bottom third, color pictures of corpses and weeping relatives above the fold, color pictures of girls in bathing suits smiling below. The remaining stories on the front page concerned two policemen assassinated in Barranquilla, troops ambushed in Caquetá, and some killings in one of the emerald mines which traffickers supposedly had taken over.

Douglas's Spanish was getting better. From reading all these newspapers every day his vocabulary expanded. Jane would have been proud of him.

In the evenings he watched American sporting events on television, or went over to the residence where he sat in on a bridge game, if one was available. He took up chess again, but found he wasn't very good at it.

Sometimes he tried to stand off and look at himself. I'm a New York cop, he thought, so what am I doing here? He was used to moving among other cops in the city in which he had been born. Bogotá was an alien place, and he was not even free to explore it.

He wondered how long this exile had to last.

He made another series of calls to the police commissioner. The deputy inspector who was the PC's secretary asked guardedly what it was about. This man of much lower rank was no one to complain to or make requests of. Nonetheless, there seemed to be no one else he could reach.

Douglas said he wondered when he might come home.

"I'll get back to you," the deputy inspector promised, and

this time he did. He relayed a message from the PC. Douglas was to hang on there until a job at headquarters opened up that was worthy of him. No call was ever returned by the PC directly.

He began to phone the chief of detectives, the chief of patrol, and others, men who were above him in rank and in no sense buddies, but men he had known for years, and they were difficult to get through to also, presumably because they knew what he wanted and had nothing they could tell him.

So one day he simply called in the movers. He stood in his living room and watched them box his pictures, the Peruvian tapestries Jane had admired, his books, his records and tapes, his blankets, sheets, and towels, his stereo and television, his dishes and kitchen utensils. He packed his suitcases. Wanting to avoid any elaborate goodbyes, any questions about his future that he would have been unable to answer, he told them at the embassy that he was off on home leave, which was true in a sense. They would learn in good time that he was not coming back—plenty of time for Bannon to ask DEA in Washington to send down a replacement.

His boxes went off in a truck. One of the embassy's armored cars took him to El Dorado Airport. He changed planes in Miami. Then he was landing at La Guardia. Then he was home. His suitcases were beside him on the stoop and he was unlocking the door and letting himself into his house. He put all the lights on. He walked through every room. It smelled musty, so he opened some windows onto the night. He took a shower and got into bed. Clean pajamas, clean sheets, and his own bed. How luxurious it felt. Then as he lay there he began to miss his wife. For the first time in weeks his wife, not Jane. But his wife wasn't coming back and in a different way neither was Jane. He fell asleep.

In the morning he phoned headquarters. He spoke to the PC's deputy inspector again. He informed him he had left Colombia definitively and asked for an appointment with the PC. The deputy inspector said he would call back, but an hour passed and he didn't. Douglas hooked up an answering machine and went out to the grocery store. He bought ninety-six dollars' worth, including a leg of lamb. Stepping into a liquor store, he bought champagne. When he reentered his house he found that during his absence his answering machine had not been called upon to answer anything.

He had phoned his children before leaving Bogotá. That night all of them came to dinner. He cooked most of it himself before his older daughter came into the kitchen and pushed him aside and took over. He poured out the champagne and they sat at the table for two hours and he caught up on what they had been doing. He was terrifically glad to see them, glad to be home—though in the back of his mind a bit uneasy as well, wondering what tomorrow would bring.

He went to bed pleased with his children but not, as he lay in the dark, with himself. He could not sit home waiting for the PC to call. Tomorrow he had to make something happen, but what?

By noon the next day, when there was still no call from the PC's office, he put his uniform on and went down to headquarters and walked the halls talking to people, being seen, hoping that Windsell would hear about it and react. And in fact this happened. Late in the afternoon he was sitting in the office of the chief of personnel listening to an explanation of the newest computer management programs. The call from the deputy inspector found him there.

"For you," the chief of personnel said, handing over the phone. Douglas took it.

The deputy inspector said the PC would see him at ten o'clock the following morning.

Douglas hung up, grinned, and went home.

The next day he was at headquarters in good time, though worried. His uniform was impeccable. His shoes almost glowed, the star on each shoulder shone, but he did not see the PC at ten o'clock, nor at ten thirty, nor even at eleven. He sat waiting in the anteroom while others went in ahead of him and he tried not to get angry or demoralized or too worried. His civil service rank was captain. All ranks above captain were temporary appointments by and at the pleasure of the police commissioner, meaning that Windsell could reduce him to captain with a wave of his hand, if he so chose. Douglas wanted to keep his star, and he wanted a command commensurate with it. For the moment he was not a high-ranking police officer at all, but a man without a job, and he was as nervous as he had ever been. He was a suitor looking for work, and the police commissioner could give it to him or not.

Finally he was admitted to the great man's office. It was by then ten after eleven. The PC did not apologize; he did not have to and he knew it. He offered no greeting either. He looked grim.

But Douglas, who had decided he must project confidence at all costs, if he could, strode up to the desk, grasped Windsell's pudgy hand, and shook it. "Commissioner, it's great to see you again," he said.

Windsell disengaged his hand. "I don't recall ordering you back to New York," he said.

Douglas was ready with a reply.

"I'd like to have stayed in South America, Commissioner, but I couldn't. Personal reasons." And he gave what he hoped was a bland smile, to which Windsell did not respond. "Anyway, I'm back, and I thought you would want a report before—" And he paused.

Windsell stared at him across the desk. The silence lasted some seconds. When Douglas did not break it, Windsell was obliged to. "Before what?"

Douglas had had more than enough waiting time to work out his strategy. All was calculated, his silences as much as his replies, and so far he was managing to pull it off. "I'm only back two days," he said, "and the press is on me already." In a sense this was true; yesterday he had met a reporter in the hall. The man had recognized him with surprise and had asked for an interview. "I guess we owe the city a report as well, wouldn't you say?"

Windsell began stirring papers on his desk. Finally he spoke. "A report, yes. Why don't you write me out a full report and I'll study it, and we'll talk again?'' He had stood up, come around his desk, and was escorting Douglas to the door.

"How long?" said Douglas. "Twenty-five pages or so?"

"Twenty-five, forty, whatever. Take your time on it." Windsell was like the headmaster assigning homework—so much homework that the student would not get out of his room for days, perhaps longer. "Take as long as you need."

But Douglas, who had entered the big office carrying a briefcase, reached into it. "I thought that's what you'd say," he remarked, "so I worked up a full report on one of the embassy computers before leaving Bogotá." And he handed it to him.

Despite himself, Windsell glanced down at it.

"The other thing we need to talk about is this," Douglas said. "I need a command."

The report seemed to weigh heavily in Windsell's hands. For a moment he only stared at it. "Why don't you take a couple of weeks off," he said. "You have the time coming to you, I assume."

"I'd rather get right to work."

Again Windsell stared at him. They were stalled there in the middle of the rug.

He was given an empty office and nothing to do. He was amazed at the extent of his suffering. His children were almost grown, almost gone. He had no wife. The police department which he loved did not want him apparently. His career, which had occupied so much of his time and energy for so many years, was certainly threatened and perhaps over.

He thought he understood the workings of headquarters, and of City Hall as well, and he tried to tell himself he was being unreasonable. In truth Windsell would not know where to place him, nor the mayor either, and being political creatures they would wait to see what sort of pressure built up before they made any decision. They would react to this pressure. As he sat in the office assigned him, which was on the ninth floor, far below the corridors of power, he told himself he could feel the pressure building. I'm going to come out of this all right, he encouraged himself.

His only visitors were reporters who had heard he was back and wanted to interview him. He referred them all to the public information office on the thirteenth floor, for he couldn't afford to seem to be courting personal publicity. Once he even telephoned the deputy commissioner for Public Information asking for instructions.

"What are you looking for, a press conference?" the man asked roughly.

He told him no, and this was true. His report to the PC was thirty pages long and not a fit subject for a press conference. It described most of what he had seen and learned while away. It was solid, thoughtful, and, he believed, undramatic. It deserved to be studied, but there were no headlines in it, no sound bites, or so he believed.

But the deputy commissioner was being pressured by the news media too, as was the mayor's press secretary at City Hall. Everyone wanted to interview Chief Douglas. Why was the police department unwilling to produce him?

Douglas didn't see this happening, but so many reporters came by his bare office only to be sent away by him, that he began to suspect it. He had his confirmation, he believed, when high-ranking commanders began to come down from the thirteenth and twelfth floors to drop in on him and chat awhile. He began to take heart. He judged that they could feel the pressure too, considered him again a force within the department, and were hedging their bets in case he should one day be promoted over them. I'm going to get out of this thing, he encouraged himself. He didn't really believe it yet, but at least he had hope.

Finally he was summoned to the PC's office. This time he did not have to wait. The four-star chief of the department was seated on one side of the PC's desk, and the three-star chief of Organized Crime Control on the other. The First Deputy Commissioner turned from the window as he entered the room.

The PC cleared his throat, and asked Douglas if he would accept appointment as chief of Intelligence, if the job should be offered to him. He would report directly to the first deputy.

The title was bigger than the job. It was not a street job. It was principally a bookkeeping job, but Douglas was both relieved and elated. He would have an office on the thirteenth floor, and would command about three hundred men, including undercover cops who had infiltrated radical groups or organized crime, and the dummy corporations that paid them. He would have many of the department's secrets at his fingertips. Within the department, information meant power. He would have fought his way back into the mainstream. Windsell would not be PC forever, and once again his career would be whatever he might make of it.

"Yes," said Douglas, "I would accept the appointment."

"It's still under consideration, you understand."

Douglas nodded.

"Now, what about this press conference business?" asked Windsell.

Douglas saw what the quid pro quo would be. The appointment was contingent on his silence. He was not to rock any more boats. "I'd just as soon avoid it, Commissioner, if I may."

"If we did permit this press conference," said Windsell, "what would you say?"

"Pretty much what is in my report."

"No dramatic pronouncement of some kind?"

The first deputy said: "You're not going to come out in favor of legalization, something of that nature?"

"No, of course not."

Windsell glanced around at the others. "We'll talk it over here and let you know," he said.

The next day a call came from the deputy commissioner for public information. The department, he said, had decided to accede to the many requests for interviews by scheduling a press conference by Chief Douglas.

"I'd rather not," said Douglas, and he meant it. Even if he were careful, the press might still twist his words. He wanted to keep his part of the bargain. He wanted that appointment.

"The press has already been notified."

"Can we hand out copies of my report?"

"Negative."

"But—"

"That's the way the PC wants it," the deputy commissioner interrupted.

The conference room was full. There were nine television cameras ranged along the back wall. Taped together in a bunch on the table in front of Douglas were too many microphones to count. The lights were blinding.

Normally at police press conferences several high-ranking officers sat on the dais, making it seem that the department spoke with one voice on the subject in question, whatever it happened to be. But nobody flanked Douglas. Except for the deputy commissioner, who stood waiting to give the signal to start, there was no other commander in the room. He sat alone behind the microphones and looked out and wondered what he was going to say to all these people that would not sound fatuous, a disappointment both to them and himself.

He was about to begin when the door in the back opened and Jane came down the aisle. She took a seat and did not look at him. He looked at her though, and his mouth went dry. She had a tape recorder in her hand and a yellow pad on her lap. She wore a dark tweed suit over a white blouse. The blouse had a big bow at the throat.

"The first job in attempting to solve a problem," Douglas began, "is to focus attention on it. If one's attention span is too short, if one's focus is not intense enough, then no solution will be found. And no solution has been found to this terrible drug problem facing us now."

He wasn't criticizing his government exactly, and yet he was. He felt pompous. It should not be the job of a policeman to make statements of this kind. He felt not only pompous but foolish. Yet the crowd in front of him seemed to hang on every word.

The focus in America was blurred, he said. People looked at the jails, whose population had doubled in the last few years, at the courts, whose caseload had done the same, at the street-corner drug dealers who had overwhelmed whole neighborhoods, at the ruined babies born to crack-addicted mothers. Fine, he said, but those are the results of the problem, not the problem itself.

He had not come home with answers, he said, but he had seen the problem—or parts of the problem—closer than most of them. He perhaps knew a little better what it was than most of them. He stood before them as an eyewitness.

"Let me tell you some of what this eyewitness saw," he said, and he began a series of word pictures that were as concise and as vivid as he could make them.

He described Peru. The rubber boats that guerrillas had shot full of holes; and the row of money changers outside the hotel who accosted everyone who went in or out for dollars, for the Peruvian Inti dropped in value every minute of every day; and the jungle cut down and burning as far as a man in a helicopter could see, because in that country at this time, the coca bush was the only cash crop anyone could count on.

Peru was a bigger problem, he said, than the street-corner dealer in the South Bronx. We perhaps had to do more to help Peru.

And Bolivia, for the jungle there was burning too. He described the one road down into the Chaparé that washed out in every storm and was not repaired for weeks for lack of money, and the program by which the United States paid two thousand dollars per hectare to any farmer who ripped out his coca bushes and planted, say, pineapples: "But no provision has been made for getting those pineapples to market." He described the border patrolmen and all the other American training officers he had met there, almost none of whom spoke Spanish. He described his helicopter ride over the desperately poor Chaparé. "Only three of Bolivia's six helicopters were fit to fly that day. Why did we give them only six? Why did we give them helicopters that were already so old?"

He glanced at Jane. She knew all this, yet was making notes. She did not look at him.

He continued. And we perhaps could do more for Colombia, the worst problem of all. A country of thirty-two million. The police there had sixteen of our helicopters. Vast areas of jungle and equally vast areas of mountain were controlled by guerrilla armies, and the cities, the very government, were controlled by a handful of the richest, most ruthless, most vicious thugs the world had ever known. If you would not accept their bribes, they killed you. The law-enforcement system did not, could not, work in such an environment. He described the bullfight he had gone to. They were all there, Marzo, Von Bauzer, all of them. "I was as close to them as I am to you. Their crimes were known. But they were able to flaunt themselves in public. They seemed to take pleasure in it. Which cop was going to try to arrest one of them amid so many bodyguards? A troop of cavalry might not have been able to do it, and even then only at unacceptable risk to bystanders."

When he had reached this point, Douglas stopped. He was embarrassed. Not because he did not believe what he was saying, but because he did not believe it was a policeman's job to say it, especially a policeman of nondominant rank. He was saying what government officials should be saying, and the fact that they weren't did not give him permission, as he saw it, to usurp their place.

But he could not simply walk away from all the microphones on the table in front of him, walk out from under the TV lights, for from the floor came a babble of excited questions, and he knew what the most insistent of them would be.

No, he did not favor legalization, he said. The Medellín Cartel controlled the product. Did anyone imagine that the legalization of the product would make them let go of it? With legalization they would become even richer, more outrageous, and probably more murderous than they were right now.

They asked what then he was proposing. The people who

made policy didn't always realize who and what we were fighting, he answered, and even so mild a criticism as this —from a cop—seemed to him risky. Cops saw certain problems—this cop and this problem certainly—clearer than most people, but most times were not supposed to speak, could be fired for speaking. He was trying to be cautious but was being forced with each passing minute into what were for him dangerous areas. He wanted to get off this dais. He wanted that appointment as chief of Intelligence. From time to time he glanced down at Jane as if asking for help, but most times her gaze was on her notes, and when she did meet his eyes her expression was unreadable.

Still the questions came. Filling our jails with street-corner dealers was not the answer, he said. There were better ways to spend our money than that. The enormous sums spent on interdiction could be allocated better. And why are we a country that needs to drug itself, anyway? he said rhetorically; he didn't expect an answer, but he wished the policymakers would at least ask the question.

Did he consider the fight hopeless? He did not, he said. We were fighting an epidemic and epidemics passed. He reminded them of the plague of the black death in the fourteenth century. So many died it was thought the world was coming to an end. But that plague passed, and if we kept the pressure on, this one would pass too.

He stood up, stepped from the mikes, and tried to get off the dais. But individual reporters clustered around him, some to renew acquaintance, some to welcome him back, some to ask for a clarification on one point or another. Looking over their heads he watched the microphones being disconnected, the television gear bundled up, the room emptying out. Most of all he watched Jane. She kept paging through her notes, not looking up. Presently the men around Douglas left him, and when he looked Jane was still there. The room was empty except for the two of them, and she approached.

"I didn't know you were back," she said.

He found he couldn't think of what to say.

"How long have you been back?"

"A little over a week."

"You didn't call."

"Jane," he said.

She peered at the floor. "You were good up there," she said, gesturing at the dais with her chin.

"Thank you."

"Really good. Congratulations."

"Thank you."

Neither seemed to know what the other's feelings might be.

"Do you really think my comments were all right?"

"Yes, excellent."

"I was afraid of sounding arrogant. As if I was giving instructions to everyone from the president on down."

"No, not at all."

"Jane—"

She was peering at the floor. "My husband and I have filed for divorce."

He remembered that she had told him this—or something like it—once before.

"I've taken an apartment of my own."

"Where?"

"Riverside Drive."

"Had it long?"

"A month now."

He wished he could stop asking inane questions and tell her what he felt.

"Living alone is rather nice."

"You don't believe that."

"No."

He looked at her.

"I've never even thanked you properly for—for what you did for me."

"I didn't do anything special."

"I asked around. It was all you. If it hadn't been for you—"

"Bannon's the one who found you."

"No," she said. "You did."

They looked at each other and he gave in to the desire to say too much: "If anything had happened to you—"

"Well," she said, not looking at him, "I have to get back to the office and write this story."

But she didn't move. Instead her eyes came up and they gazed at each other. A minute passed, perhaps longer. By that time neither was in doubt any longer.

"How long will it take you to write?"

"I'm not sure."

"Mind if I wait?"

DON'T MISS THESE EXCITING NOVELS
FROM BESTSELLING AUTHOR,

BILL GRANGER

- ☐ **HENRY McGEE IS NOT DEAD**
  A35-621 ($4.95, USA) ($5.95, Can.)
- ☐ **THE INFANT OF PRAGUE**
  A34-780 ($4.95, USA) ($5.95, Can.)
- ☐ **THERE ARE NO SPIES**
  A34-705 ($3.95, USA) ($4.95, Can.)
- ☐ **HEMINGWAY'S NOTEBOOK**
  A30-284 ($4.50, USA) ($5.95, Can.)
- ☐ **THE EL MURDERS**
  A35-209 ($4.95, USA) ($5.95, Can.)
- ☐ **THE NOVEMBER MAN**
  A32-473 ($4.95, USA) ($5.95, Can.)
- ☐ **PUBLIC MURDERS**
  A34-406 ($3.95, USA) ($4.95, Can.)
- ☐ **NEWSPAPER MURDERS**
  A34-290 ($3.95, USA) ($4.95, Can.)
- ☐ **LEAGUE OF TERROR**
  A36-126 ($5.99, USA) ($6.99, Can.)
- ☐ **THE MAN WHO HEARD TOO MUCH**
  A36-086 ($4.95, USA) ($5.95, Can.)

**Warner Books P.O. Box 690
New York, NY 10019**

Please send me the books I have checked. I enclose a check or money order (not cash), plus 95¢ per order and 95¢ per copy to cover postage and handling,* or bill my ☐ American Express ☐ VISA ☐ MasterCard. (Allow 4-6 weeks for delivery.)

___Please send me your free mail order catalog. (If ordering only the catalog, include a large self-addressed, stamped envelope.)

Card # _____

Signature _____ Exp. Date _____

Name _____

Address _____

City _____ State _____ Zip _____

*New York and California residents add applicable sales tax.

411